WARRIOR KING
AN ANCIENT FAMILY SAGA

EGYPT'S GOLDEN AGE CHRONICLES
BOOK ONE

LAUREN LEE MEREWETHER

LLMBOOKS
PUBLISHING

LLMBOOKS
PUBLISHING

For permissions and to visit the author's website, see:
www.laurenleemerewether.com

Library of Congress Control Number: 2023907787
Paperback ISBN: 978-1737905042
Hardcover ISBN: 979-8372964594
eBook ISBN: 978-1737905059

CONTENTS

EGYPTOPHILES UNITE!

Grab some Ancient Egyptian swag and free ebooks at
www.laurenleemerewether.com

INTRODUCTION
HISTORICAL CONTEXT

Warrior King is an ode to the women behind the throne during a tumultuous time in Egypt's history: the last of the Second Intermediate Period and the Seventeenth Dynasty, when Egypt is divided between the Lower and the Upper. The Lower is controlled by foreign kings and the Upper is full of rebellious Egyptian princes seeking to retake their lands.

Warrior King begins with those living in the Theban province—Waset—where the rebellious princes have declared a divine king and consolidated efforts in the war against the foreign kings—the Hyksos—called the Hekka Khasut.

The "A Look into the Past" section at the back of the book provides a more detailed dive into the history behind the story. Afterward, the glossary provides definitions for locations, names, concepts, gods, military ranks, etc.

WARRIOR KING
EGYPT'S GOLDEN AGE CHRONICLES
FAMILY TREE

1575 BC TO 1548 BC

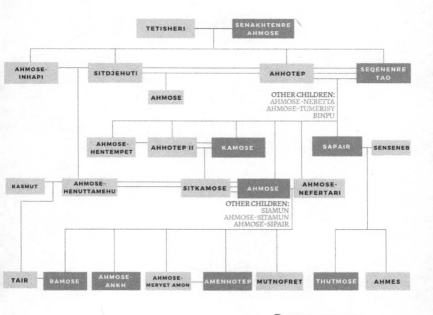

LEGEND

MALE   FEMALE

**BIRTH ORDER OF
SEQENENRE TAO'S CHILDREN**
AHHOTEP II
KAMOSE
HENTEMPET
AHMOSE-NEFERTARI
HENUTTAMEHU
AHMOSE-NEBETTA
AHMOSE (SON)
SAPAIR
AHMOSE (DAUGHTER)
TWINS: AHMOSE-TUMERISY, BINPU

1

A TIME OF DEFEAT | AHHOTEP

SEDJEFATAWY, 1575 BC

Ahhotep could not withdraw her eyes from her brother-husband's gaping mouth—open in a final silent scream. Her knees weakened as the enemy's servants lowered his mangled body before her; the double ax wound in his forehead and above his right eye blurred in her sight. The wails of her children, called to witness their father's defeat, faded in her ears. But the small whimper from her mother's closed, pinched lips pierced the quiet veil Ahhotep had fallen under. Her eyes slid to Tetisheri standing beside her. The whimper had come from her, had it not? Yet through her peer at the woman's stone countenance, she second-guessed her perceptions. Her mother would not show any weakness to the *Aamu*, the Asiatic enemy who had brought her son home.

Ahhotep returned her sights to her brother-husband, and the burning flame at the back of her throat incinerated the yell of agony she held there. She swallowed its ashes and blinked back hot tears. She had to stand strong, if not for the enemy, for her children, for *Kemet*: Egypt.

A red hue overcame her darkened cheeks. They had called her children to view their father's corpse as it was when he was slain. No dressing had occurred. No cedar dust to preserve his flesh had been sprinkled. Not even a wipe of the blood splattered around his wounds had been afforded. Such dishonor. Such disdain. Such disgust.

She would give the enemy the chance to speak for their actions against her family, but in the end, she doubted she would let them leave *Sedjefatawy*, their palace, even if they were only messengers.

The four Aamu servants who had carried her brother-husband's body into the throne room and laid it before the dais on which she stood backed away, allowing two royal Aamu messengers to step forward. One stood at the dead man's head and the other at his feet. Their knee-length pleated shendyts were tied with blue lapis-embedded leather belts. Their collars rivaled the celestial blues and golds of Ahhotep's and her mother's. The stolen wealth spoke for itself.

The Aamu clapped twice—hard—to demand the attention of those in the pillared throne room. Yet only the young naked children silenced out of fear.

Ahhotep's breath came shakily out of her nostrils, afraid of what would happen if she were to speak. Her mother, as shrewd as she was, always knew when to step in for her.

Tetisheri raised her hands, and the room became quiet at the Great Wife's unspoken command. She raised her chin and eyed the Aamu. Her voice—bold, as usual—pounded in the new silence.

"You bring home the body of my son and solicit us with a clap like we are dogs?" Her eyes narrowed. "There will be no such—"

"You and the *nomes* of Upper Kemet are the defeated," he simply said, regarding the provinces in rebellion. "And our King sends this message."

He pulled a clay tablet from his sling and read aloud.

"With the slain Prince of Waset, Seqenenre Tao, it is King Aegyptus' expectation, Waset and the other nomes' princes of Upper Kemet lay down their weapons and again submit into peaceful accord . . ."

He read on, but Ahhotep did not hear him. She snapped her gaze from her husband's gruesome, ashen face to the messenger speaking and interrupted. "You dare ask for our cooperation after slaying the true King of Kemet?" The break in her voice garnered the averted eyes of the royal guards and the Waset soldiers in the throne room. Her lip curled in disgust at herself for showing weakness but also at the enemy, who smirked back. The break had been unexpected, but her eyes, welling with searing tears, choked her words. Her mother leered in disappointment at her.

The messenger scoffed and held the tablet out so one of the Aamu servants could take it. "Your *prince* is slain, and your rebellion perishes with him." After the tablet left his hand, he firmly gripped the handle of the superior weapon on his belt: the khopesh. The long, thick bronze body with a sickle at the end sharpened to take a man's head from his shoulders. "King Aegyptus has sent home the bodies of your prince, his general, and admiral as an offering of peace, Chief Wife of the slain Seqenenre Tao. As you well know, traitors to the throne are burned, so they never have immortal life in the *Field of Reeds*. But he has spared this sentence for your family. Do not make King Aegyptus shed more blood in this matter. Do not sentence your kin and soldiers to eternal restlessness."

Ahhotep's fingers curled into her palms, and her tongue grew thick in her mouth. Every muscle strewn tight, she kept her tears from falling, but the room blurred despite her efforts. She knew the Aamu King of the *Hekka Khasut*, the foreign rulers, would not be so generous if they were to fail again. The subsequent slaying would end in burning, a true death, an inevitable cruel sentence for the person's *ka*—their spirit. They could never begin their journey west to the afterlife.

The Aamu locked eyes with her as he spoke again. "Think of your son, the heir to the Waset prince's crown. Would you have his blood spilled too? Are you willing to sacrifice your son's immortality in the Field of Reeds in a useless attempt to drive us out of Kemet? Nay, baseless attempt. We have lived there for hundreds of years. Your family's ancestors left the Lower and ceded the lands to us. It is our land, and it is not for the taking. So again, I say to you; you have lost your father and your husband in this senseless rebellion. Shall you lose your son too?"

The question lingered in the stale inner room air, and her children's eyes turned to her, all except her eldest son's. Kamose. Her gaze shifted to him. The blood had drained from his knuckles as he wrenched a dagger in his hand. A scowl lived on his lips. Hate boiled in his eyes.

Tetisheri turned to look at her daughter. She straightened her back and lifted her chin. "What is your answer, now that you are the Great Wife of the last King?"

Ahhotep swallowed the paste that had accumulated in her mouth. She was no longer Chief Wife but *Great Wife* because her husband was no longer in the land of the living. She was also now God's Mother. After all, her son would soon be the divine king. It was an odd feeling, one she had not expected to feel until she was much older. Her sights returned to Tao.

Although grateful her husband would have his body to achieve immortality in the afterlife, the audacity to send two messengers alone into the heart of the so-called rebellious lands showed the Hekka Khasut did not trust she would consent to their offer of peace. It also meant they could not spare soldiers in a show of power behind enemy lines.

She again looked at Kamose. He was young and full of vigor. He would take his father's place. He had a daughter already; he could have a son to continue the royal line. His hand holding the dagger trembled from rage; the other clutched in a tight fist, waiting for her word to strike. Would he be returned to her as Tao? Her heart dropped to the pit of her stomach. No, he would return victorious. He had to.

She stepped from the dais and stooped to touch Tao's body. She ran her fingertip down his smashed and bloodied cheek; the touch flaked off the dried blood. She studied his face with its misshapen nose and destroyed eye socket. He would have been killed in vain if she accepted the peace offering, as would the slain soldiers and their general and admiral. Her son wanted to fight. He knew what was at stake, and so she stood and returned to the dais. Her mother narrowed her eyes at her. Tetisheri wanted to fight; she had always wanted to fight. Ahhotep sucked back her breath, taking her pending tears away with it. There would be no break in her voice this time.

Before she answered, she prayed in a silent plea to Anut, the protector goddess of the god-kings, that she keep Kamose safe and protect his afterlife. She scanned the room. Her sights fell on her sons, Ahmose and Sapair, boys of five and three—naked and clinging to each other. Their big brown eyes opened wide toward her. The urge to vomit rushed up to the top of her throat. What would she sacrifice to see a united Kemet? Kamose was well-trained. Ahmose, still a boy, had never wielded a training ax. Would Kamose gain victory over the Hekka Khasut, or would he be burned on the battlefield as a traitor? If he perished without an heir, would the crown fall to Ahmose, a boy, or would the nomes war with each other over it?

The past had not been kind to the royal family, the true royal family of Kemet. Stuck between the Hekka Khasut to the north, the Kermans and Kushites to the south, and the *Dashret*, the red sand desert to the east— Kemet had grown weak. The Hekka Khasut suffocated them by restricting trade from the *Great Sea*, the Mediterranean. The Kushites did the same from the trade routes across the Dashret. They kept the true citizens of Kemet in the dark and left the royal family to rot away inside Waset while both kingdoms flourished from trade and gold. Kamose was determined to take all; she could see it in his eyes. He would make Kemet great once again. He would reinstate Kemet to its former glory and beyond —what Tao wished to do. But at what cost? How much more blood would be spilled? Would it be worth it?

If she surrendered to the Aamu messenger standing before her, she would guarantee they would keep their lives and bodies for the afterlife. Still, it would be under the rule of the Hekka Khasut, who continually choked the life out of their once great nation. They *needed* to be free of the foreigners—those who came into their lands and stole their traditions, customs, beliefs, and wealth— the imposters.

One united Kemet. That was her father's vision, and

that was her brother-husband's quest. No matter the cost. Her chest swelled with a new breath, and without further thought, she spoke in a voice as bold as her mother's.

"We do not acknowledge your King, simple messenger. We have given him the name King Apepi after the evil serpent, Apep—he who brought chaos and darkness over our lands. As Apep steals the light in the sky, so the Aamu have taken Kemet from us. As Re fights the serpent to restore the sun disc every morning, we too shall never relent until the true King of Kemet returns over the Lower and the Upper." Ahhotep pointed with a firm finger at each of the two men before her. "To King Apepi, I say, this is your only chance, O Great Hekka Khasut, to leave and return to the Levant whence you came. Leave and spare your own blood. For when we gain victory over you, it shall be *you* who is burned."

Mitry, the royal scribe, scribbled the hieratic onto the papyrus scroll to record the Great Wife's words as they poured over her lips in a confident display of power.

The messenger's jaws fell ajar, but a sneer soon replaced their surprise. "Who are you, *woman*, to command King Aegyptus?"

It was then they sealed their fate in Ahhotep's judgment. She slipped her gaze to Kamose and squinted in a secret signal before focusing again on the enraged talking messenger.

"We will take your threat back to the royal residence, and there King Aegyptus will launch a strike to raze Waset to the ground and end this rebellion, once and for all. Be prepared to *die*, for the same pardon of traitors' punishment will not be extended again!" The messengers turned to leave, but Kamose's war cry echoed in the pillared hall.

Spears hurdled through the air and pierced their targets. Ahhotep and Tetisheri stood tall, watching their enemies fall to their knees. The messenger looked back at Ahhotep. "You dare kill a messenger?" He groaned as he fell to his hands and gurgled blood.

She glowered at him, uttering, "You dare threaten a Great Wife?"

Kamose headed straight for him, dagger in hand. The messenger's eyes closed as if accepting his fate but snapped open in defiance. The spear in his back wobbled as he coughed. He yanked his khopesh from his belt in one last attempt to defend himself. "I'll take your son with me!" he yelled amid the swarm of guards ending the rest of his Aamu counterparts. He pushed up to his knees and tried to stand but failed.

Kamose picked the khopesh off the lifeless second messenger's body and swung it in the air to attack the kneeling Aamu. Its sickle end glinted from the flame of the alabaster torch lamps before the clang of bronze against bronze reverberated through the throne room. The Aamu blocked, but Kamose knocked the weakened messenger's blade from his hand and sent a swift foot into the man's belly. A yell cut through the commotion as the spear completed its journey through the man's chest as he fell backward.

The Aamu convulsed as he breathed his last breath, but Kamose took his dagger across the dying man's neck. He stood over the Aamu with nostrils flaring and his mouth curled in bitter disgust. He spat at the Aamu before looking up at Ahhotep. His eyes burned black.

She nodded her approval. "It seems he will not be taking my son with him," she muttered.

Kamose's deep voice defeated any clash or cry in the room. "I will avenge my father, the King Seqenenre Tao, and I will reclaim what is ours, Great Wives, Ahhotep and Tetisheri. I will unite our land where my father could not." His chest heaved, and his words rolled in revenge.

Ahhotep stepped forward and placed her hand on the arm of the golden-covered throne. "Call the priests of Amun. We have a coronation to conduct." Her eyes drifted to Tao's body at her feet. "And the priests of Anubis, for we have a King to send to Re." Her hand covered her womb, having birthed twins only ten days, a *decan*, prior. They would never know their father, but if she and Kamose were victorious, they would see him again in the Field of Reeds. And if not, she was sure they would all wander in unrest for eternity.

2

A TIME OF
PERSUASION |
AHHOTEP

SEDJEFATAWY, 1575 BC

A hhotep watched her son Kamose stand in front of his Sedjefatawy throne with the blue woven khepresh crown firmly placed upon his head. She had wanted him to wear the white *hedjet* crown of the Upper, but he chose the celestial *khepresh*, the crown of war. His fingers gripped the handle of the royal mace in his hand. The color drained from his knuckles just as it did when he slew the Aamu messengers at her command.

She glanced at the spot where Tao's body had been laid only a few days earlier before she lifted her eyes to the pristinely painted reliefs that wrapped each of the throne room pillars, depicting Tao and her father smiting their enemies.

The princes of Upper Kemet's nomes had gathered, and what was left of the military leaders stood in front of Kamose, waiting for him to speak. Toes tapped in leather sandals. Arms crossed over bare chests. Kohl-lined eyes stared at them from beyond the dais.

Even though she and her mother stood in support behind him, beads of sweat formed beneath his silversashed diadem. It's shining band with the twin encrusted lotus blooms on the back reminded her of the gods' divine renewal of their appointed one. Kamose glanced back at her and Tetisheri. The diadem's golden cobra, poised to strike, cast a shadow down the bridge of his nose. His eyes, dark as the fertile soil of the Nile after the flood, called to her. She envisioned them as they were when he was a young child, and his arms outstretched to her in need. But as an adult, there was confidence in his eyes, not worry. He did not need her anymore. Yet as he looked back, a flash of anxiety sparkled in his irises.

Ahhotep gave a reassuring nod before Kamose turned to face the throne room's crowd again. He would always be her son—her firstborn son. A part of her heart was reserved only for him.

His twenty years of life had prepared him to take the crown, but she had hoped it would come after his father defeated the Hekka Khasut. Perhaps it was his destiny to expel the foreigners and not Tao's. She had bound him to this path, had she not? She gave him the silent command to attack the Aamu messengers. If he were slain, as was Tao, his blood would be on her hands.

A lump grew thick in her throat, and the torchlight in the room spun. She shut her eyes, grounding herself in the silence of the room. She pushed the fear of losing her child from the farthest reaches of her mind. Kamose had wanted to fight; he saw the vision Tao had. But how was he going to accomplish such a feat? He was only twenty years old, and Tao was not even in his tomb yet.

The last eight years of his life had been spent training for war. And now, his training would be put to the test. But there was a void that needed filling. Tao's general and admiral were slain, and such positions could not go empty—that should be the first order.

Once a general and admiral were by his side, they needed to create a strategy—one far better than those employed by Tao and her father. Kamose could not win a war with obsolete weaponry and tactics. They needed warriors, not farmers with axes, yet that was what they had. For this reason, Tao had been doomed to fail.

Ahhotep shifted in her son's silence.

What words would Kamose speak as his first command? How would he say it? What if they came out in error? The contrasting fear for his future yet confidence in the legacy he would leave grabbed ahold and twisted her belly as she envisioned both the worst and the best of what was to come.

Have faith in your son, she told herself and opened her eyes. *He can do this.*

As if reading her thoughts, Kamose relaxed his shoulders. The white alabaster curve and golden base of Kamose's royal mace threw the room's torchlight across the faces of those gathered before the King.

Kamose pointed his royal weapon at the fleetsmen. "Who among you has had the longest tenure in the King's Fleet?" His voice commanded even the gods' attention.

Well-spoken. Good first words, she thought, and her hesitations diminished, replenished with pride. Why had she worried? Her son was mighty, trained, and prepared. This was her beloved son, with whom she had always been well-pleased.

Kamose swung the mace and pointed it toward the army soldiers. "Who among you?"

Ten men stepped forward, but all were of low rank: a Greatest of Fifty, a fleetsman, a Boat Captain . . . Their collars were simple, no evidence to indicate valor or other feats—no golden fly, no lapis jewels . . .

Ahhotep scanned the men dressed in soldier's uniforms. Farmers. Simple farmers. How would her son beat the Hekka Khasut with men who did not know how to lead? They were not warriors; they would not do.

He lowered his mace. "You are to leave the throne room. Only the highest-ranking officers will remain."

Ahhotep nodded in agreement, and Tetisheri's chest puffed, seemingly satisfied with her grandson's decision.

Those who would not do left the throne room, leaving four men standing before the King: one from the army, three from the fleetsmen.

The last battle with the Hekka Khasut had been a monstrous defeat. Some princes wanted to withdraw from the rebellion, but she and her mother had urged them to stay the course. All of the princes now watched from the back of the throne room, some rubbing their shaven chins in anticipation of how this new king would ensure their promised victory.

He looked at the lone soldier. "Rank?"

"Troop Commander."

It was three ranks below General, but the others had been slaughtered along with Tao. Troop Commander was an honored position, one usually awarded for might, victory, and selflessness in battle.

Ahhotep ran her eyes up and down the smaller man's body. He did not appear mighty. It did not seem he could have had many victories, but his looks could be deceiving. Tao had not been a large man either. She looked upon her son; Kamose was taller than her but shorter than most men.

Kamose nodded at the Troop Commander. "Name?"

"Pennekhbet."

Kamose swung his mace and sat on his throne, slamming its wooden handle into the golden-covered arm of his wooden chair. "Then Pennekhbet, you will be my General, for my brother is too young for the honor, and the former General had no sons. Let Pennekhbet be dressed in the golden collar and the bronze and leather armor uniform of the General."

When the servants and stewards obeyed his command, Kamose focused on the three fleetsmen. "Ranks and Names."

The first man spoke. "We are all Captains of the Fleet. I am Baba; this is Mahu and Thaneni."

Ahhotep scanned the fleetsman named Baba. He looked like a mighty man with a well-decorated collar and well-defined features against his oiled burnt-umber skin. His eyes shifted to meet hers, and in them, she found a softness, a warmth, a similar sorrow. She blinked, and his gaze returned to her son, who spoke.

"Why do three of you stand before me when there is only one Troop Commander?"

Mahu and Thaneni's eyes fell to the floor, but Baba stepped forward. "We were holding the ports already conquered. Seeing the Hekka Khasut sails flowing freely up the Nile in force, we knew our fellow soldiers had fallen. We retreated to the Upper to save our men's lives so we could all fight another day. If we were in error, take our lives in dishonor."

Mahu and Thaneni's eyes grew wide, and they shuffled back.

Baba glanced at them and then cleared his throat. "Take *my* life in dishonor. There is no sense in taking three lives when we have so few to spare."

Kamose chewed his lip as he thought. Ahhotep considered the three men. Of the three captains, Baba had the most lapis gems on his collar. He was brave, and he was right. Had they tried to stop the Hekka Khasut, they would have been slaughtered—the few of the fleet retained to hold the position. As much as it pained her to acknowledge Tao had made a foolish mistake, an all-out surge on the next city down the Nile could only have ended in failure. He should have stayed and built a perimeter before advancing.

"Was it your order to retreat, Captain Baba?" Kamose's question rang out.

Baba nodded. "Yes, my King, and I will take full responsibility, whatever the consequences." Baba stood tall—confident in his decision.

Mahu and Thaneni shifted their weight behind him and glanced at the guards in the room, perhaps afraid to lose their comrade. Kamose pointed the mace toward Baba, but Baba remained calm.

He would make a good officer, one who was steady in moments of stress, and Kamose spoke what she thought he should do. "This man shall be my new Admiral. Dress him in leather and a collar fit for such a position."

Kamose scanned the officials. "Vizier, is the transport for the slain Aamu ready to be sent?"

Tao's vizier, Tetinefer, stepped forward. He had served the prior king well, so Kamose had allowed him to keep his position at the suggestion of Tetisheri.

Tetinefer bowed. "Yes, and the Aamu's khopeshes have been withheld, per your command."

Kamose nodded. "Who among our ranks is interested in weapon design, to study the khopesh and produce them for the armies of Kemet?"

Silence befell the throne room. Kamose looked to the princes, still quiet. "No one in all the nomes?"

The princes looked at each other, remaining silent with leery eyes.

Ahhotep knew the answer but sensed none would

give up any more men for the cause—not after the slaughter they had endured.

Baba again spoke. "My son, although young, has shown exceptional skill with all weapons. He is fascinated by their design and would give his life in service for the greater Kemet."

"Then bring him to the fortress tower my father built, Per-djed-ken, south of the palace, to begin his analysis," Kamose said and turned his attention to the nomes' royalty in the back.

Ahhotep eyed the princes, who remained silent. They were skeptical; it was clear. She narrowed her eyes, debating whether she should give Kamose a chance to remedy their doubts or ignore them in case they were substantiated. But any uncertainty would increase the wedge between Kamose and their support, so she made a decision and spoke for her son. "Speak, princes. What have you to say?"

A prince among them lifted his head, so the torchlight flooded his frustrated face. An overabundance of kohl was fresh around his eyes, and his skin was excessively oiled to a superior shine. "It was disappointing to see yet another Waset royal fail in his attempt to retake the Lower."

Heads bobbed. Murmurs reverberated in the room.

Tetisheri shifted on her feet and lifted her chin at the prince. Her eyes narrowed at him, and Ahhotep did the same. Had she spoken in error? No, it was time to put the doubts to rest. Her son was prepared to be king, and they would believe it by the end of the day.

Kamose pushed off his throne to stand, and the crowd quieted. "Prince Tetian of Ta-Seti," he said. "It was disappointing to see yet another battle take place without the full support of the nomes." He swung the royal mace and pointed it at Tetian. "Had the nomes given their all for the cause their words so nobly support, perhaps my grandfather would have been firstly successful, and perhaps my father's body would not have been brought home in disgrace."

Some princes averted their gaze, knowing it to be true, yet others, such as Tetian and Metjen, stared full in the face at the Waset royal. Kamose continued. "Especially the trade-rich and flourishing nome of Ta-Seti. Perhaps you do not support the unification of Kemet under Re, King of the Gods? Perhaps you would prefer the Set-worshipping imposters in the Lower to continue their reign over—"

Tetian slammed his fist into an open hand; its resulting smack drew the gazes of those in the throne room. "I worship Re. Do not dare insult my obedience to the supreme god." He threw his hands to his sides. "We all wish to see the Set-worshippers gone and our land reunited—"

"Then why do you hold back your trade, resources, and men, Prince Tetian, Prince Metjen, Prince Setka?" Kamose's deafening question made a few princes cower.

Kamose's breath was ragged, and his knuckles again drained of color as he held fast to the royal mace.

If they had provided, Tao's body would not be in the tents of Anubis.

Metjen sneered. "Because the Waset family has never gained victory!"

Setka added more respectfully, "Your grandfather spoke great words, but his ax never saw battle. Your father struck without strategy after a few simple taunts from King Apepi. And then you, King Kamose, slew two royal messengers when they came with an offer of peace. Where is the victory warranting—"

"We had no choice," Kamose defended his family's actions. "It was a justifiable act of war."

He looked at all the dissenting princes one-by-one and then finally addressed Prince Tetian as he would make the perfect example.

"Not all the nomes are as trade-rich from the south as Ta-Seti. The Hekka Khasut squash our trade from the Nile's north. They parse the crumbs of trade to us after eating their full course. Every generation, we grow weaker. Soon, the Hekka Khasut will continue their infestation south, and we, the true inhabitants of Kemet, will be forced to be wanderers in the Dashret." Kamose found the eyes of the princes of those nomes. "Do you wish for your children's children to be wanderers in their own kingdom or to worship Set, the god of chaos and darkness, as the King of the Gods?"

Heads shook, and Kamose continued.

"Then give me your resources; give me your men! I will lead us to victory. I will restore the kingdom of Kemet. I will ensure our future will not end but live on. I will raise Kemet into one great nation under the rightful gods, but I cannot do it alone!"

Prince Paser of the nome Herui, the nome just north of Waset, raised his hand, balled tightly into a fist. "Herui is with you, King Kamose."

"Ta-Ur as well," Prince Setka said in an uncomfortable decree.

"Because you have an Admiral now from my city of Nekheb, then my nome of Nekhen will be by your side," Prince Nakht said in reserve.

"Meseh will supply all able men and send our sons to train at Per-djed-ken," Prince Baufre said with a yawn and a rub of his round belly.

Ahhotep licked her lip in anticipation of what was to

come. But the offers of aid stopped there. The remaining four princes said nothing. The dissenting voices had sway over the others. At least, they had the support of four nomes, only one of which was enthusiastic. Kamose's speech had turned Setka, for the time being.

She narrowed her eyes at them while Tetisheri stepped forward to stand beside her grandson. She opened her arms wide—her dress's translucent, pleated sleeves diffused the sunlight from the ceiling's vents, basking her in an aura of divinity.

Her sights were on Tetian. "The princes who have not offered aid seem to support this vision with their words, but their actions speak louder in dissent."

The four princes leaned back, crossed their arms, and remained silent. Tetian, though, shifted his weight and averted his eyes from God's Mother, the queen mother of Seqenenre Tao.

Ahhotep shook her head at the hypocrites as she joined her mother in line with her son to reinforce the stance of unity. The wealth, if given only from Tetian's Ta-Seti, would cut the war short, but as it was, his greed and hoarding, along with the other three princes, would prolong the struggle. No, they would need to secure a significant victory before seeing any more wealth or men flow in from the nomes.

Kamose seemingly ignored the dissenters and gave a firm nod to the princes who had joined him, raising his mace in the air. "Your names will be remembered, princes of Kemet, who aid the divinely appointed in his hour of need!"

He looked at his new general and admiral before peering at his mother and grandmother for their approval and blessing. Ahhotep gave a slight nod, and his grandmother's face remained as stone, but the pride was evident in her eyes. Yet her gaze seemed to go past him toward Tetian. Perhaps she was happy at how Kamose handled the dissenter, and that was how she thought of it. Kamose's first commands as King were good. Now, a far more difficult task lay before him—no, lay before *them*, for she would never let him bear this burden alone.

"Adjourn to the council room so that we may decide how to overcome the Hekka Khasut," Kamose said and led the way to the adjoining council room.

Ahhotep assumed, without all the nomes' full support, it would be years before they could reclaim what they lost, much less retake the Lower in full. They needed a victory—a decisive victory—to collect the contents of the four princes' storehouses. She doubted the princes would give anything until the complete Upper Kemet was retaken and they could push into the Lower.

She grimaced as the servants lit the torches in the council room. They couldn't even spare oil to burn all the torches for the day. They needed to be wise with their resources and make them endure, not just for months but years. Full-out surges on the large cities would end in failure, just as Tao's final attempt had shown them. A much slower pace and more efficient and effective strategy would have to be enacted.

Kamose sat down in his chair and glanced at Tetisheri, his officials, and, lastly, Ahhotep.

She would help him be the King he needed to be. Together, they could do what Tao could not, or at least she hoped, else they be conquered and punished as traitors.

The princes stood along the wall. They were usually

not privy to these conversations, but the Waset royal family needed them to see Kamose's stewardship.

Be confident in your son. He is divinely appointed. Be good to Kemet, and the gods will bless us, Ahhotep told herself as she found a few princes' harsh glares upon Kamose. *And I must be ready, for the road to winning this war will be a long one.*

3
A TIME OF STRATEGY |
AHHOTEP
SEDJEFATAWY, 1575 BC

Ahhotep eyed the eight princes lining the wall of the council room as Tetian opened his mouth to speak to the King. The silence had been maddening after Kamose had asked for suggestions on how to proceed. She bit her tongue to see what the dissenter would say.

"Kamose, Given Life, our great King," Tetian began. His words were right, but there seemed to be an undertone of mockery. "What shall we do in our struggle against the Hekka Khasut, you ask? Surely your many years of wisdom will provide a plan for us. You are our king, after all. Why should you ask us?"

Ahhotep glanced at her mother, who stood up. "You will respect the throne, Prince Tetian." Her stony glare lingered upon him, but his eyes only narrowed at her.

He opened his mouth, but Tetisheri lifted a flat palm to him.

"Silence your tongue if you cannot speak with the reverence due to the King of Kemet," she said.

Metjen and Setka snorted at the rebuke, but at

Tetisheri's sharp glare, they pressed a polite smile on their lips.

Tetian refrained from speaking, but a sneer arose on his face, along with a shake of his head. Ahhotep could have stood and said the same, but Tetian would not have closed his mouth and done what she said. She had tried to control the room many times when she was on the throne while her husband was off to battle. Some of the princes, Tetian as one of them, had only mocked her until Tetisheri stepped in. She wondered at her mother's power over them. Why had they given her mother respect and, to her, nothing? Specifically Tetian. Did she need to earn it? And if so, how? As she thought, she placed a finger alongside her lips and stared at the outspoken objectors. If she could uncover their motivations, then she may be able to sway them to their side and give up their wealth for the cause.

While ruminating, she looked at Tetian's sneering face, Metjen's pressed smile, Setka's cold eyes, and Baufre's vacant stare. She noticed each of their heads sat right under the feet and smiting mace of her father's image etched into the wall above them. She snorted. And if she couldn't find out their motivations, would they be enemies in their midst? She cracked her neck with a sharp twist of her head. She hoped not. Any more division and they would surely fail.

Kamose stood and again asked his question. "In light of the failure of my father's strategy, does anyone have insights into how we should proceed? We have few fighting men and few resources. The weapons of the Hekka Khasut prove to be superior: the horses, the chariots, the khopesh."

Silence.

He spoke again. "We have the son of Admiral Baba

who will study the two khopeshes we took from the Aamu messengers in hopes of supplying our troops with them. But we do not have chariots or horses. How do we gain an advantage over superior weaponry? Those who have fought against them, what weaknesses do they possess for exploitation?"

Baba cleared his throat and glanced at the new general Pennekhbet before speaking. "The chariot cabins are large. The wheels are small; they cannot turn sharply without turning over." He chopped a hand in the air to demonstrate what they could do as he once again met Ahhotep's gaze. "Their strength comes from a fast approach."

His full lips turned downward in the sense of a knowing sympathy. He was sorrowful she had lost her brother-husband.

Ahhotep's heart fell into her stomach at his second gaze that day, his motivation dawning on her. She forgot to breathe as her last image of Tao's broken body was revived again in her memory. She loved Tao as her brother but also as the father of her children. He had been irrational at times, small in stature, rash . . . And had easily fallen to provocation. She had tried to calm him many times, but he had never listened.

Nevertheless, Tao was still her brother and husband. She missed him. Were her emotions obvious enough to solicit the comfort of the new Admiral? She hoped not, for then her mother would scold her for showing weakness.

Baba continued as if he had never looked at the Great Wife. "The horses are weak at the knees and the neck. They cover their beasts in little armor, which seems to give them a faster approach."

Kamose adjusted the royal mace in his hand. "Then it

24

seems we need to capture a chariot, study it, make it faster, more agile. Or we need to be able to get close enough to kill the beasts, the horses." He took a deep breath.

Ahhotep sensed the overwhelming task in front of him. She had done this to him, her firstborn son. *Think*, she told herself, ignoring the Admiral for the moment.

"Both of these require men who can fight," Kamose said and glanced at the four silent princes.

An idea sprang upon her. "What of the *Medjay*?" she asked aloud. All eyes turned to her.

Tetian scoffed. "Now you want to bring the Kermans into this struggle? Shall we invite the Kushites too? Why not all the land of Wawat? Or even better, how about the gentle Apiru in the Lower? They will all surely run the Hekka Khasut out."

Baba and Pennekhbet jolted from their chairs, wrenching their necks to see who spoke to God's Mother with such disrespect.

But Ahhotep stood up in elegance and grace. The vulture of her royal headdress had an open golden beak ready to strike.

"Prince Tetian, leave your scorn in Ta-Seti," she said and quickly hurried to speak again before he could mock her. "The Kermans have long been allies and trading partners with all of the Upper. Why would they not fight for us? The Medjay are elite warriors, mercenaries, and all mercenaries fight for a price. It would even benefit them if we were to take back our lands and restore our trade flow up the Nile again."

The room was filled with bobbing heads.

Baba added, "They are masters of the bow and spear. They shoot greater distances than we are able. They can perhaps take out the charioteers before they begin their charge."

Pennekhbet also spoke with a nod to Kamose. "We can hire the Medjay as well to train our men." Then he added, glancing at the four princes who withheld support, "The few men we have."

Setka scoffed. "And how will you pay for these Medjay? Elite warriors do not come cheap."

Metjen and Nekhen lifted an eyebrow as they waited for a response.

Ahhotep's mind raced. She had hoped the suggestion would bring about support from the princes. It hadn't. She debated what to say: they could cut down rations even more and use fewer ships or pay the soldiers less grain than they already had.

Paser of Herui stepped forward in her silence. "I have already offered my men and resources. However, this I say to you, we do not have much, King Kamose, but what we have is yours."

Kamose lowered his chin in gratitude. "Your offering is much appreciated, Prince Paser."

Metjen stepped forward, glaring at Paser. "I think the loudest unspoken question in this council room is this: Should we give you our resources, or are you going to waste them like your father?"

Kamose responded in confidence, "I am divinely appointed and the good steward doing what is best for Kemet. The King is the defender of our land, is he not?"

Tetian smiled with thin lips spread across his face. "Yes, King Kamose, but I ask you, like Metjen, my fellow Prince of Bat, will you waste our resources like your father, who was also divinely appointed and a good steward, and all the rest?"

All eight princes waited for what Kamose would say.

Ahhotep remained silent. Her son had to answer, and she prayed to Horus that he be with his living embodiment, for this answer could gain the princes to his side or lose them forever.

Kamose pushed the chair back and paced the front of the room, royal mace swinging in his hand. "My father was rash. I am not. My father had not studied strategy and entered this war without the proper training, yet I have been trained in war and strategy since I wore a shendyt." He stopped and eyed the princes.

"My father struggled for years attacking Apu, Shashotep, Zawty, and other large port cities. He lost many men trying to bluff his might over the Hekka Khasut. As Defender of Kemet, I will attack the smaller ports north of the larger cities. Cut off the Nile trade, starve them out, ransack them for resources, and move ahead to the next smaller port."

Setka shook his head. "Your strategy will take decades to complete, and what happens when the Nile fans out in the delta before it reaches the Great Sea? How will your strategy work then?"

Kamose lowered his mace. "It won't. But," he said, "we will make a path to King Apepi's magnificent city of Hut-Waret and lay siege until we can drive him out."

Metjen scoffed. "What makes you think the other Hekka Khasut colonies will not come to Hut-Waret's aid?"

Kamose lifted his chin. "They might, but we will have already proved our might by reaching Hut-Waret in the first place. They will cower."

"You make a big assumption, King Kamose," Tetian said, retreating under the firm stare of Tetisheri.

"This is my strategy, with or without your support," Kamose said. "Thus, it is written."

Ahhotep nodded in support of her son. He would be a great King. His strategy would work at least until they breached the Lower, but they would need time. She scanned the four princes who withheld support. Maybe once they regained what Tao lost, they would provide their much-needed resources, especially once they entered the Lower, where the Hekka Khasut's influence was far greater.

Her gaze returned to Baba as all left the council room at Kamose's command. "Walk with me, Admiral," she commanded.

Her maidservants, Meret and Nena, followed them at a close distance, and Ahhotep led Baba to the courtyard where Tao's statue was being completed. She stood facing her brother-husband's stone image with Baba beside her.

"You made a wise decision to retreat," she said, and Baba opened his mouth to thank her, but she cut him off. "I will pray to Anhur that you will continue to be a model warrior making wise decisions for my son."

Baba closed his mouth and nodded.

"You may speak if you wish," she said.

"I thank God's Mother for her prayers to Anhur."

They stood silent until Ahhotep asked a question she probably should not have asked. "Why do you glance at me, Admiral Baba?"

He cleared his throat and shifted on his feet. She hid a soft smile at his antics but remained in her regal posture. Part of her wondered if he would deny it, but he did not.

"My wife, Lady Ebana, traveled to the Field of Reeds several years ago," he said.

"I fondly remember Lady Ebana. May her ka live forever." Ahhotep thought of the noblewoman from

Nekheb, the nome of Nekhen. She had never realized Ebana's husband was a fleetsman; she had always assumed he would have been a priest or scribe, given Ebana's status. But if Baba had captured the heart of Lady Ebana, he must have been much more than his occupation in her eyes. If Ebana thought enough of Baba to make him her husband, Ahhotep could trust him as Kamose's advisor. The tension in her shoulders dissipated at the thought. Kamose had chosen his Admiral well.

"My son and daughter remain with me in the land of the living," Baba said. "I only glance at God's Mother because I share in her loss of losing a spouse."

Ahhotep blinked away the coming tears as she traced Tao's eyes carved into the stone. So she had been obvious, and a sigh escaped her at the scolding she would receive from her mother.

"I do not wish to resurface your pain," Baba whispered, misinterpreting her sigh. But she would not allow him to know the true reason.

"Then do not," she said and turned to face him.

His gaze remained with hers before his head dropped in a bow. "As God's Mother commands."

He stood taller than her, so she could still see his face though his head was bowed. The vision of Kamose being brought home in the same manner as Tao or, even worse, hearing of his execution in the flame caused a thick bitterness on the back of her tongue. She swallowed it down.

She wanted to tell him to make sure her son came home alive, not to cause her more pain, but in doing so, she would make her son appear weak. He was not weak. He was intelligent and capable. So, she remained silent.

He lifted his head from his bow, and again the

warmth of his gaze filled her as if he was telling her not to worry about Kamose. Or, perhaps, it was merely what she wished he was trying to say to her.

Tetisheri's light footsteps sounded on the mud brick path surrounding the courtyard. She stood in Ahhotep's line of sight and observed the shared stare between Ahhotep and Baba.

"Come, God's Mother," Tetisheri said, and Ahhotep broke her gaze with Baba.

"Thank you for your service in the King's Fleet," she whispered. "I pray you will gain victory over our enemy."

Without another word, she left Baba in the courtyard. She followed her mother toward the royal harem's economic center to begin dividing grain and gold for the wage of the Medjay.

But she peered back at the Admiral and caught his gaze once more before she rounded the corner and entered the royal harem.

4

A TIME OF PRIORITY |
AHHOTEP

SEDJEFATAWY, 1572 BC

T he sun's rays pricked Ahhotep's skin as she rested in a rooftop courtyard. She sighed underneath the heat of *the Aten*, the sun disc. It had been a long three years.

The crumbling mud brick walls of her grandfather's palace stared back at her. A jagged crack forced its way down to the wall's base, and a few workmen were there to patch it. Royal body servants stood in front of her so they would not gaze at the Great Royal Wife or otherwise try to do anything but fix the wall. Her maidservants, Meret and Nena, knelt beside her. With a firm grip, she clutched the cool faience amulets of Isis and Hathor and pressed them against her chest. She remembered her days as a little girl when her father laid out plans to expand Sedjefatawy, the northern palace, and then again as a woman when her husband expanded it into a fortress. Yet through the years, this had always been her courtyard, even though the women's rooms were on the other side of the harem. This was her place of rest.

The shade of the palm branch glided from her head to her eyes as a servant girl fanned her in a soft, fluid motion. Its breeze was a welcome respite from the sun's prick. Her tongue longed for wine or water or even beer at noontime, but she said nothing—her teeth clenched and her jaw clamped tight. The amulets indented in the palm of her hand as a tear budded in her eye.

Mother of the Gods and Lady of Magic—grant me healing. Grant me protection. Grant me peace. Marvelous are your ways, she prayed but could not finish the silent plea.

She could not bear to attend the *Kap*, the royal nursery and school, not after hearing what the royal physician-priest had to say about her youngest son and daughter, twins at birth, born in the days that preceded the news of her husband's brutal end.

Their palace sat on the edge of the Nile, north of the city of Waset, named after their nome. If Kamose had lost at any port, she would be sure the Hekka Khasut would charge their way to Sedjefatawy without much thought of the other nomes. The fear of burning and never seeing the Field of Reeds chilled her blood and made sleep elusive. Perhaps, it was only the fear of envisioning Tao's contorted face and what the Hekka Khasut king could have done that day that distorted her sense of security within her palace walls. Her son had shown to be a competent and patient king, not rash like Tao. He took much after his grandmother. He would endure the war. He had to. He was going to.

A sigh escaped her, and the heat of the Aten's rays made her eyelids droop. She revisited the continual fear in her mind: burning, her and her family. No afterlife. Wandering in eternal restlessness. Always tiring but never able to rest. Always hungry but never able to eat. That would become them if Kamose lost even one battle, but their strategy had worked . . . so far.

So why am I worried about an imminent attack? She

swallowed the lump in her throat. Tao's body had been brought home less than half a day after Baba and Pennekhbet had returned with word of retreat. Not enough time to evacuate. Not enough time to do anything.

She wished to sleep, but she had to be alert if the palace should ever come under attack. They would only survive if she, in the few moments she would have, were able to get her children and herself to Per-djed-ken and sneak away under the guise of locals.

But Kamose was winning, slowly, very slowly, but still winning. They left a full force behind them at the last conquered port in case they lost the smaller one to the north. Enough time would be afforded to the royal family if the army surrendered. Yet, Kamose would be slain in that event. She envisioned his face marred by ax wounds and wrapping her arms around her slain firstborn son, the pride of her loins.

Stop, she pleaded with her heart. *I cannot endure this.*

The distressing thoughts swirled and muddied her mind as she questioned her actions three years ago, just as she did every day. What had she done, giving the order to slay the Aamu messengers? If she had not, they could be at peace. She could have her son home. They could all live long lives and certainly travel to the Field of Reeds.

She could sleep.

Her eyelids slid closed as the budding tear reached full blossom and ran down her cheek. Another servant girl wiped it away, and all at once, she wished to be alone. The smell of the workers' mud pitch and the repeated soft *scrape* of their bronze trowels intensified her desire until the muffled shouts came from the main gateway below.

She sat straight up and strained to hear.

"Are we under attack?" she asked, her heart beating hard in her chest. Why was she jumping to such conclusions? It was such a similar sound when the Aamu boats docked at the palace with Tao's body in tow.

Settle, she ordered her heartbeat. But as with every time before, when a clamor sounded below, it did not settle.

Her maidservants looked at each other with wide eyes. She pushed the young palm bearer from her side and ran to the door with the body servants close behind. She ordered them, "Go to the King's children; hide them should our enemies be upon us." She pointed a finger down one of the two long halls of Sedjefatawy's palace. "Come quickly, Meret and Nena," she commanded of her maidservants.

They hurried to the throne room on the first floor of Sedjefatawy and pushed open the doors. Empty, save for the usual guards and her daughter and mother. Her finger tapped on her thigh. She took her place next to Kamose's chief sister-wife, her daughter Ahhotep Tasherit called *Tep* by her family. Tetisheri sat in the back, hunched from age. She told herself there was nothing to fear and strode in under a calm facade.

Tep rubbed the corners of her eyes, and her steward, Iset, tended to the smeared kohl. "Mother, I am afraid," she whispered as the shouting grew louder.

"Do not be afraid, child." Ahhotep hushed through her shallow breaths and tingling fingertips. The imagined flame's burn teased her body, growing beads of sweat upon her brow.

Tetisheri rasped, "I am not afraid, and she is not a child."

Ahhotep turned to admonish her mother but instead

gave her a solemn stare and left the chiding unspoken: *I know she is not a child, but she is still my child.*

She soothed her grown daughter as she did when she was a babe: "The Field of Reeds is peaceful if this life ends today," Ahhotep said.

A royal messenger burst through the throne room doors and came before the queens, only to fall to his knee. His flustered face ripe from the sun's burn meant he had come in haste. Her shoulders tightened, and her jaw grew taut, bracing herself for the worse.

The messenger's voice shook with breath. "King's Chief Wife, I come bearing word from Buhen."

Ahhotep's shoulders sank, relieved it was news from the south, not the north.

"Speak your message," her daughter said.

"The Kushites have attacked and now make their way up the Nile. What shall you command of King Kamose's army?"

Tep turned to her mother, staring wide-eyed. *What do I say?* Her eyes spoke her plea. A small whimper escaped her lips. "They are coming here?" Her voice shook with fear.

Ahhotep drew a sharp breath while the tingle in her fingertips vanished at the sight of the royal messenger having come alone. At least they were not there attacking already. She calmed her mind and thought through the options.

To pull back meant leaving their Kerman allies without a defense since their Medjay were with her son. Yet, to stay meant death as they did not have the numbers to keep the Kushites at bay.

Her mind debated: *We cannot lose the Medjay. We cannot lose their loyalty. But we cannot lose our men either.*

Ahhotep cleared her throat to speak in a loud and

firm voice as required of a queen. "From the mouth of God's Mother, send word to evacuate the Kerman Kingdom to . . ."

"Abu." Tetisheri's shrewd voice cut through the momentary pause of Ahhotep's speech.

"Yes, Abu," Ahhotep said with a slight grimace at her mother's continual lack of confidence in her. Once, a perceived aid, but now, a constant display of disappointment.

"Hold our forces there," Ahhotep continued. "Do not let the Kushites north of Abu. Carry the command to General Pennekhbet, royal messenger and servant of the King."

The messenger's head fell in a sharp nod of reverence. "As God's Mother commands." He stood and exited with the same urgency he had come.

The doors closed, and as much as Ahhotep wanted to rebuke her mother again, this time for speaking for her, she knew she could not. At least not in front of Tep. So instead, she landed a heavy fist on the wooden throne.

"To Ammit with those Kushites," she yelled. She stared at the empty sockets that once held precious gems, picked out to fund the war with the Hekka Khasut. The throne's soft inlay of glittering gold remained as a last resort. She wished Ammit, the demon beast, would feast on the hearts of their enemies.

"Curse them," she whispered. "Staking their claim on what is left of the true Kemet kingdom while we are rendered vulnerable from our dealings in the north."

A soft snicker came from the back. "You were always so dramatic, my daughter," Tetisheri croaked, shook her head, and sipped karkade tea from her clay-fired cup. Refreshed from the cooled tea, her voice regained its usual rich, sardonic tone. "It is good to see nothing has changed."

Ahhotep's fist uncurled at the insult, and she swept a finger down the smooth golden metal to appease her temper. She turned to face Tetisheri, who seemed to care more about Kemet than any of her own blood. It had been her goading that prompted her father, husband, and son into this war.

At least I care. The rebuff to her insult halted behind closed lips, and Ahhotep swallowed it. She opened her mouth to refute the older woman's words in a more respectful tone, but Tetisheri quickly cut her off.

"Where were you, Ahhotep? The throne is empty, and you were needed." Her dark eyes narrowed, and the cold of the coming season set into them.

"The throne is not empty." Ahhotep's lips pressed thin. "My daughter is here in her husband's place."

Tetisheri sipped her red tea again. "Where were you, Ahhotep? You were needed here." The monotonously repeated questions could have rendered any heartbeat still.

"I did not sleep well, Mother. I needed time in meditation with Isis and Hathor." Ahhotep lifted her chin and took a deep breath at her mother's unamused stare. "You served as regent in Father's absence. You do not need me here with you all the time."

Silence.

Ahhotep continued. "Tep does not need both of us here."

"She does." Tetisheri gestured a hand toward her granddaughter. "Do you not see the look of fear on her face?" She slowly stood from her chair, holding her empty cup out for a servant to take away; the silent command was executed swiftly. With hands folded in front of her belly, she strode up to her daughter, her back straight and her head lifted. Her long fine linen dress draped about her upper arms and wrapped tightly at her thin waist. The blue faience beaded collar draped around her neck. Her grey braids, tightly plaited with false black hair to give an illusion of youth, supported her vulture headdress.

Ahhotep stood just as tall in her matching regality. The woman would not intimidate her as she justified her will to stand firm.

"And yes, daughter," Tetisheri began. "I stood as Regent for your father while he was at war. I *earned* respect due me. You will have to do it for yourself as well. That means you must speak without hesitation, control your emotions, and issue the best commands without delay. As I see it, you have yet to master any of these abilities."

She scanned Ahhotep's frame, causing Ahhotep's shoulders to shrink from the lack of approval momentarily. "I helped you in my son's absence, and now I am a tired old woman. You shall advise your daughter in Kamose's absence. She struggles to keep herself controlled and eloquent amid these tense circumstances."

She inclined her head as if daring Ahhotep to speak again. "Much like you were and still are to some extent. It will take much work, but at least you have learned to control yourself while in the presence of guests in the throne room . . . a majority of the time and seemingly much more quickly than my eldest grandchild. It is hard to think she comes from the same blood as the rest of the family."

Ahhotep forced a polite smile at the weathered-skinned woman instead of pointing out that Tao was just as emotional and rash. She let Tetisheri walk away without another word. Her mother left, her maidservants close behind.

"As you command, Great Wife of my father," Ahhotep muttered with annoyance under her breath so her daughter could not hear. Even though her mother had been the one to whisper in both her father's and husband's ears about the state of Kemet and the vision of a united land, she was still worthy of respect even when she held very little for her.

Tep's shoulders were drawn tightly inward at the indirect lashing she received from her grandmother. Breathing deeply with a pinched face, she crossed her arms at the wrists in front of her belly and tried to regain her composure and keep from crying.

"Do not bother with her words, Daughter," Ahhotep said and stared at the empty throne, turning over their situation in her mind.

Because of Mother, we are near desolation. Kamose can only go forward once the resources from the larger port are taken. My father is slain, my husband is slain, and now my son may be slain as well. She pushed that thought to the back of her mind, reassuring herself that Kamose was a competent and level-headed King. But they were weak, and the Kushites took advantage. If they captured Waset, they would not let them live either.

Her finger dug into an empty socket where a lapis once decorated the throne. The small dark hole was like that of an empty tomb where she would likely be placed if such events came to pass. She sighed. *Pride and power, Mother.* She lowered her forehead to the throne; the soft gold cooled her brow as she thought—*all of this war for pride and power. You tire of it? I tire of it. You shall journey west while I live to pick up the pieces of the war you helped begin.*

Her eyes closed. *And in a moment of weakness, I continued the war and bound Kamose to it. Would it have been so bad to live as simple Waset royals and let the Hekka Khasut keep our land and trade?* She grimaced. The answer remained unknown to her.

Tep's timid voice piped up, interrupting her thoughts: "Mother, what if our forces cannot hold the Kushites at Abu?"

Her eyes narrowed as the question repeated in her mind. She rested her forehead on her hand. *There would be nowhere to run,* she told herself.

Her gaze slowly lifted to meet that of her frightened daughter's. "Then we shall end as your father, and Kemet will be only a forgotten empire in the sand, split between the Hekka Khasut and the Kushites." She could not endure the fear in Tep's eyes, so she shifted her sights to the reliefs behind the throne and walked toward them. "I will not hide the truth from you, my daughter. I suggest we all learn how to wield a spear or an ax . . ."

Her voice trailed off as she thought of Per-djed-ken, the fortress her father had planned in anticipation of the war with the Hekka Khasut—finished by Tao. It had been built north of the city of Waset and south of the palace. They never thought their peaceful and flourishing Kushite neighbors to the south would turn on them. Perhaps they should have built two fortresses.

The smell of stagnant oil from the torches lining the throne room filled her nostrils. The torch lamps had sat unburned for days to conserve them for when they needed them. "Tao, I wish you were here," she whispered to herself. "Even though your rashness got you slain, you had such passion. I need you to help me. What do I do?"

"Mother, who should learn to wield a spear?" Tep's voice rose in concern. "Children and women are to fight too?"

In a soft voice, Ahhotep answered. "The Kushites will kill the royal children and take the women as their slaves. Give the order: all shall learn to fight by the end of the season. I must attend to Per-djed-ken. I need to see if the khopesh is ready for distribution, and I shall return with a number if they are."

Tep shuffled on her feet behind her. Her voice, again timid: "Spears and axes can be thrown, Mother. Swords cannot. Why do you waste our time and resources with the khopesh?"

It was a good question. Ahhotep took a fingernail to the itchy scalp at the base of her wig before turning around and speaking to her daughter. "The khopesh can take a head from a body. Spears cannot. Our archers need to be used better in battle. They do nothing once the ground troops have advanced." Her mind raced on how to solve such a dilemma. They had received a broken chariot and injured horses last month from Kamose, and she sent him more of the boys who had completed their training. She sighed. It seemed an impossible task. Tep only stared at her; she opened her mouth to question her mother again.

Ahhotep did not want to argue and said, "I will return before the sun rises tomorrow. Make the decree that all shall learn to fight, Chief Wife of King Kamose."

She stepped from the royal dais and commanded the servants in the throne room. "Prepare *The Rising* for my journey to Per-djed-ken." Two servants left ahead of Ahhotep. Her maidservants escorted her to the port, Nena ahead and Meret behind. The river had flooded, and the plain between Sedjefatawy and its southern tower was covered in the Nile's life-bringing waters.

The sun's harsh rays beat against her eyelids as she blinked in rapid succession upon stepping from the throne room. The servants and a royal fleetsman helped Ahhotep board her small boat called The Rising, and soon they sailed up the Nile to the south tower of Per-djed-ken.

She surveyed the small village between the palace and the southern tower or what was left of it. She watched the people stop and look at the royal barge. She sat up straight and held her chin parallel to the water. She gripped the armrests of her throne seated at the center of the boat. They would not see a weak royal family. Even though her back ached with each lap of the Nile's waters, she kept straight for her people.

The village was dilapidated. The people used all their possessions to fund and supply the sacred war. The women and children lined the streets and the fields, scraping together what they could for food and clothes. Of the men, only the old remained—the young, off to war. A lone Medjay trained up the young common boys and another in the Kap for the royal and noble boys. Ahmose would soon join them per the command she told her daughter to give. As well as her other children . . . except Binpu.

Her heart twisted for her youngest son. He would not last in this life much longer. His twin sister, Ahmose-Tumerisy, might not either. She wished for their little breaths to be on her chest and their little fingers wrapped around hers.

She was a Great Wife, however. Her time was needed elsewhere, yet Ahhotep wondered if they would pass into the Field of Reeds not knowing their own mother. She swallowed the lump in her throat. *At least Ahmose-Nefertari stays with them; they will know her love.* The vision of her third-born daughter came to mind—always quiet, but she had a way of soothing her siblings.

With such lonely thoughts, The Rising docked at Per-djed-ken, and with one last heavy sigh, she renounced any desire to return to the palace so she could run to the Kap's nursery.

I am needed elsewhere, she thought and forced her mind to focus on the task at hand.

Soldiers ushered Ahhotep in and up the steps of the tower. She peered out a window that oversaw the King's fleet, being readied to sail south to Abu.

"Take me to Ahmose, son of Ebana and Admiral Baba." She commanded upon entry of the main room.

"At once." A soldier dipped his chin and led her to the supply room.

The young man of about eighteen turned when she entered. "My Queen, God's Mother, what commands your presence here at the fortress?" His head bobbed in the uncertainty of how to appear before the queen.

"Ill tidings, I am afraid." She turned her chin to her shoulder, signaling the others to leave. Only her maidservants remained. "The Kushites have captured Buhen. They make their way here. I have ordered our forces to hold with the Kermans at Abu."

"Yes, word has just come. I ordered the fleet to be in Abu by sunrise," Ahmose-Ebana cleared his throat, and his shoulders shrunk back as if second-guessing his actions.

But Ahhotep pressed her lips into a warm smile at the young man. He had made the right decision. He was becoming a capable leader.

"Admiral Baba should be proud of such a son," she

said and saw the gleam in his eye at her words. Ahmose-Ebana took after his late mother, but he held the same deep, dark eyes as his father's. She had often found solace in the Admiral's eyes over the years as they each shared the feeling of losing a spouse. He had said nothing else after their first encounter in the courtyard. He had done nothing out of the line of an Admiral, but she was sure he conveyed all he needed to with the warmth in his gaze. It had been enough for Ahhotep to envision Baba saying and doing more than he should ever do with the Great Wife.

She averted her eyes from Baba's son to cut her thoughts short. Her gaze fell upon the weapons of the Kermans, Hekka Khasut, and Kushites disassembled, showing the wear of study. She swallowed the lump in her throat at the pang of guilt pressed against her mind's eye for her thoughts of the Admiral.

Her gaze drifted back to Ahmose-Ebana. She studied the young man's beaming face at her spoken words of praise while she remembered why she had come to Per-djed-ken.

"Captain Ahmose-Ebana, where are the khopeshes? Have we perfected their design? Have we them ready for distribution to our soldiers?"

Ahmose-Ebana's gaze fell. "No." It was the only word he could utter before he turned to grab the second of the two original khopeshes taken from the Hekka Khasut; the first was with Kamose. He laid it before Ahhotep. "We have not the bronze to make these in mass. Bronze requires tin. The Hekka Khasut have cut off our trade with those who have tin. We have tried importing across the Dashret, but the Kushites have taken our caravans."

Her lip quivered. *Control your emotions,* she thought.

"I see," she told Ahmose-Ebana with a smooth tone.

Her sights fell to the large, heavy khopesh and then to the spears lining the wall. They had fallen obsolete over time while the Hekka Khasut grew stronger.

"But I have made this," he said and drew another weapon. "Its blade is thinner, and the end is more curved, making its tip and sickle sharper. It requires less bronze, but it's just as strong. I have a thousand of these ready for war, but we can make no more."

The corners of her mouth threatened to rise in a grin. "Then let us use them. Keep one hundred here to supply the soldiers of Waset and Per-djed-ken. Send five hundred to King Kamose and your father in the north and send the remaining to Abu with General Pennekhbet." The rays of Re fell through the wall-vent and sparkled in her eyes. Now, they could give their enemies a good fight.

Ahmose-Ebana bowed before Ahhotep. "As God's Mother commands."

"What of the chariot and the beasts?" she asked, an urging in her voice. She was hopeful there was another excellent response.

"I have only disassembled the chariot, and the horses require time to breed. I do not know how long it takes for a horse to breed and grow for use in war. Neither do I know how to train it."

She nodded grimly, seeing the look of dishonor crawl across his face. "Never worry. We shall take one at a time. You have done well with the khopesh. Start next with the chariot. Improve upon it so that our archers may make use of it. I will pray to Thoth for his wisdom in how to deal with the beasts."

Ahmose-Ebana bowed low. "You are most gracious, my Queen."

She took one last look around the room. "You have

45

done well, servant of the King." He arose with another beam on his face.

She allowed herself to return a warm smile before speaking again. "Now, I must give offerings to Amun in favor of victory for his divinely appointed." She whipped around, her sheer white dress swishing around her legs. "To The Rising," she declared to Meret and Nena. "I must go to Amun's temple."

5

A TIME OF TRAINING |
AHMOSE

THE KAP AT SEDJEFATAWY,
1572 BC

The heavy wooden training ax burned his hands as he squeezed his small fingers around its handle. An itch on his leg, where his shendyt met his knee, made him want to scratch it, but the leopard-waisted Medjay named Ketti stood at the forefront of the Kap's training yard, staring at him. It wasn't the time to indulge an itch.

"Prince Ahmose!" Ketti barked in a heavy Kerman accent and pointed at them. Ahmose straightened up, garnering his tutor's approval nod for his form.

Ketti turned his fierce attention toward the tiny naked boy beside Ahmose. Ketti's shoulders dropped, and he shook his head before yelling: "Prince Sapair!"

The dark-skinned Kerman warrior put fear in Ahmose, but at the lack of Sapair's response, Ahmose glanced at his brother.

Sapair admired a cloud and swung his training ax without a care in the world.

"Sapair," Ahmose shot between his teeth. His eyes darted from his brother and their annoyed tutor at the front of the training yard. "Sapair!"

That got his attention, and the boy of five stared wide-eyed up at his brother of eight. "What?"

"We are to spar."

Sapair sighed with a breath worthy of Shu, the god of the wind. His shuffling feet kicked up the sandy dirt as Sapair turned to face his brother. The ax sagged in his hand, and its training blade dragged by his feet.

Ahmose dipped his chin to his brother. "Lift your weapon. Block me or attack me."

Sapair only stared blankly at him.

Ketti yelled out, "Fight!"

Ahmose lifted his ax giving his brother ample time to raise his own weapon, but the child did nothing.

Smack.

Sapair howled in pain and gripped the side of his arm as he toppled over to the side, screaming for help.

Ahmose dropped his ax and stood observing the mass dramatics. "I did not even hit you that hard, Brother."

But his words were lost on Sapair as the child's body servants ran to him.

Their half-sister, Ahmose-Henuttamehu of fifteen years, sat in the shade along with Sitkamose, the daughter of Kamose. Sitkamose was eleven, almost the age of marriage. She had not yet had a blood moon, so she still wore the sidelock of youth instead of a bountifully braided wig like Henuttamehu. They both shook their head at Ahmose.

He shrugged his shoulders. "What? Tutor Ketti told us to fight, and he did not fight."

"He is a child, Ahmose!" Henuttamehu leaned forward and shouted, but Sitkamose placed a gentle hand on her shoulder, reigning her back.

"Next time, Ahmose," Sitkamose called in a smooth,

calm tone, "if he does not resist, do not hit." Her eyes shimmered as her sheer linen dress swayed at the ends by her feet in the soft breeze.

Even with the serenity in her eyes and voice, a hot hue blossomed on Ahmose's cheeks beneath Re's sun. Embarrassment and anger built within him until he spat, "Will the Hekka Khasut be as gentle? What of the Kushites?" He shoved a harsh hand toward his still-wailing brother, being pulled to his feet by his body servants.

Another sister, Ahmose-Nebetta, at twelve years old, entered through the Kap's training yard gateway. "He is still your brother; hold your strikes," she said and shook her head at his presumed folly. The royal pet cat sat snuggled in her arm. At the tone in her voice, the cat lifted her sandy spotted head. Nebetta stroked her fur between the ears. "*Shh*, Kit. All is well." The cat lowered her head again, satisfied with the princess' soothing.

Nebetta flicked her newly acquired woman's wig with the tips of her fingers. "And you are greater than a mere Aamu or Kushite; you are a prince of Kemet."

Ahmose sneered. "Aren't all you *girls* supposed to be in the temple? Why are you here in the *man*'s yard?" He stooped to grab his ax and turned to face Ketti.

He heard the flutter of rebuke bubble up on their tongues and shut his eyes tight to bear the verbal lashing, but Sitkamose shushed them. He drew in a deep breath and released it.

That is why I like Sitkamose more than I like any of my empty-headed sisters . . . well except, Ahmose-Nefertari. I like her too.

His eyes opened, and he swung the ax in his hand. *It is quite amazing they even listen to her since she is the youngest. Perhaps it's because she is Kamose's daughter.*

His little brother wiped the tears from his eyes, and his body servant handed him his ax.

The burgeoning red spot on Sapair's arm had turned dark, radiating purple and blue. Ahmose's jaw grew taut as he stared at his brother's arm, and guilt churned in his stomach, knowing he had caused the bruise. Maybe he had hit him harder than he thought. He wrapped an arm around Sapair. "Brother, listen to me. If you do not learn how to fight, you will be killed in battle like Father. Is that what you want?"

Sapair's eyes popped wide open with fresh, budding tears while a grimace twisted his lips. The same vision probably filled his head as it did Ahmose: the three bloody ax wounds to the head, the crushed face, and the broken limbs. They had all been summoned by the Hekka Khasut to see their father's body and hear King Apepi's plea to stand down and return to the status quo: a prince of their nome, each nome to self-govern and pay tribute to the true King Apepi. Ahmose had been five years old and did not remember much else about his life then, but the image of his father's bloodied corpse and the Hekka Khasut messenger's bold voice would stay with him forever as he imagined it would for Sapair too.

"Well? Is it?" Ahmose asked again and squeezed Sapair's shoulder.

Sapair's little head shook fast back and forth.

"Then, fight me."

Ketti cleared his throat at the end of the training yard. "Prince Sapair, ready your ax as I have taught you."

Sapair pushed Ahmose away and readied the ax.

"Good, Brother." Ahmose nodded and readied his ax in response. "Attack or defe—"

Sapair's wide arc came out of nowhere. Ahmose lifted his weapon just in time to avoid a straight hit to the head. He stumbled backward and parried the fast, angry strikes from his brother. But the ax was heavy, and Sapair's anger-fueled vigor soon wore out. And Ahmose took the opportunity. He swung hard, wrenched Sapair's ax from his hands, and halted his ax in front of his brother's nose. "Ketti never said to start," Ahmose said as he caught his breath.

"Will the Hekka Khasut and Kushites give you a time to start the battle?" Sapair said and pushed away Ahmose's wooden ax head. He took a deep breath as well.

"No," Ahmose said and grabbed Sapair by the shoulder. "Spar once more?"

Sapair received his ax from his body servant, who had fetched it. "Yes," and he jabbed the end of it into Ahmose's stomach, sending him to the dirt. "For hitting my arm, Brother."

Ketti started marching toward Sapair with his papyrus switch. "Prince Sapair!"

Ahmose rubbed his stomach and rolled to his knees. He looked up at his brother. "Fine, we are now even. No more strikes like a coward?"

"Good," Sapair said to show his agreement and readied his ax just as Ketti approached with his switch held high. He swatted both of them on the backs of the legs. "Enough of this foolishness. Ready your training weapon."

Ahmose looked to his sisters, who all sat giggling at him. His eyes narrowed, and Sitkamose again shushed them. The corner of his lips rose at his friend. Somehow, Sitkamose knew when to speak and when to shush. She would make an excellent queen for the next king. Her mother, Tep, still could not have another child, much less a son. Their mother had ensured Kamose married his elder sister, Tep, and his secondborn sister, Hentempet, for they were the only ones old enough to have blood moons by the time Kamose took the throne. She had wanted Kamose to ensure the lineage, but it seemed Kamose's other sister-wives were not able to bear children. So, without an heir, whoever married Sitkamose would be the next King. Divine royalty ran through her veins.

Ketti's voice rang out: "Spar!"

Ahmose brought his ax to defend against his brother charging like the Apis bull. "I was not ready," Ahmose yelled.

"Well, I was!" Sapair yelled back and struck again. The glare of the sun paled compared to the fire in his eyes.

Ahmose grinned at his younger brother fighting him with every bit of strength he could muster. He swung back hard and gave him a good fight.

"Good, Brother. Good," he whispered to Sapair once Ketti called for peace. He patted him on his shoulder. "You may just live if we are attacked."

Sapair glared at him and pushed his hand from his shoulder. "And so might you." He threw his ax on the ground and ran his forearm against his leaking nose. "You did not have to bring up Father," he said and spat at Ahmose's feet before leaving.

"I had to, Sapair. You were not taking this training seriously," Ahmose called after him.

Ketti called after Sapair as well. "We are not finished here."

But Sitkamose slowly stood and stared at Ketti until he dipped his chin to her and went about his duties in the training yard. Her gaze drifted to Ahmose and nodded in the direction where Sapair had run off. Her large shoulders and boyish face lifted to the sun disc, the Aten.

"The princes are finished here," she told Nebetta and Henuttamehu. Then she turned to run her hand along Kit's furry back. "Come; my mother has decreed we shall learn to fight too."

AHMOSE WATCHED SITKAMOSE AND HIS SISTERS TAKE UP training sticks before he turned a corner. Their body servants stood close to them as Ketti instructed them with their grips, careful not to touch the royal hands. Sitkamose's boyish figure with broad shoulders deceived those who thought she might be strong. Her frail fingers gripped the training ax, but its head was firmly on the ground as she tried to lift it.

Ahmose sighed and hoped she would get well soon, for it seemed she had been sickly since he first knew her. He kicked the dirt off the toe of his leather sandal as he walked and came upon the nursery. He glanced inside at his older sister, Ahmose-Nefertari, holding his youngest sister, Ahmose-Tumerisy. Her sweet vocal melodies of a hymn to Hathor calmed him as it did Tumerisy. Her little body lay limp in Ahmose-Nefertari's arms.

Binpu lay motionless in the nurse Lady Rai's arms. His half-sister Ahmose, or as they called her *Mosi*, was tightly curled under a light blanket on a cot on the floor. Her hands pressed tightly under her cheek. All three were born the month before receiving their father's body back from the Hekka Khasut.

His gaze fell to the floor as he walked past. First, his father had gone, and next would be Binpu and Tumerisy.

At least they would be in the Field of Reeds soon and not in pain anymore.

The sound of their pitiful coughs followed him down the corridor until he saw Sapair crouched in the corner at the corridor's turn. He covered his heart with a hand as he walked toward Sapair to shield any harsh thoughts from turning into words.

Unlike his father and youngest siblings, if the Kushites killed them and destroyed their bodies, he saw the grim end and eternal restlessness just as the Aamu messenger had said.

Sapair kicked at him when he drew near. "Leave me, Brother."

But Ahmose put his back against the cracked mud-brick and slid down next to him. "Sapair, you know I will never leave you." He threw an arm around his brother's shoulders. "It is you and me until the beginning of the next life, and then we shall be together in the Field of Reeds."

Sapair sniffled and wrapped his arms around his drawn-in legs. "I wish this war would end. I have dreams of seeing Kamose come home as Father did."

Ahmose leaned his head back. "Me too." A twitch overcame his eye as the sight of his father's mangled corpse again flooded his vision. "But if he does, I will strike every one of those Hekka Khasut down. I will avenge them and fight along with whoever is appointed King. I will finish what they started. And if I am struck down like Kamose and Father, you will finish what we started."

Sapair snapped his gaze to Ahmose, who looked off at the trickle of sunlight falling through the wall vent. "Then you will have left me alone in this life."

Ahmose met his brother's eyes. "I will ask your

forgiveness when you are with me in the Field of Reeds."

Sapair pushed Ahmose's arm off of his shoulders. "Then that would make you a liar. You lie to me today. You caused me pain today. You are no brother of mine."

Ahmose gritted his teeth and spoke in defense when he should have comforted. "I did what I had to do. The Kushites may come, and you need to fight. If Kamose fails in the north, the Hekka Khasut will be here with the next Nile flooding, intent on putting us in our place. Do you think they will honor you as the son of the Waset prince who was declared the king of Kemet? Do you think they will give you your body for the afterlife after Kamose slew the royal escorts that returned Father's body? Will there be any of us left to send you off and open your eyes and mouths for the westward journey if they leave your body untouched by the flame?"

Sapair jolted to his feet. "Stop it, Ahmose!" He threw his hands over his ears. "I want . . . I want—"

"What you want is not what we must do!" Ahmose stood up and pulled Sapair's hands off of his ears. "You will wear a man's shendyt in the next season like me. You will no longer be a child."

"You are still a child too! You are not that much older than me!" Sapair yanked his wrists out of Ahmose's grip.

"But I have to be a man. I am the oldest son that remains in the palace. Who will protect the throne if they come? You? Until today, you cared more about playing senet with Mosi." Ahmose took a step backward, shocked such a tone came from his mouth.

Sapair's eyes filled with tears. "I want to play senet with Mosi!" He growled. "You know nothing!" His hot breath blasted Ahmose's face before he ran off again.

Ahmose threw his hands in the air, and an exasperated breath forced its way from his chest. His hands fell to his hips, and he kicked dirt in his brother's direction. "Why must you be so difficult?!" he yelled at Sapair's diminishing shadow.

Ahmose-Nefertari stuck her head out of the nursery and eyed him. His cheeks turned red at his sister's silent rebuking. He shrugged and crossed his arms, hating having older sisters who did nothing but giggle at his failings and scold him for his errors.

She walked from the room and motioned Ahmose to walk alongside her. She stood only a head taller than him even though she was ten years his senior. Born from their mother, only Tep and Hentempet were older than her. She would marry Kamose when he returned since her blood moon came late after Kamose had already left for war three years prior.

Ahmose glanced up at her as they silently walked down the corridor. "What do you wish to say to me, Sister."

"Let Sapair be a child while he still can be." She stopped and squared her shoulders to Ahmose. "We let you be a child until you wore the shendyt of a man. Let him. You both saw something which you should never have seen." A glisten overcame her eyes, and her gaze turned inward. "One more season of innocence for Sapair will not hurt the future palace." She shook her head with a despondent sigh at Ahmose's crossed arms. "And Ahmose, consider this: how would a child fare fighting against an armed Kushite or a khopesh-wielding soldier of the Hekka Khasut?"

Ahmose's arms twitched at the thought, but still, he kept them crossed, too prideful to answer.

She reached out and touched Ahmose's cheek. "You have such heart, Ahmose. Such passion. Sometimes others cannot bear such passion. It hurts them."

The same churn of guilt twisted his stomach upon realizing he had hurt his younger brother. "What should I do?" His arms dropped to his sides.

Ahmose-Nefertari's hand fell back to the folds of her pleated royal dress. "Love your brother. Live the principles of Ma'at and be sure your heart does not weigh heavy." She pressed her lips into a thinned smile. "I am going to tend to Tumerisy and Binpu with Rai and the other nurses." She looked back down the corridor. "I will give my love to them before I marry Kamose and be tasked with the burden of war like my sisters and Mother before me." She placed a hand on his shoulder. "We are all sacrificing in this war. I know you think you are doing good by helping Sapair see why he needs to pick up the training ax, but let him be for now." She popped the underside of his chin in a playful gesture and walked away.

Ahmose watched her slender frame walk toward the children's room and, with a rough swipe of a flat palm, took her touch from his chin off his jaw. *I hate when they do that to me. I am not a child anymore.* But his shoulders rolled forward. Ahmose-Nefertari was wise beyond her years, and she was right *most* of the time.

He repeated her rhetorical question: "How would Sapair fare against a Kushite?" He shook his head. "Not well, and probably nor would I." His mouth twitched. "Am I still a child too?" His toes wiggled in his leather sandals, and his fingers fidgeted with the white linen of his shendyt. *Perhaps.* With that thought, he went to the Kap's courtyard to find Sapair, most likely playing senet with Admiral Baba's daughter, Senseneb, to calm himself down. He smiled at the childhood game. It would be fun to play it once more.

6

A TIME OF
HOMECOMING |
AHHOTEP
PER-DJED-KEN, 1571 BC

A hhotep stood at the port of Per-djed-ken to await the ships she had seen coming from the tallest point of the tower. She had rushed down to meet them, but the towering walls of Sedjefatawy's two-story structure in the near distance blocked them from her sight. The heat emanating from her maidservants suffocated what little breeze the god Shu afforded her. The weight of her golden vulture headdress grew heavier by the moment under the sweltering afternoon sun. The kohl lining her eyes stuck in a thick plaster against the delicate skin as she peered off to the northern bend of the Nile. Her heart beat hard against her chest as the royal warship, *The Wild Bull*, came peeking around, followed by a small portion of the fleet that left three years prior. The last time The Wild Bull had come home, her husband was not aboard it.

She kept the upward turn of her lip and the hope in her eyes at bay until her son was in her sights. The soft linen of her dress clung to her legs as the ship pulled into port. She held her breath. Her arms held firm by her side until she saw the glint of sun bounce off of the silver diadem, secured to her son's upright head—its shining golden cobra poised to strike. A shaky breath blew from her lips, and her fingers traced the linen folds of her dress as she brought her hands together in a clasp over her belly. It was then that she allowed the corners of her lips to rise.

"Mother," Kamose called as he stepped from the boat.

She envisioned him as a child as he came straight to her, but he was a twenty-three-year-old man, the King of Kemet. He stopped short in front of her, and she dipped her eyes as was her place.

"I am glad the gods have blessed you and kept you safe, my son, King Kamose," she said, her voice unwavering.

"The gods have only answered your many prayers and offerings, Mother." He lifted her hand to his lips and placed a soft kiss on her wrist. "I am sure I would not have been kept safe if it had not been for you." Then he wrapped her in his arms and kissed her cheek.

She tensed, knowing that was not what the King should do, but selfishly, she wrapped her arms around him, thankful for the heat of his body pressed against her to further confirm he was among the living. "I am glad to have you home, Son," she whispered in his ear, and a small tear budded in her eye.

He pulled away with a beam. "As am I. I have come home to celebrate our victory against the Hekka Khasut." He lifted his hands and brought them to rest on her shoulders. "Father would be proud. We have slain the one who had slain him. We put to death the traitors and sent the bodies to Apepi in disgrace."

It pleased her heart to hear her husband's murderer had been killed, but as her eyes lifted to the golden cobra on her son's silver diadem, it did not bring Tao back.

Kamose continued speaking. "We stopped an alliance between the Hekka Khasut and the Kushites by intercepting the messenger and destroying the Oasis to prevent any further communication between the two." He let out a satisfied breath. "And I have retaken what Father lost. From Ta-Seti to Mednit, the nomes are under our command." His smile faded, and he added in a disgruntled mutter, "Only took three years."

"What is important is we are winning," she said with a pressed smile. "We shall feast. I have already sent word to the nomes' princes to join us and discuss our neighbors to the south."

Kamose grimaced. "Those Kushites. Right when we claim victory before the Lower's border. But I hear General Pennekhbet is holding position at Abu."

Ahhotep nodded. "He will need your reinforcements. The Kushites are even more fierce than the Hekka Khasut. We will see what the rest of the nomes say, especially our newer princes and, of course, Ta-Seti." She scoffed. "It is sad. Only the poorest nomes give their full support, and the wealthiest give out crumbs. They are no better than the Hekka Khasut and the Kushites."

"Mother," Kamose said in a soft chiding. But he kissed her cheek and patted the top of her hand in his. "We can ask for more at the feast since we have won the entire Upper. The nomes should have no hesitation."

Baba appeared behind Kamose and lowered his chin to God's Mother. His admiral's blue beaded collar dazzled in the sun and lit up his dark, soulful eyes that locked with hers. He was safe as well, and amid the busy port, peace overcame her. The sun's warmth rose on her lips in a beaming smile, grateful to him for bringing her son home alive and returning unharmed as well. But then, it faded. She wished for this moment to live on, past its time, and never move on to the next one, where an uncertain future awaited her. Would they both come home the next time they went off to war?

Baba's shoulders appeared to roll forward as if he wanted to wrap her in his arms, but Ahhotep quickly dismissed the deception her eyes had shown her as a wild imagining. He had never made such an advance toward her, nor would he ever take such action toward the Great Wife of Seqenenre Tao. At the thought, her faded smile fell off her lips. Her tongue grew dry, and words were lost as her son peered over his shoulder at the Admiral and then at Ahhotep again.

"Feast? Oh, oh yes," Ahhotep responded, finding her words again. A false smile replaced her lost one.

Baba's brow furrowed. He could see through her, she reasoned in a state of unease, and quickly said, "Will you join us, Admiral?" Ahhotep gestured to him with an elegant open hand. "Both your daughter and son as well?"

Baba gave a single nod of his head. "You are most generous, Mother of King Kamose."

Ahhotep allowed him to leave to tend to the fleet with a simple glance toward The Wild Bull and a soft smile. He turned to go and follow her unspoken command. His strong arms and back were hewn from years as a fleetsman—rowing royal ships upstream, sailing downstream, and fighting with an ax. She rubbed her thin arms, imagining what it would be like for his to wrap around her. But she pushed the thought away, for it would never be. Her hands fell to her sides. She was the Great Wife.

"Mother, are you well?" Kamose asked while raising a hand to her shoulder.

"I am only happy you are home," she said and squeezed his hand.

Kamose's gaze drifted between his mother and her maidservants as Baba's footsteps on the pier became distant. His voice was light after his heavy breath. "It seems our nome is suffering. I did not see many working the fields on my travels to our palace."

Ahhotep turned and walked to The Rising for their short boat ride to Sedjefatawy, trying to forget her imaginings of Baba's strong arms around her. "Most of the nomes are suffering, my son. The few that give their full support are suffering much more than ours." Her chin held parallel to the floor while her words barely escaped her lips.

"Then my victory is not as sweet," he whispered and boarded The Rising.

She faced him. "We must not let the other princes know how hard this war is on us. They will see weakness as a probability of failure and abandon us."

Kamose nodded and looked in the direction of the city of Waset, home to the temple of Amun. "Let us pray that not be the case," he said, adjusting his royal collar to center its golden-encapsulated lapis on his sternum.

7

A TIME OF FEASTING |
AHHOTEP

SEDJEFATAWY, 1571 BC

A few of the nomes' princes arrived at Sedjefatawy in the splendor their nomes could afford to send them. At the same time, Kamose and Ahhotep walked up to the grand double entrance of the palace after departing The Rising.

Ahhotep smiled as the three of them approached. "Ah, Prince Baufre of Meseh, Prince Metjen of Bat, and Prince Tetian of Ta-Seti." She hoped the princes and the ones to come would not show division with the new princes Kamose had liberated from the Hekka Khasut rule. They needed to show a united front.

"God's Mother," Baufre said and bowed, but only slightly. The large man's belly slung over his leather belt, prohibiting the full show of respect due her and her son.

Metjen glanced at the jiggle in Baufre's belly after rising from his bow. "I see our patron goddess Hathor blesses Meseh while she neglects Bat." He rubbed his thinned stomach, lean with measly muscle, as he envied his neighboring prince's well-fed belly.

Tetian snorted. "At least Khnum does not bring Kushites to your borders." His eyes shot toward Kamose, speaking of Ta-Seti's patron god, source of the Nile, and creator of the bodies of humans and gods. "Perhaps our King Kamose is not divinely appointed, or else the gods would not turn us over to the hands of the Kushites."

Ahhotep kept her eyes from flinging toward the sky in obvious disgust as she thought: *Tetian's nome is the richest of us all, having access to the southern gold mines for all these years. A few months of little trade has turned him into an embellisher.*

Kamose took a step forward in Ahhotep's lack of action. "You will watch your tongue, Prince Tetian of Ta-Seti. Amun has given us victory in the north, and he will give us victory in the south. The gods are with my family. I am the Strong Bull, Given Life, and they are with our beloved Kemet."

"We shall see, King Kamose," Tetian murmured with a narrowing eye. He glanced over his shoulder at the small town between Sedjefatawy and the Per-djed-ken fortress. "It would seem Waset is not faring well either. My journey through your nome from Ta-Seti did not evoke feelings of pride or prosperity."

Ahhotep clasped her hands over her stomach as she eyed the slender man with skin as dark as her mother's. "Feelings have no place in war, Tetian. Our forces have held the Kushites at Abu—"

"God's Mother," Tetian scoffed and raised a hand, "Abu is the border city between my nome and the Kerman domain. The Kushites are too close. If you wish for my support in the north, you will retake Buhen and re-establish the Kerman border at the Nile's second cataract."

A tone of finality vibrated with the rays of the sun falling into the space between them. Baufre and Metjen shifted on their feet, their gazes bouncing between the royal mother and son and the seemingly equal prince standing beside them.

Ahhotep's jaw grew taut at the forward threat. *How will I respond to this blatant disrespect for the royal family?* She tilted her head back as she stared at Tetian. *We need his help; we need his men and rich resources from his gold trade, the little he gives—the hoarder.*

She decided to avoid the threat altogether. "Shall we prepare to feast?" she simply asked. "To celebrate the prosperity the gods have granted our King and his victory over the Hekka Khasut even without the full support of the richest nome of the Upper?"

A corner of Tetian's lips lifted in a polite smile. "As we were invited, God's Mother." He stared at Kamose as he walked past him, glancing up at the golden uraeus upon the silver crown.

Baufre and Metjen followed. Their murmurings echoed back from the narrow corridor beyond the grand double doors of the palace.

Ahhotep stepped in line with her son. "We should adjourn to the throne room and not greet them outside the palace as a common man."

Kamose spun on his heels without so much as a word. His cheeks simmered red as he strode into the shade of Sedjefatawy's towering walls. Ahhotep followed him to the throne room, suppressing the beginnings of a blossoming anger welling in the pit of her stomach. She should have rebuked Tetian directly.

"Mother would not have hesitated," she mumbled to herself.

Tep stood on the dais with Tetisheri seated behind the throne. The burden on Tep's shoulders dropped upon seeing Kamose. "My King, my brother! My eyes are glad to see you among the living," she blurted out and ran to him.

He strode up to her and pulled her close. "As am I to see you, my chief wife. How does our daughter fare?"

Tetisheri coughed with annoyance and stood up. A small beam upon her lips. "She ails some nights, but she is a strong young woman," she answered for her granddaughter; however, her sight set upon Ahhotep, having little tolerance for small conversation. "Have the princes arrived?"

"Some. We are still awaiting a few more. They should arrive soon." Ahhotep dared not bring up the lack of respect for the crown in front of her mother. Tetisheri was not a woman to be trifled with.

"They were to arrive by midday, and it is now past." Tetisheri's gaze shifted to Kamose, still embracing his chief wife. A small sigh of dissatisfaction with their behavior left her nostrils. "If they tarry in their nomes, we shall eat our evening meal without them. Come, come."

With nothing else to say, she strode out of the throne room—as if the smell of mutton and pork commanded her utter attention—and took to the dining hall with her maidservants trailing close behind.

Ahhotep watched her leave. At least with her presence at dinner, the dissenting princes should keep their mouths shut in front of the others. Tetisheri's advantage made Ahhotep wish she was her mother at times. Tetisheri had no problems commanding respect.

Her daughter's voice cut through her thoughts. "Mother—"

"We need to join your grandmother," Ahhotep cut off whatever Tep was going to say, fearing it would be something foolish again. "It will not be perceived well if she is to dine with them alone."

They walked into the dining hall from the pillared throne room along the freshly painted and patched corridor. Ahhotep had ordered that anywhere the princes may wander was to appear as if the palace was not falling into disrepair to create a facade of wealth and stability.

A table awaited the King and his Chief Wife as well as his mother and grandmother, and the princes were to sit on the extravagantly woven rugs on the floor. Yet Tetian sat at the table in Ahhotep's place, tapping his fingers on the wooden surface. His head tilted as he stared at Tetisheri, who sat on the other end of the table.

Ahhotep sighed. *At least he is not in Kamose's seat.* She released fisted hands by her sides to steady her annoyance. *Clearly, Mother has said nothing to him.* Tetisheri's hard stare fell upon her. *She is waiting for me to stake my claim as God's Mother: to take her place for my son. I must show no weakness.*

A sure step and another took her to Tetian's side. She merely cast her gaze down at him and stood as still as the cracked statues in the restricted halls. Her headdress' vulture wings cast a shadow over her shoulders, and the strong beak, a shadow over her eyes. The soft breeze from the raised wall vents sent a few strands of plaited hair across her neck. The gentle jangle of the beads at the strands' ends sounded in a soft meter with Tetian's slow tapping fingers on the table.

He stared back, unblinking, while the musicians played the soft rustling sistrums, the lyrical lutes, and the ethereal harp strings. The dancers danced among the woven mats to entertain the princes before the meal.

But it all faded to silence as she summoned the courage to speak to the prince.

"You dare take the seat of God's Mother?" Her words were swift like a dagger to the throat.

A slow grin took his lips. "I dare not," he said and stood up. He brushed past her. Too close for her liking. "I dare not insult God's Mother by sitting in her place of honor," he whispered over her shoulder, so much so that the tip of his nose brushed a lock of hair.

Yet you already have, she thought but did not acknowledge his third gesture of disrespect and took her seat. Servants brought bread and figs and placed them before her. She dipped her fingertips into the water bowl and allowed a servant to dry them for her. Usually, she would flick the water from her hands, but they needed now more than ever to maintain an appearance.

Admiral Baba, General Pennekhbet, and their families arrived just as the servants brought food to the princes. Kamose took his seat next to Ahhotep along with Tep on his right, who sat beside Tetisheri.

Soon, the other princes arrived, and Ahhotep counted them: twenty-one. She recalled the nomes from Ta-Seti to Mednit. "There should be twenty-two now," she whispered to herself. She scanned them again each and noted the only prince missing was Prince Sarenpet from the nome of Mednit.

Ahhotep spoke between her teeth to Kamose as she smiled politely at Baba's young daughter, Senseneb, who had watched her scan the guests. "One could assume after you liberated Mednit's capital city of Tepihu from the Hekka Khasut, they would at least send their prince to our victory feast."

"They do not see it as liberation, Mother," Kamose said under his breath before he took a bite of mutton. She peered at him in confusion. After he swallowed, he whispered, "We slew many traitors in Tepihu. I would argue many of their numbers, including their prince Sarenpet, are loyal to the Hekka Khasut. It was the reason Admiral Baba urged me to leave many men there for our border while we deal with the Kushites."

A pit opened in her stomach to devour the reality of the statement. Her mouth, now dry, forced a gummy swallow of the sudden lump in her throat. "Do not let the princes know this," she whispered. "They would not send their men to battle for our people who do not wish to be liberated."

Kamose nodded his head as he took another bite and finished chewing. "If we continue down the Nile to Men-nefer and beyond to Hut-Waret, we will only encounter more traitors."

Ahhotep sat back in her chair. "Then we must liberate Kerma as quickly as possible. We need their gold and their warriors."

Tetian caught her eye. He had barely eaten and sat with his fingers pressed together, poised in front of his mouth. His black, beady eyes stared straight at her.

A slithering tendril of the coming winter's chill slipped down her spine at his unsettling behavior. Why would he look at her so? Was this all about Abu? His precious Ta-Seti had been left unharmed, and it was not like he was helping secure his own border. He had been nothing but disrespectful since he had come. At least Kamose's progress had satiated Setka and Nakht, but Tetian remained unappeasable. She spat a slight huff. *Why would I expect anything different from that man? Why does he treat my family in such a way?*

Kamose lowered his mutton and stood up, causing a

swift silence over the dining hall. All eyes turned to him except Tetian's, whose gaze remained on Ahhotep.

As if her mother sensed Ahhotep's discomfort, Tetisheri stood and cleared her throat. "Your King is about to speak." She looked pointedly at Tetian. "Give *him* your attention." Then she sat back down with a hard stare on her weathered face.

Ahhotep knew that would be the last time her mother spoke for her. *I must earn my respect. No fear. No fear,* she repeated in thought as she stared at Tetian.

A corner of Tetian's mouth popped up in a playful smirk before he slid his gaze from Ahhotep to Kamose with a tilt of his head.

Kamose held out his hands. "We have victory in the north. We have secured the nomes to Mednit—"

"Yet, where is their prince?" Baufre spoke up while rubbing his large belly in a slow circle.

Ahhotep shot up as her mother had in her father's absence. "You dare interrupt your King?" Flame burst to life in her eyes at the blatancy of disrespect. *And I selfishly thought this part of the unification was over, and from Baufre, of all people?* she thought and said, "Guards."

Two royal guards approached Baufre, who shrank back and lifted his hands. "I dare not interrupt the King," he said in a shaky slur of words. His shoulders hid his thick neck, and his wig-covered head bowed low so the top of it was all anyone could see of his head.

Perhaps Baufre only has the mind of any empty room. Hopefully, his disrespect is born of dimness, not from disdain like Tetian's.

Ahhotep remained standing as if daring anyone else to interrupt her son again. A slight nod of approval came from Admiral Baba and General Pennekhbet.

Yet Tetian stood and pointed a long finger at her son.

Ahhotep hesitated. *Should I stop him from speaking now? What do I do? What is he going to say? Mother would stop him.* She opened her mouth to speak, but it was too late.

"You have secured victory in the north, King Kamose," Tetian bellowed and commanded the attention of all in the room.

The breath begged for release within Ahhotep's chest as she waited to hear what else Tetian would say.

His bold voice continued. "Yet to the south, the Kushites take advantage of a war-torn Kemet—"

Say something, you fool! She choked on a flurry of words in her throat as Tetian continued.

"—You are no king of mine who lets my nome of Ta-Seti be overrun—"

"You, Prince Tetian," Ahhotep's voice cut through the tense dining hall, "as all of you have taken an oath to my father and your father to his father. You named Seqenenre Tao Lord of the Two Lands, and he took his Great Wife, Tetisheri as his Chief Wife. You all thereby gave an oath to his progeny. You declared your submission to the great unification of Kemet. You should honor this divine bloodline more than any other."

Kamose continued where she paused. She had failed to prevent the threat to the throne and Tetisheri's beam now firmly rested upon her grandson as if disowning Ahhotep at the moment. Ahhotep clenched her teeth in anger at herself while Kamose spoke:

"Through their blood and my marriage to my sisters, Ahhotep Tasherit and Hentempet, and my forthcoming marriage to my third sister, Ahmose-Nefertari, I have sealed my divine right to rule Kemet. Do you question your oath before Re? Before Amun? Before my father and his fathers before him?"

71

Tetian pursed his lips yet remained silent. A few princes shook their heads, but others lifted their chins and crossed their arms. They glanced between Tetian and Kamose.

Ahhotep let her son speak, who continued for the nay-sayers. "As my forefathers before me, we had proven our lineage from the great Kings of Waset, Rahotep and Sobekhotep, who restored the temple of Amun and who first spoke of a united Upper and Lower as it once was before the foreigners overtook our fertile delta and from them rose the Hekka Khasut. You gave an oath to Amun, to Re, to Hathor, and Isis. Our family was to be Re's hand and rescue the two lands from the Hekka Khasut. But because one nome suffers defense from the Kushites after years of plenty, you break the will of Re? We celebrate this day for the victories of adding five nomes to our cause. Tomorrow, we will sail upriver and secure the faithful Medjay's homeland. They have shown more loyalty to the crown and to Re than some of the princes before me now, who have never seen war."

He paused to let his last statement reverberate through the hall.

"Thus princes of the Upper, this, on my divine appointment, I will not forget Ta-Seti."

Tetian's eyes narrowed. "As the King commands. We will be *most* grateful for the King's rescue of Ta-Seti." His statement ended in a throat-born whisper.

Baba and Pennekhbet stood up and faced the princes. Baba spoke: "Kamose, Given Life, Living Horus, will fulfill Re's desires of a united land. We set sail tomorrow. You are free to join us in battle, and if you feel you cannot, send your resources to support this campaign or send your capable men and boys to Per-djed-ken to train up as soldiers under the Medjay and secure their place under our god Anhur's protective hand. We will need more soldiers, for we left a strong border at the cusp of the Lower."

Pennekhbet eyed the few who remained cross-armed, and his gaze came to rest upon Tetian, who still had only contributed very little to the cause despite his nome's bountiful trade with the gold-resource-rich Kermans in the land of Wawat. "And if you cannot do any of them, it is advisable you still your tongue."

Tetian sneered at the implied command as he eyed the two highest military officers. He sat down and dug his teeth into the mutton before him as his gaze shifted to Ahhotep. His tongue slid over his lips to lick the meat's juice from them.

Ahhotep looked away to Baufre. The guards she had summoned to threaten him glanced at each other before down at Baufre, who was eating with a gleeful forgetfulness that they were even there. His mutton rested on his ample belly between bites.

"The Meseh nome is with King Kamose," Baufre said, lifting his leg of lamb in the air and seemingly unaware of the political tension in the room.

Metjen glanced at him in disgust. After his soft scoff, he shared a glance with Tetian before returning to his meal.

What plans do you have, Tetian and Metjen? I know you are upset about Abu, but that is no way to treat or speak to your king. Ahhotep calmed the thoughts and knots in her stomach by scanning the room. *And a dim prince could be easily swayed from his support,* she thought as she watched Baufre take another bite. But the tension waned once Tetian began to eat from the King's court once more.

"General, Admiral," Ahhotep said with a soft gesture of her hand. "Please, sit, eat."

They lowered their heads.

"We are most gracious for the King's and God's Mother's generosity," Pennekhbet said and sat next to his wife, Nebt, and ten-year-old daughter, Kasmut.

Baba sat similarly between his eight-year-old daughter, Senseneb, and son, Ahmose-Ebana. He glanced at Pennekhbet's wife before glancing to the empty spot where his late wife should have been sitting.

Ahhotep felt the same sting in her heart, but it was not for Tao, not anymore. Baba turned his eyes to her, and she realized she was staring at him. She should have averted her gaze, but she naturally gave him a small, pressed smile of sympathy. He lifted a corner of his mouth with an appreciative nod before giving his attention to his children.

THE FEAST ENDED LATE IN THE NIGHT, AND THE PRINCES WITH full bellies went to the guest apartments on either side of the palace for the night. Nebt took Kasmut to their villa, and Ahmose-Ebana took Senseneb to theirs when Ahhotep requested the general and admiral to stay behind and speak with her and her mother.

They sat in the council room on the palace's first floor next to the throne room. The firelight in the alabaster torches lined the room's back wall as Ahhotep leaned forward on the table to speak.

"I know the day has been long, but we have a matter that needs tending before the campaign to retake Buhen," she began. "Tetian and a few others will not support us until we secure its fortress."

Tetisheri remained unusually silent but cast a

disappointed frown toward her daughter. Ahhotep ignored her.

"The matter needing tending is regarding the horses?" Baba asked. "And chariots?"

Ahhotep nodded. "I know very little about this animal. Many of our numbers are perplexed by it." Ahhotep looked off at the reliefs in the walls showing her grandfather as a mighty ruler over the Upper, knowing the exaggerated truths it depicted. It was what he wished for, but it had taken two lifetimes simply for the Upper to be united against the Hekka Khasut, and even then, the unity was fragile.

Tetisheri hummed, and Ahhotep snapped, "What have you to say, Mother?"

"I have nothing to say, *Daughter*," Tetisheri said with narrowed eyes at her disuse of titles.

She was a liar. Ahhotep pressed her lips into a thin, polite smile. Left her to suffer without aiding the conversation, she supposed.

Baba sighed. "We could send a caravan across the Dashret and build a ship in the abandoned port on the Red Sea. Steal across the water and contact the Bedu people who raise these animals daily."

"It is a risk. They may not even listen to us or help us. They may kill our messenger and escort. Steal the barter goods." Pennekhbet crossed his arms.

"What choice do we have?" Ahhotep asked. "It will take resources away from our fight in Abu and our border in Mednit. We would need to send the escort, a shipbuilding crew, the materials, camels, food, water, beer . . ." Her voice trailed off. "Much gold and grain to pay the Bedu."

Kamose sighed. "Much gold and grain that we do not have as it will be spent in retaking Buhen."

"Ta-Seti has it, but Tetian will not hand it over," Pennekhbet said.

"At least until we retake Buhen," Kamose nodded, not having to repeat the cyclic situation they had found themselves in.

"I doubt he will follow through even if we have victory there," Ahhotep said.

"The man's heart will be heavy with greed on the scales of Ma'at," the general added in a harsh undertone.

Ahhotep looked to her mother, who returned her stare with an expressionless face.

Say something! Tell me what to do. I need your help. But she would never say those words aloud to Tetisheri. For one, it would make her look weak. And two, the woman was frustrating, and her help would come with some demeaning remark and lifelong reminder.

Kamose glanced around. "Where is my wife?"

Tetisheri cleared her throat. "Chief Wife Ahhotep Tasherit felt ill after eating. Could not stomach such disrespect and tension from the evening's meal." She clicked her tongue in obvious disapproval. "Disappointing."

The word was left for those in company to ponder if the Great Wife meant her granddaughter or if the situation at the meal was disappointing.

Ahhotep figured it was the former. It was not the first time she had voiced her disappointment with her firstborn grandchild.

Kamose shifted in his seat. "What should we do?"

Ahhotep shrugged. "We only have one choice that will yield the most optimum result. We will save what gold and grain we can to send to the Bedu. I would only rather send one caravan. We will send for these trainers when we can afford to barter."

Baba and Pennekhbet nodded in solemnity.

"How do we continue the war against those with superior weaponry?" Kamose asked. "We lost many men in Nefrusy, Hardai, and Tepihu."

Baba nodded. "We did, and we will lose many more until we can afford to meet the Hekka Khasut on similar terms. But the Kushites have no superior weapons, only an excellent source of resources. We need their gold if we have any chance of winning this war."

"Agreed," Pennekhbet added. "We cannot push much farther into the Hekka Khasut lands without considerable force from the local people. Their princes are not loyal to you, King Kamose. How are we to unite a people who do not want to be united?"

The question lingered in the small space between them and repeated in Ahhotep's mind. She pushed it away, for she knew not the answer. "Let us move north after we secure the south. Kushites have no horses, and our khopesh is superior to their spear."

"In close distances," Baba clarified. "Their numbers are as many as their spears."

"And at night, the Hekka Khasut's paler skin gives them away under the moon. We will not have such a luxury with the Kushites." Kamose crossed his arms. "We have no choice. We must meet the Kushites at Abu and push them back. Conquer them before Apepi re-establishes communication with them and brings them into an alliance. As Mother says, we must secure peace in the south before we head north."

He sighed.

"Let us meet in the morning to discuss our campaign strategy for fighting this foe and smite any hope of alliance between our enemies." Kamose hid a yawn. "I tire and need to renew my energy."

Ahhotep pictured the Nile's path. She had never been south of the nome of Ta-Seti. She had never even seen the first cataract at Abu. But she pictured the Kerman homeland following the river. Past Abu was Toshka and then Arminna, and after a long stretch, Buhen, the trade fortress, near the second cataract. Much gold was there. They had to retake Buhen. It would again prove the divine's appointment of her family's right to rule. It would garner all the princes' full support, or so she hoped. Though if victorious, Tetian could no longer use any doubt in the princes for his advantage, whatever his motivation was: greed or hate, she still did not know, but she did know Buhen was essential. Buhen had to be recaptured, no matter the cost.

No matter the cost? she thought, second-guessing her ruminations. It was the same reasoning she gave when the offer of peace came from the Hekka Khasut. And four years later, they were still at war. She glanced at her son, once again imagining him brought home as Tao was. *Not that cost. Never that cost.* And she turned her head away, unable to bear losing a child, slain by the enemy, or worse, burned.

"As the King commands," Pennekhbet said with a bow, breaking her thoughts.

Kamose dismissed him and Baba: "In peace, sleep well."

Ahhotep watched Baba as he exited the room, hoping he would steal one last look at her, but he continued to walk out, not looking back. A small pit opened in her stomach. Her gaze fell downcast.

He would never make such an advance on God's Mother. Why cause herself to endure more disappointment than she already had? *Leave it*, she commanded herself.

Tetisheri yawned after their shadows disappeared in the night. "You did well, my grandson," she said with a pat on his shoulder but said nothing to Ahhotep. There would be no forgiveness after her slip at dinner. Ahhotep sat with eyes still downcast, distressed and disturbed Kamose would perish like his father. As her thoughts drifted to Tao to push away the visions of Kamose's mangled body, she couldn't help but wonder if she would ever feel a man's touch again as the room's emptiness sealed her feelings of loneliness. How could her mother endure after losing her husband and son and still treat the rest of her children and grandchildren with such apathy, save for Kamose, of whom she was most proud?

No one ever spoke to Tetisheri for fear of being demeaned. Her mother demanded competence in its perfect form, and many fell short. Ahhotep's fears could not be voiced around the one person who could probably help her in her role as God's Mother and tutor to Tep as she commanded in Kamose's absence. She sat back in the chair, watching the flickering torchlight cast shadows on the wall reliefs. It made it look like the depictions of her father and Tao were moving and living up to the greatness the walls recorded. She took a deep breath and shook her head, wondering if she would ever be the queen her mother wanted her to be, the queen Kemet needed, or if lies and exaggerated truths would have to be recorded about her as well.

8

A TIME OF VAIN LOSS |
AHHOTEP
SEDJEFATAWY, 1570 BC

A year passed, and Ahhotep stood in the throne room with General Pennekhbet, who had returned from the northern border. Tep stood on the other side of the throne while Tetisheri sat in the back sipping her cooled karkade tea, waiting to see how Ahhotep would respond.

The General waited for her command. His words repeated in her mind as a growing stiffness overpowered her curled fist: "*The Hekka Khasut have retaken Tepihu. Their prince Sarenpet paid tribute to King Apepi. The nome of Mednit is lost from our borders.*"

Vizier Tetinefer cleared his throat at her silence and shifted on his feet, glancing at the throne room guards.

In a moment of hesitation, she yelled, "Scribe."

But she closed her eyes and regathered herself. They would not rush her.

She looked beyond the General's head to the throne room's doors. The eastern sun flooded the corridor beyond. Her father and husband lay entombed in the West of Waset at the private shaft tombs of the royals and elite. Neither lived long enough to construct a pyramid in their honor. And the Tepihu traitors in the north did not honor what her husband and son did for them.

The blood in her vein bulged over her right eye and prompted her forefinger to smooth it out in a soft, pressed circle upon her skin. When the bulge was gone, her finger curled back into her fist.

"Royal blood was spilled for Tepihu's liberation from the Hekka Khasut." Her fist fell to her side in a heavy thump. "In return, they spit on their tombs? It shall not be. Amun as my witness, I shall take blood for blood," she said as the thud in her heart dropped to a steady pace. "Hold our border in the nome of N'aret Pehtet. Once the Kushites are put down," her eyes glazed over, and her jaw grew taut, "we will go into Mednit and slaughter them all."

Her gaze drifted back to the general. "We will start anew and repopulate those slain with our people loyal to the true King."

She wished to peer over her shoulder to see if her mother was nodding. As if to answer her question, the soft slurp of tea behind her signaled her mother was apathetic. *Ignore her,* Ahhotep told herself. *I do not care what Mother thinks of my decree, right or wrong. The traitors will pay with their lives.*

"As God's Mother commands," General Pennekhbet said with a raised eyebrow.

It did not go unnoticed by Ahhotep. "What else do you wish to say, General Pennekhbet?"

The General's muscles tightened, but with thick pinched lips, he said, "King Kamose and Admiral Baba are due to return after obtaining victory at Arminna."

Tep breathed a sigh of relief, letting her head and shoulders drop. "I am glad to hear they both live," she blurted out and placed a hand over her heart.

Ahhotep glanced at her namesake. "Control yourself, Chief Royal Wife."

She visibly straightened and lifted her chin. "I am sorry, Mother."

"You do not apologize. And you shall call me God's Mother." Ahhotep shook her head. *Has the girl lost sense of all her training? Yes, I feel the same, but I do not show it,* she thought, and her gaze cut over to her daughter.

Tep nodded and remained as still as a statue. A glisten overcame her eyes after the chiding in front of Kemet's general and vizier.

A part of Ahhotep's heart shriveled at the lack of discipline in her daughter, but she could not confront those feelings now. She stepped forward so that she was ahead of the empty throne. "Prepare a feast to honor our King's victories at Abu, Toshka, and Arminna. Invite the nome's princes so they may join us, and we can secure additional men and resources for this unification." She lifted a finger. "As well as celebrate the new uniting of King Kamose and his marriage to his new sister-wife, Ahmose-Nefertari."

The royal scribe Mitry and the head palace steward Ranofer bowed at the waist and left to perform their tasks. But she did not dismiss the general. His eyebrow raised. There was something he wanted to say to her.

She turned to her daughter, "Chief Royal Wife, stand in my place until I return."

"Yes, Mothe—God's Mother," Tep winced at her mistake.

She was still learning. Ahhotep relaxed the tension in her shoulders at the thought and stepped from the dais.

As she passed the General, she whispered, "Walk with me, General."

Her maidservants stayed at length behind her as the duo walked into the courtyard. With the sun rising overhead, she glanced up at him. "What else do you wish to say? Do you think I am in error?"

He shook his head. "No. Mednit is filled with traitors, and they deserve to die."

She stared at him. "But you think something else? Should we call a council meeting when King Kamose returns to decide this path further?"

His eyes narrowed. "No. I worry for your heart, God's Mother. You are right in dispatching traitors, but I fear your motivation is in revenge. And revenge heavies your heart for the afterlife."

Ahhotep snorted and snapped her gaze to the nearby Acacia tree. Even though he spoke the truth, she spat, "My heart is none of your concern, General."

His head lowered, and his gaze dropped to the stone floor of the courtyard. "Please excuse my familiarity, God's Mother. I am at your mercy."

Her thoughts accompanied a shaky breath. *I want revenge on Mednit. It was there in Mednit that their precious Hekka Khasut slew my husband. It took my son years to reach and liberate them. All for what? Betrayal.* She shut her eyes tight. "You are dismissed. Call for a meeting of the council at the King's return."

"As God's Mother commands," General Pennekhbet said, leaving with a tight turn on his heels.

She stared at the Acacia tree and a statue of her husband next to it. Kamose's statue was in the process of being built. The workers glanced at her but kept their distance from the royal woman.

She glanced at the image of her husband's face. *I miss*

you, Tao. What if my heart is full of revenge and fear for our son? I shall not lie and say that it is not. What happens then?

9
A TIME OF PREPARATIONS | AHHOTEP
SEDJEFATAWY, 1570 BC

Ahhotep sat at the table in the council room with her eyes downcast, reliving the feast. Tetian again had come, and instead of celebrating Kamose's victory, he had only belittled her son for returning without Buhen firmly under Kemet's control.

Tetian's words replayed in her mind: *"You dishonor Kemet. Any one of us could have retaken Buhen by now. We give you resources after resources, men after men, and yet you come home with the small towns of Toshka and Arminna, but no Buhen? We need a stronger King!"*

Ahhotep had lost control and yelled back at the fool instead of placating the concern and instilling pride in its place. Even as she thought of it, her body trembled with anger. Her fingertips tingled with rage. Her cheeks lit with embarrassment. The musicians had stopped playing; the dancers had stopped dancing. And then the smirk on Tetian's face made her wish for his permanent absence. She was sure the princes had gossiped about her behavior once she had excused herself from the feast soon afterward.

She shook her head. Why did she do such a thing?

She let Tetian gain the upper hand. The nomes had been independent under the Hekka Khasut for too long; each did as they pleased as long as they paid tribute to the king of the Hekka Khasut. Yet now, even more than ever before, she needed to consolidate the power and authority of her bloodline. Something Tetisheri had done well, but it waned under her transition. She rubbed her forehead and closed her eyes. "How am I to demand respect like my mother?" she whispered and then chuckled with contempt. "Well, it's not by losing my temper in front of all the princes of the Upper."

Kamose, Tetisheri, Tep, Baba, and Pennekhbet entered the council room, followed by the First Prophet of Amun, Thuty, and the vizier, Tetinefer.

Mitry, the royal scribe, entered and took his place on the floor in the corner, chisel at the ready to record the King's decrees.

Tetinefer said before taking his seat, "The princes sleep soundly in the guest apartments adjoining the palace. Their bellies are full from the feast."

Ahhotep felt the hot stares, but upon scanning the room, it seemed as if all purposely avoided looking at her. She took a deep breath and grimaced, hating her mistake at the feast even more.

Kamose spoke. "We are all here and can begin."

Ahhotep rose from her seat. As calmly as she could muster, she said, "My King, I have invited your soon-to-be royal wife, Ahmose-Nefertari, to be a part of this council."

A wave of relief passed over Tetisheri's eyes, but Kamose's brow furrowed. "*Why?*" was the question she was sure he wanted to ask, but ultimately, he refrained.

I cannot tell you, my son, Ahhotep thought. *Your Chief Wife is not yet ready to be Chief Wife. Hentempet is even less prepared than her. I want to see how Ahmose-Nefertari performs.*

Her third oldest daughter entered the council room. Ahmose-Nefertari's eyes glanced over the ruling elite, and she almost shrank back.

But Ahhotep locked eyes with her and motioned for her to sit next to Tetisheri. Ahhotep spoke in justification for her actions: "The divine's blood runs through our veins. She is the King's soon-to-be royal wife. She should be present for these discussions at least for now as was Royal Wife Hentempet when she first wed the King." She watched her nineteen-year-old daughter sit beside her grandmother amid the head nods of the gathered council and remembered when Hentempet did the same almost five years ago. She had done less well than Tep in the council meeting and did not become Kamose's chief wife at the urging of Tetisheri. Poor Tep, though; she could never quite reach the expectations of her grandmother.

Ahhotep's gaze meandered to Tep. Even in providing a female heir, her womb was not birthing any more living children. The night of rushing to her room as she screamed out in pain took hold of Ahhotep's recent memory. Kamose's child was born a season early and had not survived. She set her sights on Kamose. Why would he not lie with both of his sister wives? Unless he had, and Hentempet's womb was closed. He desperately needed an heir. This was the fifth year of his reign, but he had been to battle for much of it. Ahhotep stared at the dark circles under Tep's eyes. He would not marry or go to Ahmose-Nefertari while they mourned their lost child. They could not wait another five years for the chance of a son.

Kamose began the council meeting, cutting through Ahhotep's ruminations. "We were victorious at Abu,

Toshka, and Arminna, but we failed to take Buhen. It is out of reach." He lifted his hand to cover his eyes and rubbed his forehead with his thumb and forefinger. "We lost Mednit, and our forces have decreased in number. The nomes' princes refuse to send more men until we retake Buhen at the second cataract."

Fine wrinkles etched in his twenty-five-year-old brow. Ahhotep sighed quietly at the weight upon her son's shoulders. Those wrinkles were not there when he took the crown.

Kamose returned his hand to the table and resumed his regal posture. "You are the King's most trusted advisors. Now speak. What path do we take?" His shoulders fell back, so they touched the woven reed chair.

Silence came over the room. The answer was clear: take back Buhen, gain more men, establish the Upper, retake the Lower. Yet, the solution which was so apparent was not easily obtained. How would they take back Buhen?

Ahmose-Nefertari cleared her throat and drew all eyes upon her but Ahhotep's. She prayed her daughter would speak with wisdom—this her first time in council.

"Why did we fail to take Buhen?" Ahmose-Nefertari asked.

The men glanced among themselves.

Thuty, Amun's First Prophet, spoke up in his usual high-pitched and whiny voice. "Why dwell on our losses at this time, King's Daughter? Why answer with a question to the King's question?"

Ahmose-Nefertari shrunk in her chair and lowered her head. Her cheeks grew pink on her dark skin.

Ahhotep glanced at her mother, who stared back. *She wants me to say something.* But before she could open her mouth, Tep spoke instead. "First Prophet, you dare embarrass the daughter of King Seqenenre Tao and sister of King Kamose?"

Ahhotep shut her eyes tight while Tetisheri let out a small, breathy chuckle.

That was not the correct comment to make. How to fix this? Ahhotep sighed and placed her hand over her daughter's. "Chief Royal Wife, our First Prophet is merely questioning why the King's Daughter would pose a question instead of responding. But I am curious." She withdrew her hand and focused on her third eldest daughter. "Would the answer to your question have given direction for a response to King Kamose?"

Ahmose-Nefertari nodded and lifted her chin.

"Well then," Ahhotep scanned the room. "Is there someone who can answer the royal woman's question?"

Baba leaned forward in his chair and glanced at Ahhotep and Kamose to obtain an unspoken blessing to speak. "Sister of the King, we failed to take Buhen because the Kushites have long spears, and they blend with the night's shadows. Even on our boats, we are not safe from their spears. We lost too many men. Buhen is far from Toshka, and we became cut off, with retreat our only option."

"Do the Medjay not have spears as well? Do they not have the advantage of the night as well? Would they still be cut off from their people? Do they not know their land?" Ahmose-Nefertari asked with a furrowed brow.

Baba winced. "They do. But the Medjay are scattered along the Upper. If we had all the Medjay with us . . ." He trailed off for a moment. "We would risk losing what we have gained. They are our elite fighting force."

"Yet it is their Kerman homeland?" Ahmose-Nefertari tilted her head.

Baba's head lowered. "Yes," he whispered with a nod. "It is their homeland."

"If my home were being invaded, I would want to fight the invaders rather than be posted somewhere foreign to keep watch over the nomes with slain traitors. Would you not as well?" Ahmose-Nefertari asked.

Ahhotep cleared her throat as a signal for Ahmose-Nefertari to stop speaking. The council had decided to spread out the Medjay, but perhaps they had been in error. She glanced at Tetisheri, who cast proud eyes upon her granddaughter. Ahhotep turned her attention to Kamose and changed the direction of the conversation, knowing many in the room would take offense at the hint of their potentially erroneous decision.

"We have reconstructed the chariots you have sent us from the Hekka Khasut and are building more," Ahhotep said. "But the animals you sent breed slowly."

"The horses," Kamose corrected his mother.

She ignored him. "And we do not know how to use them, much less train with them," Ahhotep said.

"The Hekka Khasut use bow and arrow in their chariot cabins, but they tip when they turn: the wheels are too small, the cabin too big, and the bows too large," Baba said. "My son, Ahmose-Ebana, improves the design as he improved the khopesh, but the design is not ready for war."

"And most of the horses are not ready to take to Buhen," General Pennekhbet said and folded his hands in his lap. "We will need all the Medjay to retake the Kingdom of Kerma. It is their land. They know it best."

"Then what of the north?" Baba asked with glances at Ahhotep. "They also would not want their brothers in arms to have perished in vain."

The General leaned forward on the table, placing his

large forearms upon its top. "We have new trainees ready for war. They will sail north under Troop Commander Uahbra and keep the Hekka Khasut at bay."

"Will they be capable of such a feat? Men who have never seen battle? Are we sending them all to be slain?"

Pennekhbet shot Baba a cold stare. "What choice do we have?" He threw his body into the back of the chair. "We are out of options. We should take what horses and chariots we have, ready or not. It may give us some advantage, at least intimidation. Before I knew what a horse was, it put fear in my heart—the massive beasts. The Kushites have never seen a horse, much less two per chariot. They wouldn't know what a chariot was, either. What did you think they were when you first saw them in battle?"

Baba's glare at Pennekhbet shifted to a soft glance toward Ahhotep. "The gods' feet," he answered monotonously. She studied his face: sorrow lived in his eyes. But why?

Kamose inclined his head toward Tetinefer after Pennekhbet proved his point with Baba. "Vizier. Can you accompany the new soldiers and have diplomatic proceedings with the princes along the way to the north? We need the Bedu to help us train our men to use the horse, but we do not have the barter they will require. Convince the princes we will be victorious and to send more men and resources. They may give more from individual pleas, especially without some princes' constant contention."

Baba snorted, breaking his connection with Ahhotep. "The princes will give us no more gold." His usual deep timbre took over. He placed both hands on the table and stood up. "As the general has said, let us take what horses we have. For intimidation, if nothing else. We will need all the Medjay and risk losing the northern nomes. If we cannot retake Buhen, it will all have been in vain."

Ahhotep traced the bulge in Baba's veins up his forearms and focused on his downcast face. He did not wholly agree with what he was saying; neither did she. Tao lost his life in the northernmost nome of the Upper. To lose it meant he was slain for no reason. He could have come home. Her gaze met his as Kamose was giving the order to bring a few horses with them to Buhen. Baba was trying to save her the grief of her husband's slaying if it became in vain. But why change his mind? Why try to spare her feelings?

As her son's words registered in her ears, she turned to look at him. If they did not give everything to Buhen, Kamose might be killed. But he would go back to war again and again until the south and north were secured. What if he did not come home either?

He had survived three campaigns. She reasoned that he would survive many more, but she noticed a new scar on his arm, most likely made by a Kushite's spear. What if he did not survive the next spear or the next after that one? Her eyes closed in a slow blink envisioning her son's body laid at her feet as was Tao's.

Do not think of such things.

She bowed her head while her heart debated what to say. If Kamose was killed, his brother was too young to take the crown as Kamose had no sons. There would be civil unrest among the nomes on who would take the throne. The only logical choice was to name Ahmose as Coregent and Hereditary Prince, so there would be no gap or opportunity for someone to seize the crown.

There were many more battles to fight, and Kamose may not live to see them all.

Do not think of such things.

Yet, in asking Kamose to name his brother Coregent, she was acknowledging Kamose might be killed. She shook her head as her eyes welled with tears.

I cannot lose my eldest son, not after losing Tao.

"Mother." Kamose's stern whisper cut through her thoughts.

She found his eyes, unsure of what he had been saying. The others in the room stared at her to respond, but what had been asked?

Her mouth opened, but she didn't know what to say. Her mother's disappointed snort sailed through her nostrils, and Ahhotep clenched her teeth at her second significant mistake that day.

Kamose smiled at her, studying her worried face. "What do you suggest we do if we lose Buhen with the Medjay, with the horses?"

Her brow furrowed as she rushed to speak. "Well, Prince Tetian would be sure to make a case that the divinely appointed should come from his nome, the richest nome, and the other princes might agree at that point."

Tetisheri cleared her throat, and Ahhotep slowly blinked at what demeaning remark she would utter.

"Then it seems you have a problem, God's Mother," Tetisheri said. She paused, waiting for any to answer her, but none did. "You must consolidate power in the throne, not the princes."

Ahhotep slid her gaze to her mother in annoyance. Her thoughts raced at what to say to rebuke the older woman. She knew that was what needed to be done. Everyone knew that. But "how?" was the question.

"It would seem so, Great Wife of my father," Ahhotep said and pressed her lips into a thin line after the contempt-filled comment was made.

The others in the room shifted in their seats at her odd behavior and blatant disrespect of Tetisheri.

Third mistake. I wish this day to end, Ahhotep thought. *I cannot stand it anymore.*

She stood up and glanced at her son. "As I continue my former suggestion: to consolidate power and keep the crown where it is supposed to be, I propose you name a coregent."

"But I have no son," Kamose said with a slight shake of his head. His hand moved to cover the recent scar from the Kushite's spear.

Ahhotep's face fell, for he knew the motivation behind her proposal. "Then name your brother as Coregent and Hereditary Prince so the crown will go to him without an heir. And if you"—she swallowed the fear and the words she did not want to speak—"there will not be a rush for the crown."

A wave of doubt crossed his eyes, and his fingers dug into the muscle on his arm. His voice was broken. "You believe I will be killed as Father?"

"No," she whispered with a shake of her head. A warm, pressed smile beamed on her lips, but her eyes remained full of fear. Her heart broke at her son's realization of her lack of faith in his future. "I believe you will retake Buhen. I believe the princes will rejoin our campaigns once you gain victory in Kerma and Kush." She blinked back the coming tears, knowing her son could see through her facade. So, she came out with the truth. What was a fourth mistake after having made three already?

"But King Kamose, I am fearful you will be returned to me as your father. He had four sons, and you have none. Such a gap in the bloodline will surely divide the princes even more. Tetian will seize the throne for Ta-

Seti. Name a coregent, so if you perish,"—a tear escaped down her cheek—"and I pray to Horus to keep you from harm," she added. "Unrest will not become us in your absence among the living."

The bags under his eyes grew dark in the moment, and his tight shoulders released their burdens. "As you wish, Mother," he whispered, defeated. "I shall name Prince Ahmose as my Coregent and Hereditary Prince."

Her heart ached, wishing to hold him as if he were a child. To tell him, she did not want him to think about this life's end at such a young age. To tell him, her heart would shrivel and die should he return home like his father.

But she remained silent as he stood up to make his decree. "Mitry, royal scribe—declare an Appearance of the King ceremony and feast in Waset at the temple of Amun. Prince Ahmose, the King's brother, will be named Coregent before The Wild Bull sets sail for Buhen. To seal his divine appointment if he is to become sole regent, he shall marry my daughter, Sitkamose." When he finished, his gaze fell to the floor. "It is settled then. The Medjay are to fight at Buhen. The horses shall come with us, but we shall leave the chariots. My brother shall be Coregent." He nodded and glanced at his mother. His eyes told her it was done.

"I must renew my strength," he whispered, indicating his need for rest and sleep. He left without another word, and soon the others followed, but Ahhotep sat back down and remained seated.

When everyone else had left the council room, Tetisheri placed a hand on her shoulder and peered down at her from a lifted head. "You surprised me, Ahhotep. It was what was needed. I believe Ahmose-Nefertari should not marry Kamose until we know he shall come back alive. Ahmose may need a competent and healthy Chief Wife given the consistent illnesses overtaking Sitkamose."

The burn in the back of Ahhotep's eyes forced her to avert her gaze from her mother's. "But Kamose is defeated. I have stripped him of any faith he thought I had for him."

Tetisheri chuckled as if any redemption Ahhotep had gained was now lost on her. "He is a grown man. He will overcome without his mother's coddling." She whisked her hand away as if Ahhotep's comment had caused her to second-guess her comforting and short-lived praise. "Now, sleep well this night. We would not want you to make any further mistakes with the princes or the council. Next time, you should control your anger and keep your ears open to what the King says."

Ahhotep shook her head at Mother's scolding. "Yes, Mother," she ground out.

Tetisheri moved toward the door. "And, Ahhotep," she said before exiting. "Next time you speak to me in front of the council, there will be no trace of derision in your voice." They locked eyes as Tetisheri's last stab of the day sunk deep into Ahhotep's heart. A hardened glare overcame Tetisheri's eyes. "Do not think ill of me, child. I do what I do for the crown, for this family. Because one day, I will be in the Field of Reeds, and you will be left by yourself, making the hard decisions on what is best for Kemet." With nothing more to say, she vanished through the doorway.

Another tear slid out of Ahhotep's eye, and she quickly wiped it away. Her maidservants, Nena and Meret, were outside the council room waiting for her. But a tall and thick shadow darkened the doorway.

Now, who comes to mock me?

🐦 96 🐦

"God's Mother." It was Baba.

She shifted in her seat and assumed he was not there to mock. "Not now, Admiral," she said, her voice cracking, unable to keep her tears from falling one after another and not wishing him to see it.

But he came in anyway and slipped next to her at the table. "Forgive me, God's Mother, for my disobedience." He placed his hand beside hers, careful not to touch the royal flesh.

She shook her head, not knowing what to say, but she was thankful for his company. They had shared understanding glances thus far but also similar pains. The most recent sting to her heart, he would not understand, but she spoke it anyway. "I have hurt my son, Admiral."

He winced. "No, you did what was needed to ensure the crown stayed where it was meant to be." A sympathetic smile arose on his lips, and his eyes were as warm as the night.

"I have still hurt him. Please make sure he comes home to me alive," she whispered, knowing it could be an impossible promise to keep. The reassurance was what she needed. He had come home when Tao had not, but neither had his general or admiral. It had been a devastating loss. She brushed a tear from her eye, remembering all those she hoped were in the Field of Reeds. "Please bring him home alive," she repeated.

Baba nodded and, after a moment, said, "I will do everything in my power to make sure King Kamose comes back to Waset alive."

"Thank you," she whispered. His presence gave her a sense of comfort. It had been years since a man was as close to her as Baba was then. She wished to hold his hand and squeeze in friendship if nothing else, hoping the future would bring better prosperity than it had been giving them. What good was a king over a poor land?

She pulled her hand away to not give in to her temptation. His arm slipped back to his side, and he sat up straight, regathering his professional posture.

A sigh came out, and she covered her mouth, wanting to tell him why she refused him, but instead said, "My behavior was unacceptable this evening at the feast and in the council meeting. I have no excuse."

He relaxed his shoulders at her invitation to converse more. "You are God's Mother. You have no need for excuses. Besides, Prince Paser of Herui defended your honor, stating it was the anniversary of the slaying of King Seqenenre Tao and condemned Tetian for speaking harshly to the King and his family. Paser will be an ally if we fail with Buhen." Her gaze turned inward, imagining her son's mangled body. "The King's council knows you, God's Mother. They know you love your son. They know how hard it was to propose what you did to him, but it was needed to keep the peace should something ill befall King Kamose. But our King is strong and brave. The gods are with him. He will succeed."

She looked at him with fresh tears brimming while trying to put away the fears of losing Kamose. "Thank you once again, Admiral."

Baba held her gaze with eyes as dark and endless as a starless night; they longed for her to call him by his name before they momentarily dipped to her lips.

It was then she assumed his true feelings for her.

He spoke with a softness reserved for her. "You do not need to thank me."

She traced his face with her eyes, and he, hers in a silent exchange. Would she remove the boundary between them?

"I have every need to thank you, my friend." She tested her assumptions by calling him a friend.

He beamed.

A rush overpowered her senses at his response, but it lessened as soon as it had come when she remembered her place. "You have comforted me many times. I shall never forget Admiral Baba, friend to God's Mother." She stood up, as did he. "Shall you walk me to the door?" she asked in her royal demeanor.

"It would be my honor," he said with a slight bow and escorted her from the council room with a contented gleam in his eyes.

10

A TIME OF DOUBT | AHMOSE

SEDJEFATAWY, 1570 BC

Instead of a royal marriage feast, there would be a coronation. The princes ate a lavish morning meal and entered the palace courtyard with other nobles of the land who had traveled through the decan to be at the coronation. Only the princes, the priesthood, the royal family, and guards were allowed to enter the pillared throne room.

Ahmose stood in his brother's splendor next to the throne. Golden leather sandals adorned his feet, and a sash of gold and silver beads wrapped his waist and held his royal shendyt. A heavy pectoral collar rested over his shoulders. Its polished blue and gold beads reflected the morning sun and torchlight into his eyes. His bald head, save for the braided sidelock above his ear, had been oiled to a radiant shine by his steward, Bakaa.

Kamose stood beside him, wearing the blue Khepresh crown to show he was endowed with divinity and protection from the gods.

I was never to be king, Ahmose thought as Thuty, the First Prophet of Amun, and Minmontu, the Second Prophet of Amun, advanced toward him down the long aisle before the throne. Between them, Pahemred, the First Prophet of Ptah, walked with a solemn face holding the great white crown of the Upper, the *Hedjet*.

Why am I being crowned Coregent and named Hereditary Prince? Ahmose asked himself as he scanned those in attendance. *Kamose is young and healthy. He can still have a son. Why would he give me the crown?*

All the princes' beady eyes fell upon him, the ten-year-old boy, and his soon-to-be brides: Sitkamose, and Henuttamehu, his half-sister, daughter of his mother's sister, Inhapi. His marriage to Sitkamose would seal his right to rule through the King. His marriage to Henuttamehu would further prove his divine appointment.

He scanned his siblings until he came upon Ahmose-Nefertari and wondered why his brother had chosen not to marry her. Kamose was making odd decisions. Perhaps, he decided not to marry Ahmose-Nefertari because there was only time for one celebration: a coronation rather than a marriage feast.

Ahmose's gaze shifted past Pahemred, holding the crown, to the princes who stood with arms crossed over their chests and furrowed brows. He gulped and took a shaky breath. He shifted on his feet, but his brother whispered to him out of the side of his mouth, "Be still, brother. Do not let them see your worry."

He stilled his feet and knees and snapped his gaze back to Pahemred. His stomach rumbled, and his mouth watered at the coming evening feast after his coronation. The year of rites and ceremonies that usually came before the crowning had been skipped because his brother needed to leave for Buhen, just as it had been skipped for Kamose since their father came home slain.

It is not hard to understand why the princes are not

impressed with us, Ahmose reasoned as Pahemred lifted the tall royal white crown and recited the creator god Ptah's responsibilities and blessings for the King. Thuty and Minmontu lifted their heads to the sunlight falling from the wall vents of the throne room and chanted the same from Amun and Re.

Ahmose's eyes bounced between the three, waiting to see who would finish first. Their words became faster and faster until Pahemred jolted the crown in the air, silencing the throne room. His chin lowered until his red-shot eyes connected with Ahmose.

"The Lord of Strength is Re, Ahmose—will you give your youth renewed by the gods to dedicate your life to the unification of the Lower and the Upper? Will you give your power to protect this land against all foes? Will you honor your vitality before Amun and Re as a contract between the divine and men?"

Ahmose nodded and cleared his throat, ready to speak the words memorized in the preceding decan. He had already shot the four arrows in the four directions that morning to symbolize his dominion and power over the earth as granted by the gods. There had been no ill signs to say the gods disapproved of him. Yet his stomach was still unsettled, and his hands were clammy.

"I." The single word croaked in his throat. He licked his dry lips to try again and kept his eyes on Pahemred to ignore the doubtful stares of the princes.

"I, The Lord of Strength is Re, Ahmose, dedicate my life to the unification of the Lower and the Upper."

Visions of his father flashed in memory, but he swallowed them back and continued: "I give my power in the protection of Kemet against all foes, and I shall pursue any attacker until Kemet is victorious. I honor the divine's contract with man, and when my ba and ka are released to the next life, I shall become one with Re aboard his ship so the sun may rise again the next day."

I was never to be king, he thought, but his lips spoke in a perfect speech:

"This I honor, my oath. This I decree."

And with the sacred oath given, Pahemred placed the Hedjet atop his head, carefully sliding the sidelock underneath its tall hollow cylinder. Its leather band fit tightly over his brow and nape and above his ears. Pahemred removed his hands, and the reed and leather crown wobbled despite the fit. Ahmose tightened every muscle in his body to ensure the crown did not move. The formed ball atop the cylindrical crown did nothing to ease the tingles down his spine.

He was now King Coregent. Ahmose scanned the princes before him. Some seemed apathetic, their face locked in an expressionless haze. Some stared with a smile of awe and pride, yet others glared at him with a deathly gaze.

The dancers twirled before them at the clash of drums, their skirts draped high on their thighs and low beneath their navels as belts. The shockwave of the reverberation of the drumbeat rattled Ahmose's teeth. The dancers' floral collars drooped low on their chest, and their wigs of long black hair fell in thick braids to the waist. The waft of sweet perfume swept past Ahmose as a dancer twirled beneath the dais.

The sistrum musicians advanced, clad in sheer yellow drapes over their shoulders and tucked into thick belts wrapped around their hips. The whistling sistrum was like that of the Nile reeds blowing in the wind. And the beating drum's hard pound sounded like the rhythmic lap of the Nile's water.

Three claps and the dancers twirled and released a

chanting cry—no discernible word—but rather a shout of joy and peace that the divine line of Kings would continue in this life.

The company traveled to the temple of Amun in the city of Waset south of Sedjefatawy and Per-djed-ken.

The courtyard of the temple of Amun bustled with the people of Waset and those who could afford to travel from the surrounding nomes.

God's Mouth, the man who walked and spoke ahead of Ahmose and Kamose, announced their names: "Kamose, Given Life, and Ahmose, Given Life—May they live forever."

They made their way through the crowds—guards made a clear path for them until they walked through the pillars of the outer temple.

The First Prophet of Amun, Thuty, opened the doors of the long, narrow inner sanctum and led Kamose and Ahmose within the god's abode. The doors quickly closed behind them to lock out the rest of the world. The shift of broad daylight to the closed-off dark inner sanctum caused Ahmose to pause. His eyes adjusted with the small pillars of haze-like illumination from the light holes in the roof. Beyond them sat the statue of Amun upon an altar in the back of the freshly-cleaned room. The smell of cedar filled Ahmose's nostrils from the burning incense next to the god. A single white stream of smoke ebbed and flowed through the sanctum's pillars of light.

Thuty laid a grain offering at the feet of the statue and chanted the ancient rites to open the mouth of the god. He bowed his head and took a few steps back when it was finished.

"My Kings," Thuty said in a throaty whisper as he shuffled to the doors.

Ahmose's heart beat hard in his ears. His eyes were to the floor, and his breath came in random spurts. Never had he been in the presence of Amun before. Kamose went before the statue and knelt to both knees, and Ahmose did the same, eyes still to the ground. Kamose brought his hands up to face the god, and Ahmose imitated. Kamose's head dipped, and his back bowed until his face and hands paralleled the floor. Ahmose, in turn, did the same, but the Hedjet wobbled again. He turned his head to keep it secured and hoped Amun did not notice.

What do we say? he wanted to ask, but fear of the god kept his tongue mute.

They stayed in the dutiful position until a crick grew in Ahmose's neck.

"Great Amun of Re, Lord of the Heavens and the Earthly Thrones, The Hidden One, Amun, Father of the Gods," Kamose began, "Set your touch upon your divinely appointed. Grant us victory over the land of Kerma and Kush. Grant us victory over our land in the Lower." Then his voice broke. "Grant us long life."

Visions of their father flooded Ahmose's memory in the seemingly long pause. *Do not let them take my brother from me,* Ahmose thought and shut his eyes tight.

"Grant us long life," Kamose repeated, resuming his reverent speaking voice. "Renew our spirits. Never let our vigor cease. Let us be content with Ma'at. Do not let our hearts be heavy."

Kamose cleared his throat. "And let each King journey safely to become one with Re, so that all of Kemet under the Aten may live on and on."

Ahmose felt a *tap, tap* on his shoulder and opened his eyes. Kamose was sitting upright, so Ahmose shot up, almost losing the Hedjet. He balanced it upon his head and readjusted it in the presence of the god as his cheeks turned as red as the paint on the walls.

Kamose rolled back to his feet, bowed his head, and shuffled back toward the doors. Ahmose did the same. The bright sunlight nearly blinded him when the doors opened, and he blinked until the central court came into view. Beyond the gate, the courtyard filled with people who were waiting to feast because the Appearance of the King was about to begin.

Ahmose locked eyes with his mother, who held a pensive smile, but then her gaze drifted to Kamose. He glanced up at his brother, who, after sharing a glance with their mother, grimaced before forcing a pressed smile.

It was then Ahmose knew why he had been named Coregent, and he spun around just as Thuty was closing the doors to the sanctum. He stared the god Amun in the face before he disappeared from sight and prayed again in an urgent silent plea: "*Grant Kamose long life!*"

11

A TIME OF PREMONITION | AHMOSE

SEDJEFATAWY, 1570 BC

The morning after his coronation, Ahmose waved at The Wild Bull and the King's Fleet at the Sedjefatawy port as the boats pulled away and went upstream toward Kush. He peered up at his mother, standing next to him. She shook her head, and he dropped his hand, keeping it at his side as she did. He supposed royalty did not wave.

"Why did Kamose have to go to Buhen?" he whispered to her. "He could have stayed here, and then he wouldn't have needed to name me Coregent."

"Not now, Ahmose," she said through her teeth before giving a polite smile to the princes who boarded their boats to return home.

Each one passed by her and Ahmose, bowing and thanking them for the feast and lodging.

Prince Paser gave a warm grin to Ahmose. "Coregent, I am honored to have you on our throne." Ahmose nodded with the white hedjet crown bobbing on his head. He quickly stopped, so it would not fall off. "It is an honor to have you . . . in the palace," he said quickly, not entirely sure what to say to the prince.

Paser's grin spread across his face as he turned his focus to Ahhotep. "And God's Mother, Great Wife, as much as my Herui can spare, it is with your family, always."

"Prince Paser," Ahhotep said with a dip of her chin, showing gratitude. "We know Herui does not have much to give, and yet in giving your all, you have given more than any other nome, for no other are with us fully."

Ahmose wrenched his head to look at his mother. "What? Why aren't they with us fully?" he asked, but his mother ignored him, as did Paser.

"It saddens me that your son, our great King Kamose, must again go to Buhen without the full support of the Lower." His brow furrowed. Ahmose noticed Tetian drawing near as Paser spoke. "The gods—"

"Why does it sadden you, Paser of Herui?" Tetian interjected and stood with his hands on his hips, far closer to Paser than what was deemed comfortable.

Paser lifted his nose high in the air but did not back away from Tetian's rude approach. "Because our King deserves our full support no matter what we have lost."

Tetian chuckled and held up his hands to him. "I am not blinded by loyalty, Paser. My king, the one my forefather pledged an oath to, will have to *earn* my support." His dark eyes shot to Ahmose. "And boys cannot do much in earning support."

Ahmose's lips curled under at the insult. His words were lost on his tongue, but he managed to squeak out, "I can do more than you."

At the same time, Paser scoffed and said, "He is our Coregent, Prince Tetian."

Both men and his mother glanced at him for his obviously childish remark. But Paser sniffed and glared at Tetian. "Do not disrespect such positions."

Tetian leaned into Paser's space and said in a hushed tone, "Your time with God's Mother is done; why don't you load up on your small boat and sail the easy path downstream to Kemet's poorest nome."

Paser gritted his teeth. "One day, Herui will be far richer than even the rich Ta-Seti because our King will retake our lands back. It is the will of Re. You deny our gods' will by refusing your riches."

Tetian shook his head as Paser spun around and left to the smallest boat in the port. Tetian took Paser's place with a small step and squared his shoulders to Ahhotep. "God's Mother." He smiled with pressed lips.

Ahmose waited for Tetian to address him as Paser had done, but it never came. His mother, though, asked in a hushed voice. "What is it, Prince Tetian? Why do you hate the divinely appointed?"

"Hate is a strong word, Great Wife." He took a step into her space, his body almost touching hers. Ahmose dropped his jaw and pushed him back, but the man did not budge. Nena and Meret stepped forward, but Ahhotep lifted a hand to stay them. "The Prince will not harm God's Mother," she said. "What is it you wish to say, Prince Tetian?"

He leaned over and whispered in her ear closest to Ahmose. "A King should be able to protect his domain, should he not? Let us see how Kamose fares against the Kushites, and well, let us hope his brother has no need to take his place."

He stepped back with a sneer on his face. He cocked his head as he ran his eyes up and down her body and snorted when he glanced at Ahmose. "You cannot even protect your mother from a Prince getting too close to her; how do you expect to fight in a war?"

He snapped his gaze to Ahhotep, and before she

could get in another word, he took a grandiose bow just as Tetisheri approached. "In peace, God's Mother and Coregent."

"Great Wife," he said with a small smile acknowledging the older woman before leaving toward the biggest boat at the port, even bigger than The Rising.

Ahmose turned his face to his mother, whose cheeks boiled red. "What has happened with Prince Tetian? Is Kamose fighting without full support from all the nomes? Why is Prince Paser the only one—"

"Ahmose." The harsh whisper was cut short by a deep breath. "There are many, many questions you will have. But I want you to finish your training in the Kap first. When you are older and ready for a granted appointment by Kamose, then I will tell you all you need to know." She placed a warm hand on his cheek. Her lips smiled, but the smile did not reach her eyes.

Tetisheri scanned the port. "God's Mother, it is hot outside; why don't you take the Coregent into the shade of the palace? I will remain here to see the princes off."

Ahhotep's hand fell away from his cheek. "Yes, Great Wife." She turned, and Ahmose followed.

"What granted appointment?" he asked.

She chuckled. "You could be appointed general, or vizier, or admiral . . . " Her voice trailed off.

There was silence between them as they walked through the double doors of the palace until Ahmose looked up at his mother and pointedly asked, "Why did Kamose name me Coregent if I will only be appointed a general or vizier?"

Her lips pressed thin. "I think you know why Ahmose," she said finally.

A rock sank into the pit of his stomach. "But Kamose

will come home." He did not want to be king. "Kamose can still have sons."

His mother nodded and seemed to rethink her prior answer. "He will, and he can. He only appointed you if he left the throne with no heir. It is merely a formality. Nothing more. As soon as a son is born, you will no longer be Coregent, and his son will be Crown Prince."

Ahmose sighed in relief and nodded. The hedjet bobbed along with the nod, and Ahmose abruptly stopped. "Good. This crown does not fit anyway." He beamed up at his mother. "Then I shall return to the Kap and finish with my tutors?"

"Yes, your sister and I will be on the throne in your stead." She folded her hands across her belly. "Learn much, my son."

He turned to leave and whistled on his way to the Kap with the words ringing in his mind's ear: "Kamose will come home—he will, he will, he will, he will. He has to." He envisioned a great future for his brother, one with many children—sons as strong as Kamose and daughters as sweet and kind as Sitkamose.

12

A TIME OF HONOR |
KAMOSE

BUHEN, 1570 BC

Again, The Wild Bull bounced against the stone pier at Buhen—its sail cut down so the moonlight reflecting on its white fabric would not give away their arrival. There were no sounds of movement within the fortress, signifying the strategy's success. The dark sentries' shadows stayed atop their high walls—the small torchlight from within illuminated the sentries' locations and the open fortress gate. The calming aroma of the Nile waters entered Kamose's nostrils with a firm inhale. *The fools must have thought we would not sail in the Nile at night, nor had they thought we would return so soon*, he thought. *It will be our victory.*

Kamose looked at the barge full of Medjay and soldiers. The whites of their eyes gave their location away. His gaze fell to his Admiral, who watched him. Kamose placed a hand on Baba's shoulder.

Baba whispered, "Kamose, Living Horus, your forces are ready to retake Buhen."

The sun had not yet risen, but the sky was streaked

with the dark blues of the coming dawn to signal its coming. The moon had sunk low in the western sky.

Kamose's celestial khepresh crown of war blended with the landscape, and he drew his khopesh from his belt. He eyed a few men before him before he turned and leaped from the boat onto the pier—his body servants just ahead of him, his Medjay and soldiers behind him, Baba by his side. Their leather sandaled feet made little sound on the stone.

They ran toward the port fortress on the light morning breeze; the best Medjay remained in the boats, picking off the Kushite shadows atop the high fortress walls with expertly shot arrows, the weapon of choice for the Medjay.

Kamose entered the fortress, and as planned, the soldiers and Medjay spread out along the wall of falling bodies of the lookouts above. They would sweep the fortress like the mighty goddess Sekhmet in her blood lust. They would leave none alive. After a few moments of slaying Kushites as they slept, shouts and screams filled the night sky as the Kushites were awoken with such bloodshed.

Kamose swung his khopesh with a forceful blow and took the head of a Kushite. He gauged they were halfway into the fortress while he wiped the blood from his face just as another lunged at him with a spear jab, but he was quick for his age, blocking it with a parry of his shield and swinging his khopesh in a counterattack.

"Admiral," he called in the slight pause, taking note of his dead body servant at his feet. *Please be alive, Admiral.* His gaze darted between the sweaty Medjay bodies surrounding him, looking for the chief officer. "Admiral," he called again. "Shoot the arrow."

He blocked a coming attack as the whites of a Kushite's eyes grew as the man neared him. "Shoot the arrow," he called out again, engaging in defense and counterattack.

Shoot the arrow. If you are alive, Baba, shoot the arrow! He thought as he focused on his training to defeat the man trying to kill him.

He pushed the Kushite back, and another joined in when a flaming arrow lit up the night as it sailed high into the streaming purple sky.

Now, we will be victorious. He grinned at the thought. The Kushite nearly had him as he momentarily took his attention to the arrow, but a fellow Medjay saved him with a quick spear jab to the Kushite's throat.

A few moments later, a rumbling beneath their feet caused the Kushites to shrink back as more Medjay and soldiers flooded the Buhen Fortress. There was only so much room at the piers, and their reinforcements had come. And they had come with the beasts—the horses.

The Kushites reeked of fear from the rumbling in the ground and the neighing and snorting of Kemet's new war animal.

Kamose raised his khopesh in the growing dawn and yelled out, "For your homeland, my Medjay brothers!"

A stream of horses ridden by the soldiers most acquainted with them burst into the fortress and hung on their backs, clutching their manes for dear life. Medjay archers ran by their sides and drove the Kushites out the back of the defense.

Kamose ran alongside the horses, and Baba fell into step beside him. With his men by his side, new vigor filled his veins.

We are going to be victorious.

The thought made him run harder toward the fleeing

Kushites past the fortress walls and into the open, striking them down from the back to ensure they stayed out and did not return.

The chants of victory at Buhen overwhelmed the pre-dawn as the dark-bodied Kushites fled and became one with the shadows of the morning.

Baba held up his bloodied khopesh and yelled with the last of his breath. He bent over, depleted.

Kamose placed a sure hand upon his shoulder, wrenching him upward. "Are you well, Admiral?"

Baba nodded. "I am not as young as I once was, my King. Two days of no rest and a night full of fighting elite Kushites—I wish for sleep."

Kamose chuckled as did Baba. Kamose looked around at the slain bodies. "Let us plan for re-establishing our presence in these lands. Then, perhaps, we can rest and return to our families before the season ends." He gestured toward the Buhen fortress. Its walls towered overhead, and the soft *clack* of the Nile's waters against the King's fleet sounded in the dark distance on the port side of the stronghold. A single victorious thunder arose from the men within the fortress, and the rhythmic chanting "King Kamose" lifted high into the air.

Kamose held a beam across his lips as Baba's eyes lit with pride. "Let us secure what we have won this night, Admiral," he said.

Baba nodded and yelled out, "Torch the perimeter. Retreat inside the fortress walls. Leave the dead til the sun fully rises. We shall not risk more life with an enemy we cannot see beyond the perimeter's torchlight." Baba's voice carried, and as the order was being carried out, the Medjay and Egyptian warriors closed in around them with arrows pointing out toward the dim darkness.

Until . . .

A whoosh of a projectile came whistling through the dark dawn sky.

13

A TIME OF SORROW |
AHHOTEP
SEDJEFATAWY, 1570 BC

Ahhotep stepped from The Rising after returning from Per-djed-ken at the close of Kamose's fifth regnal year. The warm wind whipped in her face and body, pressing her fine linen pleated dress against her flesh. It pressed her so much that she believed the god Shu was speaking to her. She turned to look at what the deity was trying to force her to see.

Sails. But as they drew closer, her brow furrowed. *Sail.* She squinted to make it out. Her heartbeat lapped like the Nile against the port, quick and rhythmic.

"The Wild Bull," she said and turned to her maidservants and the fleetsmen of The Rising. "The Wild Bull has come home!"

Kamose's face lit in her memory, and she pictured the same return as before—his bright smile underneath the silver diadem and blue khepresh.

But as she stood at the port, she shifted on her feet. Her lips trembled, debating whether to impress a smile or a frown of worry. Why was there only one boat? Where were the others? Was Kamose victorious? Or . . .

Her tongue grew thick and dry in the heat of the day, and her gaze fell to the waters lapping in rhythm with her thoughts: *Either I have lost my son, or we failed to take Buhen. And we have lost our army. And there will be no more support for the unification. And Waset will be weak, open to invasion from the other nomes.* She licked her fast-drying lips as unshed tears burned in the back of her eyes. *Or . . . Or . . . The Wild Bull simply sailed faster than the others.*

The wounds upon Tao's body and head were too gruesome to remember, but she pictured the same upon her son.

"The Wild Bull," her voice cracked.

"Sailed." The word barely made it past her lips.

"Faster. Than. The. Others." Her breath came out in hard gasps.

Her vision blurred from the lack of air as she tried to believe the very possible situation she had presented aloud. The ship had simply sailed faster than the others, yet a whisper in the wind and a hole in her belly contradicted such a reasonable explanation.

Not Kamose. Not like Tao. Anut, Goddess of War, Protector of the King in Battle—twice you fail them? She shamed herself at the thoughtful plea turned accusation as soon as she thought it. Both kings' bodies were brought home to journey west and become one with Re. The Goddess was not to blame. She shut her eyes tight. No. One king's body. There would not be two, she told herself in vain. Not Kamose. Not like Tao.

The voice of her maidservant, Nena, broke her thoughts. "The sun ails you, God's Mother. Should we proceed to the throne room to receive King Kamose from The Wild Bull?"

"Yes," she stuttered. She forced herself not to breathe

to reset her chest and mind. *Hold it together.* The silent command forced a rigidity along her spine. *I am a royal woman; I must be like my mother.*

"Yes," she said again with a clearer voice. "We shall receive King Kamose in the throne room." Only Nena and Meret could have heard the slight tremor in her voice. Ahhotep's nod of reassurance did little to the aching instinct only a mother could have.

The doors to the throne room opened, and she walked in as if on a cloud, on another plane in the living world, unwilling to face the possibility her son was no longer alive.

But Tetisheri saw through her. "Your knees are weak. You have stayed too much under the Aten's rays." She gestured to a nearby servant. "Bring some tea for God's Mother."

Tep and Ahmose-Nefertari stepped from the dais to help her to her place, but Ahhotep waved them off.

"The Wild Bull has returned," she said with a monotone voice.

Tep's face lit up, and Ahmose-Nefertari smiled. But as Tep began to chatter about seeing Kamose again, Ahmose-Nefertari studied her mother's face, and her smile faded.

"What is it, Mother?" Ahmose-Nefertari whispered when Ahhotep was upon the dais.

"The Wild Bull comes alone," she whispered back, and Tep's chatter died as soon as it had arisen.

Tetisheri drew a sharp intake of breath through her wide nostrils. The clink of her tea cup against its saucer reverberated in the silent throne room.

"Well, what does that mean, Mother?" Tep asked, gripping Ahhotep's arm.

Ahhotep glanced at the empty throne. "Summon your brother, Ahmose. He is Coregent and should be on the throne this day regardless of what it means." Her eyes searched the floor of the dais as if the washed stone held an answer.

Tep released her arm and sent a servant to bring Ahmose forth. She came back to her side. "He is in the Kap. I said he should be there."

"He is Coregent and should be on the throne." The curtness made her daughter take a step backward.

"Yes, Mother," she said with a dip in her chin. "I have sent for him."

Tetisheri tilted her head; her long, plaited false hair jangled with golden beads. She was judging her. She lost her son, and she remained calm. She did not shed a tear. She had to remain as a strong image in front of war-torn people.

Ahhotep turned to her daughters. "No matter the word from The Wild Bull, we must appear powerful." Her words were as weak as her mother's instinct was strong. "We must master our emotions," she said in a hurried whisper and pointedly stared at Tep. "No matter what comes."

Both daughters nodded with pensive countenances as a servant brought her tea. She took a sip and then a gulp of the cool liquid before shoving it back toward the servant.

The throne room doors were thrown open, and time stopped until God's Mouth came in and announced, "Ahmose, Given Life, to enter his throne room." The boy king came in with proud shoulders and a lifted chin as instructed, but Ahhotep saw through the facade—a scared little boy was underneath that hedjet crown. He walked up to the throne and climbed in while the doors shut. His feet dangled in the air, not able to touch the floor.

She took a deep breath, hearing more feet in the corridor outside the throne room. Stooping to whisper in Ahmose's ear, she paused. She told herself they simply sailed too fast as one last bout of assurance.

"My son," she whispered. "No matter what we hear or see in the coming moments, you are our King Coregent. You must remain calm." Her voice shook. "You must remain silent unless I ask you to speak. Do you understand?"

The hedjet bobbed on his head as he nodded. "Mother, why are you frightened?" His big eyes turned toward her.

"I am not frightened," she lied and stood up as the doors opened once more. God's Mouth entered. "The Wild Bull has returned with King Kamose."

She expected after that to see Kamose striding into the throne room, but the priests of Anubis came first. Her eyes drifted to what they held: the ends of round poles carrying a litter with a body. The first image she saw was the shining blue crown with the gold uraeus poised to strike the sun disc above.

In the heat of the day, chill set into her arms and seeped into her core as the priests neared her. The morning meal came to the top of her throat as they pivoted the litter parallel to the dais.

The cries of agony hurdled through her belly as she watched the priests lay her eldest son's body before her. Yet she restrained the commoner's grief with a tight jaw and stood tall.

Her heart cried out, "*Isis! Hathor! Horus! Anut! Re!*

Amun! Why?" yet her lips remained sealed. The hot sear of restrained tears burned the back of her eyes and scalded her throat, preventing air from flowing. Her gaze lifted to Baba, whose knee was bent and head was bowed before her son's body. Her thoughts lashed out at him: *You! You come back twice alive, yet my husband and son come back slain? Where were you? Where were you?!*

Tep fell to her knees, releasing what Ahhotep wished to release. A single stream of audible pain coursed from her daughter's open mouth. Tep's arms wrapped around her stomach. Ahmose-Nefertari's head bowed with a stream of tears down her cheeks while her knuckles turned white. Ahmose sat in the chair, wide-eyed and jaw ajar, his small hands gripping the chair arms as if the great immortal snake of the sky, Apep, was only moments from devouring him.

The chant of the priests commenced as they waited for Ahhotep's command to begin the burial preparations officially, but Ahhotep stood silent, staring at Kamose.

The soft *tap-tap-tap* of Tetisheri's footsteps drew closer as she approached until she stood next to Ahhotep and spoke for her to those in the room: "The Hekka Khasut slayed my son, and the Kushites, my grandson." She shook her head. "Ammit will have their hearts, but my kin will be one with Re. Anut has kept her protection over the Horus king and brought back his body to journey to Re."

Tetisheri patted Ahhotep on the shoulder and whispered, "At least, know this, God's Mother," she whispered and wiped a fallen tear from her daughter's eye. Ahhotep blinked, not realizing tears ran down her cheeks. Her mother's lips moved, but the words were as in a well, and they lagged more each moment.

"It will help with the pain of loss," Tetisheri whispered.

Tetisheri glanced at her granddaughters, Tep and Ahmose-Nefertari. "I mourned my son under Nut's night sky, but," she titled her head toward Tep, who continued to wail, "we cannot be seen as vulnerable. Not now. Tend to your daughter."

"Tend?" Ahhotep's gaze was upon her son. Seeing Tao's mangled corpse sent her heart to her stomach, but upon seeing her son's body, her heartbeat ceased. Words were only words in the moment. Ahhotep stooped and reached out a hand to caress his flaccid cheek, ignoring his sunken eyes and the cleaned and dressed spear wound to his chest. His cool skin became nothing. The sharp cedar scent in the air faded to nothing. Her once racing mind thought nothing. The remnants of the bittersweet karkade tea on her tongue dulled to nothing. Her mother's words dwindled to nothing. Her vision blurred to nothing.

Time again stopped as she stared at the discolored body before her. The dark splotches in his dry, sun-parched skin took her back to Tao. This body was her son's, but it bore no resemblance to the man who had greeted her at the port two years earlier. That would be the vision she kept of him: his dazzling smile upon seeing her and his immediate embrace.

That is my son.

Tep's wail broke her from her haze, causing Ahhotep to cry out, "Silence."

The break in her voice caused those in attendance in the throne room to avert their eyes and bow their heads even more so that their chins rested on their chests.

She closed her eyes and calmed the burn in her

throat. "Silence," she said again. Her daughter's cries became whimpers.

Ahhotep lifted her head, stood up, and raised her gaze toward those in the throne room. The last time a body had been brought before her, she had nearly collapsed upon the floor. The gruesome sight of her brother-husband flashed in her memory as she thought.

My husband and my son are now both killed in this goal. But each was committed to better this land, our land of Kemet. To take back what is rightfully ours. She closed her eyes as a new breath surged through her nostrils.

"Prepare the King's body; he shall join his father in becoming one with Re." Her words were bold; her face, fearless, yet the trails of tears smudged kohl in lines down her face.

The priests of Anubis gathered up Kamose in the litter while chanting the rites. They carried him out to a room in the palace where they would begin the body's preparations for the afterlife.

Ahhotep glanced at her second eldest son, who sat beside her. His ten-year-old frame of a boy looked back at her with horror in his eyes. She placed a hand over his to soothe him, but all it prompted was a quiver in his lip. The warmth in his touch soothed the chill from touching Kamose's cheek.

"The Coregent is now the sole King."

Ahmose held his gaze with his mother; fear wrapped around his irises, bleeding the light from his eyes.

I know, my son. I know this pain, she thought.

The crown loosely fit upon his boy-sized head, and her mind flashed to her two younger sons, Sapair and Binpu. Must she lose them all to retake Kemet? she asked Amun in silence.

"No," she whispered. "I shall not lose them all."

Ahmose's short, skinny figure was still far from manhood. How would Ahmose command? He was but a boy, and Sapair and Binpu were even younger. Kush was at their door to the south, and the Hekka Khasut still hid in Hut-Waret like the cowards they were. Would they lose all that they had gained with her husband and son? Would their slayings be in vain? Would they be overrun and wiped out? Shall the great Kemet end with Ahmose?

Her shoulders pulled back, and she swallowed her sorrow to the pits of her *ka*.

No.

Her eyes lifted to the grand double doors of the throne room at Sedjefatawy.

No, it would not end; Kemet would begin again with Ahmose.

Heat surged in her cheeks at the injustice shown to the crown. *We will not be weak. We will persist. Their slayings will not be in vain!*

At the thought, she took her stand. "Royal Scribe. Send this decree to the princes." Her voice carried across the mud brick floor and reverberated through the pillared hall.

"King Kamose gave his life to gain victory in Buhen while they sat fat in their nomes with plenty to eat and drink and with men and resources to spare. Will they choose to let the nome of Waset take this burden alone? Will they let the nome of Waset, the royal family to whom they have pledged loyalty, suffer alone?"

Her voice grew with vigor.

"I say it is not so, for if it is, their oaths be lies, and their hearts will weigh heavy on the scales of Ma'at and be devoured by Ammit when their journey west begins."

She stood straight and focused on the doors through

which her husband and son had both been carried. Her chin lifted. Fear no longer held her tongue.

"I now call their oaths to be satisfied—there shall no longer be the request of men and resource, but a divine command from God's Mother. Amun will be our patron god for the Lower as we retake the Upper with his chosen one, Ahmose, Given Life, The Lord of Strength is Re, Living Horus. The nomes will send tribute to Amun's temple and their King, and Amun will lead us to victory!"

14

A TIME FOR MEMORY | AHHOTEP

SEDJEFATAWY, 1570 BC

Ahhotep slipped along the corridor to the palace temple, past the apartments of the sleeping princes, until she came to the doorway, which danced with shadows from the inner torchlight. Kohl lined her cheeks as she peered around the doorpost.

The priests of Anubis wore the jackal heads, the snout long over their eyes, as they prepared Kamose's body for the afterlife. The canopic jars had already been sealed. The former king's dark skin peeked out from underneath the remaining white natron spread over his body. The priests slowly and carefully brushed the last of natron off Kamose's cheeks. It would be the last time she saw his face, but she turned away when the natron was removed. His face was dry, sunken, and false eyes were put in place. The sharp cedar oil filled the room as they rubbed it into his skin. She turned back when the haunting sound of a rip of linen pierced the morning silence. They intricately wrapped Kamose's face, laying diagonal strips of cloth with tender care.

Ahhotep took a deep breath and continued past, unable to see her son in such a condition. The sun tipped over the eastern horizon as she made her way to The Rising. Her sister-wives, Inhapi and Sitdjehuti, were waiting for her to go to the temple of Isis.

They boarded with their servants in silence and let the fleetsmen take them to the temple in Waset. They could not approach the goddess unclean. Her freshly bathed skin radiating with kyphi perfume rivaled that of her sisters. Its sweet and spicy aroma repelled the stifling Nile water's scent.

Even though her mind should have been on the prayers she was to speak, her mind drifted to Kamose. She had scraped together what she could to provide her son with a burial. He had only five years on the throne, most of it spent at war, with nothing to build a pyramid or supply any tomb meant for a king.

Such injustice for him, she thought.

The Rising pulled into port at Waset, and the three royal women departed the boat and walked into the temple of Isis, leaving their servants and fleetsman guards behind, for only priests and royalty could approach the divine. They laid an offering of grain before the goddess' image and awakened Isis' spirit with the incense of myrrh. The three royal women, trained as priestesses of Isis, kneeled before the goddess and gave time for her to partake of the grain after she awoke.

Ahhotep pressed her hand against the amulets of Isis, Hathor, and Bastet, swinging from her neck to still them and rub them between her fingers to evoke the divine.

"Mourn with me, my sisters," Ahhotep whispered to Inhapi and Sitdjehuti. "Plead with me, my sisters."

The three women raised their hands with bowed heads. Ahhotep was the first to speak: "Mother of the Gods, Isis, Mistress of Magic—inspire comfort within my heart and chase the fears from my mind. Give a plea to your sister Nephthys that she may rebirth the heart of my son and allow him to live again. In your light and her darkness, may the son of Seqenenre Tao, the King of Kemet, the divinely appointed of Amun and Re, live forever. Bastet and Hathor," she said with a hitch in her voice as she began her prayer to the two goddesses. She clutched the amulets tighter in her raised hand, "Lady of the Home, Children, and Women's Secrets—Protector of Women—comfort my heart, keep my secrets, defend against the evil that threatens my children . . ."

A tear choked out her words, and Inhapi continued for her. "Give us strength that we may endure. Be with our sister's son Ahmose as he becomes the sole regent. Be with our sister's son Kamose as he becomes one with Re."

Sitdjehuti finished the prayer: "Gentle Hathor, transform yet again to Sekhmet—grant our sister the vision to see what needs to be done to unite our land and expel the Hekka Khasut and reclaim that which was taken from your brothers and sisters."

Ahhotep drew in the sweet, smoky myrrh with a deep breath through her nostrils. Its spice burned the back of her throat, but she resisted expelling it. Instead, she thanked the goddess for hearing her and rose along with her sisters.

The morning sun attacked her eyes when they stepped from the temple.

Ahhotep stared at the Aten, full-face. "Today, we will travel to the West of Waset and entomb King Kamose, but after this day, I will lose no more sons," she vowed.

15

A TIME OF FAREWELL |
AHMOSE

WEST OF WASET, 1570 BC

Ahmose stood with thick kohl around his eyes and the tall Hedjet crown on his head. The sun poured over him, warming the chill underneath his skin. It had been seventy days since his brother's body had lain at his feet. The dark hole in the ground was like a giant mouth waiting to swallow him.

Donning the panther skin cloak of the Sem-Priest over his shoulder, Ahmose, as the King, the High Priest, performed the Opening of the Mouth and Eyes ceremony. It was the first time the Sem-Priest had not conducted such a ceremony, and all eyes were upon him, the ten-year-old boy king, as he descended the stone-hewn steps to the burial chamber.

Once there, his voice shook as he repeated the rites in the torchlight: "Pure, pure, pure. You are as pure as Horus, and Horus is as pure as you." He touched the stone on each of Kamose's hands and then his heart and nose to awaken the spirit within the preserved body.

"Pure, pure, pure. You are as pure as Osiris, and Osiris is as pure as you," Ahmose said and repeated with each divine name.

He waved the fish-tail-shaped stone over Kamose's mouth and touched the linen-wrapped lips to open them. "I have opened your mouth with the Meskha of Anubis." The First Prophet and Sem-Priest wiped the former King's eyes with kohl to open them, and Ahmose touched them with the stone. "I have opened your eyes."

The priests placed Kamose in the wooden coffin. Ahmose reached out and touched the smooth edge before the top was laid. Because Kamose had not had enough time to build a proper burial place like their father, the tomb had hurriedly been hewn to completion. The inscriptions for the afterlife had been painted with haste with smeared lines, and the thick edges of the paint, still wet, glistened in the torchlight. Servants and stewards surrounded the coffin with food, drink, and what little riches his mother had been able to secure for him. Only a few pieces of gold and silver. Ahmose's shoulders drooped as he stared at the painted face atop the ungilded coffin.

Nothing spectacular. Nothing meant for a king. Ahmose rested his hand over the coffin any man could have been laid to rest in. The royal uraeus to adorn the coffin's head was not even finished in time for his brother's burial.

The coffin was placed in the stuccoed sarcophagus along with a few of Kamose's prized items: a bronze mirror, a dagger, a pectoral, amulets, a scarab . . . and then the funeral party began to leave out of the narrow passageway of the chamber. The servants who held the torchlight ascended with the rest, but Ahmose remained in the dimming light and whispered to Kamose:

"My brother, I did not know you well once you left for war. But I knew you were a great king, and you will find your way to Re. You will ensure the sun rises in the morning. I seek only to . . ." His voice trailed off, and his eyes ran over the burial chamber's walls.

Will this be me? Ahmose shook his head. *Will I be sent to the afterlife like this? Will Sapair open my eyes and mouth for the afterlife?* He stared at the painted stucco face of his brother etched into the sarcophagus until a light touch fell upon his shoulder.

"My son, we must ascend and leave Kamose to his journey," Ahhotep whispered and pulled him along. His fingers grazed the top of the stucco until distance separated them from the smooth surface. He peered over his shoulder one last time and passed the tomb servants who began to wall up the chamber once they walked past.

They emerged in the sunlight, and the mourners and dancers stopped their wailing. The priestesses representing Isis and Nephthys stilled. Ahmose stood at the tomb's entrance with the monotonous drumming of rocks and stones echoed from the chamber behind him. In the moment, he forgot what to say. The eyes of the priests, the nobles, the princes of the nomes, his mother, his new wives, his sisters, and Sapair's were all upon him.

He lifted his hands in the air. What had the Sem-Priest done for his father? He had been there, but what had he said? *Why can't I remember?* Ahmose's cheeks grew red, and he knew they all thought him a fool.

He cleared his throat as the stacking of rock behind him drummed more potent in his ears. "King Kamose." He shouted over the noise, yet his voice shook.

My brother is no longer in this life, he thought, and the crown's weight impressed his head. *But I cannot be King; I don't want to be King, yet, I am.*

His arms still outstretched, he repeated, "King

Kamose." The tips of his fingers tingled and numbed. *My brother is gone.* His eyes darted between the glares and glances and averted gazes setting upon the hard stare of Tetian.

Say what you are supposed to remember, he chided himself, but the prince's dark eyes seemed to see straight through his facade, take hold of his fear, and choke the words from escaping his lips. All he could remember was Tetian's words at the port: *You cannot even protect your mother; how do you expect to fight in war?* A lump grew thick in his throat. And here he was, taking his brother's place. He would have to go to war. He took a shallow breath as his mother approached in his silence.

No, no, Mother. I can do this. I have to do this. I am King, he pleaded with his eyes. He shook his head at her, but she came still. So he blurted out under Tetian's stare, "The King's eyes and mouth are opened." She stopped, and he settled his pumping chest at the apparent accuracy of his statement. "King Kamose will journey well to Re." He gulped.

Seventy days I had to prepare, he thought, *and I still cannot believe he is no longer in the land of the living.*

He dropped his hands to his sides. His shoulders rose with a deep breath. "Let us return to the palace and feast before his image so King Kamose may return to it as a vessel."

He ripped his gaze locked with Tetian and looked upon his mother. Ahhotep pressed her lips into a thin smile, seemingly satisfied at his first decree as the new king. However, no pride-filled beam took her face; there was only a countenance of sadness and fear for the future.

She quickly turned away to face the people who had

gathered. "Come, let us feast and celebrate King Kamose's journey to the afterlife."

God's Mouth walked in front of Ahmose; his mother and his wives walked behind him as they led the company back to Sedjefatawy.

Ahmose sat in his brother's place in the palace courtyard before the statues of Kamose and their father, Seqenenre Tao. He forced himself to eat, not because his belly urged him to, but because it kept his mind from wandering too much. He chewed the mutton and stared at Kamose's stone visage, wondering if he would see battle at ten years of age. What would the men do without their King, Living Horus, with them on the battlefield? He held up his small hand. Yet he could not even grip a khopesh. How would he inspire the men to victory?

Sitkamose's gentle hand covered his and brought it back to the table. He feared a chiding from his new Chief Wife, but there was only silence. When courage welled within him, he peered at her.

Would he be slain in battle? Would he never see manhood? Would he be as Kamose?

The courtyard seemed to shrink, and he was unaware of his arms shaking until Sitkamose laid her other hand on him.

"*Shhhh,*" she hushed. Concern lived in her bloodshot eyes. Sunken cheeks and dark under-eye circles replaced her usual plump face. She had her father's strong jaw and manly shoulders, but she was imbued with frailty.

Ahhotep shot them a stare with a silent command to stop and eat. Sitkamose removed her hand, and Ahmose scanned the feast.

Tetian was speaking to some other princes, Baufre? And Metjen? Setka maybe? Perhaps Nakht.

Ahmose winced, not able to recall all the princes' names. Admiral Baba stood with General Pennekhbet. He glanced at the general's daughter, Kasmut, who had been studying him, and she quickly averted her gaze. The Admiral's daughter, Senseneb, sat next to Sapair and his other sisters. But Sapair ate while gaping at Ahmose with eyes full of fear. Ahmose scowled and snorted at his brother.

Are you afraid I will leave too? Then you will be King? He sent his thoughts with a harsh glare. *Well, I have this burden now. I cannot carry your fears too.*

He broke that connection and continued to scan the unusually quiet feast. His other wife and half-sister, Henuttamehu, sat beside him, having not noticed the brothers' exchange.

Tep ate nothing but stared off aimlessly, lost in her mind. Ahmose-Nefertari picked at her food; her brow furrowed in intense focus on something important to her.

His mother and grandmother ate as if nothing fazed them, smiling and receiving the praises for Kamose with grace.

I am glad they do this in my place, and I do not have to pretend to be happy my brother is gone. I wish him well in the afterlife, but I also want him here, just like Father.

After the feast, he began toward the Kap, but his mother blocked his path. "You are the King now, Son," she said softly. "You sleep in the King's apartment."

He glanced up at her. "But I am still a child."

Her back straightened, her arms tightened, and her chin lifted. "You are King," she said after a pause and pointed toward the King's apartment. "You sleep in the King's apartment." She nodded to the guards in an unspoken arrangement. "Sleep well, may Bes—Master of Secrets, God of Dreams—be kind to you this night."

She spun around and left to the harem with her maidservants. The sun had set, and torchlight lit the corridor. A slight chilly breeze blew past him, and it wrapped around his legs. The sudden, short-lived shudder made him wonder why his mother was acting distant. "Is it because you think I will be slain too?" he whispered.

The guard cleared his throat. "Lord of the Two Lands, shall you retire to the King's apartment?"

He nodded and walked to the room on the opposite side of the Kap. In the nights prior, he would always fall asleep next to his brother and sisters. Now, he would sleep alone.

He pushed the door to his room open and saw Sitkamose sitting in a chair waiting for him. Her new woman's wig was neatly arranged on the room's grand chest, and her thinning hair fell past her cheeks in tight coils.

A thin smile crept over his lips. *I will not have to sleep alone.* He ran to her, but she did not stand as he approached. The door's creak behind him slowed him to stop and look back. Closed.

No body servants, no guards? He swung his head to peer at Sitkamose. Would she comfort him or tell him to be a King?

The shadows from the candlelight enhanced the dark circles under her eyes. Her hands were folded in her lap with an elegance fit for the daughter and wife of the king.

"At the feast, you were shaking," she crooned. Her lips barely moved as if it took too much of her energy to move them.

"Yes," he said, stricken with a sudden barrage of thoughts and images of his father and brother. The thought he might be brought home carried by priests of Anubis paralyzed him. *What will end life for me? A sling's bronze stone? An arrow? A mace? An ax? A swift cut of a dagger from navel to the throat? Burning?* The thoughts choked him.

The afterlife was a grand vision, but this life, he knew. This life, he wanted. He did not want to end up like his brother and father. No, he wanted them there with him. But they had been brutally taken from this life. *Yet, Mother smiled? Yet, they feasted in celebration? Kamose did not even have a gilded coffin! Yet, they were to be happy?!* He shoved his forearm across his leaking nose.

"Ahmose?" Sitkamose mouthed, too tired to speak in full timbre.

"I...I..." He blubbered his words, sucking back unshed tears that threatened to fall.

It was her father who was slain, yet Sitkamose opened her thinned arms toward him, her uncle, and her husband. He took the invitation and rushed forth into her gentle embrace.

Seventy days had passed since he had seen Kamose with a spear wound to his chest. Five years had passed since he had seen his father with an ax wound to his head. But tears ran fast down his cheeks, and an unrecognizable moan escaped his lips. "My brother," he cried. "My father," he whimpered. The need to unite their land seemed trivial. He would rather have his kin beside him, with him, not in the next life without him.

"*Shhhhh,*" Sitkamose hushed with swollen eyes. Her limp hands ran up and down his back like his nurse's hands when he was a naked child. "Be glad for them,

Ahmose," she said in a weak whisper. "Be glad for their journey to Re."

But despite her words, her tears wet his shoulder, and he cried more. He pulled away and looked her in the face. "Don't leave me, Sitkamose. I love you so."

She forced a comforting beam underneath weary eyes. "I will never leave you, my little Ahmose." She touched her forehead to his and pressed a fingertip to his chest. "As I love you too."

His lips bounced between a frown and a smile until he rested his head on her bosom. "What will happen now?"

Rather than answering, she hummed a sweet song until he fell asleep, as she had done every night he had needed her comfort.

16

A TIME TO HOPE | AHHOTEP

SEDJEFATAWY, 1570 BC

Ahhotep stood next to the throne that once held precious gems and a soft inlay of gold. Her ten-year-old son sat upon it, yet she was the words for his mouth and the whisperer for his ear. Her hand rested on his shoulder and gave him a squeeze of reassurance as the sound of stone masons' work sounded outside Sedjefatawy. His gaze came to her, and she smiled at him, taking in his big, round eyes. Visions of Kamose as a child filled her memory.

Vizier Tetinefer bowed before the royal duo. "Ahmose, Living Horus, and God's Mother, the council awaits your presence."

Ahhotep said, "I shall join them in a moment, Vizier." She peered down at Ahmose. She would not lose him too. She would go in his place. Command the men from Sedjefatawy and Per-djed-ken. He would never see war. He would wear the crown, but he would never pass on the crown in his youth. He would begin the journey west as an old man, having lived a long and bountiful life. He would have many sons and ensure the crown stayed where it belonged: with their family.

Given the day had been slow, she lied to her son. "King Ahmose, you are needed here on the throne. I will go alone to the council."

Ahmose tensed. "What do I do if—"

"Your grandmother shall be here," Ahhotep said and gestured to Tetisheri, who sat in the back in her usual chair, the arm worn from resting her tea-drinking forearm upon it.

Tetisheri shook her head. "I already told you I will not—"

"His chief wife is not here, as was your condition," Ahhotep snapped at her aggravating mother. "Unless you would like me to order Chief Wife Sitkamose to be pulled from her bed to stand in frailty and illness beside her husband?"

Tetisheri leaned back in her chair, sipped her tea, and squeezed out a grin. "Good," she whispered and sat her teacup on its saucer. She lifted a hand to Ahhotep and flicked her fingers at her: "Go, and I will remain with King Ahmose."

Ahhotep opened her mouth to rebuke her mother, but she refrained after her mother's words were repeated in her head. All that time, all she had to do was be firm with her mother to get her to do what she wanted? Her mouth clamped shut. Why would her mother grin like that? Did her mother think she had done a good job? Why did she say "good?"

She cleared her throat and shifted on her feet as she stared at Tetisheri. Was she becoming what her mother wanted her to be? Demanding respect and putting her mother in her place? But was she not reprimanded for that when they discussed the second campaign to retake Buhen? Why "good" now?

Her eyebrow lifted. It did not matter. Her mother's opinions of her did not matter, so she told herself.

"Good," Ahhotep repeated with strong shoulders pulled back in a confident posture. She smiled at Ahmose in reassurance and left to the council room.

She entered the room full of men, and all stood. She sat next to the King's chair, and they all sat. *Demand respect* . . . like her mother did. The mantra repeated in her mind. She placed her hands on the table like a sphinx.

"I have called this meeting of council to discuss the horses."

Tetinefer and Thuty glanced to each other and then to Baba and Pennekhbet, who had done the same. Thuty lifted a finger and opened his mouth to speak.

But Ahhotep was quick. "First Prophet, I know the assumption behind this meeting was to discuss King Ahmose and his plans to further what his brother and forefathers began."

Thuty lowered his finger and gave a slight nod of his head.

"King Ahmose will not be joining this day as he has other important matters to attend to. He has granted me full power as Royal Commander to act on his behalf. So, to continue the plight of our past Kings, we need horse trainers." She turned her attention to her son's vizier. "Tetinefer—have we enough gold to barter with the Bedu peoples?"

Tetinefer folded his hands and paused before responding. His glance at the King's empty chair meant he did not wholly believe her lie, but he spoke anyway. "Yes, God's Mother—"

"Royal Commander," Ahhotep corrected. She had to ensure—no, demand— respect, just like her mother.

Tetinefer pressed a polite smile and nodded. "My mistake, Royal Commander. After your decree was sent, fifteen of the twenty-one nomes sent more resources than they ever had before. I might add, Prince Tetian of Ta-Seti sent the same: his usual hekat of grain, an amphora of wine, and a few deben gold."

Ahhotep looked up to the wall vent allowing fresh air in and the stale inner air out. "While he sits on a mountain of riches," she muttered. "Why does he do this? Does he wish us to fail in Re's divine will to unite our land?"

Tetinefer leaned forward to answer her. "His family has never believed the crown belonged in Waset. They gave an oath and agreed when your grandfather spoke of unification, but they believed Khnum of Ta-Seti would bring victory as the Creator of Life rather than Amun of Waset, the Hidden One. Your father chose your mother as his wife to appease the Ta-Seti family's constant complaints and gossip."

Ahhotep's gaze fell to the vizier, as did the general's and the admiral's. Their jaws hung ajar, and their eyes narrowed in confusion.

"What?" she whispered under her breath. Why had her mother never told her this history, her Ta-Seti roots? Surely, she should have made sure her daughter knew of it. A man who did believe the divine ruler was divine was named among their allies. A man who had shown little respect for the throne with no consequence due to his resource-rich nome was not willfully fulfilling his family's oath. Had it been that he only tolerated her family due to Tetisheri's origins in Ta-Seti? That he only respected Tetisheri because she was from Ta-Seti? Would she never gain his respect or loyalty due to her Waset roots? What would happen when her mother went to the

Field of Reeds? The richest nome with trade ties to the Kushites and all the neighboring tribes could rise against Waset and easily take it, especially in their state. Fighting a war to the north and the south as well as a war within? The future turned dim. How would they survive?

Tetinefer shifted under the dazed stare of everyone in the room. "I apologize. I was under the assumption everyone here knew about the Great Wife of King Seqenenre Tao."

Ahhotep swallowed the lump in her throat and spoke slowly with clear words: "Will Prince Tetian be a threat to us once my mother journeys west?"

Pennekhbet glanced around the room as Baba nodded beside him. "He very well could be," he said at last. "But other than handing him the crown and dishonoring Amun, I have no suggestions for how to deal with this threat. As long as Great Wife Tetisheri lives, he will be no threat to us," he said, confirming her thoughts.

"She is aged already," Ahhotep said. "What then when her life becomes the next?"

Baba cleared his throat. "We will fight back when that time comes should he commit treason and rise against the crown. I doubt he would risk such an act against the divine order or the human order for that matter. But now, we must focus on defeating the Hekka Khasut and keeping Buhen from being retaken. We can give offerings and supplication to Heh for the Great Wife's long life and hope he grants our plea."

She did not like that answer, but they did not have the men to march into one of their nomes, nor would they have the support of the loyal princes in commanding such an action. Attacking a prince simply because he disagreed and had shown no other outward form of hostility would not bode well.

"Then we need to act now," Ahhotep said. "Prepare a shipping crew, prepare the royal caravan, and take a troop of soldiers to protect them at all costs. Gather the nome's resources, supply our soldiers and the Medjay their overdue rations first."

She snapped at Mitry, the royal scribe. "Write this letter to the King Hazael of the Bedu peoples: King Ahmose of Kemet is brother to King Hazael of Bedu. We fight a war to retake our lands stolen from the Aamu and are in need of horse trainers. Send two horse trainers, and in return, we have Kushite gold, and when we take back our kingdom from the Hekka Khasut, we will not pursue them into your realm, and you may do as you wish to them."

Mitry's chiseling ended, and he bowed, signaling he was finished.

Ahhotep pointed to Baba and Pennekhbet. "Each of you, prepare a Captain to protect this effort, and Vizier," she turned her attention to Tetinefer, "assign an official to oversee it."

Each man nodded before Tetinefer spoke up: "With this new trade route through the Dashret, we could also import tin again for more bronze."

Ahhotep smiled and nodded. Why had she not thought of that? They had been starved with no trade coming upstream from the delta, Ta-Seti holding the trade at the border, and the nomadic Kushites attacked the usual trade routes in the Dashret. "Yes, Vizier, where there is no path, we will forge one."

She stood up with fingertips placed on the table. Her thin linen dress draped over her shoulders beneath her collar in a regal posture.

"We will live out the will of Re." She eyed every man in the room, her gaze lingering on Baba. She traced his tightly defined jaw and strong nose and brow. Why had he not saved Kamose? He said he would bring him home to Waset alive. She had not spoken to him since he brought his praises and offerings to her son's statue after Kamose was entombed.

"Agreed, Royal Commander," the First Prophet Thuty said, drawing her attention to the man who had said nothing since she entered the council room.

"And First Prophet, we will need Amun to be well fed and well taken care of in the years to come, even more so than we have been," she said.

Thuty nodded. "We will need to add to our number."

"Make it so," she said. "The vizier should help you gain support from the other nomes. Perhaps giving the princes' qualified men and women opportunities at the temple of Amun will strengthen their loyalty to the crown."

"Very wise, Royal Commander," Pennekhbet said.

Ahhotep raised her hands. "Dismissed." She watched Baba wait to stand while the others hurriedly left. Perhaps, too quickly. Had her lie been too obvious? There had not been a boy king in any annals she had ever known. What else was she supposed to do? The men filed out, but Baba was last to leave with heavy feet.

"Admiral," she called boldly, and he remained. "Come here."

He did as he was told. She peered over his shoulder to ensure they were indeed alone. Nena and Meret stood just outside the door. She studied his countenance: furrowed brow, dark eyes, strong cut jaw, thick lips.

"There seemed to be hesitation with my appointment as Royal Commander?" She lifted her eyes to his. Baba would not lie to her, or so she hoped. She had called him a friend to her, but she had not exchanged many warm glances with him since he came back from Buhen.

He shifted his weight, and his words escaped slowly, "King Ahmose is . . ."

"A boy," Ahhotep finished his sentence with finality.

"Yes," he said with an unsure nod as she crossed her arms. "But he will be a man. A man amid war." He spoke with gentleness, his deep voice dripping with empathy.

She knew Ahmose would grow to be a man soon, but she ignored Baba.

"I. Will. Not. Lose. Another." The hate-filled words spat from her mouth like a cobra's venom. Her eyes pierced him. In her right mind, she knew Baba did the best he could to save Kamose. It was war, after all, and spears were projectiles. But in her grief, Baba was responsible.

He sucked in a bated breath. "If I may be so bold as to ask a question."

She nodded, fearful her voice would break.

"Does the Royal Commander blame me for King Kamose in Buhen?" he asked. His shoulders rolled forward, and his head dipped.

Yes, no, she debated in her mind. "Of course I do," she said through clenched teeth. "You promised me."

Baba closed his eyes. "I promised God's Mother I would do everything possible to bring her son home alive. It was night; we were attacking in stealth. We made it to the other side of the fortress—"

"Do you think I want to hear this?" she yelled and pushed him away from her.

He shuffled back and remained at the new distance.

"I only want you to know if I could have come home in King Kamose's place, I would have."

Tears glistened in his eyes as she caught hold of his gaze.

"Then why didn't you?" she asked, squeezing her arms around her belly.

"He was by my side—his body servants in front. The Medjay were all around us. We had already won the fortress and were retreating behind the walls. A spear came out of the pre-dawn sky. I tried to push the King out of the way, but it was too late."

Ahhotep turned her face away—afraid her tears would fall. They had already soured her tongue. "Did he breathe his last in peace?"

Baba nodded. "In my arms. He was as a son to me, if I may say so. I had fought by his side for five years. He was a good king, a good man. You should be proud of his legacy—"

"I am proud of his legacy," she cut back, her voice growing to a growl. "And I will be proud of King Ahmose's as well, but his legacy will be long, and he will go to Re as an old man."

Baba stepped forward. "May I speak freely, Royal Commander?"

She scoffed at what she perceived to be a ridiculous question. "We are alone, are we not?"

But Meret's shuffling outside signaled they were not truly alone. Hidden from sight, perhaps. Ahhotep's voice had risen too much and caused a stir between Meret and Nena.

Baba took a tentative step toward her. "Yes, but you are still the Great Wife, and I, the Admiral." Another step.

The warmth from his body radiated to where it touched her nose and cheeks. She wanted to hate him but also wanted to cry in his arms. Kamose was gone because he had not acted in time.

"I do not wish to bring you pain," he whispered.

She bit her tongue. She could say nothing. Her unshed tears ran down the back of her throat. No, Kamose was gone because a Kushite had thrown a spear.

"You once called me a friend to God's Mother," he said. "I cannot remove the burden you bear, but I will help you carry it until my last breath in this life."

A rogue tear ran down her cheek, and then another. "He was my son, Baba." His name slipped from her lips without his title, but she did not care. Her knees grew weak, and she steadied herself with a hand on the table.

Baba opened his mouth to speak, but Ahhotep cut him off. "Ahmose will not end like his brother and father. I will do anything to ensure it, and if this council full of men cannot stand behind me, then I shall find a new council for my son."

Baba relaxed his shoulders. "Great Wife, we will all stand with you. I believe there was only some hesitation because never has a queen been named Royal Commander when a king sits on the thr—?"

"What shall I do then, Baba?" she interjected. "Pluck him from the harem where he plays with his sisters? Or from the Kap, where he learns to hold a stick and shoot arrows at targets made of reed?"

Baba held his tongue, clearly debating whether or not to speak freely again. The slight grimace on his lips made her search his eyes. He disagreed with her.

She had to make him see. "King Ahmose is young and not capable. He is but a boy, Baba!" She had done it again, three times now. "Admiral," she forced out, but it was too late.

He saw her weakness and took one last step forward

into her space. The sweet susinum's cinnamon and myrrh notes filled her senses. It was a commoner's perfume, but on him, it made her mouth water. He stood a head above her, looking down into her full face, and whispered, "But he is our King."

"He is my son," she said. Her voice broke. She envisioned him brought before her, carried between Anubis priests.

His small grimace turned full bloom. He reached out to graze the sides of her arms but dared not touch her skin.

Yet she longed for his embrace. Someone to touch her, hold her, feel her heartache, and soothe the stings to her soul. In his eyes, she found the understanding that she did not want to lose another son. What she endured was hard enough, yet she had endured it alone thus far. Though, she hoped and envisioned Baba would hold her in that moment and help her in the hard decisions she would make with Ahmose on the throne.

But his fingers curled into his fists as if he resisted his desire to touch her. The corners of her mouth fell more than they had before.

He whispered, "Though he is your son, King Ahmose wears the shendyt of a man and the crown of divine royalty. He should—"

"As did Kamose," she said with a quivering lip. "My son."

A darkness passed over his eyes, and he lowered his forehead so it almost touched hers. "Blame me, God's Mother. Though it tortures me, I will endure your hate for not saving your firstborn son in time. I will never forgive myself for not being in his place. But please, hear me. Ahmose is King now. He must be seen as King. What will happen in ten years when he leads an army, and the army does not know who he is because all they know is your name?"

"I know he must be seen as King, for he is the King," she said as coming cries shattered her voice. Baba's eyes brimmed with tears, encompassing her agony as his. She covered her nose and mouth to choke back the would-be wails as she imagined the worst: son after son laid at her feet—all of them, each killed in some gruesome method of war. Each boy's face sunken and hollow like Kamose's. How? How was she to live while they perished? She ripped her hand from her mouth to her side, determined to regain her dignity in front of the Admiral.

"I will unify these lands, and I will not lose Ahmose. For then, who shall I lose next? Sapair? Then Binpu, who is not going to survive the season?" Another rogue tear escaped down her cheek at the thought of entombing her youngest son alongside her eldest son. "After I lose all my sons, who will succeed them? Tetian from Ta-Seti? He will force my daughters into marriage—"

The scorching tears choked her to silence. She imagined a crippled Kemet—one that would never see unification under Tetian. He was too greedy to spend any of his riches on a land that did not want to be unified. He would never love or treat her daughters with respect. He would mock her sons in their sacrifice, and the anger from such a thought burned her cheeks.

The sun glinted from the gold vulture crown and was lost in the kohl around her harrowing eyes. She did not want to hear what Baba said but knew he was right, even though dread filled her.

Baba's hand hovered up her arm, over her shoulder, and under her chin. "God's Mother," he whispered, and after a pause, he crooned her name. "Ahhotep."

She grew weak at the knees at his tenderness. "Do

not let them take any more of my sons, Baba," she moaned in hushed tones.

He shuffled closer, so close that their bodies would meet if she rocked on her toes. Both of his hands cradled the air around her face—the heat emanating from them almost made her believe he had touched royal flesh as he spoke.

"King Ahmose will one day lead his army in battle. He should understand why and how." Baba's eyes glistened from tears. "Be his mouth, but let him have his ears. Bring him to the council and let him understand why his brother and father were slain."

The battered bodies of Tao and Kamose flashed in memory one after the other as if the past moments were stitched together one at a time by a hasty seamstress. She swallowed the lump in her throat.

Baba was so close to her as she searched his eyes for something he could not give her. She wanted him to shield her from what was to come, but he could not do such a thing, just as she could not shield Ahmose from his destiny as King.

She pushed away her love for her son and did what was best for Kemet. "They will know the name King Ahmose," she finally said, straining to speak in a royal tone. "I will bring him where he should be to prepare him to lead his army when he is of age."

When the words were said, her ka hollowed. Was she sacrificing her sons to this endeavor like the heathens in Canaan who gave up their children to their god Molech? The heathens burned their children alive in Molech's bronze belly; was she not allowing the Hekka Khasut an opportunity to burn Ahmose as well? She had accused the nomes' princes of sitting fat in wealth while Kamose was slain at Buhen, yet she sat in Sedjefatawy behind fortress walls while sending her sons to war. But what was done could not be undone; she had sealed their path five years ago when she ordered the Aamu messengers slain.

"You are making the right decision." Baba's velvet voice entered the silence between them.

She closed her eyes and lowered her head at his reassurance. The side of her forehead touched his lips when she lowered. Her body tensed at the accidental brush. No man's lips had touched her since Tao was last home.

But she didn't pull away. Baba, though, froze—his hands still in the air around her face.

She half-smiled at his nervousness and let her body relax. "Then it is decided," she spoke with a wavering voice as she kept her brow to his lips. "I will lead in King Ahmose's stead as Royal Commander. I shall be his mouth, but he shall have ears in the council."

Baba turned into her a little more, the anxious rigidity melting fast.

Ahhotep knew every word she spoke sealed Ahmose's fate, and she hated herself for it. "We will consolidate the Upper while he is young. Rebuild wealth with our new trade route through the Dashret. Keep the Kermans well-fed and loyal. Reinstate our authority in the border cities of Kush and the Hekka Khasut. And then"—a tear plopped onto her gold-beaded collar—"we will see if Prince Sapair takes his place as King in his youth."

"King Ahmose could have a son first," Baba bargained, speaking against her flesh. His hands slid to the back of her neck, seemingly no longer strong enough to hold back his desire. "A son will ensure the lineage once the King goes to Re an old man, victorious in every quest."

Another tear ran down her cheek. She wished it would be as he said, but the gnawing fear of losing her son in battle sucked away those visions of victory.

"You comfort me with false hopes, Baba," she whispered back.

Baba pushed a thin braid of hair behind her ear, beneath her vulture headdress, and lifted her countenance to his. "Hope is always hope. It cannot be false."

It was a soothing sentiment. She could always hope, whether the desired outcome was likely or not. "You are wise, my friend," she said.

His lips rose in a timid beam before he lowered his forehead to hers. "You are courageous, my queen."

She closed her eyes, relishing his touch. Could she have another man? Her mother certainly had not. Her fingers slid up his defined belly, strewn with muscle. She was losing control again. Her mother would not approve of her being comforted by a man who was not her son, the King Seqenenre Tao, nor would she approve of her fallen tears in the company of a subordinate.

But with his breath on her lips, she did not care what her mother thought. She finally felt heard, seen, and loved. He caressed her cheek and shuffled closer, so their bellies touched through her sheer dress.

She parted her mouth to receive his kiss, but someone cleared their throat before their lips touched. Baba's hands dropped as a rock thrown in the Nile—his warmth instantly gone—and he stepped backward. "God's Moth —Royal Commander," he rushed. He bowed his head and turned around. Tetisheri stood in the doorway.

"Dismissed, Admiral," she hissed, standing as still as the statue of her son and grandson in the courtyard.

"Yes, Great Wife," he mumbled and slipped past her petite frame in the door.

Ahhotep's heart beat fast in her chest, and she forgot how to breathe. "Mother," she said in a facade of confidence. Her mother looked at her from head to toe.

She tossed a linen cloth toward her. It floated to the table before landing in a heap. "Wipe your eyes, you child. Have a bath too. That man's hands could have been anywhere and on any woman."

Ahhotep stared at the linen cloth only a few steps away on the table, bent and wrinkled. It mocked her pain in mimicry.

"I came to tell you, while you tarried with the Admiral, your son needs you. I tire and need to renew my energy," she said, holding back a yawn with a closed mouth.

Her mother's stare grew more intense as she expected a reply, but Ahhotep would not raise her eyes and focused intently on the linen cloth meant to demean her feelings about losing her husband and son and maybe finding love in a friend again. Her mother had experienced the same loss, yet she did not weep or fall into the arms of a man.

Tetisheri, as if reading Ahhotep's thoughts, glanced at Tao's image upon the council room walls. "Disappointing, Ahhotep," she mumbled. "So disappointing. You scorn your brother-husband in his own council room." She slipped away and down the corridor without another word.

Ahhotep stood alone in the empty room as a chill replaced the warmth Baba had been to her chest and face. At that moment, she realized she missed him.

Them. Baba and Tao. Tao would never hold her again, for he had become one with Re, and Baba would never hold her again, not after her mother dismissed him like a child. She closed her eyes, reliving Baba's hands on her neck and his lips pressed against her forehead. It would have to satisfy her desires. After a while, she took a few steps toward the cloth and picked it up, knowing Ahmose should not see her with kohl-streaked cheeks.

Baba walked into the room just as she was about to wipe her tears. He strode up to her while she stood in disbelief and gently plucked the cloth from her hand.

"You came back?" she asked in a stutter.

"How could I not . . . Ahhotep?" he whispered, almost inaudible. He dabbed her tears away to remove their faint kohl trail. She pressed her hands against his chest in a silent plea to continue what he was about to do before her mother interrupted. But he only pressed a thin smile and whispered in her ear, "We have peering eyes." He pushed a braided lock from her cheek before stepping back, allowing Ahhotep to see Nena peer into the room.

"Don't I always?" Her sadness lingered, but Baba only grinned.

"Not always," he whispered before asking, "May I escort you to the throne room, Royal Commander?"

Ahhotep softly chuckled to herself at his awkward grin and outstretched hand. "You may, Admiral," she responded, and he walked beside her, hand hovering over her lower back, making sure not to touch the royal woman.

17

A TIME TO GROW |
AHMOSE-NEFERTARI
SEDJEFATAWY, 1569 BC

Ahmose-Nefertari's arms grew stiff, holding the six-year-old girl in her arms. Tumerisy coughed with a pitiful effort as she had the entire night prior. Ahmose-Nefertari pressed her lips to her sister's warm forehead and rubbed her back. The nurse Rai popped a honey herb drop in Tumerisy's mouth.

"Roll it on your tongue, King's Daughter," Rai whispered and sat at Ahmose-Nefertari's feet. Rai's bountiful braids and smooth, darkened skin deceived her admirers' hopes for a young wife. But her smiling eyes gave her age away as she glanced up to Ahmose-Nefertari. The wrinkled creases would never be found on a girl. "I can look after your sister while you attend to your duties."

Ahmose-Nefertari looked to the open door of the Kap's nursery. She could be on the throne with Ahmose, but she was not his Chief Wife or even his wife. She thought her mother and grandmother were testing her the couple of times she had been invited to the throne room or to the council meetings. Dread in going made her feign illness a few times. Out there, the world was scary. Kemet was divided: some sacrificing for the great objective, some hoarding their riches for the eventual failure. How could one weak nation keep two warring neighbors at bay? She sighed at the dim future. It seemed so beyond hope and repair. How would victory come to them? How *could* victory come to them? Trade was pitiful, choked from the north and the south. As evidence, the alabaster torch on the wall remained unlit during the day casting a gloomy dimness in the inner room. The wealth from the new trade routes across the Dashret was stashed and stored as war reserves or used to maintain what Kamose had gained.

Her gaze drifted to the half-sleeping Tumerisy in her arms. Tumerisy buried her head in her chest, rolling the honey herb drop in her mouth. Her breath was thick with cinnamon and mint when she coughed. Ahmose-Nefertari lowered her head and kissed Tumerisy's cheek before pulling her closer.

But here, in the Kap's nursery, she was needed. She made a difference in her siblings' lives. She glanced at the empty cot where Binpu once laid.

Had made a difference.

Rai followed her glance. "Prince Binpu," she began and patted Ahmose-Nefertari's hand. "You did the best you could for him, Daughter of the King. You gave him all the love in Kemet." A warm beam impressed upon her lips. "He is not in pain anymore. He lives in the Field of Reeds."

Ahmose-Nefertari nodded, but an emptiness filled her chest and eyes. *Yet it was not enough,* she thought. *Nothing will ever be enough.*

Rai rose to her knees and cupped Ahmose-Nefertari's cheeks without touching the royal flesh. Her black eyes, as deep as night, found Ahmose-Nefertari's ka in her gaze.

Rai's aging voice was still as smooth as she remembered it as a girl. "I nursed you, my 'child of the moon.' I raised you, my little 'beautiful companion.' You hide your worries from me. Tell Lady Rai what ails your thoughts?"

Her cheek lowered into Rai's open hand. *Where to begin? What to tell?* she thought and shook her head. "Everything, Rai. Everything," she whispered. "I have horrible dreams of all of us looking like my father and brother. I cannot rid myself of the nightmares that bring decaying bodies and wounds of war."

Rai's eyes bore into her own, so intensely she had to close her eyelids. If Lady Rai had one quality that the gods gifted, she could listen intently.

"Does our god of dreams, Bes, speak to me?" Ahmose-Nefertari whispered. "Is this what is to come?"

Rai pushed a few of the tight braids behind Ahmose-Nefertari's ear. "If he is, then there should be no anxiety, for you have already seen the future."

Ahmose-Nefertari's gaze drifted down.

Rai dipped her head to recapture her hold of Ahmose-Nefertari's eyes. "But he could be sending those dreams as warnings. Perhaps you have a bigger part to play in the future of Kemet, and he is showing you what will happen if you do not do your part."

A sad smile arose on Ahmose-Nefertari's face. "But I am only a daughter of the King, not even his wife. Consider my aunts, Royal Wives Inhapi and Sitdjehuti. Their part is to pray to Isis and Amun and chant before their images. They have no role in the throne room like my mother. Shall I sing with more volume, chant with more vigor, pray with more reverence?"

Rai's brow furrowed, and her soft gaze turned cold. "Now, King's Daughter, we do not mock those who serve the—"

"I'm not mocking," Ahmose-Nefertari shut her eyes tight and shook her head. "Who am I? What am I to do? Kemet is torn apart. How am I to bring it together? I am a royal daughter, a royal woman, nothing more."

Rai scoffed and touched the bottom of Ahmose-Nefertari's chin to lift her head. "Open your eyes, my 'child of the moon.'"

Ahmose-Nefertari obeyed to reveal a glisten of tears. Rai's brow smoothed, and her voice dipped low. "You are the King's Daughter. I am a nurse. What am I to do? My role is to ensure the King's children leave the Kap as confident royals who can face whatever may come, yet never forget their heart and compassion for the people of Kemet."

She leaned back to take in Ahmose-Nefertari's rounded face: her broad, plump lips underneath a straight nose. Kohl wrapped tightly around the eyes— the irises only evident from the bright whites surrounding them. The room's dimness made her oiled skin glimmer in the little morning sunlight that made it through the light hole in the ceiling.

"You, my child, have yet to know your role. But always be prepared. Have no fear." Even though Lady Rai called her child, Ahmose-Nefertari held no ill will toward her. She felt like her child in many ways, though she came from the Great Wife's womb.

A royal steward at the entry of the nursery cleared his throat drawing the women's attention.

Lady Rai stood up and went to speak with the steward. They spoke in hushed whispers, and the steward glanced at Ahmose-Nefertari. The steward took a step back, and Rai came to her side to deliver the message.

"Your mother is not well. Chief Wife Sitkamose sleeps again. Great Wife Ahhotep Tasherit refuses to be on the throne, fearful of another chiding from your grandmother. King Ahmose is all alone with her and does not know what to say. He wishes you to be by his side."

Ahmose-Nefertari looked at Rai in confusion. "Does he not wish for Royal Wife Hentempet?"

Rai pressed a smile and stooped to speak in a quieter whisper. "She was Kamose's wife. She is in the temples with your aunts."

"What of his royal wife, Henuttamehu?"

Lady Rai gave a soft shake of her head. "You are Ahmose's eldest capable sister. He would not ask for you if he wanted another."

Ahmose-Nefertari squeezed Tumerisy in her arms a little harder. She wanted to stay. Her grandmother was a candid woman. No mistake would go unnoticed. There was a reason her eldest sister always felt like a failure. Her mother did not escape her grandmother's chiding either. "My role is in here."

"Your King and brother has requested you at his side," Lady Rai said, unamused. "Rise, go. I will take care of King's Daughter Tumerisy."

Ahmose-Nefertari pressed a lingering kiss on her sister's warm forehead before she switched places with Rai.

She left toward the door when Rai spoke. "King's Daughter, remember, you have a role to play. Bes sends you a warning; if not, you should have no fear, for the future has already been shown to you. Go confidently as I have brought you up."

Ahmose-Nefertari nodded her head with a solemn face. What would she do? What would she say? Who was she to do anything of importance?

"Lift your head like a royal woman," Rai said as her last command.

Ahmose-Nefertari lifted her chin, so it was parallel to the floor, and the vulture's beak of her headdress cast a shadow from the sunlight from the light hole in the ceiling.

Rai beamed. "You can now face anything."

A timid smile returned, and her gaze drifted to Tumerisy. She would do her best, so if Tumerisy lived in this life, she would have a future. She hoped Bes' dreams were merely a warning.

She took her place next to Ahmose after acknowledging him and Tetisheri, who was seated in the back and sipping her tea.

Ahmose leaned over and whispered to her. "The princes come today to pay their monthly tribute to me. Prince Paser just left. He is nice. He pledged his loyalty to me. I like him."

Ahmose-Nefertari's eyebrows raised. "Then perhaps after your victory over the Hekka Khasut, you should reward his loyalty as you see fit. Perhaps do the same to the other princes who support your campaigns?"

Ahmose nodded his head. "You are wise, Sister." He peered up at her in a playful narrowing of his eyes. "As always," he whispered.

His devious grin made her chuckle, but she stopped and stood straight at Tetisheri's sharp slam of her teacup against her saucer.

Her harsh rasp came quickly after. "Prince Tetian of Ta-Seti is due to arrive any moment. You will show him respect and demand it in return."

Ahmose-Nefertari glanced at her grandmother's stern face. "I will try."

"No," Tetisheri said. "You will perform as the most important advisor, FanBearer on the King's Right Side."

Ahmose-Nefertari gulped. That was a significant role; she had only been in the throne room a few times and the council once. And her mother had signaled her to hush. "Yes, Grandmother," she said as the doors flew open.

"Prince Tetian from Ta-Seti arrives in the throne room of King Ahmose, Given Life," the guard at the door announced.

The prince strolled up to the dais with his stewards behind him, and they bowed deeply at the waist. Golden and lapis rings adorned all of his fingers, and silver wrapped his thumbs. His wig braids jangled with golden beads as he rose from his bow.

"King Ahmose, Your Majesty, I have come in person to send the sympathies of Ta-Seti to the royal family for the passing of Prince Binpu." His gaze slid to Tetisheri in the back before they reached Ahmose-Nefertari. "Such a young life to enter the Field of Reeds, but surely he was comforted by loving hands in his final moments?"

Ahmose-Nefertari shifted on her feet. She had lain beside the twins in the nursery and woke to find Binpu cold and stiff. "He was surrounded by love all of his life," she said, her voice meek.

He tilted his head at her and clasped his heavy-laden fingers over his belly. "I am glad to hear it."

His gaze was penetrating, but she firmed up her stance and quit shifting on her feet. Tetisheri sat behind them, watching. She had to perform and advise her brother, perhaps even speak for him, if warranted. The task made her mouth dry.

For Kemet, she told herself.

Tetian's gaze swept down her long pleated dress and back to her eyes. "Has the King married another sister?"

Ahmose shook his head and opened his mouth to speak, but Ahmose-Nefertari interjected.

"The King has not. He has asked me to perform as the FanBearer on the King's Right Side," she said, lifting her chin and feigning confidence on why she should be there.

A crooked smile erupted on Tetian's face. "And Great Wife Ahhotep and Chief Wife, Sitkamose?"

Tetisheri sighed. "Their whereabouts are none of your concern, Prince Tetian." Her stare erased his smile but did not keep him from advancing further.

He ignored Ahmose and set his sights on Ahmose-Nefertari. "So, you are yet unmarried?"

Her eyes darted to the stewards who had come with him. Their eyes were downcast, and they were as still as the pillars in the hall. The guards, who did nothing, said nothing either. Her brother looked at her to speak.

How to answer this emboldened question about her marital status? She swallowed the lump in her throat.

"It is none of your concern, Prince Tetian," she said, echoing her grandmother.

But Tetian only stepped closer to the dais. "Of course, King's Daughter. He reached for a bag on his belt and laid it at her feet instead of Ahmose's. He released the sack to reveal gold. There were three more bags tied to his belt. "For the young Prince Binpu's journey west."

Her cheeks burned at the sight of the gold offering. "Yet, you did not give any gold for King Kamose's journey west? You have three bags still."

Ahmose snapped his head to Tetian. "You sit on your gold while the rest of Kemet suffers."

He glanced at Ahmose before again turning his attention to Ahmose-Nefertari. He stepped onto the dais and opened his hands to her. "If it is gold you want, I will give it to you if you become my wife. You can share in my nome's prosperity."

Ahmose swiveled in his throne to look at his grandmother, but Ahmose-Nefertari felt her judging stare on her back. Was it a test of her competence beside the throne? Tetian knew what he asked was absurd, so she stated it. "You ask me to become your wife, but royal women are not given in marriage to anyone outside the royal family. I was to become King Kamose's wife, and I believe I will become the next king's wife. This you know, so why do you ask?"

He glanced at Ahmose. "I only thought you may want a man instead of an eleven-year-old boy."

She stiffened at the hateful remark of her brother. "I will marry the King when it is time."

Tetian nodded with pursed lips and stepped over the bag of gold he had put at her feet. A short chuckle escaped. "As I would expect so," he murmured and wiped his hand over his chest, his finger brushing the elaborate beading of his collar.

"Prince Tetian," Tetisheri crooned from the back, and he stopped his advance. But he was still too close to Ahmose-Nefertari.

He pulled the three remaining bags from his belt and lifted them by his face in an offering. "As condolences for your almost husband who was slain in war."

Her brow furrowed. It was a little late to be offering gold for his journey west. The tomb was already sealed.

"And your almost husband who will be slain in war," he added with a forced frown.

She glanced to Ahmose, whose eyes grew wide at the statement about him.

She refuted. "He will—"

"Although," Tetian interrupted, lowering the bags of gold to his side. "Your almost-husband is quite young. Will he grow old enough to father a child with you before he is slain like his brother and father before him?"

His eyes again drifted over her body. "You are what—ten years his senior?" He shook his head. "Doubtful. With no heir and now another brother on his way to the Field of Reeds, who then will be left to sit upon the throne?"

Her gaze bounced from each of his irises as she thought. He was right. Sapair would be the only brother to remain, and he was younger than Ahmose. But she would be a fool to let him know her thoughts. He was becoming a nuisance to her and needed to be put in his place. She wanted him off the dais. He did not belong there, nor would he ever sacrifice what her family had sacrificed for the greater of the kingdom. Her heartbeat fueled the courage to speak.

"Yes, King Seqenenre Tao and King Kamose perished in the war for our land of Kemet. Yet you still stand, Tetian, having only now brought forth a small portion of your share in this cause." She eyed the bags of gold, knowing the rumors of storehouses full of traded gold in Ta-Seti. "Whoever sits upon the throne, be it my brother or his heir or his named Hereditary Prince, they will have given much more to Kemet than you."

His grin fell at the insult. He threw the bags of gold at her feet. "Graciousness would be becoming of such a royal woman as yourself, Chief Royal Wife." He placed his hand over his heart. "Many apologies. *King's Daughter*."

Her eyes raged at his attempt at a counterattack. He would not have the last of the banter. "See to it, Prince Tetian, you utter the correct titles of the royal family."

He came close to her, and she smelled his malt-born breath from the morning's meal. "I am still a Prince," he sneered. He glanced to Tetisheri, who allowed him to continue.

"My fellow princes and I have every right to this throne, as well as your unmarried bed, should your brothers leave us without an heir. Seeing as I am the wealthiest prince of the Upper, I will win all support without hesitation."

He turned his nose into her bountiful wig and sniffed her perfume. "So be grateful, King's Daughter, you are not yet married to a boy and could be married to a man."

The sudden chill ran down her spine, but she refused to honor its usual shake. "Remove yourself from the royal dais, or I shall have you thrown off." Her eyes snapped to his, her face as stone. *He will not intimidate me. I am Ahmose-Nefertari. Royal woman. Divine blood runs in my veins.*

He chuckled and stepped back after casting a glance at Tetisheri behind her. He bowed his head in a facade of respect. "As you wish, Ahmose-Nefertari."

She opened her mouth to rebuke him for not using her title, but the corner of his slipped into a smirk.

He snapped his fingers at his stewards. "Prepare the Prince's boat to return to Ta-Seti."

He brought his finger and pointed it at Ahmose-Nefertari's face. "My prayers to Isis and Nephthys that your father, eldest brother, the youngest brother, and perhaps your last two brothers all journey well to become one with Re." Having said the last of the banter, he spun on his heels.

Once his back was turned, Ahmose-Nefertari's hands curled into fists by her sides as he left without waiting for dismissal. The hot flame within her chest choked her breath until she finally sucked in the stale air of the closed-off throne room. Her chin dipped low—her gaze stuck on the open doorway where Tetian exited.

"Was that a threat, Prince?" she muttered before whipping around to face her grandmother. "You let him speak to me and about our family in such a way? He obeyed your voice. You could have stopped him at any time."

Tetisheri groaned and pushed out of her chair. She strode up to Ahmose-Nefertari with a soft smile and a slow shake of her head. Her hands folded in front of her belly when she reached her granddaughter. "Yet you stopped him all by yourself by threatening to throw him off the dais." She said nothing more and walked to the throne room doors.

Ahmose-Nefertari was left in a confused daze. Had she stopped him? Could she have just said as much as her grandmother, and he would have never stepped onto the dais? Only a few insults and a threat had made him leave. She spun around and called out before Tetisheri reached the corridor. "Where are you going, Great Wife?"

"To rest," Tetisheri called back with a gentle hand wave. "You have my confidence, FanBearer on the King's Right Side."

Ahmose-Nefertari's eyes grew wide as the doors closed. Had it been a test after all? She snapped her head to her brother, who sat smiling at her.

"What?"

He shrugged. "You are wise. Grandmother even thinks so, which is rare." He bobbed his head. "I want you by my side every day when Sitkamose and Mother cannot be."

"What of Tumerisy? Who will hold her?" she asked.

"Lady Rai," Ahmose said and shrugged again. His head fell. "I know I am selfish, but I need you too, Sister."

She drew near him, wrapped an arm around his shoulders, and squeezed. "You will be a great King, Ahmose. You have so much passion, as I have told you before. We are all here to help you. I will be by your side when Mother and Sitkamose cannot be."

But as the words passed her lips, she only wished to be in the Kap's nursery and never set foot again in the throne room.

18

A TIME OF GRIEF | AHMOSE-NEFERTARI

SEDJEFATAWY, 1568 BC

Screams swept through Sedjefatawy and forced Ahmose-Nefertari's eyes to pop open. The dying moonlight fell through the wall vent. She jumped out of bed, knocking her wooden headrest to the floor with a thick *thunk*. The linen blanket twisted around her legs, but she broke free and grabbed the ax by her door. Her sisters Hentempet and Nebetta looked at her, each still in their beds. The moonlight illuminated the whites of their eyes.

"Quiet," she ordered before they could speak. The ax's heavy bronze head scratched the mud brick floor as she crept into the courtyard. She looked around, confused at the lack of movement. The screams came again, but rather, one familiar scream: a boy's.

"Ahmose?" She spoke his name under her breath.

Another scream. She took off with ax in hand toward the King's apartment as her imagination went wild with visions of attacks on his small frame—his twelve-year-old body no match for them.

Have assassins come? The Kushites? The Hekka Khasut?

She skidded around the corridor and stopped short

at the guards outside the King's room. They readied their spears at her shadow.

A soft *shhhh* came from the interior of Ahmose's room as she approached, lowering her ax. "It is I, King's Daughter," she said and stepped into the torchlight. They stood at ease and bowed their heads to her.

"The King's Chief Wife will not wake," one guard said in a whisper.

Her breath caught in her throat as she considered all the possibilities. Sitkamose had been fragile all her life and had been difficult to wake on many occasions. Could she only be in a deep sleep to renew her strength? Could she need food to revive her? Or could it be something much more sorrowful?

Ahmose-Nefertari drew near amid Ahmose's painful shrieks coming from within the room. She handed her ax to a guard and peered past the mud brick doorpost. The candlelight on the room's grand chest cast flickering shadows against the wall.

Her mother stood by the King's bed, stroking Ahmose's shoulder. The boy king kneeled on the linen-wrapped mattress, with Sitkamose's head pulled tightly to his bosom. Her limp arms sagged against her motionless body.

The squawk of a falcon echoed in the pre-dawn night as if to signal the Chief Wife's *ba* had survived—her spiritual manifestation to grace the land of the living when she began her journey west.

Ahmose-Nefertari heard shuffling feet behind her and peered over her shoulder to see Tep stop and stare at her. The eldest sister hung her head, and the short spear she held in her hand drooped—its point toward the floor. "Is it only a nightmare?"

Ahmose-Nefertari shook her head with eyes

glistening and turned back to face the room. How would she tell Tep that her daughter would be joining Binpu?

Tep shuffled up beside her and stared in. Her jaw drifted agape. "My daughter too?" Her words choked in her throat.

Ahmose-Nefertari lifted a tentative hand and placed it on her shoulder. How to comfort her? What to say? But Tep yanked her shoulder out from underneath her sister's embrace.

"No!" she yelled. The short spear tumbled to the floor. Its tip hit and rattled on the ground until it stopped. The echo reverberated down the brick corridor.

Their mother peered over her shoulder at the two sisters. Tep screamed until her chest emptied of air. Her hands gripped her chest as she stumbled backward into a guard. He did not budge, but she tripped on his foot. He caught her, but she shoved him away. "No!" she screamed with a renewed breath, stumbling and falling into Ahmose-Nefertari.

"No!" she cried out again. She grabbed Ahmose-Nefertari's shoulders hard enough to bruise, and a grimace washed over her face while she groaned indecipherable mutterings.

Ahmose-Nefertari grabbed her sister's hands and squeezed. The indecipherable mutterings became groans of agony. She pulled her into an embrace and slid her hands around to her back, gripping her in a way to absorb her pain.

The guards' eyes drifted down the corridor as her sister slid to her knees. Ahmose-Nefertari stooped to hold her sister's head against her bosom while she cried. The black kohl stained her white linen gown.

A shadow fell and blocked the light of the candle

from the room. Ahmose-Nefertari glanced up to their mother, who stood tall over them.

"Hush," she commanded. A glisten lived in her eye, but her voice held no sympathy.

Tep snapped her face to her mother's. "I will not hush, Mother!" she yelled, emphasizing the rebellious words with harsh jabs of a pointed finger toward the Great Wife.

Ahmose-Nefertari held her breath in the tense moment between mother and daughter. The guards turned their back on that which was not to be seen. Ahmose cried out in sobs, and the short, thin braids on Sitkamose's uncovered head bobbed as Ahmose shook her. "Wake up," he whimpered in the silence at his apartment's door, oblivious to everything.

Her gaze drifted to her mother standing over them. Her jaw was taut, but her shoulders lowered. She spoke softly. "Great Wife of Kamose and Mother of Chief Wife Sitkamose, let us grieve elsewhere." She offered her hand, but Tep slapped it away and jumped to her feet.

"I hate you," she whispered through clenched, grinding teeth. "I will never be the daughter you wanted to stand beside the throne, yet you cursed Kamose to be slain by asking him to name Ahmose as Hereditary Prince. Now you tell me I cannot grieve my own daughter, my own flesh and blood? Who are you, Great Wife? Who are you!? What right do you have in telling me when I can and cannot feel? When I can and cannot grieve my husband and child? Is your heart heavy, or has it turned black? Is that why you do not shed a tear or—"

The succeeding slap shut Tep's mouth, if not out of pure embarrassment of the savage insult she had slung at her mother. She shrunk back as Ahhotep advanced, stepping on and then over Ahmose-Nefertari's linen dress. Her face fell somber while Ahmose-Nefertari stood and stepped out of her way.

A tear rolled down the side of her mother's cheek, and Ahmose-Nefertari lowered her head not to reveal she had seen it.

"My namesake," Ahhotep said and gripped her eldest's jaw. "I feel more deeply than when Isis lost Osiris, yet I do not have the goddess' divine magic to bring them back to life." She released Tep's jaw and pulled her into a slow embrace. "You will see them again in the Field of Reeds, lest you forget," she whispered and kissed her daughter's cheek.

Ahhotep slid a finger under Ahmose-Nefertari's chin to raise her face and look her in the eye. "Tend to your brother. I need to walk with your sister." She took her eldest and left down the corridor speaking in hushed tones.

Ahmose-Nefertari watched their shadows disappear from the torchlight's farthest reaches before she glanced at Ahmose. She asked in a whisper so the guard could hear her, "Did Great Wife Ahhotep already send for the priests of Anubis?"

The guard nodded. "Yes, King's Daughter."

Her belly twisted. "Then, do not speak of the cries that may come from this place when they take the King's Chief Wife from him."

The guards nodded and said in unison. "Yes, King's Daughter."

She stepped into the room and walked past the chest and chairs to the bed at the end of the narrow space. She slipped her hands on Ahmose's shoulders. "Brother," she crooned and slid her hands down Ahmose's arms. She wrenched her fingers to intertwine with his and gently guided him to lay Sitkamose on the bed without further disturbance. He screamed as she took control of his hands. The boy was strong and resisted her with sharp tugs and jerks of her body. She rested her chin on his shoulder. "Brother," she crooned again, settling him a little. "Brother, Ahmose—Sitkamose's ba has already left. I heard the falcon shriek. She has begun her journey west."

His chest pounded with each breath, and his arms gave way to her direction. She led him to place Sitkamose's head into the headrest with its wrapped and cushioned crossbeam directly under her neck. Ahmose whimpered amid his harsh breaths but let her do what she wished with his limbs. They stared at the chief wife with her jaw ajar and eyes glossed until Ahmose-Nefertari swallowed the lump in her throat and whispered, "We will see you in the Field of Reeds, our dear friend."

She reached over with Ahmose's hand and closed her eyes, so it appeared Sitkamose was only sleeping. At that moment, Ahmose turned and slammed his body into Ahmose-Nefertari. He gripped her linen gown and pulled it to his face to muffle his cries.

Their mother and elder sister returned. Tep fell to her knees before Sitkamose's body and grabbed her hand, placing her forehead there. The Anubis priests followed and took the body away. Ahmose-Nefertari could not watch while Tep sat on the bed, who stared at anything and held a far-off look in her eyes.

Their mother took ahold of Ahmose and nodded toward Ahmose-Nefertari. "Go rest, my daughter, for it will be a long day when the sun fully rises."

Ahmose's fingers grazed Ahmose-Nefertari's arm as their mother slid him off her. At the last moment, before their hands disconnected, Ahmose-Nefertari clenched Ahmose's hand in hers. "We will see her again, Brother."

He sniffled and nodded and then released her. She hurried out of the room, glancing back only once at the quiet place and the dwindling candle. Another falcon's shriek sounded in the night, and her face snapped to the sky. The lasting call reverberated in her ears. Another traveler west? So soon after Sitkamose? Her feet quickened as she returned to the royal harem. Whom could it have been? Visions of Binpu stiff in his cot by the morning hastened her heartbeat. She shook her head, but still, she chewed her lip and changed direction from her room to the nursery.

Her shadow loomed into the dark interior as she stood at the doorway, squinting to make out the figures on the floor.

Mosi slept on one side of the nursery and Tumerisy on the other. Binpu's empty cot lay waiting for the next child of the King. She quickly looked away to avoid the chill that accompanied the memory. Lady Rai lay still in the back of the room.

Ahmose-Nefertari crept in and stooped next to Tumerisy, envisioning cold flesh until her fingers grazed the child's warm cheek. It was still not enough to calm her worry. Her hand slipped to the girl's chest to feel the gentle rise and fall. Three times. Steady breaths.

She closed her eyes and withdrew her hand.

Alive.

Her shoulders slumped, and she sat back on her heels. How much more could their family take? How many more would they send to the Field of Reeds in their youth?

She stood up and released the tension in a slow, full exhale. It would be a long day yet. Those were her mother's words. What more could the day bring already? When she had watched Tumerisy breathe a few more times and stir in her sleep, Ahmose-Nefertari left the nursery, satisfied her sister would see the Aten rise. She touched the doorpost of her room, but before she stepped inside, the sun's preceding lights struck red in the sky and tipped over the eastern palace wall. She lowered her head onto the back of her hand and heard the bustle of the palace begin. The call of duty urged her to the temple to pray, but her feet took her to her bed.

FRESHLY BATHED FUR SLIPPED ALONG AHMOSE-NEFERTARI'S nose, prompting her to brush it aside. She rolled over in bed as the cat nestled by her belly. Ahmose-Nefertari's naturally coiled ringlets stuck to her neck in a warm sweat as she opened her eyes.

"In peace, Kit," she whispered and rubbed the cat between the ears. A soft, pleased *purr* responded. She surveyed her room. The blanket lay bunched by the bedpost and the headrest still on the floor as she had left them when she got up in the night.

I shall never sleep without my headrest again, she told herself and wiped the accumulated sweat from her nape.

"How long have I slept, Kit?" she mumbled and sat up. She massaged the ache from her neck as she watched her steward, Men, draw near the bedroom door through its open crack.

The cat jumped down and ran off when Men threw the door open. He bowed before her. "Great Wife Ahhotep requests your presence in the throne room."

Ahmose-Nefertari sat still slumped. "I am no one's royal wife. Why must she call me again?"

Men rose from his bow and stared at her with an unamused stare. "You are more important than you realize." He pointed to her sisters' empty cots. "Your sisters will always be critical to the harem, but you will be critical to the throne. Now, let us bathe you and get you dressed." He opened the chest and pulled the items he needed from it, and a few servants came in to help.

She stood up. "Henuttamehu is Royal Wife to King Ahmose. How will—"

"Your mother has requested your presence." Men spun around to face her with eyes ablaze. "She has granted you this pardon to rest. See to it that you obey the Great Wife."

Ahmose-Nefertari's eyes narrowed at the forthright man. He would have been a better fit for her grandmother's steward. But Tetisheri had assigned him to her, and everyone had to follow the Great Wife's charge in the harem. She licked her dry lips. "I am not disobeying Queen Ahhotep. I am merely asking why you believe I will be critical to the throne when my half-sister is a Royal Wife, and I am but a King's Daughter?"

Men stepped forward. "You were chosen by both Great Wives, Tetisheri and Ahhotep. Now let us bathe and dress you for your day ahead."

"Chosen for what?" Ahmose-Nefertari stood her ground. "And what about Great Wife Ahhotep Tasherit?"

Men simply snapped at the servants and turned from the room. The servants gestured for Ahmose-Nefertari to follow him. She clenched her jaw and shook her head at the steward, who had turned his back on her.

If she did not follow, the servants would most likely be chastised. She would not have that, so she forced herself out of the dim interior to the bright sunlight. She reached an arm overhead to shade her eyes from the

Aten's blazes until she reached the palace's baths. Men had already ordered a maidservant to stand next to the bathing stone slab with a bucket of water and three more beside her.

"It wasn't a dream," Ahmose-Nefertari whispered and hung her head. She stood in a numb trance until Men cleared his throat.

"We cannot dally, King's Daughter," he said with an annoyance wrapped around his words.

It didn't faze her, though, as he left and the maidservants stripped her of her linen dress—Tep's black kohl smear from the night before still in its threads.

She kneeled on the stone slab in the corner of the room. The water gushed over her head, two buckets over her body, and the last over her legs. The water tendrils ran down her back and tickled her feet. The sweet smell of lotus blossoms perfumed the air as the servants rubbed the infused oil into her skin. They combed her hair and wrapped her dress and belt around her. Placed the wig upon her head with her vulture headdress. Painted her face with kohl and oiled pigments and laid her beaded collar around her neck.

They rushed her to the throne room's double doors and opened them wide. She drew a deep breath and strode in after the guard declared her arrival. Her brother sat red-eyed on the throne, her mother stood in a regal fashion beside him, and her grandmother reclined in the back, sipping tea again.

What could they want from me? she asked herself.

She stopped short of the dais, bowed her head, and lifted it. "The Great Wife Ahhotep summoned me. I have come."

Her mother descended the dais with pressed lips. "Your brother is without a Chief Wife, my daughter."

"Henuttamehu is his royal wife. Would she not be elevated to the status of Chief Wife?"

"She would, but she is three years your junior, and she is the daughter of Inhapi. You are my blood. I want you as Ahmose's Chief Wife. Will you serve your family?" Her eyes pleaded, and her voice shook. "Will you become what we need for Kemet?"

"Why me, Mother?" she asked in a whisper.

Ahhotep's fingers brushed a few braids of her daughter's wig. "You are wise. You will be able to help your brother. I see how you care for my children when I cannot be there with them. You will show the same care to the children of Kemet. Your grandmother is more proud of you than any other of her living grandchildren. Kamose, she was the proudest." Ahhotep's eyes averted, and her jaw trembled as if she wished to say more, but she never did.

Tetisheri stood up and rattled her teacup on its saucer. "King's Daughter Ahmose-Nefertari, will you become Chief Wife to King Ahmose in his time of need?"

Ahmose leaned forward on his throne. His bloodshot eyes begged her. The fear in his face pleaded. How could she say no? So she bobbed her head. "For my family, Mother," she whispered.

"Then you shall be married today," Tetisheri said, offering her teacup to a servant. She clapped her hands in two quick summoning claps. "Prepare the gifts to Amun and Re. Prepare the feast for this evening."

"What of the princes?" Ahmose-Nefertari asked.

"They will receive word when they receive it, but we must act quickly. Sitkamose's passing will not stay on mute lips."

Servants scattered to do the Great Wife's bidding, and Ahhotep stepped closer and whispered in her daughter's ear. "You will do great things, my daughter. The gods will bless you. It will not be easy, but we sense a strength in you."

"You sense something I do not," she whispered back.

"In time, Ahmose-Nefertari. In time." Ahhotep patted her daughter's shoulder. "Go prepare your last day before your marriage."

Ahmose-Nefertari dipped her chin and caught sight again of Ahmose, whose flushed cheeks rivaled his relieved sorrowful grin. At least she could be there for her brother. She left the throne room and returned to the harem. In the economic center, she saw Tep in a plain dress, seated and working with flax with the other non-royal women of the harem. The vulture headdress was not on Tep's head. Ahmose-Nefertari had almost walked past her, but the familiarity of her face gave her pause enough to recognize her sister.

"What are you doing here?" Ahmose-Nefertari asked. Her shadow fell over Tep's working hands.

She did not look up but kept working, so Ahmose-Nefertari came closer and stooped down. She placed a hand over her sister's. "What are you doing here? Why are you not in the throne room taking Mother's place or at least allowing Grandmother to rest?"

Tep picked up Ahmose-Nefertari's hand and placed it away from her. She began working again.

"Tep—"

"The evil spirits curse me, Sister." Her voice was low and broken. "My father, my husband, and my only child —my sweet little girl . . . all gone from this life." Tears brimmed in her eyes as she rolled the flaxen thread to smooth it out. "I want no more of it. I am happy to help my cousins in the harem make textiles for our King's army and navy." She never looked up and focused on her task. "Leave me. I asked to be relieved of my position. Mother granted it. Grandmother was, no doubt, thrilled."

"Sister—"

"Leave me," Tep groaned and tirelessly worked the flax. Their other cousins, unmarried male and female, sat in the shade, making royal fabric, thread, and pottery. The harem was a unique place, always a sanctuary for the members of the King's family. Much good work came from the harem.

Ahmose-Nefertari scanned the working members before her gaze dropped to her sister's hands. Again, she placed a hand over hers. She kissed the top of her head. "I wish peace for you, Tep."

Tep said nothing as Ahmose-Nefertari expected but kept working. Ahmose-Nefertari stood up and continued on her way to the nursery.

"Poor Tep," she muttered and wondered if she would end up the same. She didn't want to be Ahmose's wife. She didn't want the burdens of being queen. She saw what it did to her mother and grandmother. Her cousins' children were playing in the Kap's courtyard, and she slowed down to watch them. She wanted to love and feel like Tep, not be stone pillars like their matriarchs. Her shoulders hunched and her feet dragged as another realization hit her deep in the belly. As Chief Wife, she would likely spend most nights in Ahmose's room or her private apartment and most days by his side. Tumerisy would be without her. Her chin fell to her chest.

Men snapped his fingers in front of her face. Where had he come from? He seemingly appeared out of nowhere.

"King's Daughter," he said. "Chin up; we have much

preparation for tonight. Come, come." He spun on his heels and expected her to follow him.

She only sighed and closed her eyes.

"I do not want this," she said to herself but followed Men anyway.

AFTER THE MARRIAGE FEAST, AHMOSE AND AHMOSE-NEFERTARI retreated to the King's room. He fell asleep in her arms but seeing him there made her long for her sister. She snuck out, quieting the guards who let her leave. She passed by her mother's room and heard soft cries. Her heart twisted, but she moved on. A falcon shrieked, and she moved quicker, hoping the shriek was a traveler from the village or Waset. She peered into the dim nursery and saw Rai giving Tumerisy a honey herb drop for her coughing.

It had been someone else's ba.

Ahmose-Nefertari sent an exhale into the room as she steadied her nerves.

"Chief Wife!" Lady Rai turned and said in surprise. "What are you doing here?"

"I had to see how she was," Ahmose-Nefertari said and stepped inside.

Lady Rai gestured to Tumerisy. "If you want to hold her, I shall see where little Mosi is and get her ready for bed."

Ahmose-Nefertari cupped Rai's cheek, knowing the proper response from Rai would have been a chiding to return to Ahmose. "You are a blessing."

"As are you, my 'beautiful companion.'" Rai kissed Ahmose-Nefertari's fingers and left the room. Tumerisy crawled over to her, and she picked up the seven-year-old petite girl and sat in the chair with her in her lap.

Tumerisy looked at her and let her head drift down to her shoulder. "I love you, Sister."

A beam grew across Ahmose-Nefertari's lips.

"What do you think the Field of Reeds is like?" she asked in a raspy voice. The flicker of the dying torchlight got lost in her deep, dark eyes.

Ahmose-Nefertari shook her head as the beam faded. "It is a happy place. One with no strife or worry or pain."

"I want to go there, then." Tumerisy coughed and rubbed her chest.

"You will," Ahmose Nefertari hurried through, trying to put happiness in her tone. "We all will, as long as our hearts are not heavy. But you will not go there today."

"Sometimes I wish I was not in pain or ill all the time. I would not be such a burden in the Field of Reeds."

"You are never a burden in the land of the living either." She squeezed Tumerisy to emphasize her words.

"Why am I always tired, Sister? Sitkamose was the same as me. Always sick. Always weak. She is in the Field of Reeds now. Maybe I could go to her."

"Not yet," Ahmose-Nefertari whispered and buried her face in Tumerisy's. "Please. I still need you here with me."

"If you say, my sister, I will stay as long as possible." She yawned, showing the yellow honey herb drop in her mouth, and coughed dryly again.

"Suck on the drop, Tumerisy. It will help your cough, and you will be able to sleep soundly." She swept back the girl's sidelock and kissed her cheek. "And you will wake to a new day."

Tumerisy's eyes flitted closed. Soon after, Ahmose

and Sapair peeked in with Ahmose's guards towering over them.

"I thought you were asleep," Ahmose-Nefertari whispered so as not to wake Tumerisy.

"I came looking for you when I awoke from a nightmare that Bes sent me, and you were not there. Sapair was crying in his room as I searched for you, so I told him to come with me." Ahmose crept in, and Sapair followed. They sat at her feet and leaned against her legs. Sapair's tears wet her skin.

She closed her eyes, taking in the soft sobs of her youngest living brother and the faint rasps of her youngest sister. Ahmose rested his temple on her knee and stroked her shin. "I am afraid," he whispered.

Her body grew weak in response. The weight of her new role came crashing around her. It was choking. How was she going to help her brother become courageous? How was she going to ensure the kingdom did not fall apart when he was away at war? How was she going to keep the dissenters at bay? How was she going to keep what remained of her family alive?

She wet her dry lips with a swipe of a thick tongue. It cooled the air she breathed as she leaned the back of her head against the top of the chair.

How did her mother and grandmother accomplish such feats? Her mother's face held many fine lines with a constantly furrowed brow, and her grandmother's weathered countenance, cold in its stare, flashed in memory. Such powerful women stood alone, withstanding the woes of war by themselves. Would she do the same, or would she fail like Tep and give up, choosing to work in the harem's economic center for the rest of her life? What if Ahmose was slain too? What if she lost all of her children? She rubbed her hand down

Tumerisy's back as tears welled in her eyes. Lost those she loved most? Would she still stand tall like her mother and grandmother? Would she want to? Would she have to?

Finally, in a soft voice, she responded to her brother.

"I am afraid too, Ahmose," she whispered. "But we cannot show we are afraid." Ahmose hugged her leg, and the brush of his cheek meant he nodded. He was still a child but nearly a man. He had already been through so much, but she knew he was about to endure much more.

The alabaster torch flickered, its oil reserves nearly gone. Tumerisy's rhythmic rasps fell in cadence with the flicker's ticks. Darkness would soon be upon them, but oil was in demand. Only the throne room would be lit once the oil went out.

Silence encased the room except for the soft whimper of Sapair and the rasp of Tumerisy. Her eyes lifted to the corridor beyond the doorway of the nursery. Body servants and Ahmose's guards stood, shifting their weight by the doorposts.

When the oil finally depleted, it was then, in the room's darkness, Ahmose-Nefertari let the tears run down her cheek. But she made not a sound for the sake of her brothers.

19

A TIME FOR KUSH |
AHHOTEP

SEDJEFATAWY, 1566 BC

The caravans across the Dashret needed to return soon, if they returned at all. Ahhotep glanced back at the empty chair behind her, where her mother usually sat, and then to Ahmose-Nefertari standing next to Ahmose, now fourteen years of age.

The messenger before the royal dais bowed low as he finished reading from the clay tablet in his hand. Ahmose peered first at his sister-wife and then at his mother as he curled his fingers into his fist.

Ahhotep remained silent, letting her son take control of the response. She had been proud of him in the past year; he had grown so much.

"Send Troop Commander Uahbra to put down the insurrection at Toshka," Ahmose decreed, and a slow exhale streamed from his nostrils. He mimicked her words from past rebellions but added his own voice, for which Ahhotep was pleased: "Make an example of Prince Aata, this Kushite rebel leader. Burn his body so his ba will never walk in the Field of Reeds. All shall know what it means to betray the King of Kemet."

The messenger bowed his head. "As the King commands," he said in pride and left.

Ahmose turned his head to his mother as if to ask if he had made the right decision. She nodded, and a pinched smile came over his face. His sidelock was gone, and he opted for the blue khepresh crown of war like his brother before him. He had reached manhood, but his feet only touched the floor by his toes. She stood a head taller than him, but like General Pennekhbet, he was mighty for his smaller size. She had watched him as his Medjay tutor Ketti trained him. There was none Ahmose could not best either through strength or strategy. She had brought him to every council meeting as she had told Baba she would and, through him, had commanded the armies of the King to reclaim Mednit and establish a border at the Lower. But some of the Kushites, who gave up their nomadic way of life—moving from oasis to oasis in Set's barren desert—settled in Kerma and kept rebelling. It drained their resources and delayed the coming advance into the Lower every time.

Ahhotep pursed her lips as she thought about the princes' latest reason for refusing to support the cause other than the minimum offering they had provided since Kamose was slain. No matter how many victories they won or the number of successes, Tetian always found something to cause hesitation among the princes. The latest was the delayed entry into the Lower.

Ahmose-Nefertari sighed. "Of all days to bring such a message."

Ahmose rubbed his lip with a finger. "The princes will arrive soon." His voice cracked, and a sheepish blush came to his cheeks. He swallowed back the embarrassment and continued speaking. "What do I tell them as to why we again delay the attack on Men-nefer in the Lower?"

Ahmose-Nefertari folded her arms over her chest. "We tell them . . ." Her voice drifted off as she thought.

Ahhotep took a deep breath and went and sat in the empty chair. She asked a nearby servant to bring her karkade tea. Her feet ached, and she stretched her toes wide in her silver-decorated leather sandals.

Her actions garnered stares from both of her children. "Continue," she said and waved them on. "Think on what to tell the princes."

Her head hurt, and she grew instantly hot. Like someone had placed her in a clay brick oven to bake. Or took molten bronze and poured it over her head. She wished for the servant girl to fan her, but the internal heat rendered her mute. Her arms fell limp to her side and endured the invisible flame until it passed. She had heard nothing her children had said, nor did she care at the moment. Her tongue longed for the cooled red tea. Her blood moon had become erratic, and she knew the end of it was drawing near. She only hoped these evil fire spirits would cease then too. The servant finally brought her the tea. She sipped it and then gulped it. Slamming the teacup down on the saucer, she shoved it back at the servant.

"Another," she rasped. She stared at the double doors of the throne room. No wonder her mother sat here and enjoyed tea all those years. Only, her mother had seemed to hold herself together more than she could.

The fire spirit finally left her, and she sighed in relief. Sweat poured from underneath her wig with beads rolling down her brow. Meret dabbed her forehead, and Ahhotep snatched her wrist and pulled her close. "Next time, when I ask for tea or sweat beads on my brow, tell the servant girl to fan me."

"Yes, Royal Commander," Meret said with a bow, and Ahhotep released her.

A moment later, the servant girl fanned her. *A little too late*, Ahhotep thought, but still, the burst of air upon her face and neck was welcome.

She closed her eyes and relaxed back in the chair. Her forearm slid into the chair's worn groove where her mother had always placed her tea-drinking arm.

"Royal Commander," someone called, but Ahhotep did not want to answer. Her title came again, and she popped open an eye to see her daughter calling her.

"What is it, Chief Wife?" Ahhotep groaned, wishing to take a cold bath, especially before the princes arrived.

"What if we tell the princes we are not delaying our attack on Men-nefer?"

"And lie to them?" Ahhotep scoffed and shook her head. "That would be an easy lie to be uncovered when we do not send an army on Men-nefer. We will tell them the truth. Toshka rebelled, and it had to be dealt with, or else the Kushites will end up at the port of Abu once again. The princes should thank us for putting down these rebellions. Especially those who give so little even after your brother gave his life to secure Buhen."

She had not told her children their grandmother was from Ta-Seti. It had been a hard truth to swallow, and as long as her mother lived, she did not want to burden them anymore with what Tetian might do once she began her journey west. She doubted he would kill another countryman as it would cause his heart to weigh heavy on the scales of Ma'at, as Baba said, but he had the wealth to hold significant sway over the princes should he ever decide to bribe them.

"And perhaps," she added. "Since the purpose of our feast tonight is to name a Viceroy of Kush who will maintain the peace with our southern neighbors, maybe Tetian should front the cost of that position since it would be protecting his precious Ta-Seti from the rebels. Let's persuade the princes to agree to that. Then after that, no more delays." She held up a finger, and her eyes darted between them. "Well, we still need at least two sons before you join the battle, Ahmose."

Ahmose-Nefertari glanced at her brother and averted her eyes, but Ahmose's brow furrowed. A frown arose on his mouth. "I am a man and capable of war. You have seen me best any sparring partner. You have seen how Ketti trains me. I have even won a spar against him." He stood up and faced his mother. "Let me go with my army."

But Ahhotep shook her head. "No."

"I am King. I can—"

"Ahmose," Ahhotep said as swift as a khopesh's swing. Visions of Tao and Kamose filled her mind. "Even your brother did not see war until he had twenty years, and he still came home with a spear in his chest!" Her fist smashed into the armchair just as her yell defeated the frown on Ahmose's face.

Ahmose shrunk back, his shoulders hiding his neck. The servant girl stopped fanning, and Meret and Nena shuffled backward at the outburst.

Ahhotep took a deep breath and settled her racing heartbeat. She unfurled her hand and stood up in royal elegance. "My king," she said, swallowing her rage and readdressing her son as she should. "It would not be wise for you to join your armies yet. You have capable leaders in General Pennekhbet and Admiral Baba, and we have commanded them well from Waset. Even other young men your age still accompany their fathers on campaigns to learn from them. *Your* father is with Re. Ketti will teach you what you need to know for the day you take your position as leader of your armies, and I am no longer Royal Commander."

Ahmose's shoulders returned to their regal position. "You are wise, Royal Commander," he said with a taut jaw.

Ahhotep stared him down. "The King would also do well to have at least two sons before he journeys off to war in case the same fate befalls him as did King Kamose and King Seqenenre Tao."

The servant came with a bowed body with Ahhotep's karkade tea and stretched out his arms to present her with it. She snatched it and sipped slowly as her mother had done, peering out at her son and daughter over the cup's rim. The cooled liquid soothed her throat and belly, radiating through the rest of her body. At her children's silence, she continued. "We must think of the crown above all else, especially in this time of war. King Kamose took precautions in naming you, King Ahmose, as his Hereditary Prince in the absence of an heir—"

"I have already tried having sons with Henuttamehu, but her womb is closed," Ahmose shot back, his voice again breaking—unable to decide to stay high or low.

"Yes, but your Chief Wife remains childless. At least the General's daughter will have a child next year," Ahhotep said, referencing Kasmut, Ahmose's new wife to honor the General. The remark was said in a curt undertone, and for a moment, she sounded like Tetisheri. She swallowed back her pride. She had wanted to sound like the woman she did not like for so long; perhaps the gods had finally granted her wish. Would that mean her children would dislike her, too, as she disliked her mother? She blinked a few times, imagining the loneliness; she was not as strong as her mother. She did not know if she could bear it.

But her mouth kept speaking what her mother would have said: "Given the line of Kings must go on and your brother is still not yet a man, you will have two sons before you leave for war." Ahhotep did not make a request. She took after her mother once again as she placed the teacup on the saucer and held her hand out for a servant to take it, even though she wanted more of its cooled liquid. The attendant executed the assumed command, and her hand fell to her side.

Her children remained silent, much like she had done in Tetisheri's presence. "I am glad we are agreed," she said with a lift of her chin. It pained her to treat her children in that regard, but she had to. Ahmose-Nefertari did not want to have relations with her brother being ten years his senior, and Ahmose was too much like Tao in his young manhood, rash and ready to fight without thinking through the consequences of his actions or what would happen should he fail. She had to do what she did and say what she said. The hollow spot in her chest grew more expansive, but to keep herself from comforting her children, she left the throne room without another word—Meret and Nena at her heels.

She blinked back tears as the sunlight fell onto her face while exiting the throne room's double doors. She kept her head upright and turned down the corridor to see to the feast.

"Steady yourself," she whispered as the shadows from the corridor's pillars passed by her as she walked. "Tetian and the princes will not anger me. I am in control of myself. I will choose to remain calm and demand respect due to me."

When Ahhotep entered the hall, Tetisheri sat in her usual place at the King's table. Her fingers drummed on the wood, much like Tetian had done when he had sat at Kamose's feast.

Ahhotep strode up to her. "You say you are tired and cannot join us in the throne room, Great Wife, but you have the strength to sit and wait for the feast?"

Tetisheri chuckled with a downcast face and rubbed her temple. "I almost liked you better when you were timid and emotional, Royal Commander." Her hand fell to her lap, and she peered up at Ahhotep. "I can always wait for good food. And besides, I haven't heard any rumors of devasting loss or utter failures in the throne room; it seems I am not needed anymore."

Ahhotep scoffed. The older woman did not put her family through this living nightmare, only to gracefully bow out when she tired. "You are Great Wife and God's Mother; I'm sure your presence will always be necessary."

Tetisheri smiled with pressed lips. "I hope I trained the Royal Commander well enough not to be needed. You will understand in time, which makes me think perhaps you still need me." She tapped a finger on her thigh and shook her head with a sigh. "After all these years, Ahhotep," she muttered. "Either you are a poor pupil, or I am a poor tutor."

"It is probably the latter," Ahhotep returned insult for insult.

Tetisheri smoothed her dress and stood up kohl-lined-eye-to-kohl-lined-eye with her daughter. "Watch your tongue, Royal Commander. One wrong word is all it takes for everything your family has sacrificed to be in vain."

"'*Your* family?'" Ahhotep whispered in retort. Was her mother disowning them now?

Tetisheri did not respond.

A few princes arrived, and the feast attendants seated them. The musicians began playing; murmurs and harmonious notes filled the hall while the two royal women stared each other down.

"Then I suppose I should make every word count," Ahhotep said at her mother's lack of speech and took her seat at the opposite end of the table.

All the princes arrived, and King Ahmose and his Chief Wife entered and took their seats amid silent reverence. Ahmose lifted his hands. "Eat and be merry, for we have an appointment to celebrate."

The music played again after the king's decree, and a soft chatter filled the hall. Ahhotep scanned the feast's attendees with a forced smile, gently nodding her head in appreciation to the fifteen princes who had fully supported their cause. As she finished her scan, her eyes dropped to her half-eaten meal of fish and figs, and her smile faded. It seemed a never-ending battle—a war that would not end.

She glanced to the spot where Senseneb and Sapair sat, speaking and laughing. *Poor girl*, she thought, regarding Baba's daughter. Her father was off to war in the north to maintain the border, and her brother was at Per-djed-ken, training as a Troop Commander to serve on The Wild Bull so he could teach the others how to use his improved chariot design. But without the horses, the chariots were useless.

Ahhotep had brought Senseneb into the Kap while her family was away, and it seemed she had grown too close to her youngest living son. Perhaps she would allow Sapair to marry her when they came of age, although if Ahmose perished, Sapair would need to marry one of his sisters as his Chief Wife; otherwise, the divine blood may not appear pure. Just as it was with Kasmut and Ahmose—her future grandchild from Kasmut's womb would not be pure. Even if the child was a boy, she doubted it would satisfy the nomes' perceptions of their divine crown. Ahmose needed to have children, sons, with Ahmose-Nefertari.

Ahhotep lifted a finger to her lips and eyed the spot Baba would have sat if he had been there. His breath against her lips that day in the council room made her long for him. But her mother had ensured they were never alone in the few times he had been home. Meret and Nena followed her mother's command as she was still the most tenured royal woman in the harem, and everyone there had to obey her. They would not leave her side to the point of annoyance. The only time she was truly alone was when she slept. She had thought about calling Baba to her room but knew surely there would be talk in the harem. How would she be perceived? What would her mother think?

Even when she commanded them to leave, they still lingered at a faraway distance, always within eyesight. Thus, she and Baba had only shared conversations and nothing more. But he was still a friend to her—a most cherished friend. She missed him, and her mother was the wedge that kept them apart.

A small part of her wished her mother would go on and journey west for the sole reason she could be with Baba, but that would spell disaster with Ta-Seti and perhaps a few other nomes with the perceived loss of power on the throne. And then the gossip of her with

Baba would only exacerbate the perception. It would only be that much more challenging to consolidate power.

She sighed, lost in her thoughts. Eventually, she would need to strip the princes of their power. They would need to become governors, *Nomarchs*, and report to the vizier. It would be the only way for the King to indeed be a King and prevent him from begging for their support. But how should it be done? She couldn't even fathom where to begin such a dangerous prospect.

They finished their meal, and as had been the custom, Ahhotep stood and spoke for her son as she, the Royal Commander, was his mouth.

"Thank you all for coming to our feast to celebrate this grand appointment." She paused, allowing the dancers to clear the room and the musicians to end their song. "And without further ado, the King appoints Si-Tayet, the high councilman in Prince Paser's court of Herui, for the privileged position of Viceroy of Kush. He shall report directly to the King as evidence of this most important position. Under him, five Captains of the Troop will be assigned to keep the peace in the land of *Wawat*, the home of the Kermans and Kushites."

Tetian slowly clapped. "Thank you, Royal Commander, for this much-needed and most overdue act."

Ahhotep sneered at him, and the resulting chuckle from Prince Metjen. It was then she made a decision to fight back and knew how to get what she needed from Tetian. "Because Prince Tetian of Ta-Seti required that Buhen be retaken before he supported the war effort instead of holding back the Kushites at his border city of Abu with his own wealth and soldiers, Prince Tetian has agreed to fund the Viceroy's efforts in Wawat."

Tetian's jaw fell ajar. "I did no such—"

"And since King Kamose perished in retaking Buhen to satisfy the desires of Ta-Seti before Prince Tetian gave even one deben gold or a single man for the King's army, he has graciously agreed to supply soldiers to replace the five units that will be taken from the north and stationed in Wawat."

Tetian's cheeks blossomed in a raging fire as the princes clapped for Tetian's past-due support, even those who gave little themselves. They held wide eyes that tentatively held a new consideration of Ahmose, given Tetian's generous support.

But as always, Tetian had to dissent. He had the upper hand, and he spoke, "And with this generous offering from Ta-Seti, one can assume we will now be pushing forward into the Lower?"

Ahhotep's jaw grew taut as all the princes' eyes turned toward her. "We could assume as you say; however, Toshka has again rebelled under the Kushite rebel Prince Aata. We received word this day," Ahhotep said and scanned the room. "And we must put it down to keep Ta-Seti safe from the Kushites once again unless, with the most bountiful wealth of your nome, Prince Tetian, you fund the additional Medjay required to put down the insurrection."

Tetian scoffed. "Am I not already supplying five units of men and the price of a Viceroy?"

Ahhotep lifted her chin. "It may seem like much, but it is less than what other nomes have already provided. If you do not wish to contribute to the requirements in Toshka—"

"I have provided much of Ta-Seti's reserves to this cause that your family has shown to be poor stewards of,

Royal Commander," Tetian yelled back with a pointed finger aimed at Ahhotep.

"You dare point your finger at me? I am God's Mother, Great Wife, and Royal Commander!" Ahhotep said, her bold voice bouncing off the walls of the hall.

Tetian obliged, curling his finger into his fist but again opened his mouth. "Are we to wait until the boy king is fully grown to enter the Lower? It seems you have excuse after excuse to delay an attack. Are you afraid to lose another son in this facade of unity where you keep stealing the nome's wealth? One could say you never mean to enter the Lower. Are you trying to usurp our power by making us all poor and weak? Time and time again, we come to Sedjefatawy with grand feasts and immaculate luxury. Where is our support going? To the soldiers and the war effort or to your great palace?"

Ahhotep rose from the table with both hands firmly placed on its wooden top as the murmurs among the princes frantically grew. "You will not speak ill of the throne, Prince Tetian," she growled in a roar, silencing all. "My father, husband, and son were slain for the unification of Kemet and in satisfying *your* condition to retake Buhen. If you dare bring our motivation to win this war into your petty arguments ever again, I shall have you cast out of your luxurious palace as a traitor to the throne by the very Medjay the rest of the nomes have paid for with everything they have. You see a grand feast but do not see the darkness overcome the palace when the princes are not here so that you may have light when you visit your king. You see fish before you because fish is plentiful in Waset. We have shared our food with the nomes who have asked for help, yet Ta-Seti sits in elite isolation. Ta-Seti contributes the least, yet is the richest nome of us all."

"If Ta-Seti is the richest nome, then the crown should be with Ta-Seti!" Tetian hissed.

"A selfish king would end Kemet!" Ahhotep roared back, thinking that would shut him up once and for all, but he bit back.

"And a young, stupid king will get us all burned!"

That was it; Ahhotep slammed her fist on the table. "Guards!" she called, and two guards approached Tetian. She should have done that from the beginning. "See Tetian to his boat, and make sure his nome understands his disgrace for his early return."

But Tetian shoved the guards' hands from his arms and again pointed a finger at Ahhotep and then at each prince in attendance. "You see how princes are treated when they voice a concern? Do you see now, my brothers?"

Ahhotep yelled out, "Concerns are welcome. It is when you disrespect the crown, Prince Tetian, that you are thrown out. Take him away."

The guards readjusted their grip on his arms and began pulling him out of the doorway as he still roared in defiance. "I will be in Ta-Seti if any of you decide this family is not as divine as they claim!" He ripped one guard's hand off of his arm and yanked his other arm out of the other's guard's grip. He adjusted his collar and strode out of the hall with the guards close behind.

Ahhotep calmed herself with a hot breath. Ahmose sat frozen in his chair, and Ahmose-Nefertari shrank back from the princes' stares. Tetisheri cocked her head to peer at Ahhotep.

"Princes of Kemet," she began, but Metjen of Bat stood up. His thin frame strode out with clenched fists. He looked sharply at Baufre of Meseh, who, after a moment, also stood up and strode out with a nonchalant gait. Setka and a few other princes narrowed their eyes at the royal family but sat still and waited to see what was to be said.

Ahhotep shook her head. What had she done? At least, Tetian had agreed to pay for the soldiers and Viceroy in front of everyone. He could not back out now if he wanted to save face. She licked her lip in the hot, dry day.

"Princes of Kemet," she began. "Do not be fooled by Prince Tetian's words. He desires what is not his, and is upset at the history between his family and that of the divinely appointed. The burden of Kemet's future is with us, the family of the Living Horus. You have sailed through Waset; you can see the lack of prosperity here. We are, as you, suffering and sacrificing in this war. I have urged King Ahmose to not go with his army until he has at least two sons by his sister-wives, so the divine family may continue if he shall meet the same fate as those before him." Her head drooped at the rushing violent images and the overwhelming weight in her chest, and in a moment of weakness, she muttered, "Be still my heart."

She sighed and took a deep breath before locking gazes with the long-time supporters and those who still held back their full support, speaking again. "Prince Tetian is a selfish fool who causes inner strife when there should be unity. A single man's greed swayed Princes Metjen and Baufre. Yet I feel your losses as I have also lost."

A tear escaped down her cheek. She thought the princes would sneer at her lack of control, but instead, their gazes softened. Perhaps, they saw her as genuine. So she became genuine. "As Prince Tetian said," her voice cracking, "I do not wish Ahmose to fight for fear of losing a second son. As his mother, I would do anything to protect him, but as your queen and acting defender of Kemet, I will send him off as a Warrior King, the same as the Kings before him. When he is ready and has two sons, I will send him. Not because I wish for you to become poor or powerless, but because that is what Kemet needs to rid ourselves of the Hekka Khasut. And as you have seen with your own two eyes, we are willing to sacrifice everything. Are you?" Her eyes searched each prince. "Are you?" she pleaded with urgency and a break in her voice.

Prince Paser of Herui raised his fist high in the air. "I am." Almost all the princes followed suit.

The resounding "I am" reverberated through the hall, and another tear rolled down Ahhotep's cheek as she gave one final decree, "We will be one united Kemet; this I promise you."

AFTER THE FEAST AND THE PRINCES DEPARTED TO THE GUEST apartments, Tetisheri approached Ahhotep, who was alone with her maidservants in the dining hall. Ahhotep sat and cradled her temple upon her fist as she repeatedly replayed the conversation between Tetian and herself. Where had she gone wrong?

She noticed her mother draw near and sighed, not wanting to deal with whatever her mother had in store for her.

But her mother did not grant her unspoken wish, and Tetisheri came to a halt directly in front of Ahhotep and said matter-of-factly, "You do not understand when you should close your mouth. Promising Tetian would give something of which he had not agreed? Are you mad?

You drove him to provoke you and, in the process, lost Metjen and Baufre's support."

Ahhotep sighed loudly and cracked her neck with a sharp twist. She rolled her shoulders and ran a hand over her neck to ease the growing tension abruptly caused by her mother's criticisms. "Then what would you have done when he began to insult our throne once again? Stay silent as you did? Let the dissenter dissent and sway more away from us? You told me I had to consolidate power; well, that is what I am doing. It is a command, not a request. I threw Tetian out of the feast for his disrespect. You would have done the same."

Tetisheri clasped her hands over her belly. "If I were in your place, Tetian would not have opened his mouth."

"Yes, Mother, because you are born from Ta-Seti blood!" Ahhotep blurted out.

Tetisheri shuffled back. Her eyes blinked as a rageful grimace grew on her lips. "Who told you that, child?" she spat.

Ahhotep's hands curled into fists as she stood up from the table. "I am not a child!" Sometimes she wanted to slap that old, weathered face across the cheek.

Tetisheri resumed her regal stance: shoulders straight, head up, stone countenance. "I will not repeat my question."

Ahhotep's nostrils flared, but she obliged the dominant woman. "Vizier Tetinefer told me years ago when Ahmose took the crown. Why did you never tell me you were born in Ta-Seti?"

Tetisheri coolly shrugged a shoulder and pursed her lips. "It was not relevant. I became a citizen of Waset when your father chose to marry me and make me his Chief Wife."

Ahhotep threw her hands in the air. "Not relevant?!"

Her scream echoed off the mudbrick inner room. "Not relevant?!" she repeated in an equally loud yell.

"Yes, that is what I said. Is your mind empty, child?" Tetisheri lifted her eyes in annoyance.

Ahhotep growled. Her mother disgusted her. "You are—I can't—" The words would not come out of her clenched teeth. She took a deep breath and relaxed her jaw. "It has every relevancy, Mother. Tetian obeys you because you were born in his nome. He will never obey us; he will never stop dissenting."

"Well," Tetisheri said. "Show him the crown rightfully belongs in Waset *if* your family is worthy of it. So act like you are worthy of the crown. Earn your respect." Tetisheri gestured toward the walls of the room depicting Ahhotep's grandfather, father, and late husband in all their exaggerated glory.

"We are worthy. It is not just my family. It is *your* family as well. We have lost more than any other nome. Our king fights with his soldiers to show he is worthy of victory—"

"Yet, two kings have been slain by the enemy. It does not appear so worthy, especially to Tetian."

Ahhotep felt the rising heat roil within her chest. "How dare you." Her fingernails dug into the palms of her hand. How could she say such things about her own blood? Her anger spewed out of her mouth. "You had it easy, Mother. You never *earned* respect. It was freely given to you—"

The resulting slap across Ahhotep's cheek surprised her into silence while her mother pointed a finger in her face.

"I earned every *bit* of respect, and you, especially you, will never disrespect me again."

Tetisheri swiftly left without another word, but

Ahhotep, fueled by the angry conversation, yelled after her for the last word.

"Or what, *Mother*?"

But Tetisheri continued walking out without acknowledging her. She felt foolish at screaming into an empty hall, but the rage in her chest would not let her mother leave without finishing what they had started. She took off after her. Her breath came out as a growl and her sight blurred from the heat in her cheeks as she caught up to the older woman. She grabbed her mother's shoulder and spun her around to face her.

"I was talking to you, Great Wife Tetisheri. As Great Wife, God's Mother, *and* Royal Commander, you will wait until I dismiss you, you who are God's Mother and Great Wife alone." Her lip quivered and spittle formed in the corners of her mouth. Never had she spoken in such a way to her mother, and her heart beat hard against her chest and in her ears. Her hands shook from rage.

"Fine, Royal Commander, what is it you wish to say?" Tetisheri sneered.

"You tell me not to disrespect you, but you disrespect my children and me. I will not have it. I will strip you of your title if you so do it again."

Tetisheri scoffed with a chuckle. "You? You are not King. You should learn your place, *Daughter*. For it is I who will disown you. You will never be remembered if you do not deserve the space in the people's thoughts and memories." Tetisheri took a step closer and pressed in. "If you cannot prove your line is worthy of the divine appointment, then perhaps the crown should be with Tetian."

"You speak of treason," Ahhotep whispered back through clenched teeth.

"I speak the truth. Prove it to me. And better yet,

prove it to them." Tetisheri shoved a finger in the direction of the Hekka Khasut. "Prove it to Tetian, Metjen, Baufre, and the rest. Gain their support, all of it, and consolidate the Upper."

Ahhotep should have stayed quiet and let her mother have the last word, but she couldn't do it. "It is easier to prove when you come from the nome that is the most dissenting and disturber of the unity."

"No," Tetisheri said, shaking her head. "It was only harder, my child. To refuse them the crown when your father and your son perished. Do not make me look the fool. Your great-grandfather claimed he was the divine king of the true Kemet. Time would tell, and so far, it seems maybe he was wrong."

"It only seems that way because you allow Tetian to stir up strife with his greed and entitlement to what is ours. With his exaggerations of all our failures and his false accusations of embezzlement and fraud. Even now, Metjen and the dim Baufre are against us."

"Then *earn* their fear and their support—all the princes. Win a victory without losing a King in the process. Establish your dominance. Earn your place in the records, Royal Commander." She sighed and shook her head. "Why is Tetian dissenting? Your husband failed to exploit anything Tetian sent—wasted it. It grew dissent. Under your son's reign, the Kushites came to Abu. Even with the progress made under you and Ahmose, he does not see the poor excuse we live in at the palace. You offered up his riches without his permission in front of everyone. You took away his power. It is no wonder he accused you of fraud, and embezzlement, and conspiracy to usurp the princes."

Ahhotep swallowed the lump in her throat. "We did not have the funds or the men to staff the Viceroy. If I asked Tetian, he would have refused just as he has done all the other times. What good is a Viceroy without an army to support him? It was the only way to ensure his funding and supply of men."

Tetisheri narrowed her eyes at her. "You say I am a poor tutor, but it seems pride is in your way of learning and executing well." She threw her nose in the air before Ahhotep could refute her. "And, Ahhotep, you will never force your hand upon me, *ever* again. You will know *your* place, *Daughter*."

Ahhotep held her breath, afraid of what would come out. Hot tears burned the back of her eyes as her mother's bountifully false braided hair hit her in the face as her mother spun around and left, dismissing herself. Once again, her mother would take the last word. Tetisheri's shadow crawled away as the Great Wife fell out of earshot.

"You have no heart, Mother," Ahhotep muttered as a few tears slipped from their cage behind her eyes. "But I will rise up and usher in a new era for *my* family, and I shall do it with my heart intact."

20

A TIME OF LOVE | AHHOTEP

SEDJEFATAWY, 1566 BC

Two months passed, and the Bedu horse trainers had come with the caravan across the Dashret. A portion of the army was sent to Per-djed-ken to learn the art of horse training and how to use the horses with Ahmose-Ebana's improved chariot design. And the royal family had commissioned Si-Tayet, the new Viceroy of Kush, to keep an eye on Tetian, for the prince would not stay silent.

But Ahhotep had not spoken more than was required to her mother. Tetisheri's words had burned the last of Ahhotep's admiration for the woman. The grating repetition of their conversation made sleep elusive.

One morning, Ahhotep rose before Re's sun barge tipped over the horizon and, after bathing and dressing, made her way to the palace's central courtyard with lotus blossoms in hand. Meret and Nena strolled beside her.

The towering statues of Tao and Kamose glimmered in the waning moonlight. She stopped in front of Tao's image and bowed her head but continued to walk until she stood in front of Kamose's. She placed the blossoms at the statue's stone base.

"Please take this offering, Kamose, my son. Imbue this image so I may speak to you," she prayed.

Her locked knees made her sway. Meret caught her arm, and Nena balanced a hand on her waist. But Ahhotep fell to her knees and pushed them off of her.

"Leave me," she told them and lowered her head to smell the closed blossoms, yet to reopen. "If you love me, please leave me to myself this hour," she pleaded.

Their soft footsteps faded in the night. She peered over her shoulder and scanned the perimeter. Alone. A sigh of relief escaped her, but simultaneously, she realized how alone she was. Her sisters worked in the economic center. Her eldest child no longer wanted to be a part of the royal family. Half of her children were in the Field of Reeds. Her husband was slain. Her mother . . . Oh, her mother.

She sneered at the thought of the unappeasable old woman. She muttered in mockery of Tetisheri's words that had stayed with her since the feast, *"Only if you are worthy of it."* She shut her eyes and curled her hands into a fist. "We are your blood kinsmen, Mother. Your husband, son, and grandson have all been slain for it. How are we not worthy? Why do you still question me?"

She lifted her face to Kamose's stone countenance. The dipping moon in the western sky cast shadows over the perfectly sculpted nose.

"My son, Given Life, are you here?"

Silence. Nothing. No wind. No breeze. No buzz of a fly.

"Then you are not," she said and wrapped herself in her arms. "But if your ka is near here, I want you to know how much I miss you. Curse the Kushite that threw that spear a thousand lifetimes in Duat with the serpent Apep." She placed her hand on the statue's foot and shut her eyes tight. His grin appeared in memory. Her mind stitched time together in a tapestry of moments. First, Kamose as a child, then as a man, then as he held his daughter and embraced his chief wife, and lastly, as he came to greet her after departing The Wild Bull. The silver diadem flashed in the sun before her recollection faded to black. No tears fell, but her hollow chest bled from pain.

"I wish you were here," she whispered and lowered her nose to the blossoms. They did not smell as sweet as they did before.

She stood up with shoulders rolled forward and a drooping head. "Four years," she said in a muted tone. She cast her gaze toward Tao's image. "Nine years; it does not seem so."

Her chest expanded to draw in the crisp pre-dawn air. She straightened herself, lifted her head, and smoothed her dress and collar as she turned around.

A shadow of a large man leaned against a pillar near the council room's entrance. His head was bowed, but the moonlight gave away the whites of his eyes.

"Who are you?" She asked. "Show yourself."

"Forgive my intrusion, Royal Commander." The familiar voice was as soothing as the cooled sunless air.

"Admiral," she acknowledged him looking around for Meret and Nena. They were nowhere to be seen.

He stepped out into the open courtyard. Her heart flickered with life at seeing his muscular build and dark silkened skin glisten in the lunar light. It had been a year since she had seen him, and she wondered if he had found someone else to love, although she never questioned if his friendship would endure.

He returned the day prior from the north, but she had not been in the throne room with Ahmose to receive him. She would have made every effort to be there if she had known he was coming. "What brings you to Sedjefatawy at this hour?"

His eyes lifted to meet hers. "I came early for King Ahmose's council meeting. I could not sleep. Ahmose-Ebana sleeps at Per-djed-ken, and Senseneb has found a friend in the royal daughter Mosi and prince Sapair. She sleeps in the Kap with them." He shrugged with a twist of his head toward the royal harem. "It was lonely in the villa."

Lonely. It was such a wonder how a single word could elicit the burn of tears in her eyes.

He drew near to her only to see their glisten. "If my words hurt you in any way—"

She shook her head. "No," she said and looked up at him. "I am glad you are unharmed, my friend, and able to return to us." He stepped closer, so his susinum scent filled her senses. "If I had known you were coming home yesterday, I would have been in the throne room to receive you," she said, rambling to keep her mind preoccupied.

He grinned and placed the back of his fingers against her cheek in a soft brush. "I missed you, Ahhotep," he whispered.

She turned into his touch and released a sigh of relief. He had not forgotten her or given up hope that maybe one day they might be able to love each other. "As I you, Baba," she whispered and kissed the palm of his hand.

He drew her close to him and wrapped his fingers around her nape as the dawn light streaked purple and blue across the sky. He lowered his forehead to hers, but the sound of footsteps made him lean back and step away from her.

"It is not meant to be this time," he said in a hushed tone.

"I doubt it will ever be, Baba," she whispered. Her brow furrowed, and her gaze fell, downcast. Alone. Always alone, and yet never alone as Meret and Nena rounded the corridor, assumedly having taken a short walk to leave the queen to open the prior king's mouth in solitude. But at their sights of the Admiral, they rushed to Ahhotep's side.

He pressed his lips together and turned sideways in a bow and an extended arm toward the council room. "May I escort you, Royal Commander?" he asked.

Ahhotep nodded, and she walked past him, unable to say anything now that there were peering eyes and ears.

But Baba did. "I love when the dawn lights up the sky," he said, peering up at the growing pink amid the blue. She stopped to admire the dawn with him.

Ever since she married Tao and became his chief wife, she had always dreaded the dawn. It symbolized another day to err, another day to fail. But as she stood next to Baba, her gaze drifted to him as he spoke.

"Even though those I love are not in my arms," he said, glancing at her. "Re's sun barge will light up the sky every morning in an eternal victory over Apep, just as my love for those I cannot be with will never surrender or lose hope that one day I will hold them again."

She didn't know what to say with Meret and Nena standing behind her. She wished to wrap her arms around his neck, but she stood as still as her son's statue.

"How lucky your children are to know such love," she finally said with sorrow buried in her words.

"And yours, as well, Royal Commander," he

whispered. He stepped toward the council room, but she remained to look at the growing dawn. It would have a new meaning for her now, and a sad smile arose on her lips. Baba stopped and waited for her until she sighed and entered the council room to hear Baba's report of dealings in the north.

21

A TIME OF DESIRE | AHHOTEP

SEDJEFATAWY, 1566 BC

That night, after the sunlight disappeared from the dusk and the palace settled into the quiet, Baba's words about her children gnawed at her heart.

Ahhotep sat on the edge of her bed. Her natural hair was cleaned, brushed, and softly braided. Her makeup had been washed off, and kohl applied to her fresh face, unmarred by the day's sweat. The delicate linen dress she had worn from the harem's bath to her room draped over her shoulders, but she could not bring herself to undress and sleep. Usually, she had felt beautiful in her natural state before laying down in bed, but that night, she felt vulnerable and wretched, as dirty as the water that had washed away the day's grime.

"How lucky your children are to know such love," she whispered, repeating her comment to Baba that morning.

Meret and Nena had gone to sleep for the evening, and she was left alone in her Great Wife's room. Only guards at the entrance to the royal family's sleeping quarters in the harem remained.

The small room was bare, save for a bed and a chest, but it was hers and hers alone. The Chief Wife of the King and the Kings prior were given a separate room for their privacy, and Ahhotep loved it but hated it. It was a prison —the only place she could be alone and out of sight from peering eyes. Yet cut off from the rest of her family. What if she slept in the room with her daughters? Would Tep have asked to leave the royal family? Would Hentempet have been better prepared to serve as Kamose's Chief Wife instead of her sister? Would Binpu have known her love before he journeyed west?

She cradled her tear-filled face in her hands and leaned her elbows on her knees. What was done was done—she could not change the past—but the questions repeated in her mind in a pang of unrelenting guilt that chipped away at her resolve to stay within the confines of her room.

"Poor Tep," she whispered as she thought of Tetisheri and her constant stream of disappointment and demeaning remarks aimed at the poor girl until, finally, Tep surrendered.

Ahhotep blinked away the rest of her tears. "Does my mother cry for us in her room, or does she sleep soundly?" she muttered and wiped her cheeks with the backs of her hands.

Ahhotep loved her children as she hoped her mother had loved her, Tao, and her sisters. But even as she gave up Kamose and Tep, they were always second to Kemet. The grinding of her teeth hurt her ears as the horrid realization came to light. Kemet would always be first, just as it was first to her mother. It was the duty of God's Mother. The closed room's door stared back at her as she shook her head.

"I will not cut myself off from my children as my

mother has done to me," she muttered. Never would she yell at her children, telling them they were not worthy of their divine appointment. She would listen when they had fears and insecurities instead of demeaning them with cruel words. Even if she had to give up her sons for a unified Kemet, they would know her love.

She stood with a clear mind and a light heart, grabbed her heavy cloak, and opened the door to her room. The moonlight fell into the harem's still courtyard as she strolled to the rooms of the royal children.

She stopped on the way to stand in front of her mother's door. *Why had she never told me she was from Ta-Seti?* she thought. *That is why Tetian respects her and why she does not rebuke him anymore, leaving me to do it. What if Mother believes we are all failures and will give the throne to her homeland nome? What if she* . . . Her thoughts faded.

"No mother could ever do that against her own blood," she whispered. Yet as she stood outside her mother's room for a long while, she recalled every disappointed look, remark, sigh, and scoff.

Ahhotep closed her eyes and reassured herself. "She would not do that. She only wants what is best for Kemet, which is why she urges me to do better." Her eyes snapped open, and she continued toward the royal children's rooms. "And I will be better. Better than her. I will be a good Mother."

The night's cool breeze chilled her arms as it coursed along the corridor after her, and she pulled the cloak tighter around her body. She peered into the first room where Tumerisy and Sapair slept alongside her niece Mosi and Baba's daughter, Senseneb. As they were all under thirteen years of age but over six, they were not considered children but also not yet adults.

She smiled at Senseneb, but soon a slight sorrow

filled her. Baba was home, but she did not want to sleep in her family's villa. *Poor Baba*, she thought. *Alone in his home as well.*

She stepped inside, stooped down, and kissed Tumerisy's forehead. The small nine-year-old girl was thin like Binpu and frail like Sitkamose. Ahhotep pressed her hand over her daughter's. Prayers to the god Heh for a long life for all her children and grandchildren came rushing upon her, but it seemed her prayers were not enough. Tumerisy had beaten the odds thus far, but it seemed she would go the way of Sitkamose, for she slept just as much.

Ahhotep kneeled beside the cots as she watched her children sleep. She ran a hand over Sapair's sidelock and kissed his otherwise bald head. He stirred in his sleep at her touch, and his face turned toward the moonlight falling into the room from the light hole in the ceiling. She didn't even know her son. He had grown so much. She had always been away at Per-djed-ken or in the throne room. As if sensing her stare, his eyes flickered open, and he shuffled back, trying to get away from the stranger in the room.

"Shhh, shhh," Ahhotep crooned. "It is your mother," she said.

Sapair rubbed his eyes as the fright left him, and his half-sleep returned. "Why are you here?" he asked with a thick tongue.

"I wanted to see you," she whispered.

A timid smile spread across his face. "You are a good Mother," he said with a yawn, laid his head back down, and fell asleep again.

Ahhotep's eyes welled with tears. *I do so little to be called a good mother,* she thought as she placed one last lingering kiss on her child's forehead. She certainly did not feel like a good mother. Her steps were slow as she left her children's room with her hands folded behind her back. She walked past their servants' rooms until she came upon the room where the royal daughters slept.

She peered in and saw dried tears glistening on Tep's cheeks. Her headrest lay mangled beside her as she slept curled on her side. Nebetta and Hentempet lightly snored in their beds—their necks perfectly elevated in the headrest's cushioned cradle. Ahhotep tiptoed inside and lightly stroked the side of Tep's face and then her brow, causing Tep to stir in her sleep. But a peaceful beam overcame Tep's face in the moonlight falling through the light hole.

"My firstborn," Ahhotep crooned with tears in her eyes. "I am so sorry," she whispered. "You have lost your husband and your child—your only child. I wish you happiness and peace in this life, my daughter. Know I will always love you." She stooped to press her lips to Tep's forehead.

With that kiss, Tep unfurled and stretched out on her bed. She murmured in her sleep, "I know, Mother."

Ahhotep paused, thinking Tep was awake from her speech, but the heavy rhythmic breathing made her think otherwise. "Tep," she whispered.

No response.

Perhaps it was Bes calling to Tep in a dream on her behalf. Or perhaps, Tep wanted to be alone just as she had requested the night Sitkamose began her journey west.

Either way, Ahhotep sighed, knowing she had done her best for Tep—letting her leave her position and keep her from Tetisheri's judgment. One day, Tep would understand, or so Ahhotep hoped. She backed out of the room in silence and then continued her stroll to the Chief Wife's room, where Ahmose-Nefertari slept.

Ahhotep gave a single nod at the guards on either side of the door, and they let her enter without a word.

She stood beside her daughter's bed, seeing a furrowed brow etched into Ahmose-Nefertari's beautiful face.

"Why are you hesitant to lead, my daughter? You are capable of great things. I wish you could see yourself as I see you." Ahhotep brushed her daughter's fingers. "You gave my children the love I could not. A true mother for whom I pray to Isis, Hathor, and Tawaret, bless your womb and give you as many children as you desire."

Ahmose-Nefertari stirred in her sleep, but her brow softened. Ahhotep took it as a sign her daughter would sleep better that night and left. She exited the harem—gaining one of the harem's guards as a silent escort. They passed the statues of Kamose and Tao in the courtyard on the way to the King's room. She wished she could hold each again in a lasting embrace. Her heart ached for them, but they were one with Re now.

As she passed, her gaze fell to her feet, walking to Ahmose's room. The guards again let her pass without a word, and she opened the door to find Ahmose sitting on his bed with knees tucked under his chin, staring at the chair in his room. A small candle's flame flickered on the chest. He shot up from his bed at the sight of her.

"Mother," he said with wide eyes. "Is all well?"

Ahhotep pressed her lips into a smile and softly nodded. "Sit, Ahmose. It seems we both cannot sleep."

He sat back down with his legs over the side of the bed, and Ahhotep came and sat next to him. Her usually straight back, slumped, and her head drooped. "Why are you awake at this hour, Ahmose?" she asked in a hushed voice.

He shrugged and leaned over—his elbows pressed into his thighs. His hands ran over his nape.

Ahhotep pressed at his silence. "Surely, there is a reason."

Ahmose's cheeks turned pink in the dim candlelight when he glanced up at her. "You will think me a child, Mother."

Ahhotep rubbed his back. "We are all children in some ways," she said and tilted her head as if trying to coax it out of him.

Ahmose dropped his head. "I don't like to be alone." He sat up and rubbed the sides of his arms.

The suggestion to call one of his wives to his room came to the tip of her tongue, but she held back. Ahmose needed to be heard.

"I am almost a man, but someone has slept by my side every night. I wish for Sitkamose to be returned to me, or at least to sleep in my brother's room as we did before Kamose . . . " His voice trailed off. He stood up and paced in front of her.

"Speak your mind, Son," Ahhotep said and folded her hands in her lap. "I will not think less of you."

He stopped and squared his shoulders to her. "I never wanted to be King," he said and rubbed his forearm across his nose. "I wish Kamose were here as I know you wish him here and Grandmother too. And all the princes."

He opened his palms and showed them to his mother. Open sores and blisters riddled them. The honey and castor oil rubbed into the wounds as a healing ointment shined in the candlelight. Ahhotep wanted to take his hands and kiss them as she would have done if he were a child, but she kept still.

"Ketti works me harder than any other. Says I will not be killed in battles like my brother and father," Ahmose said and pulled his hands back from Ahhotep's sight. "I am afraid to go to war, yet I want to be a king you and the princes are proud of." He gnashed his teeth. "I do not want to be placed in a tomb as plain as Kamose's; I do not want to be burned as a traitor to King Apepi. Yet I do not want to cower in this room alone." He rubbed his knuckles over his chest as if to soothe his heartache. "I will never be a King as my brother. He had such a voice of reason and a head of strategy, and I have that of a boy's," he said. "Just as Tetian said," he muttered. He ground his fingers into his palms, and his gaze drifted to his hands. "I cannot do this, Mother."

Ahhotep sighed and stood. She placed her hands on his shoulders. "Look at me, Ahmose."

He obeyed after a delay. Tears were brimming in his eyes.

"You are fourteen years old. You have done so much since Kamose left us, and you will do much more. Tetian is a selfish, jealous prince, and you should not listen to him."

"But Mother, I cannot please you. And Grandmother," he shook his head, "I will never please her. You are my voice; you are my words. How am I to ever be more than what I am today?"

Ahhotep pursed her lips, remembering those same feelings as her mother scolded her, corrected her, and perfected her. Tears welled in her eyes. She would not do that to her children. Not anymore.

"Then find your own voice, Ahmose. You are the king of your life, and you are the king of Kemet. Your destiny is there for the taking." She caressed his cheek and held his gaze. "I have acted out of fear of losing you too. If I could control you and your armies, I thought you could stay with me and be safe. But I see now that I am only crippling you. And when you do go to war, I will have made it more likely you will be brought home like your brother."

Her breath hitched, and tears escaped down both cheeks.

"You were so young, Ahmose; I did not know what else to do but only what my mother taught me. Even now, you are young for the crown. Such a heavy burden."

She pulled his forehead to her lips, and he lifted his head to face her. "There are so many variables to consider," she said. "And I will let you consider them. I will be there to advise you, as will be Ahmose-Nefertari. Find your voice, Ahmose. I know an uncertain future can make us afraid but remember you are divinely appointed, and the gods will care for you if you perform the King's duty and defend Kemet." She cupped his face. "It was your father's destiny to begin this war to unite our lands and Kamose's destiny to retake Buhen and gain support from most of the nomes. And perhaps it is your destiny to end this war once and for all."

She kissed his nose like she did when he was a child.

He took a deep breath and hugged her with a strength she did not know he had, but she paused in his embrace, cherishing the moment. When he released her, he smiled and nodded. "Thank you, Mother. I shall sleep better this night."

She tilted her head. "Maybe you would sleep the best alongside Sapair."

His brow knitted. "Grandmother would not have—"

"I will deal with your grandmother." She patted his

cheek. "Now go," she whispered and glanced at the closed door.

"I love you," he said, throwing his arms around her. She buried her nose in his neck and enfolded him in her arms.

"As I love you, my son."

He left shortly after, and his guards went with him. The door was left open, and the harem guard stood sentinel across the corridor.

She sat in the king's room alone and remembered sleeping alongside Tao in the same bed on which she sat. "This room has seen far too many kings in too many short years," she muttered.

Her fingers brushed the woven linen of the bed. At the touch, she thought not of Tao but of Baba's strong silhouette that morning and the heat of his breath on her lips so many years ago. She had missed being loved, being held, being kissed. Seeing Baba when he was home but unable to do anything more than have a conversation tugged at her heart. But there had been longing in his eyes and his almost kiss that morning. There was more love, comfort, and understanding in his countenance than there had ever been with Tao.

She ran her thumb over her fingernails in thought until she called out to the harem guard. "Have a messenger go to Admiral Baba at once in his villa. He is to meet the Royal Commander in the council room immediately."

"As you command," he said with a nod and carried out the order. She waited until he returned, and they made their way to the council room. A servant, half-asleep, brought an oil lamp to the room and set it on the table in front of Ahhotep.

Its small clay base disappeared into the room's

darkness while the flame lit up the lotus blossoms etched into its lid. The servant sat a bronze doubter to extinguish the flame when they were finished in the council room to reserve the oil.

Little time passed until Baba's familiar voice called out to her, "You summoned me, Royal Commander." His built frame shadowed the doorway, but the lamp's light lit up his face and jeweled Admiral's collar. His cloak was tied at the neck.

"Thank you for coming in the middle of Apep's night."

"There is no need to thank me. The Royal Commander calls, and I am honored to answer," he said —his voice unwavering professionalism.

"Admiral, sleep is elusive," she said. "And God's Mother needs counsel."

He bowed and sat next to her, where her mother usually sat. "What is required of me?"

A shuffling of the harem guard's feet came from the doorway. Ahhotep sighed, but an idea struck her. She could be alone with Baba.

"Guard," she called out, and the guard stood at attention in the doorway. "You will leave us to speak in privacy."

"Great Wife," the guard said, his eyes darted to Baba sitting where he should not be sitting. "You want me to leave you *alone* with the Admiral?"

"Surely, you trust the Admiral?"

"Yes, Great Wi—"

"And there is now only one guard at the harem's entrance where all the royal women and children sleep, including the King?"

"Yes, Great Wife," the guard said with eyes downcast.

"Then retake your post. I will return when I have

spoken with the Admiral and heeded his advice on why I cannot sleep at this hour."

The guard gave a curt nod of his head. "As you command, Great Wife," he said.

Ahhotep lifted her hand to dismiss him, and he spun on his heels. When they were alone, Ahhotep closed the door, engulfing the room in darkness, save for the light of the small oil lamp.

Baba remained seated as she drew near to him. She leaned her hip against the table and crossed her arms over her chest.

"Baba, I truly need your counsel, for I fear I am failing," she whispered.

"You are not failing, Ahhotep," Baba said and rubbed her arm.

"My son told me I was a good mother for checking on him during the night when I had never done it before." She rubbed her forehead with her thumb and forefinger. "And my mother does not believe us to be worthy of the crown, even after everything we have lost. I confronted her about her Ta-Seti origins; all she could tell me was to prove our appointment." She shook her head. They were alone for the first time, truly alone, yet she only wanted someone to help her carry her burden.

"I see your tears," he said, standing up in front of her.

She wiped her cheek, and it was wet. "These accursed tears," she muttered. "God's Mother is strong and demands respect." She wiped another tear away. "God's Mother does not cry," she repeated her mother's constant scolding in mimicry.

"Then do not be God's Mother this night," Baba whispered and lowered his forehead to hers.

"I want what is ours. What is Kemet's. But I do not want the cost of it. I have not told Ahmose or Ahmose-

Nefertari about their grandmother, for I fear it would drive them away. They would be as Tep." She hugged her arms around herself.

"Then do not tell them," he crooned, his dark eyes gazing into hers. The lamp light was lost in them.

"I wish Tetian would stop dividing us. I wish my mother would hear me, see me. I want Kamose. I want Binpu and Sitkamose." Small tremors took over her body.

At Kamose's name, Baba shrunk and dropped his head.

Ahhotep caressed his cheek, still seeing the guilt in his eyes. "I do not blame you for Kamose, Baba."

His lips thinned. "I have always blamed myself." He brought her hand to his lips and kissed her fingers. His tear splashed against her skin. Her heart tore at his confession. All these years, he had lived with thinking he was to blame.

"There is no blame to be made. If Kamose had been like the coward king in Hut-Waret, we may never have retaken Buhen and gained the full support of fifteen nomes. I only do not wish Ahmose the same fate. I want the head of the Hekka Khasut King and that of the Kushite leader on stakes in front of the palace." Her lip quivered as her tears now freely ran down her cheeks.

He wiped under her eyes with his thumbs.

"No one has said King Ahmose shall be slain."

She squeezed his hands that cupped her face. His eyes held hers. An optimistic comfort lived there; he would not lie to her. For a fleeting moment, she realized the assumptions she was making. Ahmose could very well live, but the thought of his demise couldn't be ignored.

"If he perishes, then maybe my mother was right,

and my great-grandfather's claim of being divinely appointed was false."

Baba pressed his forehead to hers, once more. "Never say such things," he sighed. "As much as I respect the Great Wife Tetisheri, there are aspects of life she does not understand."

She closed her eyes; she was not the only one who felt that way about her mother. How could this man speak her thoughts? How could he read her so well?

He kissed her cheek and whispered in her ear, "I promise you, splendor will be returned to Kemet, and you shall not lose another son, not while I command Pharaoh's Fleet, not while Pennekhbet commands his army. I promise you, Ahhotep."

"Do not make promises you cannot keep," she said and leaned upon his collar. The beads pressed into her flesh, causing her to wince and pull away.

He smiled with a sorrowful grin. "Yet, I have already made it." He slipped the knot from his collar and set it on the table as quietly as he could, and he pulled her onto his bare chest. Her cheek rested on his sternum, and he enveloped her in his arms. She savored his embrace and the warmth it brought to her body and her heart. All these years, she had prayed to be held again, and here she was in Baba's strong arms, the goddess Bastet having granted her secret plea.

"You are a true friend to the crown," she whispered, reaching her arms around his waist and pulling him closer.

"Only a friend?" he asked while his fingers stroked her back.

No, she wanted to say, but she was the Great Wife of Seqenenre Tao. She pressed her palms against the skin of his back and listened to his steady heartbeat, cherishing each moment, knowing they could never be. She should be thankful Bastet allowed her his embrace, his comfort, in her time of distress once again.

But she wanted more. If she allowed him, would it still be against the law for him to touch royal flesh? She didn't know. Her mother had kept him from punishment the first time. What would she do if she saw them right then—arms wrapped around each other, hands underneath cloaks? She doubted Great Wife Tetisheri would grant a second pardon. Ahhotep could order servants and guards to silence, couldn't she? Or would they tell the superior wife? She sighed, knowing she could not order Tetisheri to do anything. Her brow furrowed as she placed a kiss on Baba's chest. She had to give him up. She had to be content with this last embrace. She couldn't ask him to put himself in danger of prison or execution.

"My mother will never let us be together." She lifted her head to look him full in the face, but selfishly kept her arms around him. "I want you to find someone else to love you, a woman who can be a good mother to your children and be home when you return from war. I will never be in your bed, and you will never be in mine."

Baba leaned in where their lips almost touched. "Yet the Great Wife Tetisheri sleeps, and we are alone."

Her breath hitched as she imagined pulling on his nape and kissing his full lips. But she restrained and spoke in between shallow breaths. "It may just be this one time. Guards will speak to my mother, and she will know by the morning that we were alone together. She will keep us apart. You may be punished or imprisoned."

Baba tilted his head, keeping their brows together. "Do you not love me as I love you, Ahhotep?" His eyes, soft, were locked with hers.

227

"I do," she whispered in return.

He pushed a stray lock of hair that had fallen loose from her braid behind her ear.

"Then I do not care what the Great Wife thinks of me or us. If she punishes me for breaking her law, then so be it."

He was willing to sacrifice everything for her, and so, she would for him too. She would be saved from punishment, but she would be ostracized, ridiculed, and left powerless in the throne room. But her daughter was capable of leading. Her mother would probably prefer it that way. The fact was Ahhotep had given him her love. Bastet knew her secret. Bastet was sanctioning him for her, or so she hoped. She said a silent prayer to the goddess that if their union was wrong in the eyes of the gods, to send someone to intervene before they went further—a guard, a servant, anyone.

"You could be executed, Baba," she said again. "I could not bear living the rest of my life knowing I was the cause of your dishonorable death."

Without hesitation, he cupped her cheek. "You would bear nothing, for it would be my decision and my action that brought about my deserved punishment for even being with you as I am right now." His fingers smoothed her cheek and down her jaw before grasping her chin. "I know what I am doing, and I know the consequences of my actions should anyone come forward with proof or witness."

Her gaze dropped to his mouth and returned to his eyes. She waited for the sound of footsteps to draw near, but none came.

He spoke once again. "And if your mother does not seek punishment because of my role in the war, but succeeds in keeping you from me, I will still hold you in my heart forever." His whispers fluttered against her lips, and her heart fluttered in anticipation. She smoothed her hands up his chiseled stomach and chest and grasped the edges of his cloak, pulling him closer—his chest to hers, her belly to his.

"And I will hold you in mine," she whispered back.

His lips pressed softly against hers, and the touch's tingle grew in desire and want. His hand wrapped around her nape while the other ran the length of her back. The world blurred from memory as she pushed everything away. This one night, she would take for herself and for Baba. This one night, she would not be God's Mother, or Great Wife, or Royal Commander. She would simply be Ahhotep—a mother, a widow, a lover.

His lips grazed her arched neck while he pushed the fine fabric from her shoulders. No one came to intervene, and a soft smile of peace arose from her mouth. His cloak fell to the floor as the oil lamp's flame flickered and went out, casting the council room into darkness.

22

A TIME OF
ACCUSATION |
AHHOTEP
SEDJEFATAWY, 1566 BC

When the morning light streaked through the crack in the door, Ahhotep stirred in her sleep with a fresh beam on her face. The wool blanket spread over her body and kept her body's heat from escaping. The birds' tweeting sounded off in the distance. The morning only lacked Baba, who she wished was beside her. Meret and Nena had come in and tried to wake her when the dawn came, but she had told them she would rise when she was ready to rise. Sleep had retaken her after that. As she stared at the light streaming into her room from the wall vent, she wondered how long she had been asleep and if the night prior had been a dream. Her smile faded. Could it have only been a dream?

She sat up and stretched, feeling the morning in her mouth. But there was a hint of cinnamon and myrrh there, making her grin. Perhaps it was not a dream.

The door to her room swung open, popping the wall behind it with a loud thud. Tetisheri stood in the doorway, yelling at her. "Why did I wake to find Ahmose in the Kap, a guard whispering of you and the Admiral alone together, Meret and Nena sitting outside your room, and you, still in bed when you are supposed to be in the throne room with your son and daughter?!"

Ahhotep sighed. Her peaceful morning was now gone. She swung her legs off the bed and stood up. While her mother stood tapping a foot, waiting for her to speak, she grabbed her clothes and royal vulture headdress.

"Meret, Nena," Ahhotep called past her mother. "Prepare my bath."

She saw them hurry off toward the royal harem's bath over Tetisheri's shoulder. Then she found her mother's eyes.

"I could not sleep last night, nor could Ahmose," she said as she tied her cloak around her neck. "I allowed Ahmose to sleep alongside his brother because it was the right action to take. I sought counsel with Admiral Baba to discuss the other reasons why I could not sleep." She pushed past her mother and followed after Meret and Nena.

Tetisheri kept in stride with her along the corridor. "Alone?"

"Mother, I did not want the whole palace staff to know why I could not sleep."

Tetisheri scoffed. "They *know*, Ahhotep," she said with a gag of contempt. "And in Tao's council room? Of all places?"

"They know nothing," she said and entered the royal harem's bath. "I only needed to speak to him without prying ears or eyes."

She undressed and knelt on the stone bathing slab as Meret and Nena poured the water over her. She rinsed her mouth under the cold glare of her mother and spat the water out before she stood. Meret and Nena dried and dressed her while Ahhotep and Tetisheri stared at each other in silence.

The maidservants lined her eyes with kohl and applied blue pigments to her eyelids. Ahhotep remained unbothered, but Tetisheri's lip curled.

"Are you going to accompany me to the throne room?" Ahhotep finally asked, knowing her mother would only stay if she had more to say to her. Otherwise, she would leave and tend to the duties of the harem.

"Yes," she said. "Since you are not capable of—"

"Yes, yes," Ahhotep interrupted. "I am not capable of anything. I am not worthy. Those were your words, were they not?"

Tetisheri narrowed her eyes at her and clasped her hands behind her back. She stood a little taller and lifted her head. "Meret, Nena, leave."

The bathroom cleared.

"You brought a man into your bed, Ahhotep, you who are the Great Wife of King Seqenenre Tao." Disgust filled her eyes, and her nostrils flared as Tetisheri cast her gaze down to Ahhotep from her high pedestal of inflated righteousness.

"As you could see, my bed was clear of any man." Ahhotep took the same stance as her mother. No longer would she cower in her sight. She did not have to explain herself to her, even if her mother was the chief woman of the harem.

Tetisheri pointed her old finger in Ahhotep's face. "You are the Great Wife of King Seqenenre Tao. You are set apart. You are sacred and honored. And you had relations with a fleetsman? Ahhotep! You do not deserve your crown."

Ahhotep stood unamused. She simply sighed. "As I told you, Mother, I sought counsel with the Admiral over items I needed to discuss. That is why we were in the council room. I did not know to whom else I could speak."

Tetisheri chuckled with a sardonic twist and shook her head.

Ahhotep continued, ignoring her mother's antics. "Only you have ever been in my position before, yet you are too busy telling me I am not worthy enough rather than speaking with me about how I should become worthy. I sought out the Admiral because he has proven to be a friend to the crown. I ordered the guard to leave because I did not want to appear weak. Is that not what you have taught me? I could trust Admiral—"

"Ahhotep. Enough." Tetisheri shot both hands in the air. "Do you think me naive or ignorant or blind or forgetful?" Her hands fell with a thud to her sides. "What am I going to do with you?" The words came out through her teeth. "If you truly only spoke with the Admiral, you could have spoken with me."

Ahhotep's lips peeled back. "Speak with you when? You were not available."

"Well, not in the middle of the night. Speak to me when the Aten is in the sky."

Ahhotep viciously shook her head. "Mother, you are *never* available. And when I try to speak with you, all you tell me is 'Ahhotep, you are not good enough,' and 'Ahhotep, try harder.' You demean my children. Tep left her position because of you—"

"Tep did not do well, and she should have left her position long ago," Tetisheri said. "Her mother failed her."

The insult was unexpected but not surprising. In times past, Ahhotep would have backed down, said nothing, and let her mother leave in her royal

233

arrogance, but this time, she would bite back. This time, she would stand up for herself and her honor and dignity. Tetisheri assumed the worst of her even then as she accused her of sleeping with the Admiral instead of hearing what she had to say. Even though she was with Baba the previous night, her mother did not need to know what went on behind the closed door. Ahhotep was not going to let this woman manipulate her anymore. She wasn't going to back down, and so she snarled. "Then that means you have failed me, Mother."

Tetisheri closed her eyes and raised her eyebrows. Her nostrils flared. "You have failed yourself. I have told you what you need to do: repress your anger, tame your tears, and restrain your rashness. Be a leader. Be a queen."

"What if, Mother, what if the princes need to see a leader who feels as they do, not one so heartless to send their sons to—"

Tetisheri shoved her into the brick wall of the bath, and Ahhotep fell onto the wet bathing stone slab.

"I have a heart!" Tetisheri yelled, thrusting a crooked finger in Ahhotep's face for the second time that morning. "And my heart will not weigh heavy. I do what I do for the best of Kemet. That is why I am more powerful than you will ever be. I make wise decisions, hard decisions, and rational decisions. I remain calm when put to the test. You do not!"

Ahhotep only chuckled and looked around her. The residual water from the slab crawled its way up the linen fabric of her dress. She slowly stood up; the soaked cloth of her dress clung to the back of her legs.

"Yes, you remain so calm, Mother," she said and patted off the excess in her dress.

Tetisheri curled her finger into a fist, and her hands returned behind her back. "You are frustrating and—"

"Great Wife Tetisheri," Ahhotep spat, intentionally interrupting her mother, "You are no more powerful than the Great Wife Ahhotep."

Tetisheri sneered and turned her back on Ahhotep, but Ahhotep would not let her leave.

"So you agree?" Ahhotep asked.

Tetisheri peered over her shoulder once she made it to the door. "No. You have yet to prove your power, Ahhotep. All this time, this is what I have tried to teach you, but you are too weak, too rash to do it. Kamose was the only child of yours I believed was capable." She took a step to leave, but Ahhotep would get the last word. This time, she would have the last word.

"That is always your response; prove it, prove this, prove that," Ahhotep said and came toe-to-toe with her mother, who stopped walking out of the door and let Ahhotep continue. "Well, I am proving it. I have always proved and will continue to prove it, but you are stubborn and unwilling to see. I am worthy. Ahmose is worthy. We are worthy, whether you choose to believe it or not."

A long silence fell between them until Tetisheri said in a hushed tone. "I doubt you, Ahhotep. I doubt your family. You make unwise decisions, such as being alone with the Admiral in the middle of the night, whether you only spoke with him or laid with him, and these decisions will collect their due. I only pray I am in the Field of Reeds when the collection comes."

"Mother," Ahhotep shook her head and paused while the wrinkles in her forehead etched deeper into her brow. She lifted her gaze to meet her mother's dark, cold eyes, gray with age. "I have done my best and know it will never meet your expectations. You will always see the worst in me."

Tetisheri lifted her chin as if to confirm Ahhotep's statement.

Ahhotep chewed her lip before speaking. She grew tired of this chest-beating and power struggle. There would never be common ground or a compromise with her mother. Ahhotep searched her mother's eyes. "Hear me this one last time, and then you can say what you wish about my family, and I will say nothing in response."

Tetisheri frowned but lifted her chin with an unfurled brow. It was as if her mother had hope for what she would say.

"Go on." Tetisheri squared her shoulders to her.

Ahhotep sighed and leaned against the doorpost. What *would* she say? Would she speak of feats of victory, struggles of loss? Would she compare her decrees to her mother's to prove her stature was as great or greater? Perhaps, she should say what Tetisheri knew to be true. Then maybe she would hear her.

"I am a woman, Mother. Yes, born of royal blood, but I am still *only* a woman. My children, yes, born of royal blood, are still *only* children. You may not think us worthy, and perhaps we are not in your eyes. But the crown . . . the crown is worthy of everything. If the people and princes of Kemet cannot respect the crown, our nation is already lost, and your husband, son, grandson, and our soldiers and fleetsmen have all perished in vain, for there will never be a united Kemet."

Her mother's jaw fell slightly ajar, and the coldness in her eyes rescinded. She peered down at her daughter with a slight shake of her head. Tetisheri said nothing and walked away in a slow stroll—hands tightly clasped behind her back.

Ahhotep watched her until she reached the end of the corridor. She never looked back, even as she rounded the corner.

Ahhotep sighed and closed her eyes. It was useless. No matter what she did or the cost she paid, she would never reach Tetisheri. And in her last plea, she had told her mother that her family was unworthy, and her mother agreed so much that she didn't want to waste any more breath on her.

"At least I finally had the last word," she muttered.

But it was little consolation.

She glanced inside the bath and saw her nightdress on the floor. Meret and Nena had not grabbed it to wash in their quick departure. Ahhotep picked it up and pressed it to her nose. Hints of cinnamon and myrrh still clung to the fabric. She enveloped her arms around it and pulled it to her bosom. If she could keep that dress from the wash, she would. If she could not have Baba anymore, she would keep her reminder tucked away in her room's chest, and she would always look to the dawn and know at least someone believed in her and loved her —someone she loved in return.

23

A TIME FOR THE CROWN PRINCE | AHMOSE

SEDJEFATAWY, 1564 BC

In the following year, Ahmose's lesser wife, General Pennekhbet's daughter Kasmut, bore him his firstborn child, Tair—a strong and healthy baby girl, a good omen for his future sons and daughters.

But in the year succeeding, it appeared the omen had been misread, for his chief wife, Ahmose-Nefertari, bore him Ahmose-Ankh—a sickly, skinny, rasping baby boy.

Ahmose-Ankh's breathing sounded more like the late Sitkamose's soft snore. It held the same dissonant chord the more ill and tired Sitkamose had become before her ba shrieked in the night. But Tumerisy's rasp had the same, harrowing dry trait, and she had lived thus far. But no one had any hope she would surpass Sitkamose's age. It seemed all those who rasped were doomed to an early journey west.

Ahmose pushed away the notion his firstborn son would go to the Field of Reeds with Sitkamose. Ahmose-Ankh would grow strong like him and his brothers, Kamose and Sapair. His wife had not let the nurse take the boy, but eventually, he coaxed her from the nursery without the child. Her presence was needed beside him as the nomes' princes were gathered in the dining hall to celebrate the birth of the crown prince.

Ahmose sat in the King's place. But there was no pride-filled beam in his eyes or on his lips. Ahmose-Nefertari sat on his right, and his mother on his left. His grandmother sat beside his wife—all with unamused stares.

What should have been a joyous occasion turned sour when Tetian sent a dead fish as a gift to the King and his crown prince.

Princes Metjen and Baufre were yet to be seen.

And now Prince Weshptah of Ma-Hedj, who had done nothing but given empty oaths and pledges, stood before him, pushing aside Tetian's messenger.

"My King," Weshptah said with a voice as frail as his arms. "The princes of the nomes from Ma-Hedj to Mednit wonder if now you will join your armies and retake the Upper. You have a son should you fail."

Ahmose gritted his teeth—tired of the same undertone of disrespect. "The Royal Commander has told all the princes that the King shall join his armies when two living sons are with us. Take this message back to the princes of Ma-Hedj to Mednit."

But Weshptah stayed; his lips twisted into a frown. "I want to take this message back to the princes, but we are experiencing many riots and rebellions from the Aamu who have migrated to our nomes, especially Mednit, as it borders the Lower provinces recently conquered by the King's armies. We wish for our king to travel to the nomes of the Lower and put down the dissenters and establish a Viceroy as he has done in Kush."

Ahhotep narrowed her eyes at Weshptah but slid her gaze to Ahmose. What to respond? His mother was letting him speak. His grandmother sighed at his silence.

It had been two years since he had put down the Kushite Prince Aata's rebellion and established Si-Tayet as the viceroy of Kush. In his youth, his tongue had always grown thick when he tried to speak, but in addressing Weshptah that day, he knew his mother had faith in him and spoke in confidence.

"The Royal Commander declared the King shall have two living sons before he boards The Wild Bull. At this moment, rather than be with the King during this monumental event, the King's armies fight the Hekka Khasut and put down rebellions from Men-nefer to the second cataract. If Ma-Hedj and Mednit were to supply men and resources to back their decrees of support, perhaps then Admiral Baba or General Pennekhbet could have enough men to fight the war and secure your nomes."

Weshptah shuffled backward, stuck his nose in the air, and unlatched his mouth to speak, but Ahhotep placed her hands on the table and leaned forward, cutting him off. "Your king has spoken, Prince of Ma-Hedj."

He snapped his jaw shut and bowed his head with a slight grimaced grin. "I will return to Ma-Hedj and see who can go to war and what grain we may supply."

Ahhotep lifted her chin. "The King is most gracious. Perhaps we shall end this war sooner with the support of all the nomes."

"Yes, Royal Commander," Weshptah said and waited for Ahmose's dismissal before turning to leave.

Ahmose drummed his fingers on his thigh as his gaze shifted back to the dead, rotted fish from Tetian. At least a deben gold came with it, but the myriad of insults was not lost on those in attendance. As king, he could not eat fish, but Tetian had sent him fish, implying he was not divine. Plentiful fish meant a good livelihood, and a single dead fish indicated Ahmose could not feed his people. Or perhaps it was another insult to the poor nomes supporting the war. The whispers filled the halls as he debated how to respond to Tetian. He appreciated his mother letting him be King, but he also hated it. She was much better at speaking than he was. His wife also remained silent most days, especially after Ahmose-Ankh was born. But upon opening the sack and finding a dead carp atop the gold, his wife's cheeks turned red hot, and she rendered herself mute.

They needed the gold, but to take it meant accepting the insult. His wife shook her head, and so had his mother. His grandmother only watched him with cold, gray eyes.

The decision that would show his divine authority would be to send it back with a message that the King does not need Ta-Seti's wealth or insults, but that would do nothing for unity. What would he do to try and reunite Tetian, Metjen, and Baufre? Or should he ignore them for now and focus on the remaining princes who had come to celebrate his firstborn son?

He looked at Tetian's messenger, still holding open the bag of gold and rotted fish. The royal scribe, Mitry, lifted his reed brush to scribe what the king said.

Finally, Ahmose swallowed the lump in his throat and said, "Put it with the other gifts, remove the carcass, and return to Ta-Seti with this message to Prince Tetian: The Lord of Strength is Re, King Ahmose, is most gracious for Ta-Seti's gift of gold to celebrate the birth of the crown prince. The divinely appointed has received the prince's plea for help and sends a barrel of fish to help feed Ta-Seti's people during this difficult time of war—"

Ahmose halted at Tetisheri's chuckle. She stood up, and Ahmose froze, wondering if he had taken the return rebuff too far.

Every eye in the hall drew to the Great Wife's odd behavior. He winced and anticipated his grandmother correcting his decree and saving the relationship with Ta-Seti. He had tried to keep the gold and not accept the insult, but perhaps it was in error. He should have just entirely rejected it like his wife and mother implied he should do. His eyes closed as he braced himself for what was to come.

Tetisheri straightened up and clasped her hands tightly behind her back. "Do what the King has decreed," she said matter-of-factly.

Ahmose's eyes shot open, and his eyes landed firmly on his grandmother.

She gave a prideful beam toward him and glanced at Ahmose-Nefertari and Ahhotep before leaving the dining hall with her maidservants at her heels. The silence slowly faded to whispers as Tetian's messenger did as he was told. The whispers grew to chuckles, and Paser crossed his arms and smiled at Ahmose with a beam reaching each of his ears.

Ahmose-Nefertari nudged him under the table and gave him a slight grin. He half expected her to bop him on the nose as she did when he was a child, but he returned the smile and sat back in his chair. He peered over at his mother, who gave him a small nod.

Well, it must have been a good decree about a fish. With the thought, his mind slipped back to the carcass. Was it an omen for his firstborn? A curse? Or simply an insult to his divine throne? The rasping of his firstborn son resurfaced in memory, but he pushed it away. *No*, he thought. *As much as Tetian may not like me, he would never curse a baby.* The tension in his shoulders dissipated.

He smiled at the musicians' song and the dancers' dance, content with the voice his mother had told him to find. He would be a good king.

24

A TIME FOR LOSS |
AHMOSE-NEFERTARI

SEDJEFATAWY, 1563 BC

Perhaps, Tetian's dead fish was a curse, for the second son of King Ahmose was a baby boy who breathed but two breaths before beginning the journey west. His name was Siamun.

Seventy days for the journey's preparation came and went; the child was entombed.

Ahmose-Nefertari paced the length of the royal harem. There were usually very few people out at night since Apep ruled the dark. Where the sun had boiled, the moon cooled. Her layered linen robe drooped on her chest as she pulled it tighter over her shoulders. Even though the dark was the reign of the snake demon, the crispness of the night air calmed her and numbed her thoughts until the dawn came. Her mother came from the entrance of the royal harem, and she stopped upon seeing her.

"Daughter," she said as she approached, pulling her cloak to cover herself, but Ahmose-Nefertari saw the small rip on the shoulder of her mother's dress before it disappeared under the heavy linen. Ahhotep rubbed her arms. "Why have you risen early?"

Ahmose-Nefertari shook her head. "Sleep eluded me, as it did you?"

Ahhotep nodded and looked toward the harem's entrance. "Yes."

"Where were you?"

"Speaking to a friend," Ahhotep said. "After Siamun's burial yesterday, I could not be alone in my room."

Ahmose-Nefertari envisioned the face of her son with blue-tinged lips. She shut her eyes at the memory. "I understand, Mother. Neither could I."

She reached out and pulled her into an embrace. Ahmose-Nefertari froze, not knowing what her mother was doing. The notes of cinnamon and myrrh mingled with her mother's traditional lotus blossom scent. It caught her off guard until she realized her mother clung to her, and in a rapid response, she wrapped her arms around her mother's waist, pulling even closer.

Ahhotep whispered, "I am sorry, my child. I should have come to you, but I did not want to wake you if you were sleeping. You have not slept much since the birth."

Ahmose-Nefertari squeezed her mother and buried her face into her shoulder. It was a rare occasion to feel her embrace. It was what she needed in the moment, and her mother seemed to know it. "This is enough," she murmured and relaxed into her mother's embrace.

Ahhotep stroked her daughter's spiraled curls as a tear fell on her neck. "No, it is not," she whispered in a tone contrary to her tears. She pulled away and cupped Ahmose-Nefertari's cheek and neck. "It will never be enough to make up for my absence in your life."

"You were not absent, Mother." Ahmose-Nefertari had seen her mother throughout her childhood and as a young woman, hurrying here and there between the throne room, the harem, the Kap, the temples, and even Per-djed-ken. She had never been absent.

But in direct opposition to her thoughts, Ahhotep said, "Yes, I was. Lady Rai took care of you as she cared for me as a child. When you fell and ripped your dress, skinned your knee, I was nowhere to be found. When your child journeys west, I am not there."

"You are here now," she said, trying to comfort her mother. Ahhotep winced, and Ahmose-Nefertari wanted to soothe any perceived wound. "You are leading a war, Mother. You speak the hard truths when they need to be spoken. I am afraid of disappointing you. I am afraid I am not as strong as you. I am afraid you will regret asking me to marry Ahmose and be his Chief Wife. I admire you and Grandmother for the strong women you are. We are well-taken care of. You had important matters to tend to for Kemet."

Ahhotep moved both hands to cup Ahmose-Nefertari's face and kissed her forehead. "You can never disappoint me, my 'beautiful companion.'" Raising Ahmose-Nefertari's face, she whispered, "My children should have been the most important matter in my life, and I left you to others." Tears—one at a time—ran down her cheeks, chasing each other.

Ahmose-Nefertari counted this as the third time she had seen her mother cry. But the first time, it had been subtle, and only a tear or two as the Anubis priests laid Kamose at her feet. The second, Ahmose-Nefertari had thought she cried to garner pity from the princes when she addressed them after the Kushite uprising led by Prince Aata and after she had cast out Tetian. And now, this third time, Ahmose-Nefertari watched the genuine tears stream down her mother's cheeks.

She didn't know what to say; the royal family's most

important matter should be the god's divine appointment to care for and defend Kemet.

"But you are Queen," she finally squeaked out.

Ahhotep wiped her cheeks and stood back. "Yes, I am, and so are you," she said. Her voice remained firm as if it did not know her eyes had shed tears. "Kemet must come first, but it does not mean I wished for it to be that way. Thank you for loving your younger siblings in my stead."

Without waiting for Ahmose-Nefertari to respond, Ahhotep turned. "Let us both go sleep. Re will be conquering Apep soon, and we must be ready for this coming day." She returned to the mother she had always seen—a pillar of stone, unwavering in the night's wind. "I will walk you to your room," she said.

"Thank you," Ahmose-Nefertari whispered and silently walked alongside her mother.

"Sleep well," Ahhotep said and turned to go to her room.

"You too," Ahmose-Nefertari replied in a hushed tone and entered her private apartment of the Chief Wife. She pressed her back against the door and stared at the dark interior. She was alone again, which was precisely why she had left in the first place.

RE HAD BEEN VICTORIOUS OVER APEP, AND THE SUN SHONE with a blinding light by mid-morning. By the evening meal, the moon began its ascent. Ahmose-Nefertari hated the shortened days, but at least the Nile's waters had receded and left the rich black soil to plant the coming year's harvest. It looked like it would be a good year. The gods were pleased with her brother as King.

Ahmose came into the dining hall after training at Per-djed-ken and collapsed next to his brother on the floor. Ahmose-Nefertari glanced at her mother and grandmother, but when they said nothing, she, too, joined them on the rug. No one outside the royal family ate at that time, she reasoned. It would not matter if she and Ahmose did not eat at the table.

She stood beside the grouping, noting Ahmose, Sapair, Senseneb, and Tumerisy—the latter made room for her. Her other siblings, half-siblings, and cousins were grouped on other rugs in the large hall.

Ahmose-Nefertari snuggled next to Tumerisy, who had not yet had a blood moon at twelve years of age and still wore the sidelock of youth instead of a woman's wig. But the girl wrapped a thin arm around her older sister and pressed her hollow-cheeked face to the queen's.

"How does the King's Daughter fare?" Ahmose-Nefertari asked, placing a kiss on Tumerisy's forehead.

"The same as I was before," she said with a toothy smile before the rasp made her cough again.

Servants brought Ahmose lamb while the rest ate fish. Tumerisy looked at Sapair and Senseneb and then at Ahmose. "Why can you not eat fish, Ahmose? You ate fish when we were children."

Ahmose's brow furrowed, and he spoke to her like she was a child. "Because when Set killed Osiris, the fish of the Nile ate his body. It is not right for the divinely appointed to eat that which consumed the flesh of the great god."

Sapair and Senseneb stared at her in disbelief.

"Why did I not know that?" she muttered while her gaze hit the floor. Her cheeks blossomed pink.

Ahmose-Nefertari ran a hand over her bald head and swished her sidelock, casting her brothers a disappointed stare. "Probably because you were ill and unable to be with your tutor," she said to Tumerisy.

Tumerisy sighed and curled up next to her plate. Her thread-like arms supported her head. "I am always ill." She picked up her bread and scooped a bean or two into her mouth.

"And we will always love you," Ahmose-Nefertari said and rubbed the girl's emaciated thigh.

She nodded to Ahmose and Sapair, who said, "Yes, sister. We love you."

Tumerisy scooped another bean or two in her mouth while her eyes glistened. "I will only ever have your love. I will not be married like you, Sapair, nor be able to ever have children like Mother."

Siamun appeared in Ahmose-Nefertari's memory. *It seems I cannot bear children either,* she thought to herself, but something else caught her attention. "Sapair, you are married?"

Sapair grasped Senseneb's hand and locked eyes with his apparent new wife. "I wanted to wait to tell you after we entombed Siamun," he said, turning to Ahmose and Ahmose-Nefertari. "But Mother allowed me to take Senseneb as my wife to give honor to the Admiral as Ahmose married Kasmut to give honor to the General."

A small smile grew on Ahmose-Nefertari's face. "You could have told us, Brother. We are happy for you and Senseneb." But in her mind, she only felt more pressure to have a royal child. Their mother had allowed him to marry a common woman for his chief wife, which meant she had to bear sons—living sons who would succeed their father.

Ahmose had been talking while she thought, and she had only caught his last words. ". . . I should not name you General and wanted you to stay behind in case I end like Kamose." He shuddered and focused on his lamb before biting into the perfectly roasted meat.

Sapair patted his shoulder. "You will come back. You promised me, remember, you and me until the end. We would go to the Field of Reeds together."

Ahmose shook his head and swallowed. "For the sake of the crown, I hope that will not be the case since my son is . . ." His voice trailed off as he locked eyes with Ahmose-Nefertari. He didn't have to say it. Ahmose-Ankh would probably not live much longer.

A messenger burst through the dining hall's doors. "My King!" he called out, looking at Tetisheri and Ahhotep at the King's table. Everyone stopped eating, and Ahmose-Nefertari stood up as the messenger frantically searched the room. What was so urgent? Had the palace been overrun? Had they lost Men-nefer? Had the General been slain?

Ahmose stood, garnering the attention of all in attendance.

"What is it, royal messenger?" he asked, his voice echoing in the suddenly silent hall.

The messenger squared his shoulders at Ahmose and bowed quickly. "I come with urgent word from the north. King Apepi has journeyed west. A new king, his son, arises in his place. The Lower calls him Khamudi. The ranks fear this new king as rumors have said he is even more ruthless than his father."

His eyes grew wide, but Ahmose-Nefertari sighed in relief. Maybe a change in kings would spell an easier victory and a quicker end to this war. She stroked a finger on the stone scarab amulet tied around her neck. Perhaps Re would protect them from death and the Hekka Khasut disease spoiling their lands.

Ahmose's voice rang out, breaking through her

thoughts. "This new king shall feel the wrath of Amun's divinely appointed, Re's chosen one. We will never acknowledge the names of our enemies, and this new king shall be known as King Apepi II after his father. Tell our soldiers to have no fear in this new king, for Re has spoken, and Amun is with us. We will strike them from our lands and retake what is ours—all of Kemet."

The messenger seemed soothed by Ahmose's words, for his lips held an honorable beam. He bowed and left to carry the encouraging word to the troops.

Ahmose-Nefertari closed her eyes and prayed in thought to Amun and Re as she stroked the scarab amulet. *Please let me have another living son so Ahmose can leave Waset and end this war.*

25

A TIME FOR CELEBRATION | AHMOSE

SEDJEFATAWY, 1562 BC

Ahmose flexed his toes over his leather sandals and hoped one day they would be gilded in gold. With the viceroy of Kush, Si-Tayet, keeping matters south of the first cataract diplomatic, trade from the gold-rich region funneled through the nomes once again after Ta-Seti took its fill. The Medjay were plentiful, and khopeshes and chariots were in full-scale production. All recruits trained with the Kerman mercenaries at Per-djed-ken, before they shipped out to positions along the Nile to keep the peace.

Yet despite the Viceroy's efforts, reports of uprisings came every season, and men from the north had to be reassigned to Kush to help put it down. And as lands were conquered in the north, riots, and rebellions from the local populace who did not want a united Kemet became frequent.

It had been a balancing act, juggling resources and men from one end of the Nile to the other. Establishing an effective, forceful presence was the only way Ahmose foresaw victory. His mother had done a good job for him, ripening it for the taking.

The army had infiltrated most of the Nile delta that fed into the Great Sea but met considerable force at Lunu, which sat on the Nile branch leading to Per-Bastet and then to Hut-Waret, home of the Hekka Khasut king. At least the populous Apiru that lived in the delta had been no trouble as of yet.

At eighteen years old, Ahmose should have been at war with the other men his age. And with Tetian rising from his bow before him, the thought of fighting far away from the throne room enticed him even more. Contempt covered the prince's crimped mouth as he stared at the king, waiting to speak.

He'd rather swing his bronze khopesh or shoot an arrow or ride a chariot full force into the enemy than deal with the dissenting princes. The worst one, Tetian, had decided to come to Sedjefatawy after two years of silence since Ahmose's return rebuff about the dead fish.

After the guard had declared him, Ahmose couldn't remember the purpose of his visit. It was just a haze, and now Tetian stood staring at him as if he were to speak.

Ahmose glanced to his left, where his chief wife usually stood, but she was in the birthing pavilion having their child. He drummed his fingers on the throne's chair arm, wishing for her presence, especially now. She had always handled Tetian and his messengers for him when his mother was not there. He glanced to his right. His mother stood straight-backed with her arms stiffly by her sides with a stone-cold face. She had not moved or spoken since Tetian arrived unexpectedly that morning.

His mother, apparently waiting for Ahmose to speak, had been true to her word and, most of the time, had let him find and use his voice. But this time, he wished she would speak for him. The clenching of his teeth chafed his ears.

Tetisheri sat in the back, sipping karkade tea as she did when she decided to come to the throne room. This time it was to await the news of her great-grandchild.

"Well," she croaked and cleared her throat. She spoke again in her usual rich tone. "Is anyone going to speak, or shall the prince stare at the royalty all day?"

Ahhotep glared at her over her shoulder and muttered under her breath so Ahmose could hear, "She wants us to be worthy of the crown but speaks like that in front of an audience?" The disgust dripped off her tongue.

She took a settling breath and placed a hand on the back of Ahmose's throne as if to claim it for her bloodline. The action garnered Tetian's attention, and he curled his lip before speaking.

"I have sailed all the way from Ta-Seti to discuss negotiations with the King and his mother—"

"Royal Commander," Ahmose interjected, correcting his mother's title. The day on the port eight years ago when Tetian revealed his true stance against his family limited his patience with the prince.

Prince Tetian smugly chuckled and shook his head. "With the King and the Royal Commander."

At least he obeyed, Ahmose mused and asked, "What negotiations need to be discussed?" He inclined his head and sat back. Ahmose wasn't a tall man, but in the past year, he had grown taller, and his feet were now flat on the floor.

Tetian popped his neck with a swift turn of his head. "We have many items that need discussion, King Ahmose."

Ahhotep took a step forward. "You do not show your

face in Sedjefatawy for years, and now you demand to negotiate?"

Tetian sneered. "It seems your entry into the Lower is slow-going yet again. I would have expected the lands to be conquered by now. You need the riches of Ta-Seti to help you win this war."

Si-Tayet's reports of Tetian's trade dealings came to Ahmose's mind. He wondered why Tetian had been taking more than his usual share of the trade goods flowing north. Was it his greed, to negotiate with him for power, or something more sinister? Ahmose needed to be civil to gain more information about Tetian's hoarding, but the hateful comments about his family's motivations at the last feast Tetian attended resurfaced in memory, and the snake of red revenge settled on his tongue, ready to strike at everything the prince said.

"What we need is for Ta-Seti to stop stealing trade goods before it reaches the rest of Kemet. You are no better than the Hekka Khasut and the Kushites."

Tetian raised both hands in defense of Ahmose's implied accusation. "You dare compare a prince of Ta-Seti to the Hekka Khasut?"

Ahmose snapped back. "If the comparison is clear, there is no dare to say it."

Tetisheri coughed dryly as Tetian glowered at her. She rose from her seat, tea in hand, and strode to Ahmose's left side. Tetian smirked as if Tetisheri would take his side.

Pitiful fool, Ahmose thought. *Only because she has let you speak freely before, does not mean she will never scold you.*

Tetisheri said in a thick voice that needed her tea, "Prince Tetian, perhaps you should share more of your wealth and not hoard it for some unseen need. It seems your king thinks you a thief." She lifted an eyebrow and sipped the floral-cooled tea.

Ahmose thought his grandmother had been more supportive as of late. She still never spoke with his mother, but at least she had not chided him. Maybe he was speaking how she believed best for the throne, and Ahmose sat up straighter at the thought.

Tetian scoffed. "I am no thief. I simply manage resources better—"

"Better than who?" Ahhotep interrupted. A note of finality rang through the throne room and echoed back from the tall pillars. Her unflinching eyes cut through the space between them.

Ahmose smirked at Tetian's pinched lips and the two powerful women standing next to him. If Ta-Seti were to rejoin the cause, it would be under different circumstances while he was on the throne. No more emboldened words.

Tetian inclined his head. "Paser of Herui, of course," he said with a smug sneer. "Why would you anticipate I would say any other?"

The smirk fell off Ahmose's face. "We wouldn't, Prince Tetian." He crossed the king's regalia—the crook and the flail—over his chest and sat back. He repeated the words his mother had taught him to say. "You came to negotiate, but the King of Kemet does not negotiate. Present your requests before the throne, and the King shall decide whether to grant it or not."

His mother lifted her head in a prideful beam and glared down at Tetian at the foot of the dais. His grandmother returned to her seat, and at the creak of the chair, Ahmose said, "Speak, Prince Tetian."

Tetian curled his lip, clearly upset at being put in his place, not once now but twice.

"I have nothing to say to you, insolent king. I was going to offer you a chance at ending this war early, but I see now you will never listen. You will perish as your brother did and your father before him, should you ever decide to leave the palace and fight alongside the men your mother commands."

Ahmose's jaw grew taut at the insult, and his breath came out hot through his nostrils. He hissed, "Does the Prince prefer the King to stay in riches and wealth while the rest of the nation fights for their freedom, such as the Prince of Ta-Seti does?"

Tetian shook his head with a prideful grin. "I support the Viceroy of Kush so that your army can focus on the north. I do my share. It would do the King well to honor such a prince."

"What honor should be bestowed upon a prince who has done nothing but prevented progress in this war by hoarding needed trade goods in selfish isolation?" Ahmose asked. "State your requests or leave."

Tetian stood and stared at him blankly. "Your mother has instilled in you great confidence, King Ahmose. I hope the gods agree with your great-great-grandfather's self-declared divine appointment." He turned around to leave as a steward entered and bowed.

The steward said, "The Lord of Strength is Re, King Ahmose, your chief wife Ahmose-Nefertari bore you a son. She calls him Prince Ramose."

A new breath filled Ahmose's chest, and the burden of the previous exchange rolled down his back. His smile grew wide but faded as Tetian peered at him with dark eyes.

"So, it seems you now have two sons, King of Kemet. Shall you now board The Wild Bull?"

Ahhotep placed a hand on the throne. "Shall you board a warship as well, Prince Tetian?"

He snarled. "I am not King. It is not my duty to defend Kemet."

Ahmose peered up at his mother. The agreement had been two sons. "I do have two sons now," he whispered.

"Not now, Ahmose," she shot back under her breath.

His gaze dropped. Why had Tetian even come? A happy moment was ruined by his speech, and he had disappointed his mother by speaking when he should not have.

"You, King Ahmose,"—Tetian pointed a finger at him —"hold the crook, the symbol to defend Kemet, yet you sit as a man with an heir and now a reserve son. You hold the flail, the symbol of fertility for the people. Yet you . . ." His voice trailed off, and then he chuckled. "Why waste my breath on you? You hypocrite of a king, still coddled at his mother's breast?"

Every muscle in Ahmose's body tightened. Is that what the army thought of him, being an eighteen-year-old man and still at his mother's side? Is that what his people thought, and Tetian was the only one brave enough to say it? He had two sons now—that was the agreement his mother declared to the princes. He should announce his going to war. But the color drained from his mother's knuckles as she gripped the throne—the bones popped up in flesh-covered ridges on her nut-brown skin. He swallowed his fears and his anger, so he would speak calmly as his grandmother would have wanted him to.

"You now have a different option, Prince Tetian. Leave, or the guards shall remove you," Ahmose said, taking the cue from his mother.

Tetian spun on his heels and shouted as he left, "It

would not be the first time your family has escorted me from your presence when others blindly follow you."

The throne room doors closed, and the crook and the flail slid down Ahmose's arms into his lap. His back sagged. "I have two sons now, Mother," he said. "I need to go to war and lead my men into battle as Father did, as Kamose did. They see me as a child still having you lead in my stead. I need to be King."

Ahhotep's grip did not falter on the chair's arm. "Do not heed that renegade's words." Her chin sunk, and she drew in a deep breath—her fingers releasing the throne one at a time. "It is paramount the throne stays with the divinely appointed. The army knows this. Ahmose-Ankh is a sickly child. Ramose could be as well. Ramose could travel west in a few days like Siamun. What if both of your living sons do not see manhood? Then what happens?"

Ahmose leaned forward, his elbows pressed into his thighs, and the regalia drooped between his knees. Losing Siamun had been like a weight placed on his belly, and it returned at the mention of his name. Ahmose-Ankh though he looked like a healthy toddler, was quite frail like Sitkamose had been. His throat itched, and he sniffed back the memories of when she did not wake.

"You need a healthy baby boy." His mother's words drew him from his thoughts.

Tetisheri coughed in the back. "Ahmose, your mother is right. If you want your line to continue, you need to produce a healthy heir, one who will not enter the Field of Reeds early in life"

Ahmose sat back and lifted his regalia to their dutiful position. He did not want to talk about such things with his mother and grandmother. There were too many hard memories running through his head. "What of Tetian? Do you think he is a threat to us? I have wondered for many months why he has been hoarding. Do you think it was for bargaining, as he tried to do today? He left quickly if that was his main motivation. Should we increase the men with Si-Tayet or . . ." His voice trailed off, hoping he would not speak the treasonous implication.

Ahhotep lifted his chin so his face was to hers. "We will need to keep a closer watch. Let's ask our neighboring prince to the south, Prince Nakht of Nekhen, to keep an account of the comings and goings of the Nile and ensure he is not planning an uprising."

Tetisheri slammed her teacup on its saucer. She lifted her chin in bold confidence. "Ta-Seti would *never* do such a thing. They are honorable people. Until the gods speak otherwise, you can expect Tetian to remain a dissenter *only*."

Ahmose glanced at his grandmother. "When would Tetian believe the gods speak otherwise?"

Tetisheri snorted at the question. "When the divine line is no more, and we are close to defeat. Then clearly, your ancestor was erroneous in his claim of divine appointment."

Ahmose cleared his throat. "Well, I have two sons, and I will stay until I have a healthy son. We are making strides and maintaining what we have won. I'd say we are far from defeat."

"Then you have nothing to fear from Tetian," Tetisheri snapped. There was a possessiveness in her voice, and Ahmose wondered what she was protecting.

His mother, though, threw her gaze upward and whispered. "It still may be prudent to ask Nekhen to keep eyes on their southern neighbor. I will ask Paser to keep eyes on Metjen and Baufre north of him. He will be able to do little if the three of them decide to rebel."

"I am old but not deaf, child," Tetisheri said. "I have already told you, Tetian is no threat in *that* regard."

Ahhotep shot her gaze to her mother. "And my ears work perfectly well, Mother. Still, I do not trust Tetian and think we should be wise concerning what he *could* do especially given his large unspent resources and the men he keeps from this war. Likewise, Metjen and Baufre have withheld their resources and men for almost four years now. We have seen their trips to Ta-Seti many times. What are they meeting about? What are they planning?"

Tetisheri narrowed her eyes. "Fine. Be an ill steward of what little we have available and waste soldiers patrolling in vain when we already have many riots and insurrections in Kush and beyond Ta-Ur."

Ahmose was torn. He could see both sides. "I will do this, Great Wives: I will simply ask Paser of Herui and Nakht of Nekhen to keep watch and alert us if they notice anything that would require more attention. We will hold off on preparing for an internal attack or defense until we have more information."

His mother looked disappointed, but she nodded regardless. His grandmother dipped her chin in apparent agreement.

Ahmose drew in a deep breath and pushed Tetian into the dark recesses of his mind. He let the breath escape and called out, "Next messenger."

The throne room doors opened, and a guard entered.

"The Admiral returns and has a report to give on Men-nefer."

Ahmose let out a small sigh. It seemed no matter how many traitors they slew, Men-nefer was ripe with opposition. He glanced up at his mother, who released a soft gasp at the officer walking toward them. Seemed his mother thought the same.

"What is your report, Admiral," Ahmose said once Baba's knee was bent, and his head bowed.

Baba regained his posture and first glanced at him and then at his mother. There was a timid smile on his lips before it faded, and he spoke. "King Ahmose, Given Life, I come with a report from the north. The Apiru have been gentle and provided food to us and bandages, but they also aid our enemy. They say they remain neutral in our conflict. Time will tell if they decide to stay neutral. We have quelled the riots in Men-nefer and in Merimda in the western delta. But Lunu, Per-Bastet, and ultimately Hut-Waret remain out of reach. The men sent with General Pennekhbet to Kush will be needed to attempt to take those cities. As for now, we hold the position. We will fail if we try without proper counts."

Tetisheri's harsh voice erupted from the back, "Admiral, direct your report to the King."

Baba turned his attention to the Great Wife, "I speak to both the King *and* the Royal Commander."

Ahmose glanced between Baba and his mother and thought it odd his grandmother would be so harsh with the loyal and effective officer of his fleet. His mother was the Royal Commander and, thus, Baba's superior. Ahmose's brow furrowed in the silence that settled in between the four of them until he said, "Continue, Admiral."

As Baba spoke, Ahmose recalled the rumors about his mother and Baba seeing each other in the council room on a few occasions. He had forced the servants and stewards into silence, dismissing their petty gossip for what it was. The Admiral was a faithful friend to the crown and was now father-in-law to Prince Sapair. Given the war, why would his mother not seek his counsel?

Ahmose nodded his head, hearing the rest of Baba's report but noticed the Admiral glance at his mother quite often. Probably because she was still Royal Commander, he reasoned. And she would be until he had a healthy son.

26

A TIME FOR ENCOURAGEMENT | AHHOTEP

SEDJEFATAWY, 1561 BC

Ahhotep stood in the Kap's nursery staring at the two twin girl infants and the newborn boy. It should be a happy time in life, having grandchildren and watching them grow, but Ahhotep only felt dread and despair.

A shadow fell into the room, and Ahhotep guessed who it was by the light footsteps. "Lady Rai," she said in a hushed tone.

The old woman walked up and stood next to her. "Great Wife," Rai said but remained still and said nothing more.

Ahhotep sighed as she stared at the newborn, Thutmose, son of Sapair and Senseneb. Baba had beamed when he saw the child earlier that day. Why would he not? Thutmose was his first grandson—healthy with fat rolls on his arms and legs, a hefty child with a good strong neck. She compared him to Ahmose-Ankh and Siamun and Ramose. Tair had been healthy too, so why were all of Ahmose-Nefertari's children so sickly? Her daughter, who loved children the most, only gave birth to ill children though she was fertile like the black soil left after the Nile floods and birthed children every year since Ahmose had consummated his marriage with her. Even only four months after the twins were born, she was with child again.

Ahmose-Meryet Amon, one of the twin girls, yawned. The other, Ahmose-Sitamun, knew what her twin was doing and yawned soon after.

"Children are the most precious and innocent of us," Rai said as she brushed a finger down Sitamun's cheek and dipped it under the baby's chin when the yawn ended.

Ahhotep nodded. "They are."

Rai smiled. "Your mother came here often when you were a babe, Great Wife. She would stare and cry, but she would never touch."

Ahhotep turned her gaze to the nurse who had raised her, her children, and now her grandchildren. "You lie, Lady Rai."

She peered at her with shadowed eyes. "My mouth is pure, Great Wife. For when I speak the Negative Confession, and my heart is weighed against the feather of Ma'at, there will be no deceit found in me. I will go to the Field of Reeds."

Ahhotep averted her gaze. "I did not mean to insult you, Rai." She took a deep breath and sighed. "I just do not believe my mother would cry."

Rai gave a coy grin and spoke with gentleness. "Your mother named you Ahhotep, 'The Moon is Satisfied,' because you were born when the moon was full. She cried when she held her firstborn daughter—"

"Because I was not a son?" Ahhotep snapped. "I have failed her expectation since the day I was born." She huffed, but after a moment of silence from Rai, she winced. "I am sorry, Rai, I . . . You . . ." Her voice trailed off as she turned to go, unable to form the words she wanted to say.

But Rai's weathered hand on her shoulder stopped her. "God's Mother does not apologize."

Ahhotep shook her head. "She should if she insults the woman who raised her."

Rai came to face her and placed both hands on her shoulders. "Then, believe me when I tell you, your mother came into this very room and watched you as you slept. Tears ran down her face, but she never held you."

"Why? Why would she cry?"

"Why do you come and stand and stare but do not touch? Why did you not come when your children were here?" Rai shrugged. "You are both mothers. You both want what is best for your children, but you are both queens and want what is best for Kemet. If you answer yourself, then perhaps you can answer why your mother cried."

"Rai . . . I don't know anymore. Ahmose is nineteen with two sons, sickly sons, and he will leave for war." Her voice trailed off again. "I do not want Ahmose to go to war because he is my son and yet also because he leaves behind two sons that may not live to see the next season. The crown will go to Sapair, who will go to war and—" Her unshed tears ran down the back of her throat and choked out her words.

Rai traced Ahhotep's face. "Let old Lady Rai tell you something wise as I did when you were young and thought everything I said was wise."

Ahhotep thinned her lips and inclined her head to keep her tears from falling down her cheeks. Rai's soothing, calm voice had not changed much. It was still as rich as she remembered as a child.

"It seems you are focusing too much on Kemet. You must find balance in your life, or you will be callous and bitter." Rai cupped Ahhotep's face. " 'The Moon is Satisfied,' my dear child"—Rai's eyes shone with the fading daylight lost in the black irises—"your poor mother never found her balance, but I pray you will if for nothing else that you have peace." She softly tapped Ahhotep's cheeks with her palms. "Now, leave the children to me, Great Wife. Have this night to yourself, take off your headdress, be a woman, and do not think of Kemet."

Rai kissed her cheek, left her, and tended to the sleeping infants, checking their linen wrappings and feeling their foreheads.

Ahhotep watched Rai for a moment before walking out of the nursery. Rai's words were on her mind. "Focusing too much on Kemet," she muttered and bumped into a servant on the way to her room. "We are in the middle of a war, Lady Rai," she whispered as she sidestepped the servant who had bowed to her.

She quickened her step, entered her room, and shut the door behind her. The day was almost done. "Have this night for myself?" she said to herself. "What shall I do? Bathe and paint my face?" she uttered in sardonic play.

"Take off my headdress?" She ripped her vulture headdress off and threw it on her bed. "Find my balance?" she cried, and with a spear-like finger, she spun around and pointed in the direction of her mother's room.

"I will never be like you! Never!" She dropped her hand in a cold fist, stumbled backward at her lost control, and shut her eyes tight. It was too much. All of it. Everything.

"Find my balance?" she whispered. She grabbed her amulets of Hathor and Isis around her neck and squeezed and rubbed them in her palm.

"Help me!" she cried to the goddesses. She thought Nena and Meret would certainly burst in—or a passing steward or servant—but the harem bustled even as the sun set. No one had heard her or cared. Maybe they had grown familiar with her outbursts in her room.

She melted into the linen-wrapped wool mattress as she pressed the two amulets to her heart.

"Let this war be over," she pleaded with the goddesses but doubtful they would hear her when she had not given them praise or called upon their name or opened their mouths.

"How much must I bear?" she asked, still in vain. She ran her hand down the side of her face.

"How much must I sacrifice? All my sons, a marital bed, my daughters, the crown?" She stopped and breathed with difficulty. She envisioned her life alone, her children all slain and her mother gently shaking her head at her. The only person she had confided in was Baba and now Lady Rai. And Lady Rai had told her to be a woman, not a queen, this one night.

A loud clatter sounded in the distance—probably a dropped plate or bowl. She listened for a while. The harem rustle did not seem to be dying down. The noise was maddening at that time of day.

"Be a woman," she repeated Lady Rai's words, but in memory, the words repeated from Baba: *Do not be God's Mother this night.*

She pulled her hidden dress from her room's wooden chest and inhaled the faint cinnamon scent. Right or wrong, she loved him. He never shook his head at her. He edified her rather than tearing her down. He balanced her. She rolled to her side with the fabric near her face. Baba was right outside the palace walls tending to the fleet while she remained in her private room longing for him.

Every time he came home, it was so hard not to run to him or pull him aside. Even as he came to see his grandson that morning, she had wanted to kiss him in his joy and tell him how happy his daughter and her son were in having Thutmose. But she could not. In a bold move, her fingers brushed his as she walked past, but her mother had seen and immediately asked him to see to the fleet.

"Yes, Great Wife," he had said and left without a backward gaze. He was probably upset he had come home only to glimpse his grandson and see his daughter for a brief moment. Ahhotep watched him leave before going and standing in the nursery for the greater part of the day. Tetisheri had made him leave his only daughter and first grandchild because of her.

Ahhotep ran her thumb over her fingers where she had brushed Baba's hand. She should have done nothing and stood at an appropriate distance, and the need to apologize to him overcame her. But how would she?

She scoffed. They could not meet in the council room. There had been rumors after they had met there a few times, and she had to stop. She had not seen him other than when he reported to her and Ahmose. It tired her heart not being able to be with him, especially when he was home.

But what if she could go to him? Could she slip past the harem's guards? Could she slip past the palace door and to his villa if he was there and not at Per-djed-ken? If not, could she have a reason to see him and leave the guards and servants at the door? How would she get back in the morning? What would she say? The rumors would be confirmed. What would her mother do? Would she exile her from the harem? The palace? Have Ahmose strip her title? Have Baba bound and whipped? She was Queen. Her son loved her. And Baba was their Admiral. He was too critical to punish. If she intervened, would the guards obey her or her mother? Would her son allow exceptions? Would she be bound and whipped as well?

The faded cinnamon intoxicated her rational thought. It was time she took control of her life; let the consequences come what may. She wanted to be with Baba, her friend and her love.

But she had to find him before the last of the day's light, for if Baba was not willing to take the chance, she would need to come back to the palace before the doors closed for the night.

She donned her cloak, tying it tight so her royal collar was hidden. Would anyone recognize her without her royal regalia? She hoped not and held her headdress behind her back, concealed by the cloak.

If she made it past the palace doors, she would figure out what came next. She snuck out of her room and crossed the busy courtyard. No one seemed to notice her. A nurse bumped into her and kept walking, barely glancing her way. She exited the harem as the guards had not yet taken their post. The sun still lingered in the western sky as the night's chill set into the air. She walked the long corridor past the courtyard of Tao and Kamose, the council room and throne room, and down the entryway to the grand palace double doors.

Ahhotep held her breath as she neared the entrance guards. Baba stood speaking to them. As she drew nearer, she heard what he was saying.

". . . message to Great Wife Tetisheri, the King's Fleet is ready to sail per her command."

The guard nodded and walked toward her. Ahhotep kept her head down as she sped up.

"Citizeness," the guard said as he passed her. "The palace doors close soon; do not tarry outside the palace."

She nodded and hurried out. Baba had turned to face the port and survey the fleet. His hands were balled into fists and pressed against his narrowed waist. She admired the slabs of muscle on his back before standing beside him.

"Admiral," she said.

"Great Wife, you should not have . . ." He peered at her, his eyes glancing at her missing headdress, and his voice trailed off. He spun around as if looking for servants or guards.

"I came alone, Baba," she whispered. "I needed to see you and tell you I am sorry for making my mother send you away from your daughter and grandson."

He nodded with a pressed smile to a guard who stared at them. Baba wrapped an arm around Ahhotep and pulled her close to hide her face.

"Ahhotep, you shouldn't have done that," he whispered as he ushered her to the side street out of the guards' sight. He squared his shoulders to her and slid his hands down her arms. His fingers brushed hers before enveloping her small hands within a firm grasp. The rippled surface of the headdress' wings made him look down.

"I am not worth a tarnished image of our queen," he told her before meeting her gaze and letting the hand that held the headdress drop so she could once again hide it within the folds of her cloak.

"You are worth it to me." She stepped closer to him.

"I hurt you this morning, and I am sorry. I have come for nothing else to apologize as a simple woman who loves you because, as God's Mother, I cannot apologize to you."

He slipped a hand behind her neck and the other onto the small of her back and pulled her to him.

"I was sad to leave," he whispered, "but you have done nothing which needs an apology."

"I only wanted to share in your joy," Ahhotep said and pressed her hand on his chest. "I let myself—"

"Ahhotep, stop," he interrupted and lowered his forehead to hers. "I wished I could have held you like this. Even though I was sad to leave my daughter's family, I cherished your touch, even if it was just a brush." He grinned with a sorrowful chuckle. "Your mother has done an excellent job in keeping us apart."

Ahhotep snorted. "That she has." Her fingers toyed with his collar. "I told you she would. I told you to find another that could be with you when you came home."

He rubbed her bottom lip with his thumb as he caressed her cheek. "And I told you, I have already chosen." He pressed his lips to hers in a kiss that made her sigh in bliss. The burdens rolled off of her shoulders as the fullness of his cinnamon scent intoxicated her. Her fingers almost let her headdress slip, but the weight of the golden vulture grounded her back in truth. The last of the day's light was fading fast in the west.

The creak of the palace's doors sounded in the otherwise quiet evening, and Baba pulled away at Ahhotep's dismay. "You need to go back before they know you are gone," he said in a husky, breathless whisper. "But I selfishly want you to stay with me." His fingers curled into his hands as if releasing her, but he gave her one more soft kiss. "You should go back. I am not worth tarnishing your image even more than I have. I know why you have not called me to the council room anymore."

But Ahhotep did not move and slipped her free arm around his waist, molding her body to his. "I am willing to take the chance if you are. They will not know if I was at Per-djed-ken or the temple or—"

"Without Meret, Nena, guards, and fleetsmen?" Baba's hushed words tingled on her lips, and he tightened his grasp on her.

The creak from the second door closing pierced the air.

His eyes were full of fire but also of worry. "How will you get back inside? They will surely notice you are missing come daybreak."

Ahhotep smiled and shrugged. "If I cannot sneak back, then I will walk back into the palace as queen," she said, rubbing the gold vulture headdress between her fingers. "I am *Queen*, I figured."

She lifted a shoulder in a slight shrug. "I should be able to do what I want. And tonight, I want to be a woman. I want to talk with you, kiss you, be with you. Whatever rumors and whisperings and punishments that come from tonight, I will endure them. But only if you want to chance the consequences with me."

He smiled with a sparkle in his eye. "Well then, maybe I should come home more often," he teased.

She playfully bit his lip. "You should," she whispered, knowing he could not come home as often as he wanted, only what the war allowed.

Then in a somber tone and a brush of his lip against hers, he said, "You are worth every possible consequence, Ahhotep."

The final *thunk* that reverberated through the air

sealed Ahhotep's and Baba's fate. The doors were closed. She could not go back that night. The answers to the questions of what would happen to them would be revealed come the morning.

Baba's smile reached both ears as he released all but her hand.

He caressed her face before he led her to his nearby villa.

"How are my grandson and daughter?" he asked as the narrow two-story villa came into view. The walled enclosure stood tall with a gate in the middle.

"Thutmose is a beautiful, healthy boy and in the good hands of Lady Rai," Ahhotep said. "Sapair is a happy father, and Senseneb sleeps after the three-day ordeal. Tawaret blessed both mother and child."

He slid his arm around her shoulders and pulled her close. "I am glad to hear that," he said and kissed her temple.

As they neared the gate, he waved to the old man whose family kept the home since no one lived there while Baba and his son were away. He was tending the courtyard and the small temple grounds in front of the main house.

"Glad you are home safe, Admiral," the old man said as he brushed away dirt from the mud-brick pathway before Baba and Ahhotep walked on it.

"Anhur is generous to his soldiers," Baba declared, acknowledging the sentiment with a smile and a dip of his chin.

The old man's eyes shifted to Ahhotep. "Pretty woman, Admiral. May I have the pleasure of meeting her?"

Baba cleared his throat, and Ahhotep froze.

"Not tonight, Nemheb. Maybe another time," Baba

said and hurried Ahhotep inside. The door closed behind her, shutting out the dusk. Baba lit an oil lamp. "Welcome to my villa, Ahhotep," he said with a slight bow.

She giggled like a giddy child. He reached for her hand, kissed her fingers, and then opened her wrist to his lips. He interlaced his fingers with hers and led her to the inner room of his villa, where the oil lamp's flame overpowered the moonlight from the wall vents. The statues of Isis, Anhur, and Nekhbet stood in their shrine encasements, and Baba placed the oil lamp on the intricately woven rug in front of them. He helped Ahhotep to sit on a plush cushion, and then he took a seat behind her, cradling his arms around her belly and pulling her close.

She turned an ear to his chest and listened to his strong and steady heartbeat as she watched the lamp light flicker on the plastered walls; its oil was already almost gone. He was spending his rationed oil on her. She took a deep breath and closed her eyes. "How much longer do you think the war will last, Baba?" she asked almost inaudibly.

His chin touched her forehead. "It took a hundred years for the Hekka Khasut to establish dominance. It will not be a quick expulsion."

Ahhotep's eyes welled with tears as her heart opened to Baba, her one true friend. "I had hoped it would be over before Ahmose went to war."

"I had hoped the same," Baba said and squeezed her tighter.

Ahhotep sniffled back her tears, remembering Ahmose's boyish frame sitting on the throne that was too big for him only a few years ago.

"He was this little ten-year-old boy, a child. The day

he would become a man—a warrior—and board The Wild Bull seemed so far off. I had selfishly thought that day would never come. As Royal Commander, I thought I could end the war in his stead; that I could save my son from seeing battle."

She rolled her head to look upon his countenance in the flickering light. His eyes were full, and his ka pulled the brimming tears down her cheeks. "And now it is time. That day has come."

He cupped her face and wiped some of her tears away with a gentle thumb. She relaxed into him, letting him hold her and press a long, soft kiss on her forehead.

"He is a man, a warrior; he should have boarded The Wild Bull when Ramose was born last year. But I delayed him by speaking of how sickly his sons were and convinced him he needed a healthy boy—a boy sure to live. And now, Tetian sends taunts that Ahmose is a coward like the Hekka Khasut king we want to expel."

Baba was quick with a reply. "Do not bother with Tetian. He is a pompous fool."

She knew that, but it made her wonder.

"Even so, was it wrong of me to ask Ahmose to stay and see the birth of Ahmose-Nefertari's next child and the next? I convinced my own son not to fulfill his destiny because I am terrified he will not return home. Am I the coward, Baba?"

"No." His voice was firm, full of confidence. He pulled her legs over his thigh and cradled her in his lap. "You are a mother—one worthy of admiration. The general and I keep a firm command of your son's armies while he is in the palace, and I have already promised you I would not let him come home as his brother. We do not see him as a coward king, nor do the Medjay, nor do the soldiers. They see him as a young king ensuring the divine bloodline continues, especially given this war."

Ahhotep curled up in Baba's arms. "Is it wrong of me to see my grandchildren as security, to ensure our family lives on? What will happen if both of Ahmose's sons perish? What if Sapair is slain and Thutmose—"

"*Shh. Shh.*" Baba stroked her arm and leg—his hands sweeping down her bare flesh, giving her warmth in the growing night's chilled air. "I think everyone sees their children and grandchildren as security. We love them, but they are our legacy. They carry us in their memories. And if all of the royal family is lost in this life, the gods will appoint another." He lifted her face to his and whispered, "They will always provide, Ahhotep. You must have faith in the gods. You carry such a large burden, but it doesn't have to be so heavy."

His words were caught in her mind, trapped, and repeated. Tears seared her eyes and ran freely down her cheeks. "It is so heavy," she cried in muted tones. "I miss Tao, Kamose, Sitkamose, Binpu, Siamun, and I fear what is to come with this war. Tep does not even speak to me anymore. I only see her when I cannot sleep and go into their room." She shook her head. "And you, I only see you and speak to you a few times a year, yet you are my only friend. You hear me . . . comfort me when no other does. And I find myself asking, Why? Why do you love me? Why, when you could have another?"

Baba cupped her face, and his gaze pierced her doubts and caused her breath to stop. The shadows flickered across his broad brow and chiseled chin and danced around his endless night eyes.

"You are courageous, strong, beautiful, a fearless leader, a loving mother, and loyal to Kemet." His whispered words brushed her lips. "And even though I admired you as our queen, I started to love you when I saw your pain and felt it as my own."

His eyes averted, and he chewed his lip, lost in memories.

"My pain?" she asked, again drawing his gaze.

"My late wife, Ebana, had been sick and was on the roof to escape the heat. She had fallen off. Her servants laid her at my feet." His eyes glistened. "I had cried out, and when King Seqenenre Tao was brought to yours, I saw the glisten in your eyes and knew you could not."

A deep breath filled the space between them. "Your mother keeps her distance, and you are alone in the palace, never allowing yourself the freedom to be. Yet you endure—your will is grounded in goodness and warmth. And that is why you will always be a better leader than your mother."

He wiped away her tears as the oil lamps' light struggled to hold on to its last bit of flame. "I will be here for you—whatever you need or want. You will never have to hide your pain with me. I see you. I *see* you, Ahhotep, and I love you for who you are. Your motives are pure, and your actions are rooted in love and loyalty. The gods could not ask for a greater mother of their divinely appointed."

A small smile arose on her lips and his. The flame went out, leaving streams of moonlight falling in through the wall vents.

"Baba," she whispered. Someone who loved her and listened to her and cared for her. *Believed* in her. Someone who had felt her agony, admired her struggle, and supported her methods. Finally, she felt understood. Finally, she felt safe just to be. Yet the time was fleeting. The morning would come soon, and again, she would be alone, forced to endure until he came back, if he came back.

The smile faded.

Her arms wrapped around his neck, and she brought her forehead to his.

"I wish we could be as this," she whispered and pressed her lips to his.

He pulled her cloak around them to keep warm on the crisp night.

"We are like this," he murmured, kissing her bottom lip.

"Always, I mean."

He kissed her top lip and ran his hands down her back. "As do I, my love."

27

A TIME FOR CHANCE | AHHOTEP

SEDJEFATAWY, 1561 BC

The dawn came and went. Baba and Ahhotep stared at the palace walls from the doorstep of his villa. His arm was firmly wrapped around her. They had overslept in their time of peace.

"I do not wish to go back," she whispered.

"As I do not wish to leave for war," he said, brushing her cloak-covered shoulder with a thumb. The season's evening and early morning were crisp, but the day did not require a cloak to stay warm.

Ahhotep knew a cloak would draw attention but so would her royal regalia beneath the layered linens. She had said she would walk in as queen, but the thought of doing so upset her stomach.

"Let me go alone. At least if I go alone, I could have been at any number of places," she said. "If you come, then there is only one place I could have been."

He shook his head. "I will not leave you alone to walk the street. I swore to defend Kemet and the royal family with my life."

An alarm horn blasted from the palace, and Ahhotep gulped.

"They now know I am gone," she said and sighed. She pulled her vulture headdress from beneath her cloak and placed it on her head while Baba untied her cloak. There was no use in hiding who she was anymore. The chances of sneaking in were gone with the alarm.

"No matter what happens, Ahhotep," Baba said and pulled her face to him with a gentle nudge of her chin. "I choose you."

She kissed him full on the mouth, perceivably one last time. "And I choose you," she whispered.

They walked hand-in-hand until they rounded the street to the palace doors when Baba squeezed her hand before releasing it.

Ahhotep chuckled. Everyone would know where she was since the Admiral was her escort to the palace, but he still wanted her image intact when she walked through the doors. Maybe it would help with perceptions too. What would she say that might be believable? Her mind came up empty.

The guards had their spears pointed out on high alert, but their jaws fell agape at the Royal Commander approaching with the Admiral as the only one in her retinue, holding her cloak draped over his forearm.

Why had she been out of the palace? she asked herself as she passed through the palace doors. *Maybe no one would ask*, she thought and pressed a one-sided grin. *I am a queen, and I do what I want*, she supposed was a potential response. *Do not ask the question for which you do not have the right to know the answer!* as another. She half-chuckled to herself, knowing she had to face her mother and her children, either answering or not answering. Suspicions would be confirmed unless she could continue holding to the fact she only sought the Admiral's counsel. She had indeed sought his advice, but it had been overnight and outside the palace. Her lips pursed, and she shook her head. What would she say?

The roil in her stomach drowned out rational thought and numbed her mind as she walked the long corridor to the courtyard and throne room. A messenger ran ahead, presumably to tell the alarm horn to stop blowing. She could only hope her mother did not care about her anymore and would say nothing to her and simply dismiss Baba to the fleet again. Ahhotep's eyes lifted in annoyance at her mother's actions the day prior as the alarm horn stopped.

The morning sun flooded the courtyard and shone upon Tao and Kamose's stone visages. They watched her come to a halt before the throne room doors. She glanced at Baba, and he gave her a soft, reassuring nod. The guards, who usually stared straight ahead, glanced between Ahhotep and the Admiral.

"As you were," Ahhotep said, and their stares returned to their dutiful positions.

The throne room doors opened and Ahhotep beheld Tetisheri, Ahmose, and Ahmose-Nefertari on the dais.

"What were you doing, God's Mother?" Tetisheri stood in her place beside Ahmose and leered at Baba.

They walked in, and Ahhotep quelled the fear of confirming suspicions and the rage that her mother still would not use her greater title, that of Royal Commander. She took a deep breath, grabbed ahold of her voice, cleared her mind, and spoke with every indignation of an accused queen. The perfect response came to her in her indignation.

"Since the Great Wife sent the Admiral away before he could truly see his royal grandson, I went to tell him about how Prince Thutmose fared and express regret for the brevity of his stay yesterday morning; however, the harem was too busy, and I could not find Meret and Nena or a guard to accompany me. The palace doors were closed as I was speaking with the Admiral. I was unable to reenter. Thus, the Admiral kept me as a guest in his villa, citing his oath to protect the royal family."

Ahmose and Ahmose-Nefertari nodded their heads in agreement, but her mother scoffed. "Even if I believed you—"

"Are you calling the Royal Commander a liar, Great Wife?" Ahhotep asked. It was not all a lie, she reasoned. Meret and Nena, or a harem guard, were nowhere to be found, although she had not actively sought them.

Tetisheri pointed to Baba. "Guards, seize him, for he has touched royal flesh."

They shuffled toward him, but Ahhotep stepped in front of him. "Belay that command," she said with a hand to halt a coming guard before turning her attention to her mother. "Your Admiral, Great Wife? Are you sentencing this war to the Hekka Khasut's favor?"

Tetisheri snapped her fingers. "Guards, seize the Admiral."

But Ahmose stood up. "Stand down. The Admiral is needed, and we have no proof he touched royal flesh."

The guards obeyed their king and retook their posts.

Tetisheri spun around. "I saw them in the council room the same year you became sole regent. He held her in his arms. Your mother has grown rash and irresponsible. You would do well to remove her from your dais and the Admiral from your military ranks, as he does not care to keep the royal family sacred and, therefore, does not honor their divinity."

Ahmose-Nefertari stepped forward. "If he did not honor the Royal Commander, why would he escort her into the palace? Would he not have let her come alone?

The Admiral has been a long-time friend to the crown and the Royal Commander's most trusted advisor. The time of which you speak was after King Kamose was slain. Perhaps he only consoled God's Mother, which, if done in privacy, I do not believe punishment is warranted."

Tetisheri snorted and shook her head at the royal duo before facing Ahhotep. She stepped toe-to-toe with Ahhotep and ran her gaze from the bottom to the top of her face.

"Ta-Seti rule would never have allowed this to stand," she spat in a hushed whisper. Her eyes narrowed to slits, but she said nothing more. The remaining words she previously would have spewed from her hateful mouth were not worth her breath. She strode out of the throne room with her maidservants at her heels.

Meret and Nena arrived and took their place on the queen's side. Meret took Ahhotep's cloak from Baba as Ahhotep looked at her children. She had fooled them, and it tore at her heart, or perhaps they had known the truth and came to her rescue? But why would they do that? She lowered her chin to her son. "King Ahmose, as I have been out of the palace, I request a bath to purify myself before ascending to the divine's dais."

He nodded, then he looked to the Admiral. "Our graciousness to your safe-keeping of the Royal Commander while she was prevented reentry into the palace. Journey well to the north, Admiral."

Baba bowed at the waist. "It is my honor, King Ahmose," he said, rising and then a bow of the head to Ahhotep. "And Royal Commander."

"May Anhur keep you well and bring you home," she said.

They both exited the throne room and went their

separate ways: Ahhotep to the harem and Baba to the fleet. She peered over her shoulder to see him do the same.

I will miss you, Baba, she thought. *Come home to me. When Ahmose leaves for war, bring both of you home to me.*

28

A TIME OF AGE |
AHMOSE
SEDJEFATAWY, 1560 BC

Ahmose stood upon The Wild Bull, facing his mother on the dock. The last king aboard its planks was brought home in a litter carried by Anubis priests. The blue khepresh crown was upon Ahmose's head, and his twenty years of life had trained him for this day: to retake and finish what his brother and father had set out to do. He would usher in a new era for Kemet in one unified land under one divine king. And if not, one of his three sons would take his place should he come home as Kamose did. He looked at his firstborn son, Ahmose-Ankh—the coughing four-year-old gripping his mother's dress—and then to Ramose—the healthier son at two years of age but still thin and weak.

His one-year-old twin girls, Ahmose-Meryet Amon and Ahmose-Sitamun, stood naked beside his mother. Lady Rai stood beside Ahmose-Nefertari, holding their newborn son, Ahmose-Sipair. He was a "healthy heir," as his grandmother had wanted, and a "healthy baby boy," as his mother had advised.

With Ahmose-Sipair's birth, Ahmose could now take command of the army per the agreement with his mother. He glanced at his brother Sapair who stood next to his wife, Senseneb, and one-year-old son, Thutmose. His mother had urged him not to take Sapair with him if his sons grew ill and passed. It was the exact reason he had not named Sapair as General or Admiral or Viceroy, thus putting Sapair in danger of losing his life.

Sapair leaned over, kissed his wife on the cheek, and squeezed her hand. Ahmose glanced at Ahmose-Nefertari and his lesser wives, Henuttamehu and Kasmut. One was his sister, one was his half-sister, and the other his friend, but it was a different love he had for them than Sapair had for his wife.

He scanned the royal family and noted his grandmother had not come to see him off. She had stayed in the harem for the past year and refused to see or talk to him, or any of them for that matter. He sighed at her stubbornness. Her presence would have instilled more faith in his voyage down the Nile to try to take Lunu again.

He shook his head at his grandmother's seemingly childish response. After everything she had put her family through, she abandons them simply because he and Ahmose-Nefertari had questioned her judgment in imprisoning his Admiral for escorting his mother home. He was not entirely sure his mother spoke the whole truth, but even if she did not, it seemed petty to him. She had a plausible excuse that could deter any rumors, and he doubted the gods would hold her heart heavy on the scales of Ma'at for speaking the half-truth. It seemed justifiable to him; why would it not be also for the gods?

His mother had been a rock, a pillar of strength. He had leaned upon her many times, but who had she depended upon? Not his grandmother or else reap a harsh scolding. So she leaned upon a friend. Even if the

Admiral had held her in her sorrow for her family, he was glad she had someone, as he had relied upon both her and Ahmose-Nefertari. After all, they were in a war, and his mother led it with courage and excellence. She deserved a close friend.

It seemed, for once, his grandmother had failed to meet his expectation until she emerged from the palace doors, escorted by her maidservants and stewards. She made her way to his mother's side—did not look at her —but lifted her chin to Ahmose.

Ahmose gave a slight nod of his head toward her, and she returned the same. *All will be well then*, he reassured himself. *She has had a year to lick her wounds. She loves Kemet and will do what is needed.* The soft rock of the boat seemed to show the gods' acceptance of the Great Wife's presence. With the entire royal family's blessing, they were sure to be victorious.

The princes had come except for Tetian, but Metjen and Baufre stood in the crowd—Metjen with a scowl, and Baufre, in a daze, smiling at the festivities.

They had both bowed and paid their respects to him as their king, but Ahmose wondered why they had come, especially Metjen, after sailing past Waset on numerous occasions to visit Tetian. The flutter of anxiety unsettled his stomach as he stared at the prince. The Viceroy Si-Tayet had also brought word from his voyage to Sedjefatawy in the last season, there were many warships on Ta-Seti's banks and many being built.

Maybe I should leave men here, he thought, but his grandmother's confidence remained in memory. Perhaps, Tetian was only preparing to make a grand entrance in his dire hour of need in the north, or come in as the hero if he should fail. It would be a probable action for Tetian's persona. He let a breath out through clenched teeth and relaxed his shoulders. He scanned the royal family, and he locked eyes with his mother.

"But just in case, I will leave some men here," he muttered to himself. He turned to a royal messenger at the ready. "See to it, a unit is left at Per-djed-ken and a second unit is left at Sedjefatawy."

The messenger bowed and ran to the Troop Commanders while Ahmose thought. *Both units at Per-djed-ken and Sedjefatawy: one if Tetian attacks from the south and another should Metjen and Baufre attack from the north.* He nodded to seal his decision. It was risky to leave two hundred men behind who would most definitely be needed in their fight in the Lower, but that nagging notion of an internal uprising hadn't ceased in the last season.

His mother saw the commotion on the ports and bowed her head at him, understanding his decision, but his grandmother shook her head and sighed. He reasoned that since she had not come to the council meeting when Si-Tayet had come, she did not know about the growing number of warships in Ta-Seti. She had kept to herself in the harem, so he hadn't expected anyone to tell her. But if she graced the throne room again in his absence, he was sure either his mother or wife would say something.

The horses' neighs filled the port as they boarded the boats and the new brightly painted war chariots behind them. The Bedu had been good to them, hopeful for their victory to ensure peace and mutually beneficial trading partners in the future. The new trainees numbered a thousand men from the nomes, trained under the Medjay, the Bedu, and Ahmose-Ebana. They looked like soldiers, trained like soldiers, but time would tell.

As it would for me, he mused. He let out a shaky breath

and licked a dry lip as he prayed silently. *Anut, Hathor, Sekhmet, bring me home. Let my destiny be to unite Kemet. I have trained since I was eight years old; I can do this if you grant me your blessings and protection.*

Baba came and stood on his left and Ahmose-Ebana on his right.

"The King is ready." The Admiral's voice bellowed across the port waters. "He is The Strong. The Bull. The Lord of Strength is Re. Given Life. The Warrior King. He is King Ahmose!"

Those on the port lifted a cheer in his name.

"You are our King," Baba whispered as he lifted a hand to acknowledge those on the port.

Ahmose noticed his admiral's focus did not move from his mother, and his mother's gaze shifted from him to Baba and back to him. Baba nodded his head once to her, and she returned a bright beam.

A sigh escaped him. "You promised God's Mother to keep me safe, Admiral?" He guessed at the hidden exchange.

Admiral turned to him and bowed his head. "I made God's Mother many promises." He lifted from his bow to once again look him in the eyes. "I am proud to serve next to you as I did King Kamose, and I am honored that my son shall also serve next to you. With my life, I swear you will return home alive so you can end this war and establish a new era for Kemet."

Ahmose's shoulders shrank as he envisioned his dark tomb, still being hewn from the rock, his pyramid only with foundations laid. He did not want to end like his brother. The archers in the chariots, the trained chariot drivers, the Medjay and their spears and arrows, and the foot soldiers each supplied the superior khopesh—all advancements his brother did not possess. Maybe he

290

would be victorious; perhaps he would come home alive and finish what his father started.

Ahmose grinned and nodded. "Fear will live in the eyes of our enemies at the mention of my name."

Baba lifted his chin in pride. "So it will be."

29

A TIME OF
CONFESSIONS |
AHMOSE

THE WILD BULL, 1559 BC

The royal boat sat tied to the dock at Sau, a city in the Nile Delta. The Nile waves gently lapped against its hull. Ahmose boarded it along with Baba. It seemed that Baba had stuck to his side more than his own son over the past year. He had almost become like his shadow or a talking body servant.

It had been quite a month, putting down riots in the delta; the latest one ended in victory at Sau, but it was not without its grievances. Servants came and wiped the blood from his armor and khopesh.

The Apiru were helping tend to his soldiers in the fields. He did not trust them entirely, nor did Baba. He had ordered his soldiers not to eat what the Apiru provided but allowed the Apiru to dress wounds. The Apiru's long linens and the women's head scarfs were very different from the Aamu, who had stolen Kemet's identity and dressed in shendyts, beaded pectorals, and elaborate wigs.

Ahmose did not look at Baba and strode to the center of the boat where the royal's meal was about to be served. Baba followed him, saying nothing.

Ahmose sat down on the King's thick dining rug, weaved with an intricate design of scarabs, and a servant handed him a bowl of soup and bread. Baba remained standing and without food, waiting for Ahmose's invitation.

He thought, *I do not want him to follow me anymore, but I cannot offend him. He is my best officer.*

He took a bite of bread and leaned back. He swallowed and sighed. "Bring the Admiral the evening meal, and Admiral, please dine with your King."

Baba knelt on a similar mat but more basic in its design. "My King is most gracious," he said and received his soup.

But Ahmose could not let it go. "Admiral, you embarrassed the King today. You called for me to fall back when I took but five steps toward a rioter. I can defend myself, especially with a rebellious Aamu citizen, if this past year has not shown you as such."

Baba sat down and crossed his legs. He took a sip of soup and drew in a deep breath. "I apologize to you, King Ahmose, for it was not my intent to embarrass the divinely appointed." He locked eyes with him. "I only fear my misstep will end with the King in the care of the Anubis priests."

Ahmose's brow furrowed, and he shooed away the servants, so the two men could speak frankly with each other. "Is this a promise you made to my mother? You acknowledged her unspoken command last year when we set sail from Waset. You never directly answered my question. You stay by my side at all times. I want you to lead our fleet, not coddle me."

Baba placed his soup down on the rug. "Do you feel I am not leading your fleet?"

Ahmose gritted his teeth. "You are doing a fine job, but you are not a body servant. You are an Admiral."

Baba tapped his finger on his knee. "Yes, King Ahmose, I am an Admiral and a friend to the crown. I promised your mother I would not bring home another slain son. I would rather anyone else, including myself and my son, go home in a funerary litter. You will stay by my side in battle, King Ahmose. It will be the only request I make of you on behalf of your mother."

Ahmose swallowed his pride. *Even Baba's son, his only son?* They sat in silence again until Ahmose sipped his soup. Baba took a bite of bread. His life was more than any of theirs, he finally realized. Because he was king, they would all die for him. How honoring and . . . humbling. He closed his eyes and bowed his head. "Yes, Admiral, I will grant your request," he said, lifting his head and finding Baba's gaze.

The Admiral dipped his chin in graciousness.

They continued to eat in silence, but another question arose in Ahmose's mind, and it slipped on his tongue. "When did you promise my mother this?"

Baba squinted, trying to recall. A soft gleam came over his eyes, and a faint smile arose on his lips. "It was before the Crown Prince was born."

"That was five years ago," Ahmose said.

"Yes, and it was a few years before that." Baba's gaze drifted to his bowl, and he sipped his dinner.

"Why would you promise to care for me when I may not have even gone to war? Neither you nor my mother knew this war would continue five years later."

"Your mother could not sleep and called me to the council room to discuss what was on her mind. She feared for you, and to calm her fears, I made my promise. When we spoke the night she spent outside the palace, I told her again of my promise because she feared for your life, even more so since you would probably leave for war in the coming year, which you did."

Ahmose nodded, and the question that he had held in the back of his mind since that night his mother was stranded outside the palace came to mind. But what would it change if his mother had lied? She was still his mother, and her service to him was greater than all others. What if the Admiral was more than a friend to her? Would it change the way he saw him? Would it sicken him or make him happy his mother had found love again? His stomach growled, wanting more food, so he answered the stubborn beast and took another bite of bread.

After a few moments of eating in silence, he decided to ask his question, bear the answer, and determine how he felt afterward. "Was it true?"

"I have spoken the truth," Baba said.

"No, what my mother said about being stranded outside the palace?" Ahmose could not look at Baba, so he focused on his soup and the glazed rim of the bowl, running his finger along it.

Baba shifted. "What she said, from what I recall, was true."

Ahmose would have believed him if he had not shifted. "Was it the whole truth?"

Baba again put down his bowl and leaned his elbows on his knees. "No, my King, it was not the whole truth."

Ahmose's jaw grew taut, and he narrowed his eyes. "What was the whole truth?"

Baba picked up his bowl again and began to eat until Ahmose turned his gaze to him. "Well?"

Baba stared off into the eastern sky; the dark realm of Apep fast approached. "Once I tell you the whole truth, you will be unable to not know it. Is that what you want?"

Ahmose nodded. He gripped the bowl in his hands, wondering if he should recant his question. Maybe he did not want to know. But maybe he did. He nodded again, seeing Baba waiting for him to indeed decide.

"I love your mother, and she loves me," he said fast as if ripping out a suture. "That night, your mother came to me alone without her royal dress, and I was glad to receive her in my home."

"And what of the council room meetings?" Ahmose asked, his stomach churning. The vision of Baba holding his mother while she cried or held sorrow or fear as a friend turned into something entirely different. He blinked a few times to get the image out of his mind before he realized what he had asked and what Baba was answering.

"The few times we could be together without prying ears or eyes." Baba sat up straight and watched him think.

Ahmose ran his answers through his mind once more. Baba had never explicitly said they were lovers. Maybe Baba was only a close friend. He didn't want to make assumptions, but what would he do if they *were* lovers? His grandmother was ready to imprison Baba for even holding his mother. Was that the right thing to do? He could stop asking Baba questions, but his mouth spoke the question that lingered on his tongue.

"So, you have touched royal flesh intimately, more than a friend to the crown would?" Ahmose said with a bitter taste in his mouth. Why had he asked that?

"Yes," Baba said before Ahmose could take the question back.

Ahmose nodded and cleared his throat. There were

no more assumptions to be made. With this knowledge, what would he do? Was there a law that said no one could touch royal flesh? She had been the divine king's wife. But Ahmose never knew his father. His only memory of his father was a faint image of the mangled corpse brought home by the Aamu. Yet he knew the Admiral, and the Admiral was a good man. He popped his neck with a sharp turn of his head.

Ahmose noticed while he thought, the Admiral did not flinch, have an excuse ready, or ask to be treated better than anyone else who broke the royal standard. Maybe that was why Ahmose was drawn to him. He accepted responsibility for his actions.

Ahmose sipped his soup. "You realize I could relieve you of your command, and have you sent back to Waset in bonds?"

Baba nodded without a waver in his voice or his eye. "I do."

Ahmose drew in a deep breath and finished his soup. "Then sleep well, Admiral. We have a long day tomorrow heading to the next riot downriver," he said as he rose from his rug, not giving Baba a chance to respond.

He went to the king's small retreat aboard the royal warship. The servants drew his opaque curtains to keep the flies out. He fell on the makeshift lounger with a full belly. The gentle rock of the boat nearly put him out as soon as he laid down, but before sleep took him, he smiled. His mother had always been good to him and chose a good man to love. The Admiral's secret would be safe with him—law or no law.

30
A TIME OF VALOR |
AHMOSE
LUNU, 1558 BC

The gentle bounce of the barge against the stone pier broke Ahmose from his haze-like visions that teetered between victory and defeat. Shouts and clamoring of pending battle lay thick in the large port city of Lunu, which claimed the sun god Re as their patron deity. In Ahmose's eyes, victory over this city would seal his great-great-grandfather's claim of divine appointment. Even though the Hekka Khasut revered Set above all other gods, the true Kemet knew Re, with his hidden one Amun, was premier. Reclaiming this city would send a message to King Apepi that their foreign reign was nearing its end and prove Re over Set. If defeated, Ahmose knew a fiery death awaited them.

It had taken two years to reach Lunu as they had to abolish rebellions on the way north and settle riots in the delta. They had tried to go around Lunu and Per-Bastet and hit Hut-Waret straight on, but the chariot wheels would not go through the marshlands. They had to go through Lunu. The next port north was Per-Bastet. They could not take it and choke out Lunu as they had done with the large cities in the Upper. But this was how his father was killed—rushing a large, fortified city.

A steady stream of cool breath flowed from his nostrils. Hot, muggy air blew from a westward wind and swept away some of the weaker flies that buzzed around Ahmose's silver diadem. The diadem's gold-bodied royal cobra cast a slight shadow down the bridge of his nose from the overhead sun. Although shaded beneath the blue khepresh crown, the top of his head felt the heat more than his bare skin.

"Lunu is full of traitors," Baba muttered, breaking Ahmose from his thoughts. "Loyal to the Hekka Khasut and not to the true King to whom this land belongs."

Ahmose turned around to face the elite soldiers on his royal boat. The black-skinned, leopard-waisted Medjay were ready to spill over the side of the barge and onto the pier. Their Kerman blood ran thick through their veins, but their commitment to his family had been proven time and time again. But he felt their loyalty was greater than just the gold and grain they were paid. They would fight and die next to him; they were *his* men as far as he was concerned.

Baba yelled out, "For Kemet! For the true divine King!" His voice bellowed across the large military barges.

A single chant rang through the air, followed by a loud cadence of spears banging on the barge's deck. "For Ahmose! For the King! For Kemet!"

With the pride of his most elite and most fierce fighting force standing in front of him, Ahmose's twenty-two-year-old body grew stronger with the great sound his forces summoned.

Ahmose lifted his khopesh high in the air, so its

sickled-bronze body glinted in the sun as he faced the Medjay. Its weight was superior to that of the spear of his father. Visions of his father's mangled face and his brother's body passed in memory, but he pushed them away as a strong breeze took the remainder of the flies with it.

"Today, Re and Amun will grant us victory." His voice carried on the waters of the Nile, and three more barges bumped against their own, giving them all a slight jolt. But each man, nimble and war-minded, absorbed the jolt with an eerie synchronization.

"Fight, men. Fight for this land which is ours," he yelled out and took the first step onto the barge ramp and onto the pier—his body servant just ahead of him and Baba beside him.

The thundering wave of Medjay rushed off the barge in a swift, fluid wave, each man trusting his brother in arms to step when he was supposed to step and be sure of foot. With his khopesh held high and his shield in front of him, Ahmose led his Medjay in rushing the garrison at Lunu.

Ahmose's lasting war cry sounded behind him as the horse-drawn chariots of the Hekka Khasut advanced toward the port forces. His shield caught an arrow, as did his body servant, who fell dead at his feet.

"Now!" He yelled, and the Medjay sent their barrage of arrows and spears sailing toward the chariots' horses, each landing their target.

They advanced again, watching the chariots behind them careen to miss the wreckage of disabled comrades.

"Cut them down!" Ahmose cried as he removed the head of an Aamu who had been flung from his crippled chariot. The King's sickle-shaped sword slung the blood droplets from his latest killing into the air. Baba stepped in front of him to slow him down in his advance as the Medjay and soldiers of Kemet took over.

Ahmose-Ebana's new chariots raced past them. Ahmose's royal chariot stopped, so he could board. The new design proved well as each chariot could get close to the enemy so the archer could shoot and whip around, dodging the fallen.

The carnage went on as the Medjay sent another wave of spears toward the advancing second line of Aamu chariots that rushed upon them. Ahmose-Ebana's improved chariots proved superior again and again until the Hekka Khasut's forces were pushed back into the garrisoned port city under a setting sun.

Ahmose wanted to crumple over as his chest rasped for precious breath, but he stood tall and wiped his leaking nose with the back of his forearm. "Lay siege," he yelled, and as his Troop Commanders repeated the order throughout the fighting men, he said on a tired breath, "Make camp."

He scanned the Medjay, all men of great prowess, carrying out his order. He had fought well, but he needed to be better. The new soldiers that had left Per-djed-ken with him two years prior mingled among the decades-long veterans, and Ahmose could not tell each apart. He had to be better.

Even the older Baba stood beside him, barely winded.

He hooked his khopesh to his shendyt's belt and palmed his face, wiping the sweat from his brow. Blood tainted the air as he took in a full breath. The usually lightweight leather and reed khepresh crown grew heavy upon his head. The silver diadem constrained his head's heat—his head begging for release from his regal wear.

His eyesight blurred for a moment, and his feet compensated for his slight shift in weight.

Baba's heavy hand fell on his shoulder. "Well done again, my King."

Ahmose nodded and peered over at his loyal military officer, feigning stability upon his legs. "They still have not surrendered. Tell me well done when we take the city," he said, still not entirely familiar with how he should act with his closest advisors. Baba had been like a father to him these past two years, and so he allowed himself to be less than what the crown dictated him be to others. Perhaps it was the same confidence his mother had in him.

Baba said with a beam, "We shall have Lunu in surrender in a few short days or decans. And we shall hope they have not sent for reinforcements from Per-Bastet."

Ahmose scanned the garrison and imagined the Aamu hiding and cowering behind their walls. "My father started with only eight nomes, and now only three remain under the Hekka Khasut's control. Two more cities to Hut-Waret," Ahmose spat and snorted, "where the King of the Hekka Khasut lives in stolen luxury and remains faceless in war."

"The coward King Apepi," Baba said with a nod. He patted Ahmose's shoulder and withdrew his hand. "Unlike ours, a King of courage and strength. The future of Kemet is bright with you, blessed by the gods." He gestured to the royal blue Khepresh crown upon Ahmose's head. "Perhaps King Apepi's cowardice will keep Per-Bastet's forces in Per-Bastet to further shield himself from your glory." He smiled. "Your name will be remembered forever as the one who propelled Kemet into a golden era."

"Yes, we will bring my grandfather's vision to fruition." Ahmose turned his face to the western sun. Its rays poured on his skin. The god Re and all of the Kings of the past were there with him on his brilliant sun barge fighting Apep, the evil serpent of darkness, to raise the Aten every morning. His father and brother were there on that sun barge, having become one with Re.

"Even though you are gone from this life, Father and Kamose, I know you are proud this day," Ahmose whispered, finding his breath.

"Yes," Baba whispered behind him, having heard him. "Very proud."

LUNU, 1557 BC

The whinny of a horse sounded in the distance after Ahmose's forces took Lunu a year later. The siege had proved a good tactic for the large, garrisoned port city and was the strategy that had provided for them this far. They had slain every Aamu at Lunu and every man of Kemet that had pledged allegiance to King Apepi. It was a message meant for the Hekka Khasut as a chance to leave or be killed, but the cowardly King had chosen to stay in Hut-Waret.

"Another stallion." Ahmose gestured with his hand to restrain it. "If it is wounded, send it back to Per-djed-ken for breeding."

"It is good," the soldier said, inspecting the slight nick to its neck.

Ahmose nodded. "Then take it with the others."

Baba gestured to ensure the command was carried

out. A few soldiers took the horse's reins and led him off to the growing corral of thirty usable horses.

Ahmose walked alongside Baba with two body servants around him who were silent and willing to die for their King.

He scanned the city walls. Re had been with them, so they did not burn the god's patron city to the ground.

"Should we establish a presence here before moving on to take Per-Bastet?" Ahmose asked, stopping at the city gate.

Baba nodded. "Given the number of rebellions in the previously controlled cities, I would establish a large presence, and maybe it will scare the coward king into leaving and ending this war in peace."

Ahmose nodded. "My thoughts too."

Baba told a nearby royal messenger to take word to Waset of their victory and then turned to face Ahmose. "A wise decision."

Once the soldiers were out of earshot, Ahmose dipped his chin to his admiral. "You were the one to voice it."

Baba smirked. "You were the one to suggest it, my King. You are too generous with praise."

The air seemed clearer as Ahmose nodded and surveyed his victory at the critical port city. He was a young King, but he had done well. But images of his father and brother in his tomb passed before him once more. His fear of a possible future haunted him, both under the Aten's light and Apep's night.

Baba whispered, "King of Kemet, what is it you think?"

Ahmose shook his head. "Nothing, Admiral."

They both looked north toward their next stop, Per-Bastet, and then, Hut-Waret. It seemed so close. Just two or three days' travel, but it would probably be at least a few more years if they were lucky to end it all. But he pushed the thought away and sighed with triumph as the Nile breeze brushed his face.

"Lunu is ours, and victory is within reach."

31

A TIME OF CURSES |
AHMOSE-NEFERTARI

SEDJEFATAWY, 1556 BC

The screams and wails of women shook the palace in the early morning. Shouts of men and splashes of the Nile waters joined in the cacophony. Ahmose-Nefertari stood on the dais with her mother. They snapped their gazes at each other, locking eyes.

"Guard," Ahmose-Nefertari called. "Find out the meaning of the uproar."

The guard bowed and hurried away, but a messenger flew in as soon as he opened the throne room doors. He did not bow, and his eyes were full of fright. "Chief Wife, your children . . . the Nile." His breath poured out in spurts.

Ahmose-Nefertari felt the bottom of her belly hit the floor. Something horrible had happened, and soon she realized she had left her position on the throne and was running alongside the messenger to the harem's inlet of the Nile.

She rounded the corridor, and she beheld Men, Bakaa, Ranofer, and Iuf were all fighting with two crocodiles. The harem guards were thrusting their spears at them. That was when she noticed the flesh hanging from the beasts' mouths. An indecipherable call of pain left her with an agonizing groan. She jolted toward the waters to get her children back, but arms wrapped around her waist and arms, holding her in place.

She screamed out, "No!" Tears blurred her sight. Lady Rai sat with royal children huddled under her arms away from the lap of water. Her screams and tears rivaled Ahmose-Nefertari's. How had the crocodiles even entered their inlet?

She fell to her knees, helpless to do anything but watch the struggle between man and beast—the tug of limbs.

Finally, the crocodiles relented and released their prey. The spears in their backs disappeared into the murky waters along with their targets.

The bitter stench of blood mixed with the muggy air. The Nile's waters turned copper as the lifeforce intertwined with the ebb and flow of their lap against the shore. Men brought the two bodies with missing limbs and placed them before Ahmose-Nefertari. He bowed his head. The steward's usual snark was gone as he spoke in heartfelt bitterness.

"The children were playing in the water as the servants washed the clothes and drew water for baths and needs of the palace. The crocodiles attacked so quickly." His voice stopped abruptly, and he sniffed back tears.

Ahmose-Nefertari reached out to close their eyes. Ahmose-Sitamun and Ahmose-Sipair were gone. Their mangled bodies blurred as she focused on their perfect, untouched faces. The six-year-old twin girl and the four-year-old healthy son were now on their way westward.

Falcons shrieked in the distance, and she knew their ba had left their bodies.

"Why Sobek?" she prayed to the crocodile god in a hushed whisper. "Why?" she whimpered. She fell over her children, wrapping them in her arms. Their blood ran up the fibers of her dress as she enclosed them close and kissed their faces. She cried out, lifting her face to Re.

"Why do you curse me?" she yelled and pulled them closer to her bosom. Her womb had been fertile but had given birth to sickly children. Ahmose-Sipair was the healthiest of them all. He was to be the one who succeeded his father when Ahmose-Ankh and Ramose eventually traveled west. Now, with Siamun, she had three children in the west. Tears streamed from her eyes. Her grandmother caught her attention standing off in the corner of the harem, having emerged from her room to see the cause of the commotion. Her eyes were dry, accompanied by an expressionless visage.

Suddenly, Ahmose-Nefertari felt the weight of the stares upon her. "I can mourn my children," she screamed at them, knowing her place was to control herself and be strong for her people. "You will not judge me!" she yelled again. "Look away if you cannot bear it!"

Her sister Tep, who had not spoken with her since she began work in the harem, stood nearby with a twisted grimace. She drew near and dropped to her knees with wet cheeks. Ahmose-Tumerisy limped toward her and wrapped her arms around her neck.

A hand fell on her opposite shoulder, and she saw her mother kneeling beside her with tears glistening in her eyes, threatening to fall. Had she been there all along? Had she left the throne room, her duties to Kemet, to come with her? Had her mother held her back from going to her children as the stewards struggled with the crocodiles?

Her mother only whispered, "Your pain is mine. We shall bear it together." She looked up and gestured. The priests of Anubis had come and were waiting with their litter. They came and bowed before the kneeling Chief Wife and held out their hands to take the little ones.

Ahmose-Nefertari clung to them and kissed their faces one more time, letting her tears fall into their mouths.

"Chief Wife," a priest said. "Their bodies need preservation for the afterlife. The open wounds will make the process harder if we do not begin immediately."

She held them away from her bosom, wanting to keep them with her, but knew they needed their bodies if they had any chance of living in the Field of Reeds. One at a time, they gently placed each child onto the litter and gathered up the limbs they could find. They left to begin the preparations.

Her children's blood stained her dress and soaked into the fibers of her regal collar. The tips of her braids dripped red as she stared at the crocodile surface in the inlet and return her stare from afar.

"Sobek, you rip my heart from my chest," she muttered in a cry and collapsed with a curdling release.

Her mother and sisters rubbed their hands on her back, and all at once, she wished to be alone in her agony, without the eyes of the harem upon her, judging her strength to rule over them. Was this how her mother felt when Kamose was brought home? When Binpu passed? Yet, her mother's lips had remained sealed. Cries of agony had not escaped them. Her mother was the strong one. Something she could never be. Perhaps she should be as Tep and ask for the release of her position, for they were both unable to stand strong amid terrible loss.

LATE THAT NIGHT, AHMOSE-NEFERTARI DRIFTED FROM ROOM TO room. She stopped at the women's room where Tumerisy and Mosi slept with their older unmarried sister, Nebetta, and her aunts, Inhapi and Sitdjehuti. She brushed Tumerisy's thin strands of hair from her forehead. The young woman was not her child, but she was in a sense. She had proven the royal physician wrong and had lived nineteen years, many years past the age of Sitkamose. Tumerisy had credited Ahmose-Nefertari's love and devotion for why she had lived past expectations.

Ahmose-Nefertari let out a soft breath and bowed her head in the dark room. She had wanted children like Tumerisy, like Ahmose, like Sapair. Children she could love for a long time, but three had been taken from her too soon.

She left and entered the children's room where Meryet Amon, Ramose, and Ahmose-Ankh slept, her three remaining children. Her stepdaughter, Tair, slept soundly beside the two rasping boys. The moonlight revealed their wet cheeks.

Tears welled in her eyes, but her chest was empty. She could not understand why. Why had she lost half of her children? Why had she been cast this lot in life? What had she done to anger the gods? Why did Sobek want to take Ahmose-Sipair and Ahmose-Sitamun? Was it a test for her strength, and she had failed?

"I did not want to be Chief Wife," she whispered

under her breath as her tears broke free. "Your test was in vain, Sobek."

She stood with clean skin in a silken white gown that pressed against her curves in the night's warm breeze.

The last of the waters drawn that day were used to clean her, Ahmose-Sipair, and Ahmose-Sitamun's bodies. Everyone else had to go without bathing. Her blood-stained dress and collar turned brown as it hung in the harem along with the other dresses and shendyts, awaiting a harsh scrubbing. Yet it stood out among the others. Her collar had to be re-beaded as there was no way to remove the bloodstains from the flaxen thread holding it together.

The workmen's call sounded in the night. They had spent the greater of the day draining the inlet to reveal the two crocodiles. They had been cornered and ushered out the way they had come—through a broken water gate. The call signified the gate was fixed. The inlet slowly filled with fresh water. The soft rush of it coming through the gate would have been peaceful to some, but she hated it. She hated the calm of the night. She hated the day's bright, glowing sun. She found no beauty in the once-beautiful creation of Re, Ptah, and Amun.

She slid down the doorpost. Her arms crossed over her knees, and her head leaned back as the tears ran free. She wished to pray but did not know to which deity to pray. They seemed so far away from her—had they abandoned her, or she, them? Her jaw grew taut, and the clench of her teeth made her ears ache.

"Bastet," she finally called out in a muted tone so as not to wake her children. "You are the protector of children. Why did you let this happen? Why were you not there? I pray to you three times a day and offer you food and lotus offerings to appease your senses and images. What have I done to anger you?"

Her words poured over shaky breaths. Her knees drew in, and she buried her head in her arms. She heard a creak behind her, and she sat up straight and turned to look. Her mother stood in a regal posture. Her natural hair was braided over her shoulder. Her hands softly clasped in front of her belly.

Ahmose-Nefertari gulped before resuming her position. She leaned forward and cradled her head in her hands. Of all people, she wished her mother and her grandmother not to see her like this. They would be disappointed in her for acting out her grief. They would think she was a poor example of a Chief Wife. She expected a scolding or a command to stand. She waited for it to come as the soft swish of her mother's dress brushed her leg. She took a deep breath bracing herself for what her mother would say.

But Ahhotep sat down next to her, wrapped an arm around her shoulders, and pulled her into her bosom. It was then, Ahmose-Nefertari let out her cries, muffled by her mother's perfectly pleated dress.

THE PREPARATIONS WERE HALFWAY THROUGH WHEN WORD CAME that Ahmose was coming home after taking Lunu and establishing a presence there.

Ahmose-Nefertari wondered if he had sent the report before hearing her communication about his children. She nodded at the royal messenger and said weakly, "Prepare for our feast for our king, who has gained a significant victory at Lunu."

She felt lifeless even though her eyes could see and her ears could hear.

Her mother standing on the other side of the empty throne, lowered her head. She said in a calm voice, turning her attention to Ahmose-Nefertari, "I had hoped to say this after the children were in their tombs, but with Ahmose coming home, I feel it pressing to say."

Ahmose-Nefertari lifted a shoulder in a slight shrug. She half expected what was coming. She was numb. It did not matter what her mother said.

"Speak."

Her mother sighed and walked around the throne to face her daughter. She placed her hands on Ahmose-Nefertari's shoulders. "Your brother will need another son as Ahmose-Ankh grows weak as Sitkamose had done. I do not expect him to live much longer. I suggest you have Ramose marry Tair when they become of age since he is the healthier one and more likely to live, and perhaps Thutmose could marry Meryet Amon if both brothers do not make it to manhood."

The thought of losing two more of her children pulled tears from her eyes. She was not completely numb. "Yes, Mother," she forced out and was glad her grandmother was not in company that day.

Her mother wiped the tears from her eyes. "We must be strong," she said. "I know your pain. I felt it when Kamose was laid at my feet. Your grandmother felt it when your father was laid at hers. I had always hoped you would be blessed with many children because you love so deeply." She pressed her forehead to Ahmose-Nefertari's. "You are a good queen for Kemet."

"Even when I cry out?" she mumbled, trying to keep her tears from falling.

Her mother nodded. "Yes, even when you cry out. I did not understand for a long time—for my mother would have never allowed it—but I have found that strength comes from pressing on, not from restraining your tears. In finding a way to continue living, not covering your cries. You, my daughter, my sweet Ahmose-Nefertari—you are a strong queen. You will endure. You will prevail. You will overcome." Her mother placed a soft kiss on her nose as she had done when she was a child and lifted her countenance to hers. "I have every confidence in you. Your burden does not have to be so heavy. I am here to help you carry it."

Ahmose-Nefertari's face twisted into an ugly visage and her body shook with tremors. She enfolded her mother in her arms, casting her pain onto her, digging her fingernails into her dress and collar, clinging to the woman who gave her life, and in doing so, she finally felt not so alone.

32

A TIME OF
REFLECTION |
AHMOSE-NEFERTARI

SEDJEFATAWY, 1554 BC

Ahmose had come back home and stayed for two
years, commanding his army from Waset.
Ahmose-Ankh had drifted into a deep sleep,
waking only to eat a little once a day. It looked like he
would not last the season. Ramose had stayed ill and
weak, but his health did not descend like his brother.

Ahmose needed a healthy boy, and Ahmose-Nefertari
had delivered him one after she gave him another
daughter, Mutnofret. Once his son, Amenhotep, was
born, Ahmose left again for war, leaving the two-
hundred soldiers in Waset. Tetian had remained in Ta-
Seti, but Viceroy Si-Tayet had still reported a growing
number of warships. When Ahmose had sent a
messenger to question it, Tetian had replied he was only
securing his border in case Si-Tayet failed in the land of
Wawat, and the Kushites were once again at Abu. It
seemed like a well-enough answer, but Ahmose had left
his wife and mother with a warning to keep vigilant
along with two-hundred men. He had left the day after
Amenhotep was born, and the warning did not sit well in

Ahmose-Nefertari's stomach as she watched him sail away on The Wild Bull earlier that morning.

Her mother had sent her straight to the harem to rest and went with Tetisheri to the throne room in her stead.

Ahmose-Nefertari loved her grandmother, but she never wanted to be left alone with her, for fear she would do something wrong and be whipped with a verbal lashing. It seemed Tetisheri felt the need to correct even more so after she rejoined the harem activities after her year hiatus from the royal family, specifically Ahmose, Ahmose-Nefertari, and Ahhotep. She had often wondered if she and Ahmose had been in error when they undermined their grandmother's command to arrest the Admiral for touching royal flesh, but was it enough for their grandmother to abandon them for a year and be even more difficult to please since she rejoined them? There must have been something else between her mother and grandmother to spark such a callous command to a plausible explanation. Her grandmother was a woman she would never understand. Her mother had surprised her on many occasions, proving to be the mother she needed and wanted.

With the musings of the day passing through her mind, Ahmose-Nefertari reclined on the cot in the Kap's nursery and held her infant son while Mutnofret, her one-year-old napping daughter, wrapped his finger in her little hand. Lady Rai busied herself, gathering Meryet Amon and Thutmose's belongings to move them to the children's room. Now seven years of age, they stayed in the nursery for a year longer than they should have, but Lady Rai needed them after the ordeal with the crocodiles, and Ahmose-Nefertari had granted her the request. Even then, two years after the fatal incident, Rai's worn hands trembled as she touched the children's old blankets and toys. Ahmose-Nefertari could say the same about her own hands when she walked past the Nile inlet every day. The soft lap of water was almost peaceful, but memory's curse made her ignore it. Rai refused to take the children to play in the waters anymore. "Never again," she had said. Her rich declaration thudded again in Ahmose-Nefertari's mind as she watched the old Rai limp and shuffle back and forth between the two rooms.

"Lady Rai," Ahmose-Nefertari said. "There are many servants who can help you."

"Child of the moon," Rai shook her head in a deep swing back and forth with lips pursed. "I have already denied any servant's help. It is my responsibility for the royal children from birth til they journey west. Lady Rai will take good care of the children. All of them."

"As you wish, then," Ahmose-Nefertari said with a sad smile. The burden of the incident had been great on both of them.

A baby's coo came from across the room and shifted Ahmose-Nefertari's focus.

Senseneb lay in the cot with her new daughter, Ahmes, born only a few days before Amenhotep. Despite the good health of her children, Senseneb's womb had been closed most of the time. She called her two children, Thutmose and Ahmes, granted blessings and answered prayers.

Ahmose-Nefertari ran a hand over the cot she lay in. It was the same cot she had slept in as a child as well as Tumerisy, Ahmose-Ankh, and Ahmose-Sitamun. She leaned her back against the wall and held her living son. It hadn't seemed fair that Senseneb was granted two healthy children, and she was granted eight, losing three, and soon to lose a fourth. So much heartache.

The two sisters-in-law remained silent, each tending to their baby's coos until finally, Ahmose-Nefertari spoke to no one in particular while Rai was in the room. "Hathor and Isis have blessed me again with Mutnofret and Amenhotep, but I am not ready to lose another child," she said, referencing Ahmose-Ankh. "I remember Sitkamose never waking up, and I know it will soon be my son, my firstborn. I do not know if I can bear it."

Rai sat in the nursery chair and rubbed her thin legs. "My child of the moon," she said—her voice deep and rich despite her age. "You have five living children and three in the Field of Reeds. You are blessed, my queen."

Senseneb nodded in agreement.

"Lady Rai, I am afraid of what is to come. I have always been afraid. I cannot withhold my pain like my mother, even though she tells me strength comes from different sources. I will never please my grandmother. She has avoided me for the last few years, and I know she disapproved of my mourning aloud." She sighed in sorrow. "If she were in the throne room as she was when Tep was Chief Wife, she would have pressed that I step down for, like Tep, I am unfit for the position of Chief Wife. She does not care about anyone; perhaps that is why she can hold her tears."

Rai shook her head. "Your grandmother cares deeply."

"How do you know?" Ahmose-Nefertari asked with a shake of her head, unable to believe her.

Lady Rai sighed. "When you have my years of observing people, you will see those most rigid, most unfeeling, are the ones who feel the most and are the most afraid. But they make others believe they are invincible and perfect so they can also hope to believe it."

Ahmose-Nefertari scoffed. "What is Grandmother afraid of? Her braid being out of place?"

"Child of the Moon," Rai chided, casting a firm glance upon the queen.

Ahmose-Nefertari swallowed her words and lifted her eyes to the ceiling at her comment. She knew better than to mock the Great Wife.

"You could ask her," Senseneb offered.

"She will only say, 'I am not afraid. Fear is not becoming of a leader,'" Ahmose-Nefertari said, mimicking her grandmother's firmness.

Silence settled in the room before Rai drew a deep breath and let it go. "Your grandmother, I believe, loves Kemet more than any other and wants the best for our people. She is the most afraid of traveling west and not knowing the outcome of this war or who will be capable of leading Kemet once she is gone. I believe that is why she did what she did to her granddaughter Tep, for she smiled when Kamose was on the throne."

"Yet she does not smile with Ahmose on the throne and married to me." Ahmose-Nefertari's gaze dropped to Amenhotep in her arms. His round face was smushed, having grown big in her womb. "Instead, she does not care to see us lead it. We are not worth her time. She is angry at us; I know it. She has been harsher since Mother returned with the Admiral and keeps to herself outside of the throne room when she chooses to come. Are we tarnishing the throne that much, Lady Rai? Are we that inept?"

Senseneb shook her head, as did Rai. "There is something your grandmother hides," Rai said. "I have not found what it is, but I think the way she treats her family has nothing to do with you." She tapped her fingers on the chair's arms as she turned to the Chief

Wife. "You, Ahmose-Nefertari, are loved by all who meet you."

She smiled in response, but it faded. "Except Tetian."

Rai chuckled, as did Senseneb. "Are you sure? The rumor was he wanted to marry you."

Ahmose-Nefertari laughed in memory. "He only wanted the throne." She buried her face in Amenhotep's belly. "But he will never get it," she whispered and listened to the baby's responding coo. She gazed at him and Mutnofret stirring in her sleep beside her. She had beautiful children, and she loved each one of them. *Indeed, I am blessed*, she thought and gave silent prayers of thanksgiving to the gods.

33
A TIME OF SIEGE |
AHMOSE
HUT-WARET, 1553 BC

The decades-long war seemed to almost be at an end. Ahmose rode his chariot from the conquered Per-Bastet and north down the Nile branch to Hut-Waret. "Ignorant King Apepi," Ahmose muttered. "They have lost. What can they hope to gain by staying?"

Ahmose-Ebana and Baba rode in their chariots beside him. No one came out to meet them in battle or surrender or otherwise. The city was bustling. They could tell from the smell of meat roasting and the sounds of farm animals, but the fortified town was apparently hunkered down.

"Lay siege," Ahmose commanded. He sighed. It would not be a short siege. Hut-Waret was the largest city in the Lower. It took a year for Lunu to fall. How many years of siege would it be until they finally won this war?

The servants set up camp and served dinner. Baba and Ahmose-Ebana dined with him. The Apiru were among the staff, aiding the wounded from the final takeover of Per-Bastet.

An Apiru woman passed by Ahmose with a baby strapped to her back, and he called out to her. "You, what is your name?"

She turned around and bowed before the king. "My name is Rivkah, King Ahmose," she said in a broken tongue.

"Rivkah," Ahmose mumbled the foreign name. "Why do you help us? What benefit do you seek? Why have you chosen to stay in your clothes of the Levant while living in Kemet?" He asked, gesturing to her thin, cotton head scarf.

"We have no judgment in your conflict," she said. "We help both you and whom you call the Hekka Khasut. This is not our land; we are only long-term sojourners. One day our God will bring us out of the great Kemet."

Ahmose snorted. "At least you will leave, unlike this foolish king," he gestured toward the fortress. He took a bite of lamb taken from Per-Bastet. The meat felt good in his belly, for he had been without it for a while. "However, I do not like it when you help our enemies." He glanced at Baba and Ahmose-Ebana. "Perhaps, that is why they stay: to find favor in whoever wins this war."

Baba nodded in agreement.

Ahmose called over a royal messenger. "Send word into the Nile Delta that if anyone, Apiru or otherwise, helps or aids the enemies of King Ahmose, they will be seen as traitors and burned as such."

Rivkah gasped. "King Ahmose?" she asked.

Because of her foreign nature, he allowed her a warning for questioning his command. "You will not question my command, woman. Either you help my forces only, or you do not help at all. Those are your choices, but you will not aid our enemy. Make it be known to your people, for I would hate to slaughter such a generous populace."

With that, Ahmose lifted his hand to dismiss both Rivkah and the messenger.

The messenger nodded and left to carry the word to other messengers that they may scatter and inform Ahmose's ranks throughout the Lower.

Rivkah backed away slowly and then left.

"Was it too harsh?" he asked his advisors, but Baba and Ahmose-Ebana shook their heads.

"You are wise, King Ahmose," Baba said. "For you are right. If they have helped the Hekka Khasut all these years, perhaps that is why King Apepi stays, hopeful the Apiru will again come to their aid or perhaps even raise arms against you."

Ahmose-Ebana said, "I only hope they do not raise arms against you for threatening to burn them if they help the Aamu."

Ahmose pursed his lips. "Do you know how many live in this land?"

Both men shook their heads again, but Baba said, "They seem plentiful, though."

Ahmose glanced around at the long opaque cotton dresses and headscarves. Mostly women, a few men, but their number rivaled his army's number. As the word spread of his mandate, it seemed they did not care and went on administering to the wounded. They would not be a threat for now. "Remind me, Admiral," Ahmose said. "When we win this war, to take a census of their numbers."

"Yes, my King," Baba said and then returned to his food.

HUT-WARET, 1552 BC

Almost a year later, morning came, and Ahmose stood outside his tent watching the dawn. Hut-Waret had proved more challenging to overtake. The Hekka Khasut would fake an attack only to draw them in and use their archers atop the walls to attack in a coward's war. With the last city under Hekka Khasut's control, it also seemed the riots had surged as a type of last stand or with the intention to disperse Ahmose's ranks enough for Hut-Waret to push back. It became discouraging, constantly sending men to put down rebellions in lands they had already taken. General Pennekhbet was somewhere in the delta. Royal messengers went missing too often, so much so Ahmose had ordered royal messengers be accompanied by a company of soldiers.

When Hut-Waret finally surrendered, it would still be a long undertaking to truly unite these lands, Ahmose thought with a frustrated sigh. Perhaps they should kill every person in every town and repopulate it with their loyal citizens.

A messenger from Sedjefatawy arrived and bowed before Ahmose. His face bore no happiness, and Ahmose already knew what would be said. He had only hoped to be home when his firstborn son traveled to the Field of Reeds.

The messenger spoke what was expected. "Your Chief Wife sends word the Crown Prince Ahmose-Ankh has begun his journey west. The succeeding Crown Prince Ramose has taken the King's Daughter, Tair, as his wife."

Ahmose paused a moment, knowing the day a message like this would be delivered, but his heart fell into his stomach even as it were. His muscles tightened, and he stared toward the west. He could not leave the siege, not under these circumstances.

Baba stepped forward and stared at the west with him. "You should return for your son's opening of the mouth ceremony. I have a good command of the men here."

Ahmose appreciated his comfort. "I will when the time for burial is closer. My presence has empowered the men."

"It has, King Ahmose. You are a superior warrior and the embodiment of the gods' will."

"Then I will not tarry on my return." He rubbed his chin and dropped his hand before speaking the message that should be returned to Sedjefatawy. "The King sends his best gold with the late Crown Prince Ahmose-Ankh on his journey, and the King honors the living Crown Prince Ramose and his wife. May they be fruitful and live long lives."

The messenger bowed and returned the way he had come while Ahmose continued staring toward the western horizon, still tinged with Apep's night.

Fitting for such a day as this, Ahmose thought.

34
A TIME OF SURRENDER
| AHHOTEP
SEDJEFATAWY, 1552 BC

Ahhotep chewed her lip as she glanced at Ahmose-Nefertari. It had been a slow morning. Not one messenger. Every day, she had hoped someone would come with word from the north. There had been silence in communication before the Aamu came with Tao's body, but it hadn't been this long. There had been rumors that the King was slain, but in her heart, she felt Ahmose was alive—a mother's intuition, perhaps. She studied the words of the gods written on the multitude of pillars in the throne room as her mind retreated to Kamose and Tao being placed at her feet. With a deep breath, she pushed those thoughts away.

"Ahmose will live," she willed in a whisper and glanced at the empty throne.

As if the gods heard the determination in her voice, the throne room doors creaked open, and the guard declared a messenger from King Ahmose had come.

She closed her eyes in relief. But before believing her son was still alive, she waited to hear what the messenger said first.

"Let him come," she said, with a reassuring nod toward Ahmose-Nefertari, who held the same worry etched on her face.

The soldier messenger entered the throne room and bowed before the regal queens.

"Chief Royal Wife of King Ahmose and Great Wife of Seqenenre Tao, King Ahmose sends word of King Apepi's impending defeat."

Broad smiles overcame Ahhotep's and Ahmose-Nefertari's faces as tears of joy almost slid from their eyes.

The messenger continued. "They have conquered the lands to Hut-Waret, where they lay siege upon the foreign king's fortress city. He will have victory within the year or sooner should the coward king choose to flee."

That was it. The war would soon be over. Over twenty years of fighting and bloodshed would be over within the year. Ahhotep's heart pounded in her ears. *Finally. Finally over.*

Amun had been with them even when the princes had not. With that thought, Ahhotep stopped her ruminating. *Even when the princes had not,* she repeated in her mind. *I will fix that now. It is time to consolidate all the power under my son.*

So Ahhotep spoke. "Summon the princes to Sedjefatawy. We shall feast and announce the gods' blessings upon their divinely appointed."

The messenger bowed as Ahhotep dismissed him. He took with him servants to accomplish the task as he left.

She turned to her daughter. "Never again should the king beg for support. He should simply say it, and it is done."

"Agreed, Mother," Ahmose-Nefertari said after taking a sweeping breath through her nostrils and giving a firm nod. "Agreed," she repeated with a knowing look in her eye.

WITHIN THE DECAN, ALL TWENTY-TWO PRINCES OF THE UPPER came to Sedjefatawy, from Ta-Seti to Mednit. The Lower princes would be subjected to whatever the Upper commanded if they survived the war.

Ahhotep looked over the top wall of Sedjefatawy, surveying the palace complex's harbor. Tetian was last to arrive, and his ships were many. She had sent a messenger boat to Per-djed-ken to keep a watchful eye, and she watched it to ensure the message was delivered. Guards stood on either side of her, and soldiers lined the roofs of the palace.

She had left Ahmose-Nefertari to entertain the princes in the dining hall with food and wine of the Upper to show them the divine work of Ahmose.

The messenger boat made it, and the Troop Commander Uahbra received it with a nod and a fist over his chest as he faced the Great Wife atop Sedjefatawy's roof.

Before she turned to leave, she eyed the warships from Ta-Seti with a soured stomach. "He comes to intimidate," she muttered and descended the stairs to the dining hall.

The princes lowered their heads to her as she entered, even Tetian. Her mother, grandson, and daughter were already seated at the king's table while she took her place.

She surveyed the nomes' royalty as the ten-year-old

Crown Prince Ramose looked up at her. "Princes, thank you for making an appearance this day. King Ahmose hopes the food was to your liking."

"Excellent, Great Wife," Baufre offered up—his plate full of likely seconds.

Wide smiles and chuckles came from the princes who agreed with him.

"We are honored to serve the best spoils to such respectable men."

Tetian shared glances with a few of the princes. "But what is the catch, Great Wife? You left your statement as if you had more to say."

Ahhotep peered at him. "Nothing. Continue to feast and be merry. We have received word that Amun and Re have been with our King Ahmose."

Tetian clapped. "Good, I thought he had been slain."

"Assumptions only make you look a fool, Prince Tetian," she said, turning her full face toward him.

He shut his mouth, but his cheeks boiled. His eyes narrowed while his hands curled into fists.

Ahhotep released the tension in her shoulders. This was not the way to begin the complete consolidation of power. "Prince Tetian, let us begin again," she said with a sincere smile. "Thank you for coming to the feast of the Great Wife and for sharing your happy sentiments upon hearing King Ahmose lives."

His hands uncurled, and he dipped his chin. But his narrowed eyes remained locked with hers.

She lifted her hands and announced, "Feast and be merry, for we have much to celebrate. I shall tell of the messenger's words after you have filled your stomachs with all that you can."

The musicians' song and the dancers' dance went on

for a while as the servants served the last of the feast's reserves, and the princes were full.

It was then Ahhotep stood up. The song faded, and the dancers and servants drifted to the back of the room. "The divine King Ahmose has Hut-Waret surrounded. The war will be over within the year. Twenty-six years and three kings—it took us twenty-six years and three kings to enact the will of the gods since King Seqenenre Tao began this war." She paused and stared each prince in the eye.

"It should *never* have taken twenty-six years and three kings. Had all of you supported your King from the beginning, many lives would have been saved. This much blood would not have been spilled, and this feast would have occurred much earlier."

A few princes averted their eyes, knowing it to be true.

Ahhotep continued. "Our bloodline claimed divinity to rule Kemet, and we have proven my great-grandfather's claim through the victories of King Ahmose. Therefore, the divine rule shall be consolidated in Waset. If you believe, as you and your forefathers gave an oath, that divine blood is seated on the throne, then give up your royalty to the true King of Kemet."

A few princes opened their mouths to speak in rebuke, but Ahhotep's strong voice carried out over them.

"No longer will you be princes, but *nomarchs*, governors of your nomes. No longer will the King call you 'Prince' unless you descend from his blood. As nomarchs, you will be subject to the King's vizier."

When it was clear the princes would not speak, she gestured to Tetisheri, Ramose, and Ahmose-Nefertari to stand beside her. So they did while Tetian eyed Tetisheri before scanning the three rebel queens and the young crown prince.

Ahhotep commanded the room and demanded respect as her mother had always wanted her to do. Even though her mother gave no notion of approval, pride filled her heart as she began again.

"To give up your prince hood and authority is the only way to have the gods' will be done. For what is a divine King with non-divine princes ruling the lands? I will give you the answer: nothing but a figurehead. For the king to enact his divine appointment from Amun, Re, Ptah, Isis, and Hathor; Horus, Khnum, Heh, Sobek, and Nephthys, the gods and goddesses who are patrons of your cities and your nomes—then you *must* give up your royalty and submit to the divine bloodline which King Ahmose has now proved." Her gaze bore into each prince. "Do you and will you submit to your King?"

Silence came from all, so much so, Paser's footsteps echoed in the hall as he walked forward. "I am honored to be the first prince to lay down his title and authority for the true King of Kemet. I shall henceforth be Nomarch Paser, and I shall give up my royal rule and submit to The Lord of Strength is Re, King Ahmose, Given Life."

Prince Nakht of Nekhen, Prince Unasankh of Sha, and Prince Weshptah of Ma-Hedj followed suit, pledging their loyalty to the divine king and removing themselves as princes.

But as Prince Setka of Ta-Ur stepped forward, Tetian yelled out. "Do you see what is happening?" His voice rang throughout the hall. "I told you all those years ago, this would happen. The Great Wife conspires to steal your power—our power!"

Ahhotep shook her head as all eyes turned to her. "There is no conspiracy, Tetian," she said in a humble voice. "This is the natural order." She folded her hands behind her back and stood with a lifted chin as her mother had taught her. The princes remained silent to hear why it was the natural order. She prayed to Thoth, the god of wisdom and the words of the gods—let her mouth speak that which would bind them together, not rip them apart.

"The Hekka Khasut appointed your line as princes of Ta-Seti, Bat, Meseh, and all the rest. With their defeat, your power becomes the true King's, that of King Ahmose and his line. We shall return to the time before the foreign kings divided us and pitted us against each other to keep us weak and submissive. Only together can we rise from this division." She scanned the room. "Only together can we move forward to the future the gods want for Kemet. Together, under King Ahmose, we have pushed the foreign kings back to their last stand in Hut-Waret. Together, under King Ahmose, we have gained victory, expelling the imposters. It *is* the natural order. Can *you* not see what is happening? To keep your power as princes, *you* divide us all. Divided, we will fall yet again to more foreigners who come and settle our land, and all the resources, men, and agony we have suffered will be in vain. Can *you* not see? We must be united. We must act *together* under the one true king and allow our king to act as a king."

The room was silent in deep consideration of Ahhotep's words until Tetian snorted and scoffed. "You speak powerful words, Great Wife. But no one, not even this so-called King, will have my power. If I were not prince, I would not have been able to amass an army to keep my nome safe from the Kushites."

Before Ahhotep could refute his selfishness of not securing the Kerman homeland and putting down the rebellions in the Lower, he addressed the princes in the room. "If you believe as I do, then come with me. If you are like sheep led to the slaughter, then give up your royalty as the weak and poor Paser has done." He spat at Paser's feet, turned, and strode out of the dining hall. Metjen followed and snapped at Baufre, who hustled himself up and casually walked behind them.

Setka looked between Ahhotep and Tetian's followers. "What are you to do with Tetian?" he asked the Great Wife.

"Leave him be," she said, not risking civil unrest with those who had not yet pledged their prince hood to the king. "When he sees the might of Kemet with the gods' blessing, he will join us. And as a reward for those who have given up their princes' title and authority, you may honor a man from your nome as the nomarch for a conquered nome in the Lower."

Metjen stopped and peered over his shoulder at Ahhotep but continued with Tetian and Baufre.

She had hoped the recompense would have kept the two princes to her side, but Metjen was set with Tetian. Somehow, they had persuaded the empty-headed Baufre to follow them.

Every remaining prince in attendance glanced at each other before surrendering their royalty to the feet of King Ahmose's empty seat and bowing their head low to the Crown Prince, pledging an oath of loyalty until their days end.

"Nomarchs," Ahhotep spoke and spread her arms wide. The pleated linen layered dress fell like waterfalls from her arms as they draped to her narrow waist, made tighter by the royal beaded belt. The vulture's beak of her headdress soared over her eyes as she lifted her head and smiled. "Nomarchs," she said again. "With your oaths and loyalty, we can move forward into a future that knows no bounds. We can—"

A war horn's resounding and oscillating blare pounded in the air. And clamors of yells and clangs froze those in the dining hall.

A soldier burst through the doors. "Sedjefatawy is under attack! Per-djed-ken as well!"

"Tetian," Ahhotep muttered under her breath. "So this is how it is to be."

Two hundred men and the guards were all that stood between them and Tetian's fleet, built with hoarded wealth and men. She stared at her mother, who nodded and whispered, "I molded you for this, prepared you every day of your adult life. Lead, my daughter, Royal Commander."

Ahhotep's jaw grew taut. Her mother had never spoken to her in such a way. With such empathy, with such encouragement. With new confidence, she turned to Ahmose-Nefertari, who stared back at her with wide eyes. "Chief Wife, take the Crown Prince to the harem and return to the throne room as my advisor. Great Wife Tetisheri, see that no one enters the harem."

They left as Ahhotep walked with purpose to the throne room, where the nomarchs followed. A soldier fell from the roof with an arrow in his neck and landed in the courtyard as Ahhotep passed by. She wanted to reach down to him and tell him to dream of life in the Field of Reeds, but her mother's teachings kept her walking with a face of stone. She strode up to the royal throne and sat on it.

"I shall again be Royal Commander in the absence of our King Ahmose while his throne is under threat," she said to the servants, nomarchs, and guards who had followed her. "We can assume Tetian, Baufre, and Metjen have raised arms against your king. My first order: archers will take to the roof to defend the palace. The workers of the harem will keep a steady supply of arrows. Not one archer shall be left without at least three arrows in their quiver. My second order: a unit of soldiers shall guard the palace entrance and secret exits. My third order: send the signal to Per-djed-ken that the highest ranking officer shall lead them."

"What of us?" Setka called out as the throne room guards left to carry out her orders.

"Send for your reserves," she said. "Hopefully, the north is clear."

Setka scoffed. "We have no reserves; they are with the king."

Ahhotep eyed Weshptah, who had withheld much. "Even Ma-Hedj?"

"I have some, as does Unasankh, but how can we get a message through if Baufre and Metjen are also against us? They come from the north. It would not be clear."

"Then let us hope Tetian acts alone."

The coward Weshptah shook his head and crossed his arms. "Surely our nomes will see we have been gone too long and come looking for us."

Setka laughed at the ridiculous statement. "If we last that long. We need to send a message, but how? You spoke of a secret exit?"

"Yes, guard, take the messenger servants to the secret exit. We will also send word to General Pennekhbet and King Ahmose that the palace needs reinforcements."

"I shall go with them," Paser said and left with the retinue.

Ahhotep gripped the arms of the throne. "You there," she called to a servant. "You will go to the roof, look out over the harbor, and report what you see."

335

The servant walked away.

"Hurry!" she yelled, and the servant broke into a full run.

"Everyone in the palace will defend this divine palace and the fortress tower."

After a while, Paser re-entered the throne room and fell to a knee, breathless. Blood smeared across his cheek. "Royal Commander," he said. "The secret exit is not so secret. We stepped through only to find the soldiers of Metjen's Bat there to strike us down. I believe only one, maybe two messengers got through, but I am uncertain if they will make it very far. The archers on the roof helped us, but there were heavy losses. The soldiers have sealed the exit."

Ahhotep's stomach boiled with indignation. "So Metjen and Tetian have secured their places as traitors to the crown. Take Nomarch Paser to see the physician-priest for his cheek wound."

The servant sent to the roof came and knelt beside Paser. "Royal Commander, I have done as you commanded and looked out into the harbor. Warships flying the sails of Ta-Seti, Bat, and Meseh are battling the boats brought by the other princes. They have blocked the north and the south bends of the Nile. A soldier muttered as I was surveying, 'It looks like a siege.'"

Ahhotep scanned the nomarchs. "If it is siege they want, then they shall have it. We are equipped for a year."

Weshptah sighed, "Surely, King Ahmose or the reserves will come within a year."

But Setka eyed Ahhotep and Paser and shook his head. "*If* traitors do not kill our messengers. Then what, Royal Commander?"

"Then we shall fight ourselves. I command you and

your servants to take to the Kap's training yard. We have a Medjay there who will teach you how to fight. The workers of the harem will be glad to supply you with your weapon of choice, for when the time comes, you will be called to defend the throne with your life."

35

A TIME OF PROMISES |
AHMOSE

HUT-WARET, 1551 BC

The second year of siege neared its end. Ahmose took in the midday sunlight glinting off the Nile waters. Riots and rebellions in the Lower had kept them occupied while trying to starve out the Hekka Khasut's royal residence.

A single white sail drifted down the river charred from black smoke. It wasn't a military boat but a *skiff*, a small vessel made of papyrus reeds—a fisherman's livelihood. But why would a fisherman venture this far into an army encampment and with the lasting thumbprint of burn marks on the sail?

Ahmose nodded toward it to garner the attention of Baba and Ahmose-Ebana. "What is that? Or, more importantly, why does it come here?"

It banked in the marshy shore, but it appeared only a lump of a person lay in the boat's belly.

Soldiers approached with spears raised, and archers pointed their arrows upriver, keeping vigilant in case of a surprise attack or assassination attempt on their king, an event that had happened twice before.

Baba's large frame stepped in front of Ahmose in case

an arrow or spear was meant for him. Ahmose turned his head down and waited to hear what happened now that he could not see.

A Medjay cried out, "It is one of our brothers!" The splash of water and the rip of papyrus reeds filled the air.

Baba led Ahmose to the leopard-waisted man they had pulled from the boat and laid on the shore. The Medjay soldier lay bleeding and exhausted. "Get him water and bread!" Ahmose-Ebana ordered, and two servant boys rushed off to get the needed supplies.

The Medjay's lip trembled. "There was an insurrection at Men-nefer." His raspy whisper made Ahmose kneel and hold the man's hand in a tight grip.

"An insurrection, you said?" Ahmose asked to ensure he understood the message through the Medjay's thick Kerman accent.

His head bobbed while the other Medjay knelt in a circle around the King and their brother.

"We were surrounded. No messenger has been able to get through. I, Tabid, have escaped to tell you. No others could make it out."

Ahmose gritted his teeth. "Fierce warrior, do you know if we are still fighting or if defeat became General Pennekhbet?"

"Fighting, but surrounded. Need reinforcements," Tabid sputtered.

Ahmose-Ebana barked an order for his legion to be ready to sail upriver to Men-nefer at once. He looked to his father as the servant boys returned with water and bread.

Ahmose allowed them to give Tabid water, but the Medjay refused the bread.

"We could not send word to Waset or you, King Ahmose." The whisper had less of a rasp. "We have taken many losses." His eyes rolled under his eyelids, and the quiver in his lip ceased. His breath became less heavy, and his grip loosened.

Ahmose closed the man's eyes. "Sleep well, brave Tabid." He stood up and ordered the battlefield physicians, a fellow soldier had brought, to care for him and heal him with the magic of Heka and the goddess Isis. As they took Tabid away in a litter, Ahmose glanced at Baba and Ahmose-Ebana.

"How long do you think we were out of communication with Waset?"

Baba let out a long breath. "The last messenger from that area came almost two seasons ago. Perhaps, then, at least two seasons."

Ahmose shook his head. "Then that is the longest time we have ever been out of contact with Waset. We need to re-establish our communication routes immediately." He snapped his attention to Ahmose-Ebana. "Take your fleet and two Troop Commanders with their men and aid General Pennekhbet. Then re-establish a link to Waset before returning here in case King Apepi decides to show his face."

Ahmose-Ebana clasped a fist over his chest. "Yes, King Ahmose, Given Life."

Baba added. "To keep the rebellions and riots from further distracting us, I suggest wiping out any Aamu from here to Mednit."

Ahmose nodded. "Give the order, Ahmose-Ebana. Once you retake Men-nefer, make them an example, as the Admiral states." But Ahmose glanced at the Apiru woman, Rivkah, in the distance, giving bread to his men. "But leave the Apiru alive if they do not resist you."

By dawn, Ahmose-Ebana had left upstream to help their brothers-in-arms, leaving half of Ahmose's army in the fields before Hut-Waret's fortress walls.

The next day, the Hekka Khasut sent out their chariots, seemingly taking advantage of the smaller army on their doorstep. But Ahmose and Baba had been ready for such an attack and met them full-force, chariot against chariot, foot soldier to foot soldier.

The air became acrid with the stench of blood and sweat. An Aamu thrust his spear in between the wheel spokes of Ahmose's chariot, flinging him and his chariot driver to the ground. Baba's chariot went on.

Ahmose rolled to his back, leaving his chest vulnerable to attack. A groan and spit flew from his mouth as an ax came swinging down from overhead. He brought up his shield to block it. The ax head thrust through the wooden shield locking it in place.

Where was his khopesh? He looked for his weapon as he rose to his feet, twisting the ax away from its wielder. Three Aamu approached him amid the surrounding chaos. His chariot driver was nowhere to be seen. Two spears and a dagger threatened him as he ripped the Aamu's ax from his shield and parried a spear thrust.

A fourth Aamu approached from the side and swung a khopesh toward his crown-covered head. He dodged it, stepping into a spear strike from another Aamu, and blocked it with his shield. The spearpoint cut his forearm as it pierced the weakened wood.

The crown's shining blue woven fabric was like a beacon on the battlefield. Blood dripped from his lip and nose after being expelled from the chariot as the enemy drew near.

Not like this, he thought. *Not like Father. Not like Kamose.*

He swung his axe at one of them and prayed there were no archers around him. Where were his men? Why hadn't they come to help him? Were they losing?

He spotted Baba's chariot whip back around and toward his position, leaving the chariot vulnerable to attack from the Aamu archers in the distance.

His heart beat hard in his chest, and the clatter of men's yells defeated any meaningful sound in his ears. The five Aamu rushed him. The ax in his hand felt heavy compared to his khopesh. Aamu archers in the distance nocked their arrows, readying for release. Baba would be too late or killed, so Ahmose released a mighty yell, swung the Aamu ax to block as many strikes as possible, and used his broken shield as if it were new. If he were to be slain that day, he would take as many Aamu with him as he could.

The pricks of spearpoint ran across his forearm as the shield weakened even more. Soon the holes would be large enough for the full force of the spear to come through. His ax's head sunk into his enemy's neck, and he dodged another swing of an Aamu's khopesh. But the attack took off the top of part of his shield, and the force knocked him back to the ground again. He swung the ax at the legs of those who came near, taking one man's leg with it. The shield was useless as it defended its king one last time. He tossed it away and sat up, bringing his legs in close to avoid a spear strike.

More Aamu had come seeing his royal beacon as he hopped up and still swung his ax to keep them at bay for a moment until Baba's chariot horses ran over a few of them. An archer from another of Ahmose's chariots whipped in and killed two Aamu with quick, rapid arrows. It was enough distraction for Ahmose to hack through and best his attackers. It was then the Aamu's arrows darkened the sky as Baba raced toward him, his shield high over his and his chariot driver's heads. The horses ran faster at the pumping of the reins.

Ahmose looked to the ground for a useable shield, but there was none. So he ran toward the chariot, knowing it would probably be futile in the end. But the chariot careened sideways, propelling Baba out in a massive leap toward him just as the arrows began to fall. Baba's eyes were filled with fierce determination, and his shield was outstretched as far as it would go, even uncovering his own head, in one last attempt to save the king.

36

A TIME OF
OPPORTUNITY |
AHHOTEP

SEDJEFATAWY, 1551 BC

Soldiers' screams and shouts filled the mid-day air in Sedjefatawy as they had for the last year. Ahhotep sat on the throne with her daughter standing by her side. The dark circles under Ahmose-Nefertari's eyes mirrored her own. Their thin frames were the result of rationing food. The year had not been kind to Sedjefatawy or Per-djed-ken, but they were all alive, for now. No word or aid had come from anyone or anywhere.

A year ago, Ahmose said he would defeat the Hekka Khasut and liberate Kemet from their rule. But there had been no word from him since and no sign of his army breaking through the northern Nile barricade. Was he dead, burned as a traitor? Had the Hekka Khasut renewed their strength and pushed him back? Or was he simply not strong enough to fight Tetian's forces?

Ahhotep sighed. They were on their last reserves, and after a year, aid seemed unlikely. Her daughter's cheeks were hollow, and Ahhotep swallowed with a thick tongue that thirsted for water and yearned for meat. They could never surrender even if Ahmose was slain, and so they would either die by sword or by starvation. Or by the grace of Horus, Amun, and Re, they would fight to victory.

As Ahhotep listened to the usual noises of siege, the soldier's screams and shouts sounded different that day. They seemed closer.

She locked eyes with Ahmose-Nefertari just as a palace guard burst into Sedjefatawy's throne room. Ahhotep held her breath as to what was coming.

The guard did not bow or pause for respect of the crown but instead blurted in a long, continuous rant, "Tetian has broken through the palace barricade."

Ahhotep glanced at Ahmose-Nefertari but spoke to the guard. "Hide the royal children and signal Per-djed-ken." Her mind raced as the guard fled the throne room to carry out the order. She stood up and hugged her daughter in case it was the last time she could do so in this life. "Be brave, my daughter. Stand strong."

Ahmose-Nefertari nodded. "I am not afraid."

"Good. Men like Tetian can smell fear."

Her hand slid over the long handle of the King's golden gilded mace hooked behind Ahmose's throne. She had hoped never to use it, but she assumed her hopes were lost in probability.

Remembering the look Tetian gave her mother when she had asked for the prince's authorities, she called to another guard. "Bring Great Wife Tetisheri." Then she muttered after the guard left, "Maybe she can talk sense into her fellow Ta-Setian."

Ahmose-Nefertari ran her hand down the throne's chair arm. "We shall not merely give Tetian the throne. It does not belong to him," she uttered in low tones as a third guard handed the two royal women each a dagger.

Ahhotep ran her thumb down the blade's handle. She

knew how to wield one, but it had been years since she had trained with it. She had opted to train with the mace and arrow. The time for negotiation would come if they could not stop Tetian from further ingress. The shouts and screams grew louder as they neared their location.

She slipped the dagger into the folds of her leather beaded belt, as did Ahmose-Nefertari.

"Horus, protect your throne this day," she said and looked at the sunlight flowing in from the open door. The remaining guards twisted their maces and spears in their hands as the roar of footsteps intensified.

Ahhotep snapped to garner their attention, knowing the fighting that was besting the guards along the palace's entrance would only end with the two queens left defenseless in the throne room. But a soldier who unjustly killed a man in surrender was sure to have his heart devoured by Ammit. She hoped no soldier would risk that, so she gambled with her next order.

"Guards, do not fight them when they arrive. Surrender. Surely they would not kill those who do not resist." The images of her father and Tao and Kamose lined the throne room walls smiting their enemies. They would be with them that day. "Hide a weapon, for they will take what is visible. And then wait for my signal."

Her maidservants bowed before their precious royal vessels as the guards did what they were told. "We give our lives to protect the women whose veins run with divine blood."

Ahhotep cupped the cheek of Nena and then of Meret. "If I live, I will ensure you, all of you," she glanced to the other maidservants of her daughter and then to the guards, "will go to the afterlife with as much as we can give."

A sudden dark shadow loomed in the throne room's

doorway like a black stain on the painted reliefs on the floor.

Ahhotep dropped her hands to her sides.

"Tetian," she said in a brooding tone.

He said nothing in return, but his shadow grew longer and nearly touched the dais as he walked forward, noting the guards at ease. His soldiers came in behind him like fire rushing upon new wood. Baufre and Metjen entered with a few of their soldiers as well.

Ahhotep's heart beat hard in her chest. *What signal am I going to give? What am I going to do? Isis, Horus, Amun, and Re! Protect this throne from the greedy.*

Underneath a stern countenance, she held her breath to keep from rasping for air. She scanned the throne room. The traitorous soldiers confiscated the guards' weapons but did not kill them. Her gamble had paid off. The white painted streaks across a handful of the invaders' faces and the solid gold circles dangling from their earlobes gave them away as the elite of the Kushite kingdom.

He dares to bring Kushites to the throne room. Has he gone mad? Has Ammit already devoured his heart?

Letting out a captive breath in slow release, she counted the number of men Tetian had brought and noticed they barely filled the throne room. But more soldiers rushed by the open doors toward the harem and the king's quarters and crossed the courtyard to other parts of the palace.

Tetian came toe-to-toe with the dais and popped his neck while staring at Ahmose-Nefertari. He bounced the head of his mace in an open palm. His clothes were unstained and unwrinkled, meaning he had never used his mace nor fought in battle.

"The throne is empty and weak, Chief Royal Wife." A smug face accompanied his words.

Ahhotep stepped in front of it, drawing his gaze. "The throne is not empty, nor is it weak," she growled.

"Then where is your son, God's Mother?" Tetian roared as Kushite and rebel Kemet soldiers drew their bows and arrows or lifted their maces and axes. "Ah yes, the great Kamose is slain, little Binpu is entombed, the man Sapair hides like a coward, and the last one, ah, Ahmose. Where is Ahmose? No word or aid has come from the king, his general or admiral, or even the now powerless nomarchs?" he asked in sardonic play.

He mocked her pain. The burned image of Kamose returning to Sedjefatawy blurred her sight and soured her tongue, twisting her mouth into a grimace.

Tetian asked again, his tone matter-of-fact. "Have you heard from our king in the last year?" His soft smirk indicated to Ahhotep that he was in control of this conversation. He already knew the answer, for no aid had come, or if it had, Tetian had been able to keep them at bay.

Ahhotep said nothing, not knowing what question to ask to turn the conversation in her favor. She glanced at the doors, hoping her mother would come soon. Perhaps he would still respect her and submit to her will.

Tetian smirked. "You had declared King Ahmose would have victory over the Hekka Khasut within the year. But it has been a year. So where is he, Ahhotep?"

The lack of her title seared her anger on her cheeks and sealed her mouth.

"Must be slain or about to be slain," he continued. "He has not come to the northern Nile barricade, Baufre has so willingly set up."

She swallowed her anger and relaxed her face. She had to stay calm. She had to be in control.

"Do I speak with truth, Ahhotep?"

She could not confirm it even though she knew it to be true. Not in the situation they were in.

Tetian chuckled and looked around at his men in the room. "No, we have not heard from the King in a year as he let his palace succumb to siege. We can assume, then, he and his army were burned as traitors, and the Hekka Khasut make their way here." He faced Ahhotep once more, glancing at Ahmose-Nefertari. "Give your son's wife and crown to me, and I will spare the rest of your lives."

Ahhotep noticed that Baufre's and Metjen's men filled more of the throne room. "If you cease your attack now, Prince Tetian, I will pardon you and Princes Baufre and Metjen for the blood you have already spilled."

Tetian laughed. "This woman believes she can win this battle."

The Kushites and the traitorous men of Kemet laughed along with him, but Baufre held a cautious countenance.

Tetian stepped onto the dais with a scoffing smirk. "Do not make me kill these men loyal to you." He gestured to the guards with his mace and then repeated his offer. "Give me the crown and your daughter, and I will spare everyone in this palace loyal to you." An eyebrow raised. "It is a generous offer, is it not? I could simply kill you all right now."

"Is this what you came to negotiate all those years ago? Your bid for the crown?" Ahhotep asked, stalling for her mother to arrive, hoping they had spared her as she came to the throne room.

The fears from the distant past resurfaced as she

remembered the sleepless nights spent worrying and planning what she would do if they were attacked by the Hekka Khasut. How she would get her family to safety, but those plans and worries faded the more Ahmose had pushed into the Lower. The notion that Tetian would rise against them nagged the back of her mind, but she had not heeded it, and she found herself greatly unprepared for this internal insurgence.

Tetian shrugged. "That does not matter anymore."

Ahmose-Nefertari stood beside her mother. "Prince Tetian, you take to violence when simple negotiation would suffice. You will never share my bed. I am sacred, the Chief Wife of King Ahmose, Given Life. You are but a greedy and jealous fool who thinks violence can replace a divine appointment."

Tetian stepped closer, but Ahmose-Nefertari's maidservant stepped in between her and him. "You shall not come closer to the Chief Wife," the maidservant said.

Tetian peered over the maidservant's head before turning his focus back to Ahhotep.

"Then tell me, Ahhotep. Where are your last remaining sons so they may fulfill your great-grandfather's claim of divine appointment? Are they still in the land of the living? Or have they gone to the Field of Reeds? Where is Ahmose's son so that he may be King in the likely demise of his father?"

Ahhotep spoke firmly and directed her gaze on Baufre and Metjen. Perhaps they could be turned back. "*King* Ahmose is alive until we otherwise hear of it. Then one of his sons will take his place if he is not."

"Which son?" Tetian opened his arms wide to ask, "Where are they?"

He looked around and chuckled. "Oh yes, Ahmose, his brother, and his sons have all perished. Sapair,

Ahmose-Ankh, Siamun, Ramose, Ahmose-Sipair, Amenhotep?"

"His name is *King* Ahmose. And you will address God's Mother as God's Mother. The princes Ramose, Sapair, and Amenhotep still live as well. Your words are spoken in error."

Tetian shook his head. "I gave orders to kill them, so they will not be living for long. It is time to end this divine charade. The power is with the princes and should always be. You overstepped by asking us to step down. You are not fit to lead—you or your sons, grandsons. It is better for Kemet to be rid of your bloodline."

At that statement, Baufre cleared his throat. "We never agreed to kill any of the royalty, Prince Tetian." His meek voice barely traveled over the stone floor. "We only wanted them to reconsider our prince's title. You said we would be poor and hungry if we gave up our prince hood." Metjen nodded in agreement.

The prince spun around to berate Baufre, and Metjen stilled. "Silence, you fool." Tetian shook his head with a curled lip. "What do you think we were going to do? Come in and ask for the throne when she demanded we give up our title and authority?" He walked to the edge of the dais. "With a legion of soldiers? After a year of siege?"

"Yes," Baufre mumbled and hid his neck between perched shoulders. "Since you said they were failing the Upper and King Ahmose was slain."

"You have blood on your hands now, Baufre," Tetian said with a sneer. "Remember that, you pitiful man of an empty mind." He faced Ahhotep once again. "Last chance, Ahhotep. Give your daughter and crown to me, and I will spare those loyal to you."

Ahhotep remained silent, looking past Tetian at Baufre and Metjen. Their soldiers looked at their princes.

There was hesitation, she noticed. Yet, Tetian's soldiers and the Kushites had bloodlust in their eyes. Perhaps, if she could turn Baufre and Metjen, they could push Tetian back.

He lifted his mace high and swung it, so the bronze hummed through the air. The threat made her speak.

"Even if I were to give you my daughter as your wife and my son's crown, even the men in this room who claim to be your supporters do not support you. I can see it in their eyes. You will have two wars on your hands—with those in the north and with those who know you will have spilled divine blood."

Tetian snorted. "I will show you, Ahhotep; these men want me for their king." He faced the throne room audience. "We need a man. A man with resources beyond fathom who can ask for a prince's resources but not need them to enact the will of the gods. A man who keeps powerful princes by his side—not throws them out of his palace. A man divinely appointed by Khnum, Divine Potter, He Who Made Gods and Men, The Great Nile God, from where he shall spring forth victory against our foes. Who is this Amun who must usurp power from the other nomes' patron gods? Who is this Amun of Waset, the Hidden One, to rival that of Khnum of Ta-Seti, who has no need to prove a divine appointment? We, the nomes, have pledged oaths to this false family and the weaker god in error."

"All the nomes believe the same?" Ahhotep took in Baufre, who stood like a child in the middle of the throne room, shoulders shrank back, eyes darting. And Metjen, who stood with ax low, hanging near the throne room door as if he were about to run away. "Or just you who stand here today with our enemies in the divine's throne room?" Ahhotep said, glancing at the Kushites through the hall's pillars.

Tetian scoffed. "Enemies?" He shook his head. "They are our neighbors."

"They killed King Kamose, my son," she said through her teeth and pointed to one of the Kushites. "And you said you built your army to protect your nome from them, but it seems you were dealing with them all this time. Your army was built for this moment, was it not? All these years, you were planning to attack the palace."

Tetian chuckled. "Very good, *queen*. I was preparing in case you demanded what I feared. If I were to give up my power and authority, it would not be to any family of Waset. Only Ta-Seti wields enough power to claim divine appointment."

He leaned in to whisper in her ear, his nose brushing past her wig's perfumed braids. "I shall let you live in return for the throne. I will know what it means to be king and allow the nomes' princes to keep their sovereignty. It is my last offer of peace, or you can depart in your falsehoods."

His body heat warmed the powder on her face before he leaned back.

"Tetian, do you not realize?" Sorrow and hate accompanied her words. "You were never sovereign under the Hekka Khasut. You were never meant to be sovereign in the land of the gods of Kemet." She leaned back to put more distance between them, however small.

"The natural order?" He spat, understanding her meaning, and rolled his eyes. "No, I will not be giving up anything and am willing to die for my right to rule Ta-Seti and for these spineless *nomarchs* and their right to rule their nomes."

The Great Wife Tetisheri appeared in the throne room doorway. The tension in Ahhotep's shoulders relaxed. Her mother could talk some sense into this man filled with a false reality. There was only one king, divinely appointed by the gods, Ahmose, and all had to submit to him.

A Kushite and a Ta-Setian soldier escorted the Great Wife down the long hall to the dais. Tetisheri narrowed her eyes at Ahhotep as if what had transpired was Ahhotep's fault.

Tetian said, unaware of Tetisheri, "It seems you are willing to die for your beliefs then too?"

"It seems so, Tetian. There will only be more blood you will have to answer for when your heart is weighed on the scales of Ma'at," Ahhotep said and glanced to her mother.

Tetian ignored Ahhotep, taking note of Tetisheri, who stepped upon the dais. The Great Wife's presence did not seem to faze him. He snapped at a few soldiers. "Find the nomarchs and bring them here. I want them to see what I am doing for them."

The soldiers left to carry out Tetian's command before he turned to pat Ahhotep on the cheek. "Do not worry about the throne in the afterlife, Ahhotep. My family is strong and rich. My sons have sons, and their sons have sons. Strong, healthy, and wise, unlike yours. We are worthy of every divine appointment, while your great-grandfather's claim wavers and ultimately is proven false."

Tetian gestured to the throne room under duress to prove his point before maneuvering around Ahhotep and sitting on the King's empty throne.

"You have been proven unworthy," he said, glancing up at Ahhotep. "Isn't that correct, Aunt Tetisheri?" His gaze shifted to the older regal woman on the dais.

The roil in Ahhotep's stomach gurgled up to the back of her throat, not registering his words. Her brow furrowed. "She is God's Mother and Great Wife. You will address her correctly. And you will remove yourself from the King's—"

Tetian laughed and leaned his head back upon the throne's chair. "You are right, Aunt. Her mind is quite empty sometimes, just as you said it was."

Ahhotep's jaw fell ajar. Time froze. What had he said? She blinked, repeating his words in her mind. She stared at Tetian, studying him more than she had before. Familiar cold, grey eyes stared back at her. Tetisheri's wide nose, the pout of her lip, and darker skin were also Tetian's.

Her breath hitched as she spun to face her mother.

No, it couldn't be. Could it?

Taking a few steps toward her, Ahhotep asked in a whisper, "Great Wife, he is your nephew? Why have you never mentioned this?"

Tetisheri scanned the room with an uplift of her chin and inclination of her head. She clasped her hands behind her back and straightened her shoulders. "I did not want to marry your father. I wanted to stay in Ta-Seti and live a life there. My older brother, whom I loved, had a son, Tetian, before he journeyed west. I raised the child as my own. But to avoid conflict with Waset, I became your father's wife and left my nephew, my adopted son, in Ta-Seti in the care of my father's house."

Ahhotep gritted her teeth, and her body grew tense. She heard her mother's words, but the response she wanted to say twisted and turned on her tongue, her lips refusing to release them.

"Do not stand there mute, Great Wife. You look a fool," Tetisheri said with a blank expression on her face.

"I am the fool?" she yelled in desperation, her voice cracking. Tears seared her eyes as the words ran out of her mouth. "You are the fool! All this time, this is why you never thought I was worthy: because your loyalty lies with your Ta-Seti family. You resented us because you were forced to marry my father; that was why we were never *your* family when you spoke of us."

Every harsh word, every disappointing glance, it was all for naught. Ahhotep and her children would never rise to her expectation. Tetisheri would never accept her as a daughter. Ahhotep was just a woman born out of forced marriage.

Silence came from the Great Wife as Ahhotep shook with a tremor in her voice. "Now your nephew—by your words, an adopted son, your blood—comes to lay claim to the throne. Have you in all this time been vying for him?" She pointed a finger at Tetian. "Wanting him to take the crown? Did you know of this? Did you know he gave orders to kill my son and grandsons?"

Tetisheri strolled to face Tetian on the throne as Ahhotep spoke, seemingly ignoring her. Ahmose-Nefertari's eyes grew wide, and she stepped backward when Tetisheri approached the throne. Her eyes pleaded with her grandmother, but Tetisheri never looked at her.

The breath in Ahhotep's chest needed to burst out; it begged release as Tetisheri stopped and faced the throne. Was she going to bow to him? Declare him King and sentence them all to the arrow and ax?

Ahhotep's gaze fell as tears brimmed her eyes. After all, in Tetisheri's eyes, they were never her family. She had never said "my family" when referring to Ahhotep's line. What loyalty did she have to them? Tetian was her blood from the land she loved. Ahhotep recalled grabbing her mother's shoulder and yelling in her face.

All the times her mother had told her she was unworthy —the family was undeserving—passed in memory. The times her mother said nothing, not wanting to waste words and breath on her, followed behind in rapid succession. Tetisheri had shown them the utter disownment after Ahhotep's dance with death by sneaking out of the palace and her children's disagreement with her command to arrest Baba. The last words her mother had spoken to her that day rushed upon her: *"Ta-Seti rule would have never allowed this to stand."*

Ahhotep stared at the throne as she stood off to its side and glanced at Ahmose-Nefertari and the guards in the room being held by spear and arrow points. She was helpless to do anything. If her mother agreed with Tetian, even the royal family would be divided. Would the guards side with her or her mother? Did it even matter?

In the next moment, they could all be slain to make way for Tetian, the nephew of Tetisheri, her blood, the son from her brother whom she loved, the son she raised and thought worthy of being king.

What were Ahmose-Nefertari and Ahmose and Amenhotep and the rest to her?

Nothing.

They were never anything to her. She was never anything to her mother. Her mouth was dry; her tongue, thick. She swallowed down the vomit that had come to the top of her throat. Had she told her to lead the forces against the siege as Royal Commander in mockery? She had known they were going to fail. She only said those words in vain.

"Stand up, Tetian," Tetisheri said in muted tones as the nomarchs filled the throne room under spear point.

"Mother?" Ahhotep choked, watching her cousin stand in pride before the woman who bore her. She shut her eyes, and her chin touched her collar. She had failed. After all the pain and sacrifice and hurt, she had lost the crown and now the lives of her family.

Her mother's words filled the throne room. "I want what is best for Kemet," she began. "And Tetian, I raised you to be better than this. You sorely disappoint me." She shook her head at him.

Tetian scoffed in a snigger, clearly not expecting that response. "What? How?"

Ahhotep lifted her head, her eyes darting between mother and nephew. Disappointed? She waited for Tetisheri's answer. Perhaps, all hope was not lost.

Tetian did not allow her mother to answer and instead yelled, "I am your blood. Ta-Seti is your home. The crown is mine. It does not belong to these Waset *fools* who want to take what was never theirs!"

Tetisheri was quick to strike back. "Yet these '*Waset fools*' have achieved victory without the riches of Ta-Seti to support them. And even more so, they have never given orders to slay any princes of Kemet nor brought the enemy into our throne room. You will *never* see the crown and cursed be Kemet if you take it."

Ahhotep's chest hitched, and a breath of relief escaped through her teeth. Tetian's actions had been his undoing. Now how to win this battle?

"You said there should be someone of Ta-Seti blood on the throne!" Tetian yelled and stepped into her space.

The mace hooked on the back of the throne grabbed Ahhotep's attention. She had to take the chance, and while the aunt-nephew debate took the attention of those in the throne room, she quietly moved closer to it.

"There is already Ta-Seti blood on the throne,"

Tetisheri said. "They came from my loins. Are you as dim as Baufre not to see that? And ordering the slayings of my grandson and great-grandsons? Are you mad, my child?"

Ahhotep's fingers gripped the mace handle. *I must be quick. Without Tetian, perhaps this can end now.* She eyed the back of Tetian's head. *Now is my chance.* She slowly lifted the mace from its hook, the weapon still hidden by the throne's chair back.

Tetian growled at Tetisheri. "I am not mad, old woman. I am the only sane one here. And if you do not agree, then step aside or be slain."

Ahhotep prayed her heart would not weigh heavy on the scale of Ma'at for her next actions, but before she could send the mace sailing toward Tetian, he stepped to the edge of the dais, shoving Tetisheri aside.

She halted—her mace still hidden behind the throne as Tetian spoke. "Who is with me? Former princes, do you see what I am doing, what I have done for *you*?"

Paser shook his head, and Setka stepped forward to speak. "Tetian, if the bloodline of Seqenenre Tao is divine and the Waset family is appointed by the gods, what you have done is an act of treason. If they are not divinely appointed, then you have ordered the slaying of the children of the prince of Waset, an unjustifiable act to the human and divine order either way. We are not with you."

Tetian threw his mace against the mud brick wall, shattering the carved reliefs into powder. The mace fell to the floor with a clang amid the mud brick pieces. "You ungrateful donkeys! Can't you see? This false family is doing to you what the Hekka Khasut did to us. We all descend from royalty before the foreign kings demoted us to princes over the nomes, and now your so-called divine king uses you, takes your wealth, and now usurps everything you have, demoting you to nomarchs?! Can't you see? Or are you all blind?"

Ahhotep settled her breath and adjusted her grip on the mace. She realized she had never trained with the mace in her non-dominant hand and prayed to Sekhmet and Pakhet her aim be true. It was then or never, so she sent the mace's golden-decorated club toward the back of Tetian's head.

But he heard the swoosh of air and shifted to the side. The crack of bone reverberated through the throne room. She yanked the mace back, and the sharp tang of blood leached into the air. The tall, greedy man hunched over with his hand gripping his bleeding and broken shoulder. He gritted, "Kill them all."

Ahhotep's ragged breath was all that was heard for the slight moment between peace and chaos. A spear and a few arrows sailed toward her, but Meret had already jumped in front of her Queen, taking the fatal projectiles upon herself. The guards rose up with their hidden weapons, taking the intruders by surprise. Baufre's large frame bolted for the door; Metjen had already slipped away, his soldiers leaving with them.

"Baufre, Metjen, you cowards," Ahhotep yelled and swung her mace toward a Kushite's head. Its golden glimmer shimmered in the sunlight as enemy blood dripped from the club.

Baufre turned to look at her with wide-vacant eyes— the pitiful fool had been led like prey into the lion's den.

"Fight for Kemet," she yelled. "Fight for the true divine King!"

She thought he would continue running, but he ordered his soldiers to fight against the Kushites: "Fight for Ahmose, Given Life!" he commanded.

The battle ensued, and a great clash of bronze against bronze rose before the midday sun.

A Kushite's arrow landed in her thigh, and she went down, screaming in agony. Tetisheri stood with head bowed, no weapon to wield. But no one touched the Great Wife. Ahmose-Nefertari sliced her dagger across the neck of a Ta-Setian soldier before a Kushite thrust a spear into her shoulder. She yelled out but cut him back before a guard did away with him. She, too, fell to the floor amid her slain maidservants, gasping for air and wrenching the spear stuck in her shoulder.

Ahhotep scanned the fighting that fell away from the dais. Nena kneeled beside her, tending to her leg. But Ahhotep pushed her away, whispering in a haze, "Help my daughter." Nena broke the arrow in Ahhotep's leg before tending to the Chief Wife.

Baufre's men, the guards, and the nomarchs were pushing the Ta-Setians and Kushites from the throne room. Tetian slipped from the doors with trickles of blood staining his perfect white tunic and golden collar.

Horns from Sha and Ma-Hedj blew in the distance, signaling reinforcements had come.

"Finally," Setka yelled out and swung a khopesh at the last of the soldiers in the throne room. Baufre and his men chased after the intruders.

As the guards closed the doors and a numbing haze overtook Ahhotep's senses, she stared at the stone visage of Kamose's statue in the courtyard while Tetian's order to kill her son and grandsons haunted her mind.

37

A TIME OF REPRIEVE |
AHHOTEP

SEDJEFATAWY, 1551 BC

Ahhotep stroked Ahmose-Nefertari's forehead as Re's sun barge again dipped low to enter the realm of Apep. She pushed her daughter's braids away and dabbed the sweat beads on her brow with torn linen from her slain maidservant.

Ahmose-Nefertari's eyelashes fluttered as she tried to keep her eyes open while Ahhotep pressed the spear wound to keep the blood from coming out too fast.

Tetisheri sat in her usual chair in the back of the dais, staring out at the closed doors.

"You must remain awake," Ahhotep crooned before kissing her daughter's forehead.

"I am afraid, Mother," she whispered.

"You have nothing to fear," Ahhotep said. "I am with you. The doors have been closed. No one will hurt you again."

Nena stooped down. "God's Mother, let me care for the Chief Wife. Take your place on the throne. The men, they need you," she stuttered but glanced to the guards and the nomarchs standing aimlessly around the throne room after separating the dead and tending to wounds. The servants that remained alive stood back, having cleaned the throne of blood spatter. Paser and a few others went out the back exit after securing the throne room to ensure the princes were safe, but they had not returned. Worry lived on the faces that glanced back at her.

"I see," Ahhotep muttered. Nena placed her hand over Ahmose-Nefertari's shoulder wound, causing the Chief Wife to wince. "Be good to her, Nena."

"As Meret gave her life to save you, I will give mine to save your daughter's."

Ahhotep nodded at Nena's oath and released her daughter into her care. She limped to the throne and sat upon it. She rubbed her thigh where the arrow had been pulled and her leg tightly wrapped. They all needed the services of a physician-priest. They would not last long without honey, stitches, and castor oil applied to their wounds. Blood from her leg soaked through the bandages and stained her royal dress. The pain permeated through her hip and leg.

"Are we all that is left? Or have we regained the palace? Has anyone come with the status of Sedjefatawy?" she asked in her daze.

"None." Setka looked at the dead with linen cloths draped over their faces and shook his head. "None," he repeated in a whisper and clutched the handle of his khopesh in his hand.

She looked at the back exit, guarded by half of the soldiers, to the small corridor that led to the king's apartment.

"It is useless," she began, causing everyone's heads to turn. "It is useless if there is no crown prince. We can hide in here, or we can go out there and be of service to the palace. We must find the crown prince and his siblings and keep them safe."

She stood up and gripped her son's mace that a servant had hooked again on the back of the throne. With a steadying breath, she walked toward the exit.

"Royal Commander, you are going on a suicide mission," Weshptah said, stepping in front of her.

"Today, Nomarch, is the day you have been called to give your life in defense of the throne. Nomarch Paser understood that when he led the small unit to retrieve the crown prince. But he has not returned and may very well be slain alongside the future of Kemet. We are of no use here. Leave the wounded to defend this location, and Nena will attend to them as needed. The rest," she scanned the able-bodied men and women, "we shall go to the harem and find the royal children and bring them back here."

Ahhotep pointed her mace at her mother. "You too, Great Wife."

After the throne room's attack and her mother's unscathed body, Ahhotep was certain no one would kill her. Tetian might, but the others would not. She was still a daughter to the former prince of Ta-Seti. She was still the mother of King Seqenenre Tao.

Tetisheri stood up without a word and led the way. Ahhotep snorted at the unquestioned obedience. Now— after all this time—now was the time her mother decided to obey her command. Ahhotep gritted her teeth and released a tension-releasing breath through her nostrils. Would she ever understand the woman who birthed her? Tetisheri had not handed them over when Tetian asked. For some reason, she had stood beside the family she thought worthless. Ahhotep wondered if Tetisheri felt any guilt that her nephew caused all this bloodshed and agony, or if she had simply cast him off as she had done to them for a time.

"But Royal Commander, you are wounded," Setka said, stepping in front of her, cutting her from her thoughts.

"I live; I can fight." The mace's handle was firmly in her right hand. If only she had been able to use her dominant hand when attacking Tetian, maybe this ordeal would have been over by now. With gritted teeth, she followed behind her mother, flanked by guards and soldiers.

The small corridor was eerily quiet, and the king's room had been torn to pieces, but no one was there. Tetisheri walked with a bold gait to the hallway and peered down the corridor past the courtyard. She glanced back. "The path is only littered with the slain. No man is living."

Their company advanced. Ahhotep's leg ached, but she would not limp. Fresh blood squeezed from her wound as she walked. Her chin remained parallel to the floor as she wrestled the whimpers in her chest to keep them from escaping. They made it to the courtyard's edge, where the destroyed images of Tao and Kamose lay in pieces on the ground. Ahhotep forced herself not to look for fear of the cry that would escape her lips. Men's grumbles and grunts sounded over them and down the long corridor at the palace entrance. Bodies lay everywhere, but it seemed the palace defenders had pushed Tetian's forces back and were securing the palace. They continued past the courtyard and around the corner to the royal harem's entrance. The stench of blood and maddening noises caused Ahhotep to stagger. The harem workers were weaving linens for wounds and carting amphoras of honey and castor oil to various parts of the palace. One headed for the throne room.

Ahhotep watched the boy run off. It seemed their brave voyage beyond the throne room was too late. The pit of her stomach knotted as she scanned the harem-working courtyards. The Ta-Seti soldiers had no honor. Bodies of women and children lay covered with cloths. She turned her face away, quelling the rage within her. It seemed they had slain every child to ensure the princes were dead and Tetian's order was carried out. Such cruelty, and all because a prince became too greedy, too self-empowered, too . . . powerful.

Never again.

Never again.

Her gaze fell on the motionless children and young men with blood-smeared cloths over their faces. Their sandals of reed and leather drooped from their lifeless toes—so many of them. The desire to crumple to the floor nearly took her knees in strict obedience. What if her children and grandchildren were among them? Her mother drew near to a young boy whose naked body resembled Amenhotep. She reached for the cloth covering his face.

Please don't, Ahhotep begged her in her mind. *Not here.* She shut her eyes tight and waited to hear a reaction. But nothing came. But of course, it would not. Her mother barely made a sound when her own son was laid at her feet.

"Royal Commander," Setka asked, drawing her thoughts away from the children's bodies.

Her head bowed low, and she opened her eyes to the ground, unable to see if the boy was her close kin. "Yes, Nomarch?"

"These people are traumatized. They do not even

notice the Great Wives as they enter. Shall we look for the princes in the harem?"

Her mind muddled, and the corners of her lips turned down. "Find the head steward, Ranofer. He should know what became of the princes."

"As you command," Setka said with a dip of his chin.

Yet while Setka still spoke, a distant "Royal Commander" traveled across the harem. The steward Men nursed a bloody arm as he hurried toward them, tripping over a worker and dodging others. He arrived out of breath but still bowed at the waist.

"Great Wife, Royal Commander"—he rose from his bow—"I am glad you have survived. The gods' blessing is great. Now, about the royal children, the princes." His gaze shifted to Tetisheri, who was going child by child, lifting cloths. She stopped and stood at Men's mention of those whom she sought. He cleared his throat when he had their attention. "We hid the princes, but they were not where we had placed them after the attack was pushed out of the harem. Nomarch Paser came and began a search for them."

It meant they could be alive. She lifted her eyes to Re in gratitude, but before the silent prayer could form in her mind, she asked, "What of the royal daughters?"

Men's mouth twitched, but he spat what he was going to say, quick and to the point: "Great Wife Ahhotep Tasherit was the only one slain." He pointed to a woman's body with a large blood-stained cloth over her upper body.

Ahhotep snapped her gaze to the woman Men pointed at. The dread in her stomach leeched onto the color of her face, draining it to pale.

"Tep?" she mouthed. *No, it can't be,* she thought. *Not Tep.*

Her mother had already advanced upon the body.

Ahhotep shifted to follow, but her leg gave way. Hands reached out to support her, but she pushed them away.

"Tep." The whimper pressed between Ahhotep's lips. She limped, dragging her aching leg behind her as she rushed to Tep's side. Her mother had already ripped the linen away, revealing a gaping, jagged wound that ran from her left jaw to her opposite breast.

The need to vomit at the sight of her firstborn commanded Ahhotep's stomach, but her tongue pushed it back into its roiling depths. She fell to her knees as she reached out to caress her daughter's cold cheek.

Heat encased her face and hands as she held the anguish in its prison until soft weeping drew her focus. In her haze, she wondered who was crying. If anyone was weeping, it should be her. She wiped her cheek: wet. Yet, someone else was crying. She looked around, and her gaze rested on her mother.

Tetisheri held Tep's hand to her face and wept aloud. Ahhotep stared at her mother. Why did she care about Tep? And now, after running her off? Tep was the one she weeps for? Not her son, not her grandson, not any of the great-grandchildren? But for Tep, the one she ridiculed and ostracized every single day of the poor girl's life? The one she was glad was not an active part of the royal family anymore? The one she thought the most unworthy of the crown?

Ahhotep closed her eyes. With those unanswered questions, she hated her mother and knew she would never understand her. Eyes fell upon her as she knelt beside Tep and her mother's weeping grew louder. Ahhotep froze, wanting to allow the whimpers and cries to flood the hole in her heart and push through an open mouth, but she was the Royal Commander. So, she bit her tongue and leaned forward to place a lingering kiss on Tep's cheek.

"You will be buried as a queen, my daughter," she whispered in her ear. Tep had been slaughtered as she stood defenseless. "If only I had killed Tetian when I had the chance," she uttered to herself. If only she had restrained Tetian and Metjen and forced them to give up their prince hood one year ago. If only she had not ordered the deaths of the Aamu servants twenty-four years ago. If only so many mistakes and actions had been taken or not taken, her children would be alive. Tep would be alive, and maybe, she could have held her in an embrace one last time before she parted to the Field of Reeds.

38

A TIME OF HEALING |
AHHOTEP

SEDJEFATAWY, 1551 BC

Ahhotep remained at Tep's side for what seemed an eternity. She could only imagine Tep's final moments. Would they have struck her down knowing she was Kamose's wife? If she had worn her vulture headdress and royal collar? Ahhotep imagined her other children and grandchildren in a similar state. Was not Ahmose-Nefertari in pain and bleeding from her wound as well?

The shouts and screams of men at war escalated from the distant hum it had been, drawing Ahhotep from her thoughts. She pulled away from her daughter but found she could not stand. Her fingers clutched the wound in her leg, making fresh blood rise through the makeshift bandage. Pain trembled on her lips in a whimper.

Men snapped at a servant. "Get the Royal Commander to the physician-priest."

Tetisheri placed Tep's hand down over her chest. She looked up and scanned the harem once again as if in a daze under the dimming sunlight.

"Great Wife," Ahhotep called to her mother, but it

was useless. Tetisheri either did not hear her or ignored her. Where was the woman who stood as a stone, unwavering in whatever tide crashed upon her? Had her first love, Tetian, her adopted son, created a cleft in her hard heart? Ahhotep snorted as two arms hooked under her armpits and yanked her up.

Ahhotep straightened as she withdrew her gaze from Tep. She had failed her firstborn. Tao, Kamose, Tep— they were all slain for this divine power struggle. Their passing would not be in vain. She snatched her arms away from the help she had received and turned around with a slight limp, masking the agony that traveled up and down her leg. "I do not need a physician-priest," she declared. "I need Tetian on a stake in the front of the palace as a symbol of what befalls traitors to the crown."

She lifted her chin and placed her hands behind her back. "The throne will not be empty while the defenders of Kemet fight."

Ahhotep limped toward the harem's exit, gritting her teeth with every step. She had to stop after making it past the nomarchs. Sweat beaded her brow.

"Royal Commander," Weshptah and Setka said simultaneously, but Setka continued. "The soldiers fight without your command for the greater of the day. Go to the royal physician-priest. Name one of us to command in your absence while the Chief Wife is injured and the crown prince is yet to be found."

She eyed each of them and wished Paser were there. Even though they all had surrendered their prince hood, she trusted Paser the most. She glanced back at her mother, who remained seated and stared in a daze at the destruction done to the harem. Tetisheri was in no frame of mind to lead.

"Nomarch Setka, command in the absence of a

member of the royal family," she finally said and allowed a servant to take her arm without touching the royal flesh.

SERVANTS HELPED HER TO THE PHYSICIAN-PRIEST'S ROOM DEEP within the palace. She scanned the room filled with hyssop and smelt of rich cinnamon incense. The wounded filled the floor, and the royal physician-priest dressed in his leopard tunic stopped mid-gait upon seeing her.

"Royal Commander." He bowed low. The tunic's plaster leopard head swung out, and as he returned to stand, it plopped back on his soft belly. "I have used the king's royal room to treat the injured. It is my decision, and I accept whatever punishment is befitting this perversion."

Her gaze jumped from each man, woman, and child filling the room until her eyes found Ahmose-Nefertari lying on one of three tables. Her eyes were open, but the irises were dilated.

"You have acted in the best interest of Sedjefatawy," Ahhotep said and limped through the bodies to the table with the help of the servants. "My leg, if you will."

He gestured to the table, and the servants helped her upon its flat top.

"Will she live?" Ahhotep asked the physician-priest and gestured to her daughter.

"Yes," he nodded, pushing Ahhotep back on the table with a gentle nudge of her shoulder. "She had a deep wound, and I had to administer a potion for the pain. I will have to stitch it up in a moment. Now, please, bite down on this while I remove the arrow." He placed a wooden bite plate in her mouth before tending to her leg.

He tenderly pulled the arrow's tip out while Ahhotep bit into the hard piece of polished wood. Sweat poured from her brow, and moans escaped past the wood. When it was over, she let the bite plate fall from her mouth as her breathing rushed past clenched teeth.

After the pricks of pain from the needle to stitch up her leg subsided, a shadow in the doorway took her attention, and she was glad for the small reprieve. Her mother stood there, scanning the room with hazy, bloodshot eyes.

The physician-priest glanced at her and bowed his head. "Great Wife Tetisheri," he said, scanning the blood stains on her royal linens. "Are you injured as well?"

Tetisheri shook her head. "Only here to speak with the Royal Commander."

The quick tug of fabric and the subsequent sting told Ahhotep the physician-priest was finished with her leg. She swung herself off the table with a grunt and groan, and he held out his arm to stop her. "You are injured. You need to stay and rest. I have already prepared the potion for pain."

"I shall not rest," she said and looked at Ahmose-Nefertari, seeing her eyes aimlessly wander in a daze. "I must have my mind about me. Stand aside, for there is no one in the throne room."

He dipped his head low. "Then I shall attend the Chief Wife."

"Very good." Ahhotep put weight on her injured leg and her knee buckled, but she caught herself on the table. She swallowed down her yelp and stood again. Breath filled her chest as she tried once more. She walked to the doorway with a sure step, ignoring the searing agony that ripped down her leg, although a grimace remained on her face.

"Mother," she gritted as she pushed past her.

"Ahhotep, wait," she said and grabbed her daughter's arm. They stood outside the room.

"Why should I wait for you? Before the attack on the throne room, you would have told me to be worthy of the crown and never leave my duty to the throne, no matter who was laid at my feet. Never show weakness. Or have you changed your mind, now that you have wept for your eldest grandchild whom you hated?"

Tetisheri withdrew her hand. The haze in her eyes returned to their usual cold grey. "I never hated Tep. I loved her with all my heart."

Ahhotep scoffed and began the journey to the throne room by herself. Tetisheri took Ahhotep under the elbow and arm and supported her while she walked.

"I was harsh, yes. I know you believe me to have a hard heart, but I loved Tep so much. I love you all." Her voice broke. She stopped and faced her daughter.

"You only say this now because your kin has failed you by ordering the death of the Crown Prince." Ahhotep tried to push forward.

But her mother's hand remained firm on her elbow, keeping Ahhotep where she stood.

"Did you know of Tetian's plans?" Ahhotep spat and snapped at her mother. "Are you to blame for this as well? Did you conspire with him?"

Tetisheri's face blanched. She looked at her hand and curled it into a fist. "I did not think my nephew would bring an army against the king. I had told him of my disappointments in you in a few of our letters." Her chin drooped. "I never knew it would come to this. Tetian is no longer my own. I disown him."

"As you disowned me?" Ahhotep jeered.

Tetisheri stood up straight and yanked her hands to her side. "I never disowned you, Ahhotep. You disappointed me greatly with some of your actions, but I never disowned you." Her voice softened, as did her eyes. For once, Ahhotep thought this harsh woman might speak something other than insults.

"I thought I could make you a better regent," she confessed. "Harden you for a day like today. Harden you for when your husband and sons could be laid before you, before us, broken and defiled against our sacred traditions. Harden you so you could still lead in spite of agony. I did not have a mother who had endured what I endured. I did not have a mother who could teach me how to remain strong and powerful in the midst of war, in the eyes of the enemy, while standing upon the divine dais. I had to learn it myself. And I did my best to teach you because I did not want to see my firstborn daughter —you—laid at my feet. For if you were laid there,"—her eyes filled with mist, and she cupped Ahhotep's face— "then I knew I had failed my family. My son always had a chance to be brought home in a litter carried by Anubis priests off to war. It was something I had accepted could happen, but if my daughter was slain, then I knew the war was lost. Seeing Tep . . . " Her voice trailed off, and she shook her head. "All my mistakes rushed upon me."

Ahhotep still did not wholly believe her mother's confession, but it was the most genuine slew of words she had ever spoken to her.

"You do not make mistakes, Mother," Ahhotep said in a gentle mockery.

Tetisheri took a deep breath, and the mist formed tears in her eyes. "I disregarded my nephew, and in my quest to teach and provide the best for you, I lost my virtue in how I treated you, Tep, Ahmose, and all the rest. I never made amends with Tep. She will never forgive me for what I have said and done. She lost her family, and I only pushed her away. I saw you that night sitting with Ahmose-Nefertari, comforting her after the crocodiles. It was then that I realized you are a better queen, leader, and mother than I ever have been."

Ahhotep choked back her disbelief and wondered who the woman in front of her was. Why was she speaking these lies? Weren't they all unworthy in her eyes?

But Ahhotep swallowed down the snide remarks she could have said and asked a question that had plagued her since the day she heard the tale. "Lady Rai said you cried in the Kap's nursery when I was a babe. Why?"

Tetisheri shuffled back, not expecting such a question. But with a quiver in her lip, she answered, "Because I knew I could never be a good mother to you. I let myself fall victim to my beliefs, and now Tep is gone from this life. My son, my grandson also . . . Do not be a victim of circumstance, Ahhotep. Do not be like me."

Her gray eyes darkened. "To be the defender of Kemet, you must rise above the challenges, no matter what they are, and you must do so with virtue. If you lose your virtue, then who are you to rule? Without virtue, people might follow you if you wield enough power to make them cower, but they will never honor you, as you do not honor me. Their hearts will be far from you, and the day will come when they will rise against you. Do not be a victim. Do not lose your virtue. Learn from my mistakes, and be what Kemet needs in this hour."

Ahhotep remained mute, unable to form a response. *What? Did those words come from my mother?*

Tetisheri grabbed her elbow again and led her to the throne room in silence.

"Who is this before me now? You are not the same woman even from yesterday," Ahhotep whispered.

Tetisheri hung her head. "Tep was slain in the harem along with all those children. I was so focused on trying to better you, thinking you could not be strong and demonstrate a powerful front in the face of hardship, that I ignored Tetian. I failed him as his adoptive mother, and because of his actions, many have been slain for no reason other than I did not stop Tetian's growing outrage. I ignored it. I was too blind to see. But you saw it all those years ago. Ahmose saw it, which was why he left two hundred men here. I thought it was a waste. My Tetian would never have done this." Two tears rolled down her cheeks. "I was wrong, and others have paid the price."

Ahhotep stared at her mother as she spoke, seeing tears fall from her stone-cold eyes for the second time in her life. Finally, she understood Tetisheri: a frightened mother and queen who hid behind a hard shell, trying her best to survive the pressure of the crown and duties to those born of her womb, yet in doing so, she had made herself an outcast in her family and a blind advisor to the king. She stood alone wearing her granddaughter's blood on the dress she tried so hard to keep stainless and pure for the sake of her royal image. Was that why she never let anyone in, for fear of seeing who she really was? They could crack that stone facade she projected. They would see her weakness. They could allow her image to be stained.

But as they walked, Ahhotep saw her mother for the first time as the woman she could have loved all these years in all her perfect flaws. She stopped and pulled her mother into an embrace.

"What are you doing?" Tetisheri whispered, wrapping an arm around Ahhotep's waist. "They will see."

They had gained servants, guards, and soldiers behind her, awaiting her command. The clashes and men's grunts and yells sounded outside the palace walls.

Ahhotep smiled. "Then let them see." She pulled away and locked eyes with her mother. "You bore me. You raised me. You taught me. You told me not to lose my virtue. I will not be weak. I will lead, and I will be victorious."

They came to the throne room, and the doors were wide open. The throne was empty. She gently lifted her mother's hand away from her.

"When sound decisions need to be made to ensure victory," Tetisheri advised as they stared at the empty seat. "When life and death depend on your decision, when there is no time for sorrow and pain—mourn the slain later. Do not let others see you struggle. Do not let those who look to you see you as weak. They need direction and confidence; they need you, who carry divine blood, to show them the gods are on their side. Lead, like I know you can do, my daughter."

Ahhotep nodded along with the cadence of Tetisheri's words. "You will be proud of me, Mother," she finally said.

"I already am, Ahhotep." Tetisheri dipped her chin to her. "Royal Commander."

With a renewed heart free of one of the burdens it once carried, Ahhotep fought through the pain with her back upright—mouth clenched—as she walked the long hall of the throne room, came to the poorly gilded chair, and sat in it. She glanced at the body of Meret alongside the other slain guards and servants during the recent skirmish.

Her mother stood beside her. The crowd that had followed her filled the pillared room. Their eyes were hungry for her presence, spoken word, and divine link to the appointed king. The castor oil and honey crystallized on her leg's bandage as she sat still. The clamoring and shouts of men still lay thick in the air.

"Do not fear, for we shall be victorious," she began in an emboldened voice as Apep's dark frame slithered into the sky. "Amun will protect his divinely appointed."

39
A TIME OF BALANCE |
AHMOSE-NEFERTARI
SEDJEFATAWY, 1551 BC

Ahmose-Nefertari's brow furrowed. Deep hums and chants pounded in her ears. Her body drifted as if she were as light as incense and yet felt as heavy as a grain sack. Even though she could hear, she could not feel anything at all. Her eyes rolled underneath their lids. She swallowed the thick lump in her parched throat.

"Be still, Chief Wife." The harsh command reverberated in her head. But she remembered her sons were being hunted and forced her eyes open.

Her arms felt detached, but she clenched her fists.

Where was she?

The overwhelming aroma of incense and green smoke filled the air. Her vision blurred. She rolled to her side, but the sudden, paralyzing rip of agony seared across her chest and back, sucking in the scream that begged for release.

"Be still, Chief Wife." The command came harsher than before, and a firm hand returned her to her supine position.

She blinked and then once more.

"No," she ground out and rolled the other way. She had to find her sons. She had to make sure they were safe. Her mother had never come back to the throne room. Maybe she was killed along with Nomarch Paser. She looked around again, wondering where she was. The pain was not as great on that side, but the floor seemed to drop off. She flung her hand out and realized she was on a table.

The firm hand came again and pushed her backward. "Be still."

Ahmose-Nefertari's head slung back around the other way, and she found herself locking eyes with a leopard. She froze. Her heart raced. A scream escaped. She jerked back. Her words garbled into nonsense as she attempted to scream past her swollen throat.

"Be. Still."

She stared at the leopard's eyes, and the more she stared, they seemed false. Her gaze wandered up the spotted body until it dawned on her: she was looking at the leopard tunic of a priest. His face was blurred, but at the sight of him, her body relaxed. She was in the hands of the royal physician-priest skilled in the god Heka's magic.

The priest hummed and shook his head as he brought down his needle made of bone, threaded with finely woven flax. "I am almost finished, Chief Wife, but you must remain still. You pushed through my potion easily. I shall have to make it stronger for you."

She watched the needle go up and back down. Blood ran along its bone body. She expected to feel a sting or a poke with each needle dive, but she felt nothing. The steady up-and-down motion nearly called sleep to rush upon her, but at last, it stopped right before her eyelids closed.

"Finished Chief Wife. Now, I will make you a stronger potion," the priest said.

"No," she sputtered, rolling the least painful way off the table. "My sons." Her words sounded as if they had been bathed in honey. Her legs barely caught her fall as she grabbed the table's edge with clawed fingers. She pressed her forehead to its cool mud brick to relieve the ache in her brow.

"Chief Wife, you cannot walk with the potion in the body. Heka's magic works best when you are still." The physician-priest grabbed her good arm and helped her stand up. "Now lay back, and I will make you a stronger potion." He picked her petite frame up and sat her back on the table. "Please lay down," he urged.

Her vision remained blurry as she glanced around at all the wounded that filled the small room.

"No," she said and pressed her finger and thumb over her eyes. The room spun around her, but her bottom was planted on the table. Her heart raced as she tried to make sense of the sensations passing over her body.

"No more potion," she said with a thick tongue. "I need my wits about me, and I feel as if I have lingered with wine all day and night."

"As you command, Chief Wife," the physician-priest said. "But you will be in pain, and the more you use your arm, the less likely the wound will heal."

She scooted off the table as a snail, gingerly touching her toes to the floor to secure her bearings. The physician-priest wrapped her arm in a sling while she steadied herself beside the table. "Do not use it, Chief Wife, or it will not heal."

She nodded and shut her eyes, regretting the movement. "I need to find my sons."

The physician-priest's firm hand became soft as he

turned her face to his. "We have already found the Crown Prince. It was why I wanted you to lay down for a while longer."

"Why? I need to see him. I need to know he is safe."

Though blurred, she could see the man's downturned lips.

"I urge you to lay down, for your own sake," he said.

Her heart beat hard in her chest as the worst images came to her mind. First, her father, then her brother, and now, her son.

No.

She would not accept such an assumption.

"Where is he?!" Her screech stung her ears, and she wondered how that sound came out of her.

"As you wish," he said and took her arm, guiding her to the third table where a boy—perhaps a young man— lay upon it.

She squinted to make out his face.

"Ramose!" She stumbled out of the physician-priest's grip. She grasped his arm, but it was cool to the touch. She yelled, "He needs warmth. Why is there no blanket on him?"

A soldier and servant woman stood. They limped to her as she eyed them. "Have you brought a blanket?"

The soldier bowed his head. "My queen, Crown Prince Ramose, wanted to be like his uncle and father and lead the guards of the harem to victory against the traitors, so he left his hiding place with Prince Sapair when we fought with Ta-Seti soldiers."

Ahmose-Nefertari's head spun, and the need to vomit pressed at the top of her throat. Her gaze drifted back to her almost twelve-year-old son as she caressed his rigid cheek. Her fingers grazed the open wound on his neck with blood thick in the crevice. She could think of nothing—the soldier did not have to continue speaking about what became of Ramose.

She grabbed his shoulder and pressed her forehead to his chest. "Why did you not leave the fighting to those charged to protect you?" The words pushed past clenched teeth. "Ramose, why?"

The soldier must have heard her, for he said with a bowed head, "He fought bravely to defend his wife, Princess Tair, and unborn child. Although sick, he fought well with the mace. He helped us push them back away from the royal children. He did not want to sit idle. We urged him to stay back, as did Prince Sapair, but he said he was a leader and would fight with us. He gave us strength that we did not know we had. We won our victory but an arrow . . ."

His voice trailed off as her knees buckled under the weight of her sorrow. Hands came from around to support her, but she pushed them away as an unmistakable moan left her lips.

"He was an honorable prince, Chief Wife. He would have made an honorable king."

Tears welled in her eyes before running down her cheeks. "Please, no more," she said with hitched breath. Control fled until she was hunched over her son, weeping. It was then she noticed the stares of all in the room. She was their queen. A second time she had failed them in her show of strength and power.

"Look away," she cried. "Close your ears," she begged in a guttural plea before uncontrollable shrieks sent waves through her ribs. How had her mother and grandmother stood silent on the dais as their sons were laid at their feet? What mystic strength did they possess to keep their cries of agony at bay? Her body sagged against the table as tears gushed from her eyes and cries poured from her mouth. The beat of her heart pounded in her ears, contrasting the still chest of her son. Her nails dug into his chilled flesh as she pulled herself up to look into his eyes—glossy and vacant.

It was enough to entomb two of her children, taken in illness, and two more, killed by crocodile. Now she was to entomb a fifth child, slain by an enemy? Her legs wobbled, and she slipped to the floor, curled on the cool mud brick. Spent—drained by her divine appointment. If this was what she had to endure to be queen, she could not do it. Her ka sought liberation from this life.

This war had destroyed her home. The Hekka Khasut, the princes, the Kushites—they had all killed members of her family. Were Amenhotep, Mutnofret, and Meryet Amon slain as well? Her mother and grandmother? All the nomarchs? Was it all for naught? Everything done in vain? Did this divine appointment mean anything to the gods? Where were they? Did they not protect? Did they not bless? Was the true Kemet to shrink into oblivion under foreign kings?

The slur of words left her tongue in a yell, "Where are you, gods?!" She tried to pull back her words, for what would those around her think of her question? She was the divine's appointed chief wife. She should not utter such questions. She should not cry out in agony. Show weakness? Never. Yet, she remained on the floor, her cries turning to muted whimpers.

Shame crept over her cheeks. Who was she to question Amun and Re and Hathor and Isis? Tears chased each other down her cheeks. She had no strength to continue until she looked up and saw the wounded soldiers and servants from the room had come and circled the table—their backs to her and Ramose— shielding her from any who would see her agony.

Her breath settled in her chest at this act of love from these soldiers, many of whom she did not know their names. Thoth, the god of wisdom, came to her then.

If the legends were true, even the god Osiris was murdered by his brother, Set. Even Isis mourned Osiris, her husband. Even the gods felt pain. Even the gods lost their loved ones.

Perhaps this path, although divinely appointed, was not meant to be easy. It was not intended to be devoid of agony and loss.

Even in mourning, Isis proved her love to Osiris by gathering the pieces of his body and raising him from the dead with her magic.

Perhaps then, the divinely appointed was meant to endure. For if she gave up, she would never have proved her love for the gods, for Kemet, for the people—her people. Her gaze scanned the blood-smeared tunics of the people who surrounded her, facing out.

These people.

A lump grew thick in her throat as the potion lost its effect on her sight. The incensed green air pleased her senses as a bittersweet peace fell upon her. Maybe this was what her mother and grandmother knew. Maybe that was why they could stand firm in the face of adversity and sorrow. She drew a deep breath. Ramose was gone from this life—Ahmose-Ankh, Siamun, Ahmose-Sitamun, and Ahmose-Sipair as well. But they were in the Field of Reeds living for eternity. They had brought joy, love, and laughter to an otherwise dim life. She cherished them all, even for the two moments Siamun was with her. Their lives in the land of the living had not been in vain. They had lived and endured until they could no longer endure. They were brave in their illness and challenges and met the afterlife with open eyes and open hearts. The thought was a balm to her bleeding spirit.

Pain returned to her shoulder. She had forgotten about that wound, but it seemed less than the anguish in her heart. But despite the affliction, she lifted herself, using the table as a crutch.

She would stand and be the queen her people needed. She would endure until her body could no longer sustain life in this land, just like her children, just like the gods.

Her recent weeping made her voice gruff, but still, she cleared her throat and spoke. "Your queen thanks you for your service to her in her hour of need. Send for the Anubis priests if they have not already been summoned for the Crown Prince Ramose."

"They have been called, Chief Wife," the physician priest said.

"Well then," Ahmose-Nefertari said and took a deep breath. "I must find my living children. Who will come with me?"

Those, who stood, turned around and bowed their heads in service. Some, who were seated, stood, and did the same.

"Good. Then let us go," she said and left that place of sorrow. A stone visage fell upon her face, just like her grandmother and her mother. Only one thought entered her mind: The gods mourned, but they were also vengeful. Tetian would pay with his afterlife.

40
A TIME OF THE DIVINE
| AHHOTEP
SEDJEFATAWY, 1551 BC

Black smoke billowed as a dark offering to the skies from the battle outside the palace. The smoke in the distance grew darker and blocked the sun, casting a shadow over the land, but at least Per-djed-ken still stood.

Ahhotep's stomach boiled up to the back of her throat as she looked out over the harbor. So much destruction. After three months of fighting, and finally, with the help of the small militias from Sha and Ma-Hedj and the converted traitors from Bat and Meseh, they were able to push Tetian and his Kushite allies up the Nile. Many of Tetian's ships sat sunk in the Nile.

With her chin lowered and her eyes locked on the southern bend of the river, her jaw clamped tautly. Her leg ached. Ahmose-Nefertari's shoulder had not healed well. Tep's and Ramose's bodies lay prepped, wrapped, and ready for the tomb, but the path to West of Waset had not been safe to travel. Their ka and ba were mad with waiting. Even though Lady Rai suffered wounds that would soon ensure her journey west, she had made sure three of Ahmose-Nefertari's children had survived.

A breeze blew the black smoke in her face causing the braids under her vulture headdress to sway. The reek of the blood-flowing Nile reached her nostrils.

"When the river runs red, it means a new divine king is known," she said to the guards and soldiers surrounding her as the Ta-Setians turned their ships to flee. "And it is not Tetian of Khnum's Ta-Seti."

"May the gods renew Ahmose, Given Life," the men said in unison.

"Amun seals our divine appointment this day." She sneered, curling her lip. "Pursue and put down," she commanded, and the soldier beside her blew a horn to tell Troop Commander Uahbra. The celebrating ships soon followed.

"I want Tetian, alive or slain, at my feet before the end of the month."

"Yes, Royal Commander," the soldier said before blowing the order on the horn—three long, blaring notes.

The lead ship took her attention. "Viceroy Si-Tayet and his five units will keep them from venturing too far south," she muttered before lifting her head under the dimmed sky and placing one hand behind her back. *That is, if they are still alive*, she thought. No one had come from the past year to report to her about the dealings in Wawat. If Si-Tayet had sent a messenger, he would have known about the siege. If then, why had he not come to their aid unless Kush had rebelled and he could not spare resources? Her other hand gripped a cane as she sighed. *Well*, she thought, *we will soon find out what became of Si-Tayet and his five units.*

She turned around expecting to see Meret and Nena, but two guards stood in their place. The familiar shadows were no more: Meret lay waiting for burial, and

Nena was given in service to Ahmose-Nefertari. But Ahhotep mused: she did not need maidservants, for she was Royal Commander. She needed guards.

Her back straightened as she began the long walk across the roof toward the stairs with a half-empty heart. So much blood. So much killing. Tears gathered behind her eyes, but she blinked them away.

Soon, she thought. *Soon, it will all be over. Soon, we will have peace.*

The new year would be upon them in the coming month, but there would be no Birth of Re Festival to welcome it—they had no food or preparations. Yet an opening of a new year brought healing. Maybe she should arrange something, however small. Yes, perhaps she would. They all needed healing from this war and rebellion, starting with Tetian's flesh burning on a stake.

THE NOMARCHS LINED THE THRONE ROOM BEFORE AHHOTEP, seated on the throne. Her leg was wrapped tightly; the pain had never left.

The royal family stood behind her, heavily guarded. Princess Tair stood with bloodshot eyes, her hand cupping the bottom of her small pregnant belly. Sapair leaned upon a cane with his head and arm wrapped. He had been badly wounded but wanted to be on the dais for what was about to transpire. His wife Senseneb held Ahmes' and Thutmose's hands. Mutnofret and the new three-year-old Crown Prince, Amenhotep, stood next to Ahmose-Nefertari on the right hand of the throne. Meryet-Amon, at ten years old, held her arm around Amenhotep's thin shoulder, and Tetisheri stood on Ahhotep's lefthand side.

The doors to the throne room opened with a creak, and the sound of grunts and groans filled the otherwise silent hall. Ahhotep stared with hard eyes as soldiers brought a bloodied and struggling Tetian before her. Metjen and Baufre were prodded in behind him by spearpoint.

Sound decisions. Sorrow can wait. Show your people the gods are with them, Ahhotep thought before clearing her throat to speak.

"Tetian, Metjen, Baufre, you have brought arms against your king, and Tetian, you have ordered the slaying of all the sons of King Seqenenre Tao and King Ahmose. The Crown Prince Ramose was killed by your command, leaving his youngest brother, Amenhotep, as the Crown Prince. Prince Sapair and Prince Thutmose live. You have failed in your quest, yet in your failure, you have proven to all the world the line of King Ahmose is divine. The gods provide for their appointed king. For such an act of blatant treason, the gods' law is eternal death."

Baufre collapsed to his knees, weeping uncontrollably. "Have mercy, Royal Commander, God's Mother of King Ahmose," he begged—his hands clasped tightly together and head bowed in shame.

Ahhotep ignored the empty-minded fool. "This day, the crown will have power over you in your treachery."

As Baufre wailed about helping fight Ta-Seti, Tetian scoffed and ripped his arms from the guards' grips. They seized him again, but Ahhotep held up her hand to halt them. She would afford him this one last luxury, not out of pity or mercy, but to prove he was powerless.

The guards sneered at the traitor and released him. Tetian took a step forward. His eyes lifted in arrogant pride. "You have no power over me, Ahhotep. You will have to slay the prince of Ta-Seti, for I will never succumb to that of a nomarch."

He spat at her feet and turned to the nomarchs, lifting a finger and pointing in their faces. "One day, you will remember my warning and wish your power returned, but it will not be. You will go hungry and starve and send your men into slavery under this line of so-called divine kings. Heed my words!"

But they remained mute and looked to Ahhotep to speak.

She scanned the hall and sighed, shaking her head at him. "I tire of this man's blasphemy. Cut out his tongue."

He spun around, wide-eyed, yelling, "I am the prince of Ta-Seti! You will not lay a hand on me."

Tetian swung his fist wildly at the first guard who approached him, connecting with an audible thud. The guard staggered back, clutching his face. Three guards attacked, wrenching his arms behind his back and pinning him to the ground. He writhed and kicked, but to no avail.

"Your heart will be heavy, Ahhotep! You commit such an act against the prince of Ta-Seti! The greatest of the nomes?" Tetian yelled as the guards made him stand and stretched out his arms and legs so he couldn't move.

A third guard approached and drew his dagger. Tetian pulled back. "You have all pledged your loyalty in vain. My grandfather was a fool, just as you are now. Look at what they have done to you! Rise up! Take what is yours!"

A fourth guard grabbed Tetian's jaw and pulled out Tetian's tongue while the other raised his dagger. Tetian squirmed and yelled as the blade lowered.

"Halt!" Ahhotep's command flung through the air, and the guard stopped before slicing the soft pink prickled flesh. All eyes turned to her as she stood in elegance and majesty. A servant approached her with her cane with his head bowed, and she received it in grace. She moved to the edge of the dais. The soft echo of her footsteps and the cane's clack trumped the sound of Tetian's grunts while the guard held his tongue and the other still wielded the dagger.

"Do you see the women before you, Tetian?"

He sneered at the obvious question.

"You took the son of the Great Wife Tetisheri by refusing aid. You took the son of the Royal Commander by demanding he retake Buhen. And now you take the son of Chief Wife Ahmose-Nefertari in cold blood. You will know the penalty for treason against the divine crown, and you will meet the flame."

He jerked his head out of the guard's grip reclaiming sovereignty over his tongue, and gritted, "No one here would burn the prince of Ta-Seti."

Ahhotep scoffed and looked around. "No one here acknowledges there *is* a prince of Ta-Seti."

His face blanched.

"Continue," Ahhotep ordered the guards. "And then burn him as an example of those who dare attack Kemet's chosen king."

"Your heart will weigh heavy, Ahhotep!" he yelled his last, before the screams of agony came.

She watched the bloody order carried out before returning to the throne to sit. It was not long before the pungent miasma of burning flesh wafted through the wall vents.

Baufre was prone on the floor, sobbing. "Please, Royal Commander. I did not know. Mercy! Mercy!"

Metjen kneeled in silence before the throne, gaze downcast, waiting for his sentence.

"Baufre, Metjen," Ahhotep barked. "Now, you shall have your future declared."

Baufre was forced to kneel alongside Metjen.

Ahhotep's jaw grew taut. She had thought about what to do with these two. Her words had been carefully constructed in the days leading up to the moment.

"These two men before the Royal Commander do not deserve to live. They do not deserve an afterlife."

Metjen glowered at Ahhotep while Baufre cried, "But we fought for you, Royal Commander. We did not know Tetian would kill anyone."

Ramose's bloodied face flashed before her. "Yet because of your actions, the Crown Prince was slain, along with hundreds of soldiers and servants, children, and citizens of Waset, Nekhen, and Herui." Tetian's fleshly stench reached her nostrils. "You could be burning by Sedjefatawy's port as Tetian is now. You should be gracious to me."

Baufre cried like a child and put his face on the floor. "Yes, Royal Commander," he whimpered.

Ahhotep regained her posture and secured the attention of all in the room before speaking again. "I spoke pardon of the blood spilled upon your first entry into the throne room after the siege from this dais; you listened, and you fought for your king. I shall keep my word, but for your willful act of treason and conspiracy with Tetian, you both will be stripped of your position and wealth. Your army is now the king's army. You shall live the rest of your long lives in disgrace for taking up arms against Amun's divinely appointed."

She stared at Metjen, wanting him to suffer more than Baufre, for Baufre was a dim-witted fool. Metjen at least had a mind about him. "You will keep your afterlife. Your tombs will remain untouched until your journey west. But until then, Metjen is henceforth exiled to the land of the Bedu with his officers. Anyone loyal to Metjen over Ahmose will be stripped of their worth and sent to farmlands in Tjenu."

Metjen lifted his eyes at Ahhotep, sneering, but bowed his head in acceptance of her sentence. She surmised he knew he had done wrong and was grateful he would be allowed back into Kemet for his internment and journey to the Field of Reeds.

Ahhotep turned her focus to the fool who sat wringing his hands. "Baufre and his officers will live in disgrace as servants to those who farm the land of the Amun priesthood. They will never be allowed to leave their servitude."

Baufre cried, not understanding the extraordinary generosity that had been granted to him, until Metjen elbowed his large belly and told him in a harsh whisper, "Shut your mouth. You could have ended up in the Bedu like me, you of an empty mind."

Baufre's eyes widened, and his jaw fell ajar as the realization of Ahhotep's decree dawned on him. He wiped a forearm across the bottom of his nose and stopped wailing.

With Baufre's sniffles in the background, Ahhotep scanned the room of nomarchs. *This can never happen again*, she told herself.

"These dared betray their oath before Ma'at. These dared betray the King of Kemet. Tetian and his followers dared betray the will of Amun, Re, Hathor, Isis, Horus, and Bastet." She squared her shoulders to them, and emphasized her last words: "If you dare to attempt the same, you will be struck down."

The nomarchs shifted on their feet, and Paser nodded. "Divine blood runs through your veins, Royal

Commander!" he yelled out, and the other nomarchs followed.

Metjen and even Baufre said nothing as guards took them away, stripping them of their wealth and visible status.

Ahhotep took a proud breath amid the cheers. Paser kneeled before the royal family, and those in attendance did the same. When all was quiet, Paser said, "Royal Commander and her son, the Warrior King Ahmose, lead us into a new era."

Ahhotep looked at the midday sun pouring onto the courtyard beyond the throne room doors. Kamose's statue had been pieced together—tied in place—until another could be sculpted. His cracked stone visage found her eyes. His presence descended upon the dais, and his embrace wrapped around her. A tear budded in her eye as the falcon shrieked. His ba was satisfied. He had not perished in vain, and her mother's instinct and the gods' victory at Sedjefatawy told her Ahmose was indeed alive.

41

A TIME OF DOMINATION | AHMOSE

THE LEVANT, 1550 BC

At the end of the third year of the siege, King Apepi left his palace out of cowardice. King Ahmose's army chased him and his Aamu people into the Levant, burning everything to ensure they could not resettle the land.

Ahmose rode in his chariot, returning to Hut-Waret from the fortress city of Sharuhen in Canaan. They had claimed victory over it and burned it to the ground, leaving King Apepi to flee like the coward he was from wherever his line had descended.

It was then the Hekka Khasut were no more, and Ahmose could return home victorious. The salt of the Great Sea filled his nostrils, and the cool sea breeze whipped past his collared chest. Though the Aten's rays were plentiful, he felt cold, having been in Kemet all his life. He looked to his right, and the leader of the Medjay named Gorte rode along beside him. He was shivering. It made Ahmose chuckle. He looked to his left, and Ahmose-Ebana rode in his chariot, hiding a slight quiver on his lip.

It seemed they were all cold past the boundaries of

Kemet, so Ahmose decided to take their attention from the elements and try to shorten the trip with conversation.

"Without the chariots and the Medjay, we would not have been victorious. We owe many blessings upon you, Ahmose-Ebana, and you, Gorte," he said.

"You are too generous, my King," Ahmose-Ebana said, and Gorte grunted in reply, "Agreed." But the cold made his chin quiver and not say much else.

"I shall establish a chariotry division of my army," Ahmose declared, hoping for something more to keep the conversation going.

"Most wise decision, my King," Ahmose-Ebana again replied.

Silence ensued. Ahmose cleared his throat.

"Like Admiral and General, I will need another chief officer for these wheeled beasts." Ahmose patted the rim of the chariot as it rolled along the sea-smoothed rock path.

Ahmose-Ebana remained silent, and Gorte only said, "Yes, it would be logical to have a hierarchy of officers too."

Ahmose chewed his lip as he glanced at Ahmose-Ebana. It was his father that had saved him. The arrows had left a scar; it seemed on both of them. Ahmose ran a finger down his chest along the scar's smooth edge, remembering the arrow that had barely missed his head and nicked him before Baba's shield covered him. The hard *thud, thud, thud* of arrows hitting the shield was nothing compared to the wincing pain in Baba's face.

He pushed it from memory, trying not to dwell on the past, and hoped Ahmose-Ebana did not hold ill feelings against him.

"What name should I have for this chief officer?" Ahmose asked.

"Chief Charioteer," Gorte offered.

Ahmose-Ebana shrugged. "Master Chariotry Leader," he said.

"Yes, good names," Ahmose said, but both suggestions did not have the important ring he wanted. He would think about it further.

Baba would have known a good name to call it, he thought. He glanced to Gorte, where Baba formerly rode alongside him. He missed Baba even with his constant hovering. He had many conversations with the man, who was almost like a father to him. And in some ways, with Baba's secret relationship with his mother, Baba was like a father to him.

His gaze fell to the ground as it swept by underneath the chariots' wheels. He would need a new Admiral soon, but he hadn't the heart to replace Baba over the last year, not after all his sacrifice.

HUT-WARET, 1550 BC

A few days later, they returned to the place they had called home for three years and found the Hekka Khasut palace razed and the city gutted. All that remained were the Apiru's homes.

Ahmose smiled at the good work as he rode through the encampment, looking for the Admiral he left in charge. His army bowed to him and parted as he journeyed through the ranks until he finally came upon Baba, whose arm was in a sling and who walked with a cane.

Ahmose dismounted along with Ahmose-Ebana.

"My King and my son," Baba said, greeting the duo with a pride-filled beam.

"Admiral," Ahmose returned. "I am glad to see you are up and walking." He eyed the cane. He had been worried the arrows to Baba's leg would have rendered him paralyzed.

Baba chuckled. "Not very well," he said. "But I will learn to use this cane much better each day." The ghastly healed wounds on his shoulder, arm, and leg were like starbursts on his sable skin.

Ahmose placed a hand on Baba's uninjured shoulder and locked eyes with him. The Admiral's military career would be over because he had been determined to save him, and the King's Fleet was worse for it. But a small smile crept to Ahmose's lips. "Let us journey back to Waset and celebrate our victory, Admiral. And perhaps, you can find contentment at Sedjefatawy and a woman of your choosing."

Baba pressed his lips into a thinned smile as if trying to contain himself. "I have been at war all of my adult life. It will be good to rest," he said. "My son, Ahmose, son of my late Ebana, is proud to follow in my footsteps."

Ahmose-Ebana bowed his head in agreement. "Yes, my King. For you, I dedicate my life just as my father. I have no greater honor."

Ahmose smiled. Perhaps Baba's son held no ill contempt toward him. But past Baba's ear, Ahmose saw a royal boat from Sedjefatawy dock at the port at Hut-Waret.

"We finally have word from home," he said, and the three men turned to face the queen's messenger, who disembarked with news from Waset.

The man grimaced, however, and his brow furrowed, giving no notice of happiness.

Ahmose's smile faded quickly, and his heart sank into his stomach—anticipating a grave message—as the man came to greet the King.

42

A TIME OF GRIEVING |
AHMOSE

SEDJEFATAWY, 1549 BC

I t had been two years since the victory at
Sedjefatawy. Ahmose had come home from his
success in the north, seized Ta-Seti, and forced the
Kushites back into submission with the help of the
Viceroy Si-Tayet's four remaining units. They had been
preoccupied with Kushite attacks for the year
Sedjefatawy was under siege. They had never known
about Ta-Seti's involvement until Ahmose had come to
aid them.

The King had returned to his palace and walked
along the path to the West of Waset and stood in front of
the re-sealed tomb of his sons and daughter. His guards
followed at a distance.

His hands folded behind his back, and his head
bowed. "I should have left five hundred men," he
muttered, his gaze downcast. "I should have secured the
Upper before returning to capture Hut-Waret." He
wanted to fall on his knees before his sons' tomb, but he
refrained since footsteps sounded behind him. He lifted
his head in solemnity, for the king bowed to no one. His

mother's sweet and earthen perfume proceeded her presence beside him.

"You would have been proud, Ahmose," Ahhotep said in muted tones. "Ramose had wanted to be like his great father. He fought with the soldiers of Sedjefatawy when they attacked the place where the royal children were hiding."

"But he was only twelve. Did no one tell him he would not be successful against the Kushite and Ta-Setian elite?"

Ahhotep pressed her lips into a thin line. "Yes, but he wanted to protect his sister-wife and his siblings."

He shook his head. "He was slain before even becoming a man." His fingers dug into the palms of his hands.

"He had become a man even though his age determined otherwise. He had taken a wife and fathered a child. Ramose was well-trained with the mace. He enjoyed his life, and now, he is in the Field of Reeds in eternal happiness."

Ahmose could not bring himself to look at his mother. The shame and guilt rose on his cheeks. "Still, he should have known he had not even reached the age to fight in the King's campaigns on his own."

His mother's voice soothed him as when he was a boy. "I once had a son of eight years who thought he could best a Kushite since the Medjay had trained him."

Ahmose pursed his lips at his mother's comment regarding himself at a young age. "Well, then. I suppose father like son."

"He wanted to be like you, the great expeller of foreign kings," Ahhotep said. Her hand slipped into his, and she wrapped her petite arm around his frame, built by years of war.

Although he had thirty-one years in the land of the living, there was still something about holding his mother's hand and being comforted by her embrace. He heard the guards shuffle and turn around.

"I should have been here to protect my family, Mother. I took all the nomes' men with us into the Lower. I left you defenseless. Because of my neglect, Tep and Ramose are slain."

"No, Ahmose. We all considered the possibility of Tetian's uprising, but we all disregarded it as improbable. The nomes would never do such a thing. We put five units with Si-Tayet in Kush to protect us from uprisings there. Without your two hundred men, I am sure Sedjefatawy would have fallen in defeat very quickly after the siege. Yes, Tep and Ramose were slain, but the palace was saved. Your divine appointment proved to all."

He tore away from Ahhotep. Was he supposed to feel happy about her words? His second crown prince was now in his tomb. Only one son remained. He had overlooked Tetian's threat. He had disregarded his presence. And it cost him dearly. Now, the Apiru in the north were plentiful, too plentiful, and perhaps that threat should not be disregarded. Never again would he assume peaceful relations. Never again would he make the same mistake. As soon as they were able, his next decree would be to set taskmasters over the Apiru. Rebuild the Lower with their labor. Show them who is King of this land in which they sojourn. Ensure there would never be another uprising again.

His cheeks boiled red as he turned to his mother. "My divine appointment may be proved, but I proved it again by sending as many Kushites to Ammit as possible. I slew every Ta-Setian soldier that did not surrender and put the rest to work in the fields. I will not let this event upon my house be lost to time. I will not let threats become realized. I will be the king that is remembered for eternity. My kin will not have been slain in vain!"

He slammed his fist on the stone face, and his heartbeat pounded in his ears.

Ahhotep straightened her shoulders. "Do what you must, King Ahmose." Her head lowered to him. "I only request you keep vigil over your heart. I see your anger. I see your guilt. You must accept that you did what you could. What if you had left one thousand men here? You may not have retaken Hut-Waret and lost the war. Do not dwell on this, for it will heavy your heart. Do not let what happened here determine the fate of your journey west. We need you to become one with Re so the sun may rise again the next day. Otherwise, you give us all to Apep."

Those were wise words from his mother. His fist loosened. "I promise to keep vigil, Mother. But I will never let you suffer because of my neglect again." He drew near her again and saw Ahmose-Nefertari coming up the path with her maidservants in tow. They held lotus blossoms as an offering to the slain children.

He placed a hand on Ahhotep's shoulder while his gaze remained on his chief wife, whose cheeks were wet with tears.

"Never again," he whispered.

43

A TIME OF AMENDS | AHHOTEP

SEDJEFATAWY, 1549 BC

Ahhotep glanced at General Pennekhbet and Baba's son, who sat in the Admiral's place. She had only a few official reasons to summon Baba or to speak with him since his son was appointed in his place almost two years ago. She had watched father bequeath the title to son in the throne room and Ahmose grant them both honors and gold. Her heart had turned in her chest as Baba left the throne room. Would that be the last time she saw him? He would no longer be a member of the King's council.

She had stressed many nights to devise a plausible reason to speak to him and summon him to the council room while Ahmose was off fighting and keeping the peace in his conquered lands. It was mainly for reports of what happened in the north. Only once had he been able to kiss her before anyone could see what was happening. So, she had been reduced to staring at his son while in council, wishing he was his father.

"Great Wife Ahhotep," Ahmose said, pulling her from her thoughts. She turned her attention to him. She had not been listening. His gaze darted between her and the Admiral's place.

She furrowed her brow, pretending to think about the following words she would say to whatever question she was asked. Then she noticed her mother's steward at the council room door. A sigh of relief barely escaped her lips before she smiled and asked, "What is it, royal steward?"

"Great Wife Tetisheri requests your presence." He looked between Ahhotep, Ahmose, and Ahmose-Nefertari. "All her family's presence."

Ahmose stood up. "We shall continue this discussion after the King meets with the Great Wife."

Ahhotep rose with her daughter, and they followed the steward to Tetisheri. She lay on a table in the courtyard with blankets draped over her aged body and a headrest under her neck. The steward bowed again before Ahmose. "She wanted to journey west under the Aten, the sun barge of Re," he whispered before leaving the royal family to Tetisheri's side.

She had ceased to eat and drink and had grown weak. The deep creases in her forehead and by her eyes and lips showed the hard life she had lived and the weight of the burden she had carried for so long.

Ahhotep saw it and felt it. She ran a finger along the side of her lip, feeling the formed wrinkles. Each woman had carried their burdens differently, but it was the same weight, regardless.

Ahmose reached out and touched his grandmother's hand. Her eyes fluttered open. "I am glad you came," she rasped. "The Aten warms me." She sniffled. "I was never warm to you, my children, or my grandchildren. I never made peace with Tep, and I hope I will make my peace with her in the Field of Reeds."

She turned her head to Ahmose. "My grandson, you have done so well. I am proud to be your grandmother. Your name will be remembered forever." With a weak finger, she warned. "But this I leave you, we overlooked Tetian's presence as a threat." Her eyes closed, and her head shook. "No, *I* overlooked Tetian as a threat. Do not make my mistake."

Ahmose grimaced as if he felt her words. "It was my negl—"

"No," she whispered and put a finger to his lips. "It was mine. I see my error and now, my grandson, heed my advice: oppress the remaining Aamu, the Apiru," Tetisheri interjected as if she only had a few words left and little time to say them. "They will rise like the Hekka Khasut. All of this will be in vain." She lifted her head to plead. "Promise me; you will not let our spilled blood be in vain."

Ahmose gritted, "I have already decided it will be so, Grandmother. My children, my brother and sister, will not have been slain for naught."

Her head lowered in satisfaction with his response. She lifted a weak hand to his cheek. "You are a good king," she said in a rasp. "Worthy of every praise, Ahmose, Given Life." A weak smile perched on her lips. Her hand fell as if her arm gave out.

She shifted her sights to Ahmose-Nefertari. "My granddaughter, you as well. The gods bless you. I have never heard one ill word about you. The people, the nomarchs, they all love you. They will need your care as your children have received."

She shifted her focus to Ahhotep, and her gaze bore into Ahhotep's eyes.

"My Ahhotep, you have my pride. You will now be

the matriarch. Lead your family well; I have no more lessons to teach."

She rasped and grabbed Ahhotep's hand. "Every time I told you that you were unworthy, I should have said, I love you, but you need to be better prepared. That has been my error, my burden, and it drove my family apart."

Tetisheri shook her head as tears streamed down into her quivering mouth. "I only wanted what was best for Kemet, but you, you wanted the same, and you have found balance and peace. I never found it until this day. I hope my heart will not weigh heavy on the scales of Ma'at."

"Mother, I—"

"I must rest now and close my eyes, for they have been opened for far too long." Her eyes drifted closed.

Ahhotep brushed her mother's cheek with the back of her fingers and smoothed away a few wiry silver stray hairs from her false braids. Her mother's breath came in spurts, but Tetisheri rolled her cheek into Ahhotep's palm. "My firstborn," she whispered.

A thick lump grew in the back of Ahhotep's throat. All those years spent hating her mother when she could have loved her if she had only spent the time to understand her. Ahhotep kneeled beside the table and rubbed her mother's brow to smooth out the hard-worn wrinkles. They had not been there when she was a child, but when she became queen, there had always been the sign of burden on her brow. Ahhotep placed her lips on her mother's forehead, envisioning her as a young woman loving her brother's child as her own and leaving him because she was forced to marry another she did not love. Standing as the regent in her young son's place without a mother or father to help guide her, while earning respect among the nomes as a queen regent for her son Tao. Leading the divine family up as best as she could, knowing the hard days would come, but seeing them through with the only strength she knew. It made her heart swell with pride for the woman who bore her. A tear ran freely down each cheek, as she whispered, "Go to the Field of Reeds in peace, Mother."

Soon after, Tetisheri fell asleep, and her chest forever stilled.

44

A TIME FOR KEMET |
AHHOTEP

SEDJEFATAWY, 1548 BC

The Aten's rays fell from Re onto the temple of Amun and on the nomarchs in the temple's courtyard.

Ahhotep and Ahmose-Nefertari stood at the forecourt entrance to the temple, their eyes downcast as Ahmose emerged from the inner sanctum. Two high priests of Amun bowed and closed the doors behind him while he proceeded down the long corridor toward the royal women.

Kemet now stretched from the land of Wawat to the Great Sea, and her son was Kemet's one divine king. Ahhotep let out a deep breath, and the corners of her mouth turned upward. She imagined Tao, Kamose, and Ramose walking alongside Ahmose down the corridor. They had been slain for this moment and would be proud to see it finally come to fruition.

Nobles and officials were tightly packed, and they waited to hear their King speak after communing with Amun.

Ahmose lifted his hands to those gathered before him. "The King's victories are Amun's victories!"

The men and women gathered erupted in cheer but were quickly silenced when Ahmose clenched his fist. Ahhotep nodded her head at the man and king he had become.

"From this day forward," Ahmose began. "Amun and Re will be one god. Re, God of the Sun, has lifted Amun, The Hidden One, the patron god of Waset, by raising up the divine in his nome as the true King. Amun-Re shall be the highest god because The Lord of Strength is Re, Ahmose, Given Life has prevailed against our enemies."

Ahhotep held her breath for his next decree. They had just ended a war; how would the people react? She glanced at him to see if he needed reassurance, but he did not need her confidence anymore. He only scanned the forecourt and the courtyard beyond and spoke in a commanding voice.

"Since the King and his armies have expelled the Hekka Khasut from Kemet, he shall now subject those who remain. Return to the great halls of record. How did the Hekka Khasut take the Lower over one hundred years ago? Aamu from the Levant settled in the best of our land as traders and gentle shepherds. And once they multiplied and grew plentiful, they took it without a battle. Out of the Aamu rose the Hekka Khasut, who forced the divine kings south. If we leave the remaining Aamu, these Apiru, as they are, they will once again produce kings, and we will once again be divided. They will unite with our enemies and destroy this new era of Kemet before it begins. Your fathers, brothers, and sons will have perished in vain, as the late Great Wife Tetisheri foretold. The god Amun-Re has spoken; we shall seal our dominion over the Lower—oppress the populous and reign over them."

The nomarchs clapped and nodded with firm agreement. No one wanted to endure another war.

Ahhotep beamed. *Well-spoken, like a true king*, she thought, but then she chided herself. *He is a true king.* Her chest puffed and her chin lifted. He was her son, and hers alone. He was everything she had hoped and prayed he would be. Pride filled her senses, so much so, she did not notice as Vizier Tetinefer approached with a golden plate with three golden flies strung with a golden chain. He presented it to Ahmose as Ahmose continued to speak.

"We shall reign over our enemies, both foreign and internal. The King awards the most prestigious accolades to the royal women who showed prowess, honor, and courage while under duress. Starting with the most coveted and esteemed military award . . ." He lifted the dazzling gold flies in the air, and the Aten's light danced on their semi-spread wings. The audience gasped at the splendor. He lowered it over Ahhotep's vulture crown and placed it around her neck.

"For valor and bravery in putting down the rebellion of Tetian and ensuring a man of Kemet shall never again rise up against his king. "

Ahhotep lifted her gaze to him. The sunlight reflected from the gold around her neck and lit her graceful countenance.

"For smiting the enemies of the King of Kemet as an enduring and tenacious victor. For consolidating divine authority in the name of Amun-Re until the King's victorious return, God's Mother, Great Wife, Royal Commander, Queen Ahhotep, is awarded the great honor . . . of the Golden Fly," he declared to the crowd.

Mitry captured the event in the words of the gods on the tablets to be entered into her tomb as the sistrums and goblet drums rounded out the encore cheer. Ahhotep bowed her head to her son in gratitude for the exceptional award. She had never seen such awards, they were so rare. Painful memories of the rebellion nibbled at the back of her mind, but she pushed them away. She would not let them steal this moment from her. Never had a God's Mother received such an honor, and she lifted her face to Ahmose in dignity.

Ahmose acknowledged her with a pressed grin before turning to his sister. "Chief Wife Ahmose-Nefertari, to you for your support, honor, and strength, you shall be God's Wife of Amun, an elevated position because Amun is elevated. You shall be the Divine Adoratrice and the Mistress of Upper and Lower Kemet. Let this great honor be known in all the land. She is now above all others. No other woman can attain her glory."

He lifted his hands to the skies.

"And for the late Great Wife Tetisheri, the great matriarch of the King's family, I order a cenotaph to record her name forever and ever."

Ahhotep smiled as the Aten's rays fell upon them. Re shone in his brightness down on his appointed one. The gods were satisfied, and a mother could ask for no greater reward.

He stepped forward to continue with the next part of the ceremony and summoned, "Nomarch Paser. To you, the longest supporter of the crown, Amun-Re, and the divine King bless you the most of any other nomarch. You shall receive a storehouse of gold and silver, servants, and a noble's house for you and all your children. You shall be the highest nomarch, the Nomarch of Waset."

To each nomarch, he awarded spoils of war aligned to the support they had given.

Lastly, he offered a feast for the morning's meal. Servants and stewards poured in from the port, bringing the finest cuts of meats and the freshest fruits and vegetables.

"Kemet shall rise this day," Ahmose said. "No longer shall we go hungry. No longer shall we scrape by with crumbs from our neighbors to the north and to the south. We are now one land with one king in a new era. Feast and give thanks to Amun-Re. Feast and enjoy the spoils of this decades-long war."

Priests brought the gold and silver libation goblets, offering tables, and precious gems retaken from the Hekka Khasut, which Ahmose had ordered to be dedicated to the temple in honor of the great Amun.

Music erupted in the morning. The people danced, drank, ate, and were merry.

Ahhotep drew near to her son and bowed before him. "All of Kemet is yours now, my son, my Warrior King," she whispered. "It was your destiny as I once told you."

Ahmose smiled at the memory. "Yet, Mother, I feel we make our own destiny. At least with the help of those who love us and with the guidance of the gods."

Ahhotep chuckled. "Perhaps you are right, wise king."

"There is another wisdom I have found as well." His eyes shifted behind her, so she peered to see what caught his attention. Baba stood conversing with his son. Baba's proud gleam glanced her way before he continued his conversation. He leaned upon a cane, wearing the tunic of a nobleman. He had saved Ahmose, and for that, she would be forever thankful to him. He had kept his promise to her and brought both he and Ahmose home alive. But she missed him. Missed his touch and embrace.

Her son's voice drew her gaze back to him. "I have arranged for the former Admiral to escort God's Mother to a private feast at Sedjefatawy."

A red hue arose on her cheeks. Did he know about them? Did Baba tell him? Did he know she lied about her relationship with the former Admiral? Why would Ahmose do such a thing?

"Ahmose," she uttered in a muted tone and looked to her side to see if anyone heard them. "The war is over. There is no official reason to speak to him now."

Ahmose pulled her into an embrace, and she selfishly returned it. "You deserve love, Mother, as much as you have given us," he whispered amid the cheers. "Make your own destiny as I have done. We, your children, will do well because you have taught us and led us. You have done the good work; now, be happy with someone you love and who loves you in return."

He released her, kissing her on her cheek. She pulled away to take in his full face. He was once a ten-year-old boy king, and in some ways, he would forever be a child in her heart. But as he stood before her as a man, her heart twisted, wishing Tao could see their son grow into manhood and take part in his victories, but as the sunlight grew brighter—Re's sun barge lit up the sky— she knew he already had. Tao and Kamose were one with Re. Her children and grandchildren who journeyed west lived without pain or worry in the Field of Reeds. An auspicious grin formed on her lips as she envisioned her family thriving and her love for Baba allowed. Her burdens were gone, the future shined as bright as gold, and she could finally breathe in serenity.

THE STORY CONTINUES

Do you want to continue the ancient family saga with
Woman King, a chronicling of how the She-King
Hatshepsut rose to power?

Be notified of release by signing up at
www.LaurenLeeMerewether.com

A LOOK INTO
THE PAST

Warrior King and the resulting series, *Egypt's Golden Age Chronicles*, take place during the 18th Dynasty of the New Kingdom. *Warrior King* specifically begins at the end of Pharaoh Seqenenre Tao's reign and concludes during the reign of Pharaoh Ahmose.

The series name comes from scholars considering the New Kingdom, Dynasties Eighteen thru Twenty, a golden age of Egypt, during which the empire reached its peak. The first king of this new era was King Ahmose.

This fictional story is based on the historical fact of that period; however, the author took creative liberties in *Warrior King,* where there were uncertainties and unknowns in the facts, or where in her opinion, the demands of the story outweighed historical accuracies, such as fictional relationships and the timing of the recorded rebellions of the Nubian Prince named Aata and the Anti-Theban—anti-Waset—Egyptian named Tetian.

Many familiar with Egyptian chronology would not agree with the 1575 BC date of Tao's demise or the 1570 BC date of Ahmose's regency; however, radiocarbon dating performed by Christopher Bronk-Ramsay at the

Oxford Radiocarbon Accelerator Unit estimates Ahmose's reign at the earliest could have started 1570 BC. Other radiocarbon studies suggest it could be even earlier, around 1585 BC. Manetho puts Ahhotep around 1700 BC. The Tempest Stela dated to the time of Ahmose speaks of events that fit with the Thera eruption radiocarbon dated to around 1600 BC, which is 30 years earlier than Ahmose[1]. Regardless of the many dates proposed by various authorities, the author selected 1570 BC as the start of the New Kingdom with the ascension of Ahmose to the throne as Coregent to fit with the timeline she wanted for this series and her existing series, *Ancient Legends* and *The Lost Pharaoh Chronicles*— the former set during the Second Intermediate Period and the latter set during the Eighteenth Dynasty's Amarna period.

King Seqenenre Tao's mummy is grossly violent. There are ax wounds to his cheek and forehead, and his mouth is open in a final gaping scream. There is also a spear point in the skull. It appears he was slain on a battlefield with the Hyksos, or as the Ancients called them, the Hekka Khasut.

Kamose became king afterward. Kamose could have been a brother, son, or uncle to Seqenenre Tao. Not much is known about Kamose. In the story, he is the son of Tao and brother of Ahmose. He campaigned north but never made it to Hut-Waret. He intercepted a Hyksos messenger in the Bahariya Oasis, who the Hyksos sent to propose an alliance with the Kushites against them, but he destroyed the Oasis to prevent further communication between the two empires[2].

In the story, Kamose gained Medjay mercenaries. The Medjay were elite Kerman warriors. Their role changed and evolved in the King's service over the Eighteenth

Dynasty as Egypt's influence and control spread in Nubia, and eventually, the Medjay became the police officers of the day, staffed by Egyptians.

In the year or two preceding Kamose's demise, Ahmose likely became Kamose's junior Coregent, as they were both titled "Given Life" in the stele found in Toshka[3]. Kamose's reign is usually dated to three years, but Kim Ryholt attributes a five-year reign noting his, not one, but two, campaigns to Nubia/Kush[4].

Archaeologists found horse skeletons dating to the time of Kamose in Buhen and suggest Kamose must have been using horses at war when he reached Buhen to retake it from the Nubians[5].

Around this second campaign, Kamose died. The victory at Buhen in the story was probably not likely since an image of Kamose was found burned and desecrated by the Nubians. It could have been after the Nubians recaptured Buhen at a later date. In the author's opinion, this desecration lends more to defeat and the cause of Kamose's death. Kamose's mummy was found in an ungilded coffin[6], but he was entombed with the items mentioned in the story[7].

The site of Deir el-Ballas has also been identified as the northern palace, Sedjefatawy, which fell into disrepair and was soon abandoned after Ahmose's reign[8]. Ahmose and his successors rebuilt the Lower with a large workforce—some assume this workforce was comprised of the biblical Hebrew slaves. Hut-Waret became Pi-Ramesses in the Nineteenth Dynasty and was later known by its Greek name, Avaris. The term "Apiru" has been long debated on whether these were the Ancient Hebrews or a term for a homeland-less or stateless people.

The Deir el-Ballas site was probably founded by King

Seqenenre Tao or by his father, Ahmose the Elder, but the true founder is not known. The author assumed either individual constructed Per-djed-ken, the Southern Palace, in his attempts to expel the Hyksos. In between the Northern Palace—Sedjefatawy—and the Southern Palace—Per-djed-ken, there was a cemetery, officials' villas, guest apartments, and a workman's settlement. The royal family seemingly used the complex as a command center for troops and the fleet in the war with the Hyksos[9].

In *Warrior King*, the author renamed members of the royal family as their actual names were duplicated and would make the story hard to follow; an example: Ahmose had a niece named Ahmose and a half-sister named Ahmose. The author reverted to another spelling, Ahmes, for the niece's name, and the author nicknamed the half-sister Mosi. Ahmose's grandfather was also named Ahmose, and so the author kept Ahmose the Elder unnamed in the story.

It is also assumed Ahmose had a sister named after their mother, Ahhotep II, named Ahhotep Tasherit (Tasherit meaning "the Younger") in the story. The author nicknamed her Tep to avoid confusion with her mother. However, whether there were two women named Ahhotep remains a debate. If there were two, the sister died during the latter part of Ahmose's reign, while the mother lived past the reign of Ahmose's son, Amenhotep[10].

In another example of duplicative names, King Ahmose also had a half-sister and a daughter named Meryet Amon. The author left out the half-sister and kept the daughter, as the daughter becomes important in the life of Amenhotep. A fourth example, King Ahmose had two sisters with very similar names, Henuttamehu and Hentempet. Only Henuttamehu became a royal wife, and Hentempet lived as only King's Daughter and King's Sister until she died at an elderly age. In the story, Hentempet was Kamose's royal wife; however, the historical record mentions no marriages for Hentempet or Kamose.

Ahhotep and Seqenenre Tao were brother and sister and had many children together, including another son named Ahmose-Sipair, whose currently identified mummy shows he was only 5 or 6 years old at death[11], yet a monument exists to Ahmose-Sipair and depicts deification, which is odd given his age and prince hood[12]. Contrary to the mummy's age, there is also a Sapair mentioned, who may or may not be the same person, and who perhaps lived to be older. In the story, Ahmose-Sipair and Sapair are not the same person, and Sapair is the father of Thutmose; however, the true father of Thutmose is unknown. Senseneb is known to be Thutmose's mother, but her relation to Baba and Ahmose, son of Ebana, was contrived by the author.

Ahmose and Ahmose-Nefertari were the second generation of a brother-sister union, and their children did not live very long. Their children, Ahmose-Sitamun and Ahmose-Sipair, were very young when they passed away and their mummies were distorted. Ahmose-Sitamun's mummy only had her head and a false body, thus implying a tragic accident such as a crocodile or hippo attack[13]. The author included this incident in the story as a heartrending end for both children.

If Sitkamose was also the product of Kamose and his sister, it could explain why she died at fourteen years of age. Because of tradition, Ahmose would have had to marry Sitkamose to seal his divine appointment and be king. However, there is no evidence that she was his chief wife, as the story depicted.

The royal children, Ramose and Tair, were never known to be married or to produce children; however, Queen Tiye, a later powerful queen, is said to have descended from Ahmose-Nefertari, and the author chose this fictional union to begin Queen Tiye's ancestral line.

Ahmose-Ankh was the Crown Prince up until around Ahmose's seventeenth year when he passed away. The crown eventually passed to Amenhotep. He and Meryet Amon were the third generation of a brother-sister union, and their only child died early, thus leaving the crown open for Thutmose, who married the last remaining daughter of Ahmose-Nefertari and Ahmose, sealing his divine right to rule after the death of Amenhotep, and thus, beginning the Thutmoid familial line of Eighteenth Dynasty rulers.

Tetisheri was common-born, but her origins are unknown. From reading what little is known about her in a National Geographic premium article[14], she was a shrewd, forthright, and politically-focused woman, but the author exaggerated these implications to build her character. She also connected Tetisheri to Ta-Seti royalty for the sake of the story.

Tetian was either an anti-Theban—anti-Waset— Egyptian or a Hyksos sympathizer who had been a dissenter of the Waset royal family[15]. He rallied the Nubians and led a rebellion, assumedly, when the Nubian Prince Aata rebelled and failed. However, per the stela of Ahmose, son of Ebana[16], both rebellions took place after Ahmose conquered Hut-Waret and came back to Nubia to put down the rebels. It is not known if Tetian was a prince, from Ta-Seti, or if he attacked Waset. From the stela of Ahmose, son of Ebana, the author assumed both rebellions took place in Nubia; however, from the stela of Karnak[17], Ahhotep was given the golden fly award for her bravery along with a golden battle ax and two barks because of her efforts in the war and putting down a rebellion. Because of this, the author wrote the story where Tetian attacked Waset while Ahmose was away.

There is no evidence to suggest Tetian and Tetisheri were related. Their relationship was fictional to provide motivation for Tetian's anti-Theban stance and to add tension to the story.

Ahmose, son of Ebana, chose to take his mother's name, which implied Ebana had been a very important noblewoman. According to his stela, his father was Baba. Both Ahmose, son of Ebana, and Baba served in the navy under two different kings. Ahmose, son of Ebana, served under Ahmose, while his father served under Seqenenre Tao. There is no evidence to suggest Baba served under Ahmose as well. There is no evidence to show Baba was an Admiral, but his son, Ahmose, son of Ebana, was a naval officer, some attributing him to Admiral. High officer positions were usually passed from father to son, so the author named Baba as Admiral in the story.

The relationship between Ahhotep and Baba is also fictional.

There is no evidence Ahmose, son of Ebana, improved the khopesh and chariot or that Ahhotep sought the help of the Bedu—the Bedouin peoples of Arabia.

General Pennekhbet was Ahmose's general; however, his father-daughter relationship with Kasmut, a known lesser wife of Ahmose and mother of their daughter Tair, is fictional.

There are only a handful of named minor characters

in the story, such as the nomes' princes and the maidservants. The author named most of the main characters after their real-life counterparts. She wanted to stay as close to the historical account as possible, yet still craft an engaging story.

In the historical record, Ahmose spent three years laying siege to Hut-Waret, mostly because of riots and insurrections in the lands they had conquered, which delayed them in expelling the Hyksos. When the siege ended, he ran King Khamudi or Apepi II, who the author assumes were most likely the same person, into the Levant. Ahmose burned his way through the Levant to prevent anyone from resettling in Egypt and to keep enemies at a distance. Based on the stela in Karnak, Tetisheri, Ahhotep, and Ahmose-Nefertari consolidated power among the nomes in his absence.

After Ahmose's victory against the Hyksos, he came home and awarded the golden fly, the highest military award, to his mother, Ahhotep as previously stated. He also generously granted gifts to the princes of Egypt's nomes that had supported him in his conquest.

Paser was a familial name in the Eighteenth and Nineteenth Dynasties, where a long line had served Pharaoh as officials. The author made the first Paser a loyal Prince who rose in importance because he supported Kings Kamose and Ahmose. A descendant from his line plays an important role in Merewether's *The Lost Pharaoh Chronicles* prequel, *Wife of Ay*.

Three last notes that helped frame this story are as follows:

1. Ancient Egyptians called their country Kemet, meaning "Black Land" for the rich black soil deposits left after the Nile flood.

Regnal years and dynasties were not used during the ancient times but were used by historians to help chronicle the different reigns and eras. The author inserted these references throughout the novel to help the reader keep track of how much time has passed and to have a better idea of the historical timeline. Ancient Egyptians seemed not to celebrate or acknowledge years of life; the author included years of life in the story for the reader's reference. The only "birthday" celebration was every month of Kaherka, which is usually identified as a month from September through December in the Julian calendar, but depending on when the Nile flooded which could be off by 80 days. Kaherka was a symbolic celebration of the king's coronation, for the gods to renew his life force. To read or listen to a free short story the author created as a winter gift for her readers surrounding this time for the later King Amenhotep III, visit her website and download *King's Jubilee*.

2. Amun can be spelled many ways—Amen, Amon, Amun—but it refers to the same god. Likewise, the Aten has also been spelled Aton, Atom, or Atun. The author chose consistent spellings for her series for pronunciation purposes. During the early Eighteenth Dynasty, Amun and Re became a single premier god to appease the priesthood of Amun and the priesthood of Re. Amun was elevated after Ahmose's victory due to Amun's status as the patron god of Waset.

3. Ancient Egyptians did not use the words "death" or "died" unless it meant an eternal death for someone whose heart and body had been lost, but for ease of reading this series, the author did use "death" and "died" in a few instances. The Egyptians instead used euphemistic phrases such as "went to the Field of Reeds," "became an Osiris," and "journeyed west" to lighten the burden of the word "death."

The author loved diving deeper into this fascinating culture and hopes you did too. If you enjoyed this story and want to find out what happens with Ahmose-Nefertari, Amenhotep, Thutmose, and Hatshepsut, continue reading *Egypt's Golden Age Chronicles* with *Book II: Woman King*.

Visit www.LaurenLeeMerewether.com for more information and to stay updated on new releases.

1. Robert K. Ritner and Nadine Moeller. 2014. The Ahmose 'Tempest Stela', Thera and Comparative Chronology. Journal of Near Eastern Studies, vol. 73, no. 1; doi: 10.1086/675069
2. James, T.G.H. *Egypt: From the Expulsion of the Hyksos to Amenophis I.* in *The Cambridge Ancient History,* vol. 2, part 1, ed. Edwards, I.E.S, et al. p.291. Cambridge University Press, 1965.
3. Grimal, Nicolas. A History of Ancient Egypt. Blackwell, 1992
4. Ryholt, Kim SB, *The Political Situation in Egypt during the Second Intermediate Period (Carsten Niebuhr Institute Publications,* Copenhagen, (Museum Tusculanum Press:1997) ISBN 87-7289-421-0
5. *Buhen in the New Kingdom - Butehamun.* http://media.butehamun.org/2018/09/Buhen-in-the-New-Kingdom-public.pdf.
6. Redford, Donald B. History and Chronology of the Eighteenth Dynasty of Egypt: Seven Studies. Toronto, 1967
7. Brier, Bob. Egyptian Mummies. p.259–260. William Morrow and Company, Inc. 1994. ISBN 0-688-10272-7

8. The Egyptian empire strikes back - ancientegyptarchae ologyfund.com. https://www.ancientegyptarchaeology-fund.com/wp-content/uploads/2017/09/Deir-el-Ballas-CWA-084-.pdf

9. The Egyptian empire strikes back - ancientegyptarchae ologyfund.com. https://www.ancientegyptarchaeologyfund.com/wp-content/uploads/2017/09/Deir-el-Ballas-CWA-084-.pdf

10. Ann Macy Roth, The Ahhotep Coffins, Gold of Praise: Studies of Ancient Egypt in honor of Edward F. Wente, 1999

11. "Sipair." *View Early Eighteenth Dynasty Mummies from DB320*, The Theban Mummy Project, https://members.tripod.com/anubis4_2000/mummypages1/Early18.htm#Sipair.

12. Dodson, Aidan; Hilton, Dyan (2004). *The Complete Royal Families of Ancient Egypt*. London: Thames & Hudson. ISBN 0-500-05128-3., p.129

13. Sitek, Dariusz. "Sitamun." *Ancient Egypt - Cache DB320 at Deir El Bahari (Western Thebes)*, Ancient Egyptian History and Chronology, http://www.narmer.pl/groby/db320_en.htm.

14. "How the Rebel Queens of Egypt Expelled the Hyksos." *History*, National Geographic, 3 May 2021, https://www.nationalgeographic.com/history/history-magazine/article/rebel-queen-thebes.

15. Grimal, Nicolas, A History of Ancient Egypt. Blackwell, 1992

16. Ahmose, son of Ebana: The Expulsion of the Hyksos - https://docslib.org/doc/2785587/ahmose-son-of-ebana-the-expulsion-of-the-hyksos

17. *Singer, Graciela Gestoso - Ahhotep I and the Golden Fly*. https://www.academia.edu/241855/Ahhotep_I_and_the_Golden_Fly

GLOSSARY

CONCEPTS / ITEMS

1. Aamu – Asiatic(s)
2. Amphora – a ceramic container usually holding wine or other liquid
3. Apiru – Hebrew(s) or person/people of a low state or no homeland
4. Ba – a person's personality; takes the form of a human-headed falcon after death
5. Bedu – Bedouin peoples of Arabia
6. Deben – the weight of measure equal to about 91 grams
7. Decan – week in Egypt (ten-day period); one month consists of three decans
8. Field of Reeds – the afterlife; Egyptian *A'aru*
9. "Gone to Re" – a form of the traditional phrase used to speak about someone's death; also: *journeyed west, became an Osiris, lives in the Field of Reeds*
10. Hin – a jar measuring about half a liter

11. Headrest – a wooden crossbeam that held a fabric-wrapped sling or curved wooden piece for the neck while sleeping; Egyptian *Urs*
12. Hedjet – the white crown of the Upper
13. Hekat – a barrel measuring ten hin or about five liters
14. Hekka Khasut – Rulers from the hills; foreign rulers (Greek: Hyksos)
15. Ka – the spirit or life force of a person
16. Kap – royal nursery and school
17. Karkade – hibiscus tea
18. Khepresh – blue crown often worn in times of battle
19. King – Other titles include Living Horus, Given Life, Lord of the Two Lands, High Priest in Every Temple, Sun, Majesty, etc.
20. Kyphi – a rich and expensive perfume reserved for royal ceremonies or used as incense in the temples; Egyptian *Kapet*
21. Natron – clay and ash soap with a scent that scented bath water for cleansing
22. Nomarch – a governor-type official over an entire province (nome).
23. Nome – a province of Egypt
24. Pharaoh – the modern title for an ancient Egyptian king; Egyptian *per-a-a* (used as a title for Egypt's King by the Levant kings during the latter part of the Eighteenth Dynasty)
25. Season – three seasons made up the 360-day calendar; each season had 120 days
26. Senet – an ancient board game
27. Shendyt – apron/skirt; a royal shendyt worn by Pharaoh was pleated and lined with gold

28. Sidelock – long lock of hair above the ear kept, despite a shaved head, to signify childhood; usually braided
29. Sistrum – a musical instrument of the percussion family, chiefly associated with ancient Iraq and Egypt
30. Steward – main person in charge of a noble's estate or care of a royal; position held by a man or a literate woman
31. Susinum – a popular perfume based on lily, myrrh, cinnamon
32. Tasherit – the younger, junior
33. The Rising – name of a royal boat
34. Vizier – highest royal advisor to Pharaoh who oversaw state affairs

FOREIGN PEOPLE

1. Aata – Kushite Prince
2. Apepi – *Aegyptus*; Hyksos King; King of the Hekka Khasut
3. Khamudi – *Lynceus*; also called *Apepi II*; Hyksos King; King of the Hekka Khasut; successor to King Aegyptus
4. Hazael – King of the Bedu

GODS

1. Ammit – goddess and demoness; "Devourer of Hearts"
2. Amun – premiere god of Egypt in the Middle Kingdom

3. Amun-Re – the name given to show the duality of Amun and Re (the hidden god and the sun, respectively) to appease both priesthoods during the early part of the New Kingdom
4. Anhur – god of war; protector of the military
5. Anut – goddess of war; protector of the king in battle; defender of Re
6. Aten – sun-disc god of Egypt (referred to as "the Aten"); a minor aspect of the sun god Re
7. Bastet – cat goddess and protector of the home, women, women's secrets, and children
8. Bes – god of childbirth and of dreams
9. Hathor – goddess of joy, women's health, and childbirth, among other aspects of life; Egyptian *Hut-Hor*
10. Heh – god of eternity, time, and long life
11. Horus – the god of kings, protector of the king; Egyptian *Heru*
12. Isis – goddess of healing and magic; Egyptian *Ahset or Auset*
13. Khnum – god of the source of the Nile and molder of humans' and gods' bodies
14. Ma'at – goddess personifying order, balance, morals, and harmony
15. Nephthys – goddess of the dead and the night; Egyptian *Nebet-Het*
16. Osiris – god of the dead, resurrection, and life; Egyptian *Auser*
17. Ptah – god of creation, art, and fertility
18. Re – premiere god of Egypt in the Old Kingdom; the sun god; the New Kingdom Pharaohs began to associate with Amun rather than Re

19. Sekhmet – lioness goddess of war, plague, and destruction; transformed from Hathor
20. Set – god of the desert, chaos, and violence; the supreme god of the Hekka Khasut
21. Shu – god of the wind and air
22. Sobek – god of strength and power; crocodiles
23. Thoth – god of wisdom and writing; Egyptian *Dḥwtj*

MILITARY RANKS - ARMY

1. General – military officer; highest military rank
2. Commander – military officer; one rank below General
3. Commander of the Garrison – military officer; one rank below Commander
4. Troop Commander – military officer; two ranks below Commander
5. Captain of the Troop – military officer; one rank above Greatest of Two Hundred Fifty
6. Greatest of Two Hundred Fifty – second lowest ranking officer of Pharaoh's Army
7. Greatest of Fifty - lowest ranking officer of Pharaoh's Army
8. Soldier - lowest rank

MILITARY RANKS - FLEET

1. Admiral – naval officer; highest naval rank
2. Captain of the Fleet – naval officer; one rank below Admiral

3. Boat Captain - captain of a boat; one rank below Captain of the Fleet
4. Fleetsman – naval officer; lowest ranking officer of Pharaoh's Fleet

MILITARY

1. Ahmose, son of Ebana – *Ahmose-Ebana*; Fleetsman; son of Baba and Ebana
2. Baba – Admiral, father of Ahmose-Ebana
3. Ketti – Medjay tutor to Ahmose and Sapair
4. Pennekhbet – General
5. Uahbra – Troop Commander

PEOPLE (OTHER)

1. Ebana – late wife of Baba
2. Kasmut – daughter of Pennekhbet; wife of Ahmose
3. Minmontu – Second Prophet of Amun
4. Mitry – royal scribe
5. Nebt – wife of Pennekhbet
6. Pahemred – First Prophet of Ptah
7. Senseneb – daughter of Baba; wife of Sapair
8. Si-Tayet – Viceroy of Kush
9. Tetinefer – Vizier to King Kamose and Ahmose
10. Thuty – First Prophet of Amun

PETS

1. Kit - royal cat

PLACES

1. Abu – the ancient name for the island of Elephantine, part of modern-day Aswan, located at the Nile's first cataract
2. Buhen – a massive fortress located on the west bank of the Nile close to the Second Cataract
3. Dashret – Sea of the Red Land; the Lower Egyptian desert located between the Red Sea and the Nile
4. Goshen – Hebrew name for the Eastern Nile Delta
5. Great Sea – Mediterranean Sea
6. Hardai – (also known as Saka) port city of the nome Input; modern-day El Qais
7. Hut-Waret – an earlier name for Pi-Ramesses (Greek: Avaris)
8. Kemet – *black land*; what the ancients called "Egypt"; the Upper is the southern half of modern-day Egypt running from Aswan (Abu) to Atfih (Mednit); the Lower is the northern half of modern-day Egypt running from Mit Rahina (Memphis/Men-nefer) to the Mediterranean Sea (Great Sea)
9. Lunu – city of Heliopolis; capital of nome Ḥeka-Redj
10. Men-nefer – city of Memphis; south of modern-day Cairo; capital of nome Inebu-hedj
11. Nekheb – modern-day El-Kab; capital of nome Nekhen

12. Nufresy – a small port city located north of modern-day cities of El Ashmunein and El Quseyya
13. Per-Bastet – city of Bubastis; capital of nome Imty Khenti
14. Per-djed-ken – royal fortress north of Waset; modern-day site at Dier El-Ballas; or specifically, the southern tower of the palace
15. Sau - city of Sais; capital of nome Nit Meḥtet
16. Sedjefatawy – the royal palace north of the city of Waset; contained within the Per-djed-ken fortress
17. Ta-Seti - the first nome bordering Nubia (Kerma and Kush; together called the land of Wawat)
18. Tepihu – the port city of modern-day Atfih; capital of the nome Mednit
19. Waset – ancient name for the city of Luxor and the fourth nome
20. Wawat – *Nubia*; name for the combined land of Kerma and Kush

PRINCES OF THE UPPER NOMES

1. Baufre – Prince of Meseh (Nome 6)
2. Metjen – Prince of Bat (Nome 7)
3. Nakht – Prince of Nekhen (Nome 3)
4. Paser – Prince of Herui (Nome 5)
5. Sarenpet – Prince of Mednit (Nome 22)
6. Setka – Prince of Ta-Ur (Nome 8)
7. Tetian – Prince of Ta-Seti (Nome 1)
8. Unasankh – Prince of Sha (Nome 11)
9. Weshptah – Prince of Ma-Hedj (Nome 16)

ROYAL FAMILY

Tetisheri – mother of Seqenenre Tao, Ahhotep, Ahmose-Inhapi, and Sitdjehuti

- Seqenenre Tao – *Tao*; deceased King
- Ahhotep – great wife of Seqenenre Tao
- Ahmose-Inhapi – *Inhapi*; wife of Seqenenre Tao
- Sitdjehuti – wife of Seqenenre Tao

Children of Seqenenre Tao and Sitdjehuti:

- Meryetamun – firstborn daughter (not mentioned in *Warrior King*)
- Ahmose – *Mosi*; secondborn daughter

Children of Seqenenre Tao and Inhapi:

- Ahmose-Henuttamehu – *Henuttamehu*; wife and half-sister of Ahmose

Children of Seqenenre Tao and Ahhotep:

- Ahhotep Tasherit – *Tep*; firstborn daughter; sister and chief wife of Kamose
- Kamose – eldest son
- Ahmose-Hentempet – *Hentempet*; secondborn daughter; royal wife of Kamose
- Ahmose-Nefertari – thirdborn daughter
- Ahmose-Nebetta – *Nebetta*; fourth born daughter
- Ahmose – secondborn son
- Sapair – third-born son

- Binpu – fourth-born son; twin of Tumerisy
- Ahmose-Tumerisy – *Tumerisy*; fifth-born daughter; twin of Binpu

Children of Kamose and Tep (Ahhotep Tasherit):

- Sitkamose – only child; daughter

Children of Ahmose and Kasmut:

- Tair - only child; daughter; wife of Ramose

Children of Ahmose and Ahmose-Nefertari:

- Ahmose-Ankh - firstborn son
- Siamun – secondborn son
- Ramose – third-born son; husband of Tair
- Ahmose-Meryet Amon – *Meryet Amon* – firstborn daughter; twin to Ahmose-Sitamun; wife and sister to Amenhotep
- Ahmose-Sitamun – *Sitamun*; firstborn daughter; twin to Ahmose-Meryet Amon
- Ahmose-Sipair – fourth-born son
- Mutnofret – third-born daughter
- Amenhotep – fifth-born son

Children of Amenhotep and Meryet Amon:

- Amenemhat – only child; son

Children of Sapair and Senseneb:

- Thutmose – firstborn son
- Ahmes – daughter; wife of Thutmose

Children of Thutmose and Ahmes:

- Hatshepsut – firstborn daughter
- Neferubity – secondborn daughter

STEWARDS & SERVANTS

1. Bakaa - steward of Ahmose
2. Men - steward of Ahmose-Nefertari
3. Meret – maidservant of Ahhotep
4. Nena – maidservant of Ahhotep
5. Rai – chief nurse to the royal children
6. Ranofer – head palace steward
7. Iset – steward of Tep

EGYPTOPHILES UNITE!

Do you love Ancient Egypt and *Warrior King*?

Grab some Ancient Egyptian swag and free ebooks at
www.laurenleemerewether.com

EXCLUSIVE READER OFFER

If you want to dive into the Amarna period of Egypt, check out Lauren's debut series, *The Lost Pharaoh Chronicles*.

Visit www.LaurenLeeMerewether.com to receive a FREE Starter Library, including *King's Jubilee*, a FREE short story in *The Lost Pharaoh Chronicles Prequel Collection*.

A secret. A brotherhood. A father's sin.

Crown Prince Thutmose's auspicious future keeps his chin high. He strives to be like his father, Pharaoh Amenhotep III, in every way until his eyes open to one of the King's biggest failures.

What will he decide to do with this knowledge when he takes the crown one day?

ANOTHER EXCLUSIVE READER OFFER

Uncover the origins of Thruna, the woman from Thrace, who captured the heart of Oceanus and became the Tethys of Ancient Greek legend.

Visit www.LaurenLeeMerewether.com to receive
The Curse of Revenge,
a FREE prequel novella for the *Ancient Legends* series.

The *Ancient Legends* series will feed into the Hyksos (Hekka Khasut) reign during the Second Intermediate period of Ancient Egypt as a precursor to *Warrior King*.

ACKNOWLEDGMENTS

First and foremost, I want to thank God for blessing me with the people who support me and the opportunities he gave me to do what I love: telling stories.

Many thanks to my dear husband who supported my late nights of writing this book.

I want to give a special thank you to my volunteer book production and launch team members. Without both teams, I would not have been able to make the story the best it could be and successfully get it to market.

Thank you to my newsletter subscribers, who voted on the story's characters and plot aspects.

Thank you to the Self-Publishing School Fundamentals of Fiction course, which taught me invaluable lessons on the writing process and how to effectively self-publish, as well as its students who gave me friendship and encouragement in supporting my goals.

<u>Finally, but certainly not least, thank you to my readers.</u> Without your support, I would not be able to write. I truly hope this story engages you, inspires you, and gives you a peek into the past.

I hope that when you finish reading this story, your love of history will have deepened a little more—and, of course, that you can't wait to find out what happens in the next story!

ABOUT THE AUTHOR

Lauren Lee Merewether is an ancient family saga fiction author who loves to daydream about times long past while sipping green tea and watching the experts on Discovery unearth our ancestors' civilizations.

She likes to dive into history and find overlooked, under-appreciated, and relatively unknown tidbits of our past to weave into her emotional sagas.

Bringing the world stories forgotten by time, Lauren lives to breathe new life into lost people as characters who love and lose, fight wrong with right, and hope in times of despair.

Grab some free prequels, go behind the scenes, say hello, and stay current with Lauren's latest releases at www.LaurenLeeMerewether.com.

- facebook.com/llmbooks
- twitter.com/llmbooks
- instagram.com/llmbooks
- bookbub.com/authors/lauren-lee-merewether
- goodreads.com/laurenleemerewether
- amazon.com/author/laurenleemerewether
- youtube.com/LaurenLeeMerewether
- tiktok.com/@llmbooks

ALSO BY LAUREN LEE
MEREWETHER

For all of Lauren's books, visit:

www.LLMBooks.com

Salvation in the Sun *(The Lost Pharaoh Chronicles, Book I)*

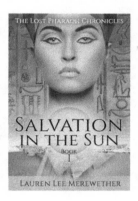

This future she knows for certain—the great sun city will be her undoing.

Amidst a power struggle between Pharaoh and the priesthood of Amun, Queen Nefertiti helps the ill-prepared new Pharaoh Amenhotep enact his father's plan to regain power for the throne. But what seemed a difficult task only becomes more grueling when Amenhotep loses himself in his radical obsessions.

Standing alone to bear the burden of a failing country and stem the tide of a growing rebellion, Nefertiti must choose between her love for Pharaoh and her duty to Egypt in this dramatic retelling of a story forgotten by time.

The Curse of Beauty *(Ancient Legends, Book I)*

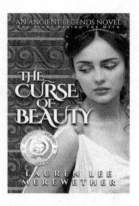

Before the Muses spoke of Medusa, a woman inspired the myth.

Perfect for fans of epic historical sagas, slow-burn romance, and mythic retellings, this standalone installment of the Ancient Legends series offers a compelling and imaginative take on the historical roots of Greek mythology's most enduring myths.

In 1650 BC, King Oceanus, a self-proclaimed lord of the sea, arrives with his soldiers on the shore of Tiryns and begins a struggle for power and dominance.

Experience the rise of tyranny, discover the power of a people amid a sea of lies, deceit, and secrets, and unveil the legacy behind the legend.

WHAT DID YOU THINK?
DID YOU ENJOY WARRIOR KING?

Thank you for reading the first book of the *Egypt's Golden Age Chronicles* series. I hope you enjoyed jumping into another culture and reading about the fictional story of Ahhotep and her sons.

If you enjoyed *Warrior King*, I would like to ask a big favor: Please share with your friends and family on social media sites like **Facebook**, **Instagram**, or **TikTok** and/or leave a review with book retailers, **BookBub** and **Goodreads**.

I am an independent author; as such, reviews and word of mouth are the best ways readers like you can help books like *Warrior King* and the resulting series, *Egypt's Golden Age Chronicles,* reach other readers.

Your feedback and support are of the utmost importance to me. If you want to reach out to me and give feedback on this book, ideas to improve my future writings, get updates about future books, or to just say howdy, please visit me on the web.

www.LaurenLeeMerewether.com
Or email me at
mail@LaurenLeeMerewether.com
Happy Reading!

Printed in the USA
CPSIA information can be obtained
at www.ICGtesting.com
LVHW042334020724
784552LV00028B/317